HAYNER PUBLIC LIBRARY DISTRICT-ALTON
0 00 30 00094932

D0875343

THE LAST FILM OF EMILE VICO

ALSO BY THOMAS GAVIN
KINGKILL

THE LAST FILM OF EMILE VICO

THOMAS GAVIN

VIKING

VIKING
Viking Penguin Inc., 40 West 23rd Street,
New York, New York 10010, U.S.A.
Penguin Books Ltd, Harmondsworth,
Middlesex, England
Penguin Books Australia Ltd, Ringwood,
Victoria, Australia
Penguin Books Canada Limited, 2801 John Street,
Markham, Ontario, Canada L3R 1B4
Penguin Books (N.Z.) Ltd, 182–190 Wairau Road,
Auckland 10, New Zealand

First published in 1986 by Viking Penguin Inc.
Published simultaneously in Canada

Grateful acknowledgment is made for permission to reprint selections from the following publications:

Hitchcock, by François Truffaut, with collaboration of Helen G. Scott. English translation copyright © 1967 by François Truffaut. Reprinted by permission of Simon & Schuster, Inc.

Joseph Conrad: A Personal Remembrance, by Ford Madox Ford (Little, Brown and Company, 1924). Reprinted by permission of Little, Brown and Company.

LIBRARY OF CONGRESS CATALOGING IN PUBLICATION DATA
Gavin, Thomas.
The last film of Emile Vico.
I. Title.
PS3557.A955L3 1986 813′.54 85-40626
ISBN 0-670-80492-4

Printed in the United States of America by
The Book Press, Brattleboro, Vermont
Set in Trump Medieval

To Claire
for her tender
ruthless criticism
of these pages,
and for her
constant love

You have an immobilized man looking out. That's one part of the film. The second part shows what he sees and the third part shows how he reacts. This is actually the purest expression of a cinematic idea.

—ALFRED HITCHCOCK

THE FIRST PART:

AN IMMOBILIZED MAN

His face would light up; it was as if he whispered; as if we both whispered in a conspiracy against a sleeping world.

—FORD MADOX FORD,
remembering his partnership with Conrad

CHAPTER
I

1. A Smudge of Ash

I SHOULD HAVE KNOWN: When a star like Vico disappears, the spotlight he lived under spills into headlines, and anyone caught there tastes the actor's secret vice. The homicide dick in charge of the case, the microscope peepers in the crime lab, even the wife who was first on the scene—they all get the treatment. You walk up the steps and the news cameras turn, photographers lurk in the precinct house hall, and by the time she's released—the wife, that is—fans under drumming umbrellas clot the sidewalk. She appears at the top of the steps, lips lavender pale the way I always liked them, only a sleepless night to shadow her eyes. She pauses, and since she is only twenty-four and in her first picture and married to Vico less than a year, she's new to the treatment and maybe wondering what she can feed those eyes to make them let her pass. Even the seen-it-all newshounds stuck on the cop beat till they're good for nothing else fix her with that thrill-hungry gape. She tightens the cinch on her raincoat. This is the shot the Movietone News will run the rest of the week. She places her foot on the first step, she descends among them. They send up a moan and the voice-over barks about Vico's lovely bride: Is she a wife—or a widow?

That's the treatment. She got it more than others, but as I said, everyone the case touched got a taste, and it's not surprising that with all those eyes staring, someone would want to speak a few lines—say whatever he knew, that the world was hungry to hear. I know what it's like. The reporter prompting at your elbow takes it all down as if you were Cagney or Gable. So much for hush-up investigations.

It was a Wednesday, Ash Wednesday in fact, and the detective who took her arm and waved people back so she could get to the car waiting at the curb must have been to an early Mass, because when he ballooned into the newsreel close-up, his umbrella wobbled back and the rain streaked the thumb-smudge of ash he wore on his brow to remind him he was dust and would return to dust. Yes, Ash Wednesday, March the second, 1938, and the first edition to hit the streets that morning already had every sensational detail. Once you unscrambled the first-things-last newspaper chronology, you could piece together a story that looked fairly complete and thoroughly sleazy. They had a summary of gossip-column tidbits, starting about six months earlier with a hint of "friction" between Vico and the fashion-model bride he had brought back from the East Coast the previous summer. Then, within a week after shooting began on *Loves of a Spy,* there were the items about a feud on the set between Vico and Bolger, the director; but nothing, oddly enough, on the Tuesday morning fistfight just before Vico's walkout. And finally the headline story—full, lurid coverage of what had happened overnight: the phone call that had brought Lisa out into the storm sometime after midnight, driving the coast road to the isolated beach house where she expected to find her husband raving drunk; and what she found instead: the open door with rain pelting in through the screen; the blood-soaked towel on the bathroom floor; and—most sinister of all—the photograph from his desktop, Vico's favorite self-portrait, crumpled and defaced.

By that afternoon Vico was only one of scores of missing people in the San Fernando Valley and the Vico mystery had been crowded off the front page to make room for the biggest flood in California history. In Beverly Glen a mudslide pushed a house two hundred feet downhill and caved in a wall on a woman and child. The husband was found a couple hundred yards farther down. He was naked in a bathtub with his wrists broken. The Los Angeles and Santa Ana rivers spilled over their banks and became shallow lakes that dissolved roads and invaded orange groves. Telephone poles marked where the roads had disappeared. A wooden footbridge over the Los Angeles River at Long Beach gave way and ten people drowned. Other bridges collapsed. In Hollywood film crews were piling sandbags around soundstage walls, and in downtown Los Angeles cars navigating the streets were washed against curbs. Stores let their clerks go at two p.m. if they had any chance to make it home. Some of them holed up in bars and tried to phone their wives and found the lines dead. In one of the bars on the Strip an old guy said it wasn't the first time God had got tired of what he'd made and somebody said, "You mean what Sam Goldwyn made," and somebody who knew his Bible said, "Yeah, but he promised Noah there wouldn't be no more floods," and the wise guy said, "*Who* promised—Goldwyn?" and the old rummy standing by the streaming window said, "You ever know anybody remember a promise when he gets good and mad?" There were twenty-six known dead and more corpses parked in the morgue every hour. A reporter for the afternoon edition asked Captain Hoensinger if he expected Vico might turn up among them. He was told anything was possible. The story got headlined "Vico Possible Flood Victim."

Telling it that way, of course, ignored the towel and the photo. But they were no-news facts anyway. The marks on the picture were the kind a Red Streetcar artist draws on the lady in the cigarette ad: thick round spectacles and a Groucho mustache. You could only make so much of it. A kidnapper's prank? The self-mocking scribble of a suicide? As for the towel—the blood wasn't enough to drain a healthy rat. Sorry clues, really—not much to build a case on. Nothing you could say about one of them would account for the other. That's why, once the waters had dropped back inside their channels and people dropped back to their old gossipy ways, the towel and the photo got forgotten. Over the broken shells of lobster boiled in Ciro's kitchen and over the greasy hamburgers of the Vine Street drugstores where actors traded news of who was casting next week and who had a friend with a contact who had promised a role, theories rose like a ripe gas. Within a week all they had in common was a single fact: since the night of March 1, 1938, Emile Vico had not been seen.

2. Several Takes of a Slow Fade

ANYONE WHO HAD been on the set of *Loves of a Spy*, the film he left unfinished, shot to celebrity. Anyone, that is, who would talk. The script girl, for instance, little Nellie Nugent with the Clara Bow lips, or the gofer who knocked on his door that rainy Tuesday with a cup of coffee he was never to drink—people who usually tagged along to the party with someone who'd been invited. Now they were phoned by the hostess herself and steered under the key light where the camera picks up every twitch and quiver. For a few minutes, maybe half an hour if they knew how to sell a story, they would sit knee to knee with the producer of *Dancing Down Manhattan*. When I saw it I found myself repeating something Vico once told me: The man behind the camera is only an eye. But an eye, Vico, can shut its lid or turn away—a knack I never mastered.

Since Vico's second picture I've been his cameraman. Which is to say: I created him. Not strictly true, but let it stand.

An early story, one I kind of liked, held that a few miles down the beach from Vico's empty summer house a killer shark had floundered into a tide pool. When it turned up its belly to die, someone had spotted a glint in its mouthful of spikes, something gold. Jammed halfway up one of the teeth in the lower jaw was a gold ring, hammered into the Janus face of tragedy and comedy. An autopsy spilled from the shark's gut a sackful of human bones. The ring, it was whispered—by those, you recall, who make drama their lives—the ring was Vico's one piece of jewelry, the gift of its maker, Picasso.

No such ring existed.

Other rumors circulated, breathed from lips to ear so fast that often the costume-department seamstress who had supposed a theory to her lover in the first sleepy bedroom talk of the morning heard it that afternoon as fact from a woman she didn't even know her lover knew. Vico, it was said, had drowned, a suicide, for reasons known intimately to the informant and every reader of fan magazines. No, not drowned, said another, but murdered: A criminal society called the Secret Six had slit his throat for betraying its secrets. You see how far they would go.

But the stories most often repeated claimed that Vico wasn't dead. One night in a downtown bar a woman with big earrings and uneven bangs had it in strict confidence, regularly breached as she migrated from table to table, that Vico would soon turn up in the Third Reich—the new director of Hitler's film industry. Somebody must have thought that was unpatriotic, because within a few days there was another version: It told of a secret mission, a plan to get Vico presented to the Fuehrer, whom he had sworn to assassinate. Nothing was definite. At the very next table you might hear of a traveler recently come back from Asia with a photograph snapped in a Buddhist monastery. Cover the shaved skull with your thumb and the features of the fourth monk down the row were clearly Vico's. Emile Vico, legs akimbo, eyes piously hooded, was spinning a prayer wheel in Tibet.

Then there was the deformity theory, my personal favorite. In an auto crash or a fire Vico's face had been "horribly disfigured"—a phrase that made me think of melting tallow. He was in permanent hiding from the world, cared for—depending on who was talking—by a lover, an aged aunt, a defrocked priest. This script was lifted straight from Vico's own film *The Mask of Don Juan.* Remember that shot of the servant girl pulling out the stopper on her vial of acid, then cut to Vico and that little hiccup of terror he gives just before the acid slaps his face. Remember how he pitches backward, tearing at his face, and how the camera peers down at him writhing between the ottoman and the samovar, then closes in for the final shot: the steam rising from beneath his splayed fingers.

We shot nine takes of that scene and that night the screams called to me in my sleep. Not a tranquil business, making movies.

I heard at third hand one of the best of the Vico theories, the only one, I suspect, that would have appealed to Vico himself. Shag Masters came up with it after people had run out of things to invent. He claimed the camera ate actors. He'd been directing nearly twenty years, he said, and he could tell you that's why most actors were sons of bitches. Everything human in them got eaten up by the camera. Most held a little back, enough to trick you into thinking there was somebody across the table from you who liked his martinis dry and smoked Pall Malls. The only place they couldn't fool you was in bed. The trouble with Vico, he explained, was that he didn't know how to hold back that little bit you needed to keep up the illusion. That's why he was so good on the screen. Most goddam naked actor you ever saw, and every yard of film they cranked was eating him alive.

Masters had a drawl flat as a Kansas plain and level blue eyes that made him the best deadpan joker in town. More than once, I heard, he got to his punch line and nobody laughed. Want to find Vico? Masters would ask and take a sip. Look in that last can of film.

3. Gila Monsters and Sunbursts

BUT THERE WERE FACTS, at least a few. At least, in those early days of the case, what passed for facts. For instance: The only person known to have spoken with Emile Vico on the night of his disappearance was his second wife, Lisa. For that fact you would look in the wire basket on Detective Captain Hoensinger's desk, where he filed the pink carbon of his daily report. It was available to my friend Al McMahon, the police reporter for the *Tablet,* and to the rest of the cop-beat vultures who picked through the basket each morning.

Of course there must have been other facts, things that

Hoensinger didn't put on paper. But from his summary you could piece together yet another theory. It was a good guess, according to the story McMahon did for the *Tablet,* that by the time of her husband's disappearance—not such a long time even by Hollywood standards—Lisa Vico was what the gossip columns call "estranged." That meant, McMahon said, she hadn't yet filed divorce papers, but was no longer keeping the bed warm. Naturally she was still showing up for work each day as female lead in *Loves of a Spy.*

Hoensinger was good at making you squirm and quick to spot the kind of motive that can fill out a tabloid headline. But anything too subtle to stick between the ears of a jury didn't stick between his. Or so I thought. I'd been worked over myself once, enough to know how Lisa felt and how much Hoensinger would miss.

It was eleven p.m. when Lisa Vico telephoned her husband to tell him that she wanted a divorce. The storm, she said, filled the connection with static, but her impression was that Vico sounded... distraught. And confused.

Confused? Captain Hoensinger's raised eyes and hovering pencil were as good as a cattle prod. Heavy-tongued, she said. As if he had been drinking or drugged. Captain Hoensinger asked how her announcement had affected Vico. Was it at this point he became what she termed distraught? No... from the moment he answered the phone. Did she speak right away about the divorce? Not for about five minutes. She needed time to build her courage. Maybe, Hoensinger said, she'd been feeling a little distraught herself. He flipped the word back at her like a counterfeit quarter. Later when I had a chance to talk with her alone, Lisa told me it was not until that moment that she realized she was under suspicion. It was a good warning, she said. It prepared her for the turn the questioning took an hour later, when Hoensinger abruptly demanded the name of the man she had been seeing. For the moment, however, she simply agreed that, yes, she had been distraught, repeating the word deliberately, her eyes meeting his.

Whatever advantage that defiance gave her she lost immediately with Captain Hoensinger's next question: What had been Vico's immediate reaction to the divorce news? His reply, she said, had been puzzling. She tried to explain: She wasn't sure he had heard her. Due to the storm. A thunderclap had deafened her. Through it her husband was murmuring, talking she didn't know what, talking nonsense, two words, she made out only two words, it sounded like he said "Gila monsters."

Gila monsters? Captain Hoensinger said. That's what *I* said, Lisa answered, and for the only time that night broke into something like a laugh. Along with the static, she explained, the line carried an echo. Vico's voice had seemed to come from far away, from underground. She told Hoensinger the next word she understood was "murder." Again the pencil hesitated. Had her husband ever before threatened her with violence? Once, she said, and on that question no amount of bullying would make her say more. Not to Hoensinger, that is. To me she told the whole story. A couple days before Vico's disappearance, they were in the middle of a squabble. The gossip-column rumors and the feud on the set with Bolger were getting him down. He was on edge all the time. Finally she told him she had to get out. Live from now on at the town house. He gave that little smile, she told me, and said, "Just as well. I killed Berenice, you know. I don't want to kill you, too." Those were his exact words, she said, and her voice on the phone got tight. "Farley, tell me," she said. "What did he mean by that?" As if it never crossed her mind that I might not know. I wonder what it cost her—always coming to me to find out what her husband was thinking. I know just what you know, I told her: Berenice was Vico's first wife and she's dead.

When Hoensinger saw he couldn't get any more out of her about Vico's threat, he asked for the rest of her phone conversation. During a break in the static, she went on, he seemed to be explaining something technical about time-lapse photography, the problems of photographing a flower opening its petals. And then something about a sunflower, because he kept saying, "Sunburst, sunburst, filling the screen." Then the connection broke. Later, during the grilling about her hypothetical boyfriend, she had the steady calm of a clear conscience, since of course I didn't count.

Another thing Hoensinger was interested in was time. The phone line went dead before eleven-fifteen. The coast road from Lisa's penthouse to the beach house was an hour's drive. Yet it was nearly one-thirty a.m. before she arrived to check on his condition. Even accounting for the storm, wasn't that a long drive? She admitted it was. Had his threat frightened her? She hadn't taken it seriously. The captain reminded her that she had said Vico was distraught. Wasn't she a little worried? They had been separated before, she said. Sometimes his ways of saying he wanted to make up were a bit... melodramatic. For half an hour, she claimed, she paced around, and at last put on her raincoat and went. It was the same one she was wearing early the next morning at police headquarters, when press photographers snapped the picture that made page one in most of the afternoon editions: her jaw slack with exhaustion and shock, hollow eyes staring at the paper coffee cup tilted from her forefinger. Five hours earlier she had arrived at the empty house, discovered the mutilated photograph, the overflowing bath, the towel soaked in blood—just the shots Vico would have used in a slow montage.

4. A Possible Scenario

I CAN ALMOST hear him in one of our story conferences, telling me what the camera has to see, sliding in front of me sketch after sketch on which, during his annual six-week retreat to the beach house, he had roughed out shot and angle and shadow for every scene of a new film. To make its purpose clear he gave each set-up a title, a habit I see I've carried over into this manuscript. Flying in his hand as he talked, a pencil would be refining the sketches, shifting perspectives, sharpening focus. And as he sketched, that voice—the one you heard on soundtracks in a tight close-up when his eyes were staring back at the lens or through it, I sometimes thought, at me on the other side; that voice a critic of his first sound film called "a river flowing through a cavern"—would be explaining just what he had selected that night for Lisa's eyes to discover. Open, he would say, with a shot of the desk top, the camera so close we see woodgrain. That close, with nothing to give away the scale, it might be an aerial shot of a desert, and then the white curtain bellies across it.

White curtains, Farley, he would say, something wispy, just enough to make the wind visible. The sound of a wind from the ocean, and on the desk as the camera pulls back: splinters of glass, the twisted frame, the photo ripped in half and crumpled. Then you tilt down onto a scrap of the photo, crumpled and smoothed flat. Go tight onto the face. Somebody with a fountain pen, the police report said, had given it huge specs, a bushy mustache, sideburns. And then you hear a *toc. Toc, toc,* and a raindrop hits the photo, the curtains flap, raindrops speckle the desk, and a drop hits the face in the photo, blurs the ink. Out of the wind, the rainpatter, we lift a long cello tone: title music. I want the stroking like something whiskey and grief do in your throat, Farley, like someone going over it in his mind for the hundreth time, and with the title (Vico's titles were always twice as long as a marquee space, till I made him whittle them down), with the title, Farley, I want something special. I want you to give me a wipe dissolve that *streaks* the words, smears them across the screen as if it were a windshield with the wipers going, and when it clears we *are* looking at a windshield, the glass streaming. And behind it, blurring and forming with each stroke of the wipers, we can make out her face. You run the star names below her eyes, let the wipers smear each one away, and— That won't work, Vico. It would have to wipe too fast for them to read. And besides, it's *stylish.* When I brought him down like that, he would purse his lips as if he were sucking something sour, then say...

You can make it work, Farley. Do the wipers in slow motion. Think of her face rippling behind the glass. If you make them want badly enough to see her face, only nosepickers will be thinking of style. After the last name wipes away, then, cut back to the photo on the desk. The rain has soaked away the phony mustache and specs, and just before a gust blows the picture onto the floor we recognize him, and it's Vico. (In these conferences he would never say, On this line give *me* a close-up, but always, Come in tight on Danglers, or the Whisperer, or Count Boris.)

In fact, a corner of the broken frame had weighted the photo to the desk top, where it was found by Captain Hoensinger. He didn't need a lab exam to spot the marks left by the pen-point. Someone had used such pressure the nib of Vico's fountain pen (brown, given him, he once said, by his father) was ruined. But Vico never let facts obscure the truth. The torn photo, he would tell me, has to fall to the floor in the spill of light from the bathroom. He would explain how the light would lure the camera inside, just as it will lure Lisa when she arrives, and the eye, my lens, must stray over the shard of glass in the sink, linger on the porcelain spotted and tracked with blood.

When the headlights of Lisa's car at last swept the private road to the house, the rain was still drumming. Under the roof of one of the darkened gable windows the drumming might have been loud enough to swallow the sound of a pulsebeat. The car rounded the hill and braked. The headlights splashed the house, the open garage door, the trunk of Vico's blue roadster. Was it only seconds that she sat behind the wheel? Later she would tell Captain Hoensinger she thought she saw a movement behind one of the attic windows. She convinced herself it was only the glint of her headlights on the glass. I was afraid, she told him. The back door was open. The hall was dark. I didn't want to stumble in the dark. That was her explanation of why she failed to cut the headlights before she left the car.

In the headlight glare, then, I shoot her running through the rain. Inside, I frame her in the doorway, shoot her silhouetted by the headlights, saying his name into the dark house, saying, Vico, where are you? When she finds the wall switch, I bring up the key light, a liko above her to aureole her hair. As she glides through the house I am ahead of her in every room, waiting in the dark while she fumbles by the doorjamb for a switch or gropes toward the lamp, and each time a light floods the room, I track in for a quick hungry study of her face.

At the stair landing she detached from the drumming on the roof another sound—a gurgle and splash coming from inside the house. She placed a foot on the first step and said his name. As she climbs the stairs I crane up alongside her as far as the banister where she paused, then let her go on alone. I peer up after her, at her silhouette rising into the steam that pours through the bathroom door. Steam, Captain Hoensinger noted, which meant that he couldn't have been gone long enough to empty the hot-water tank.

Before describing to me the final shot of a scene Vico would often let the tip of his tongue graze the triangle of flesh at the center of his upper lip. Background in deep focus, he would say, water cascading off the rim of the tub. A two-second cut to the overflow drain, a washcloth jammed in its mouth. Then get behind her, low angle so the backs of her calves fill the right foreground. She takes a step, and... What, Vico? What would be best? A cut to her foot maybe—yes, in one of those beige pumps that squeeze out the tips of three tantilizing toes; her foot coming down on that oddly piebald towel that lay in the water pooling across the tiles, her foot squeezing from the towel into the water an inky cloud of blood.

5. Iris Out

THAT OR SOMETHING like it, something maybe a bit more grotesque, was how Vico would have filmed it. That or something like it is what the press reported Lisa Vico told the police. What she *finally* told them, after she discovered the dead phone line and got out to her car and found that dead, too, water splashed into the wires, and hiked through the storm to a house a couple miles down the road. Why hadn't she used Vico's car? Hoensinger asked. We have two cars, she told him.

Ours and his. I only had a key to ours. What it came to was that a rare Hollywood genius—the genuine article, who made producers rasp the word as if it meant some kind of beast it would be safest to cage or kill—an acting genius, directing genius, scripting genius, whose genius stamped every frame I shot for him with what that famous *Life* cover story termed "his unique vision of the beauty in monstrous hearts"; this genius, I say, apparently opened the back door of his house and walked or was dragged—barefoot and possibly bleeding—into the worst rainstorm in southern California history. The rain closed around him like an old-fashioned iris out. From a stretch of clay in the path leading down to the beach the police took three casts of a naked foot that would have fit one of Vico's shoes. Beyond the path was a sand beach that held no prints and beyond the beach was the long gray swell of the Pacific. The next day, along with the other flood debris, the planks of a sailboat that had broken up on the rocky point half a mile away washed ashore. Stories of a body in the hold proved false. The boat, like many others, had simply slipped its moorings in the storm. I waited. I still wait. I wrestle my bedsheets into knots and wait for the tide to give up its secrets. The days fill up with rumor—rumor and gossip, like water filling one of Vico's footprints and slowly seeping away.

CHAPTER
II

1. The Don Juan Look

EVEN BEFORE HIS disappearance the images of himself that Vico molded out of shade and silver light seemed to go on acting in people's minds after the screen went dark. The whispers started after each new film, tugged from the film's guts like a tapeworm. After *The Mask of Don Juan* you heard that he had stashed in various parts of the city no less than four mistresses—and had a different kind of nasty fun with each. What's more, he now and then brought his ladies together for exotic parties. Here the details would vary depending on who told the story. None I ever heard were wild enough to compare with Vico's *real* tastes. His choice perversion was fidelity, of a kind. While Berenice was alive, I never knew him to sleep anywhere but home. How much satisfaction that gave her I'm not sure. When I saw he was serious about casting Sarah Russell in *City of Sapphires*, I reminded him that she read a line of dialogue as if she were translating from Sanscrit. Don't worry, Farley, he said, we'll let the camera do her acting. She's got a face I can play to. He played to all his leading ladies, on screen and off. All through a shooting he would be drunk in love, like one of those soldiers who need to be stinking drunk to climb out of the trench. Once the last yard of film was in the can, he'd pull back. At the cast party she'd cozy up and slide a hand under his arm, thinking now the work was over he'd get down to business, and Vico would shift his shoulder as if he'd felt a spider crawling inside his shirt. Drunk in love all right, but like a drunk, he had blackouts. And hangovers: Watching him untangle himself from all the little promises he must have whispered in someone's ear during the binge, you could see his temples throb with self-loathing. Who would blame him for taking a hair of the dog? Hair of the dog, sure, but he was never one to mix his drinks.

I used to wonder where people got that crap. But all you had to do was think of that moment in *City of Sapphires* just after Stanhope slugs him to the floor. As his cronies hoist him by the arms, a thread of blood tracks from the corner of his mouth. He swallows hard, his tongue explores his cheek. While he keeps Stanhope fixed in that concentrated glare, his hand wipes away the blood. And then, like a preening cat, he grazes the bloodied back of his wrist with his tongue. In gestures like that an audience glimpses its own secrets. Think of him condemning Princess Eulalie's lover to the firing squad, think of his eyes. They branded in celluloid something you couldn't look away from no matter how you tried. But what? What was it locked your stare to his? The heavy-lidded glaze of a lizard in the sun? Or some ruthless wisdom that didn't blink even at death? And what would you not believe of the man who could offer you these alternatives?

Was it true that for a lavish party he once emptied the swimming pool of his Beverly Hills estate to make a pit for a cockfight? Or that his strongest personal attachment was to a street peddler's blind and deaf daughter whom he had once jostled in a crowd, and that after dabbing his handkerchief at her tears he had tried to buck her up by buying her an ice-cream cone, a private tutor, a home with her parents in Beverly Hills? That one, despite the Chaplin-style bathos, rings true. I can't think of anyone not blind and deaf whom Vico would need more than a glance or a word to seduce.

And the crux of it was that face. It made any rumor credible. I think he was aware of its power—and did his best to despise it. Notice his makeup, each role a new disguise. He had a huge head, nearly a mongoloid's bubble, but refined, and in one film he would slick his hair tight to his scalp to make those frontal lobes bulge, and in the next he would frame them in ringlets. When he ignored his skull, you would find him slapping a mustache over his lips, pushing them into a pout. That odd nose was his one vanity. In left profile some old break or the asthmatic's thickened septum knobbed the bone just below the bridge. But the right profile rolled straight and dull down to a fleshy lump and had no grace. He never failed to stick a wad of makeup on that straight bone to balance the left-side knob. Nothing he did to deflect your attention, though, could keep you from his eyes, and a single glance put you behind them, where all the strangeness of the face fit like your own flesh.

It was that power to trap you inside him that kept Vico afloat through what I sometimes at first thought of as lapses of taste, scenes no other actor could have dared. Remember that moonlit garden in *City of Sapphires*, and Vico climbing down a trellis from the bedroom balcony of the ambassador's wife? Not even Fairbanks could make that look romantic anymore, and Vico did it with a rose between his teeth. I fought him about that one, said it would be ludicrous. No, Farley, he told me with that sweet patience I hated, Fairbanks would be ludicrous, because he is so pretty. But I'm going to play the rose and the moonlight against my mug. It worked, too, but only because he was Vico. Which I guess was his point.

But he went too far even for Vico with the terrier. As he crosses the garden, the terrier rushes out of a hedge, yapping and snarling past the lighted window where the ambassador is just adding a sliver to his matchstick cathedral. His hand pauses in close-up. He almost looks over his shoulder into the garden. Ah—no need; the yapping stops. Cut to Vico, squatting as if he's about to give the mutt a pat; then back: Serenely attentive, the ambassador completes his gesture. A banana-peel scene, you would think, something spliced in from an old Harold Lloyd picture. But when you saw Vico snap his hands around the mutt's neck and drag it behind a bush, there was nothing funny, not even the rose still between his teeth. He insisted, I remember, that we get a good close-up of the terrier's hind leg twitching, and another of a silver thread of spit drooling from the rose stem in the corner of his mouth. Then a second later, just as Sarah Russell comes to the window, we got a full shot of him rising with slightly rumpled jauntiness, the hedge at his knees hiding the dead terrier, and who but Vico could have taken that rose in his hand to waft his lady a final salute before vaulting the garden wall? Once audiences believed that scene—and the Hays office believed it enough to shorten the terrier's agony by quite a few frames—Vico must have despaired that anything people read or heard about him would seem out of character.

While *City of Sapphires* was still in release something happened that you forget about until later. Vico was having a quiet dinner with Berenice—making up after one of their fights—when they noticed the maître d' in a rumpus with another customer. A big jowly man was glaring at his feet and blushing behind his cigar, but all the same standing firm, while his wife declared that she would not be seated near that horrible man—meaning, Vico at last gathered, himself. The next day he made a joke of it, but I could tell it bothered him, and later, thinking how he must have felt when Berenice died, I remembered that night in the restaurant, remembered how worried, how downright scared he was to think that someone could confuse him with those shadows he made on the screen.

If I had thought earlier to look in Vico's films for the pattern, I might have seen flashes of it in his next one. When a man casts himself as Don Juan, he's telling you something. But exactly what he was telling depended on the twists, and Vico's Don Juan was full of them. With a genius it's hard to know when he is being very canny and when he does something original simply because he can't see what's obvious to any competent hack. But Vico ought to have been aware that if he did a Don Juan, it would be a character role. In looks, any dimestore Valentino outclassed him. The first twist, the one that follows with flawless Hollywood logic from that fact, is that Vico's Don Juan flops at his vocation. He's got all the standard seductive virtues: He's cultured and ruthless and prickproud. But the only woman he can drag to bed is his lady's lady-in-waiting. Who douses him with her acid cologne. Through the scenes where he wanders the waterfront taverns and that great shot of him sobbing in the alley behind the whorehouse (which the Hays office insisted we call a dance hall, whatever that is), I played a striptease with his face. Never gave it more light than a sliver along the cheek, like a new moon. That all paid off when he finally finds the alcoholic surgeon and says, "Are you good enough, then, to fix *this*?" and sweeps off the hat that shadows his face. Any actor with a good makeup man, and Vico never trusted anybody to work on his face but himself, could have punched that gasp out of the audience. Only Vico would have given the monster a coy arch of the head and those schoolgirl fluttering eyelids.

Here is where the twists get complicated. Because when he says, "Give me a face she can't turn away from," he must know every woman in the audience is thinking of Fairbanks or Robert Taylor or Valentino. So when the surgeon unwraps the bandages, it must be Vico's joke to show us a smooth, rigid mask of Vico's own face. Not a real mask, just heavy white makeup. He had taped a couple strips of adhesive on his cheeks, mostly to remind him to keep his face stiff. Was he counting on that single expression of stoic amusement to be what fascinated? What did it say about Vico's notion of women that he could have his Don Juan walk into a ballroom and make them all wiggle inside their stays just by wearing a face like a plaster cast?

At a party once a writer, one of those who use a pipe for a portable tit, was grunting and umming through a deep analysis of Vico's Don Juan, and I overheard Vico tell him the film was nothing but his comment on Robert Taylor's acting. The crack got just the right kind of third-martini chuckle you would expect, but in order to believe there was any but the most superficial truth in it you would have to forget the film's ending, when Don Juan finally meets the woman who won't tumble into bed with him just to see if she can crack his makeup.

He bows to her refusal. Not even the eyes betray the mask. And when he gets back alone, he shrugs his cape into his manservant's arms with no explanation, only a muttered something as his back glides out of the frame, and it's only when he's upstairs looking in the mirror and says it again that you catch the words: "It's itching." Puzzled, he seems, not even worried yet, and that's all we needed to plant the idea, so that throughout the scene in the portrait gallery where he stalks her the next day, you're aware of every time his fingers stroke his cheek. I've yet to meet anybody who could stand aside and smile at that final scene, when he hammers at her door until she opens it and we cut to a head shot of him with his flesh hanging in strips. Sure it's melodrama, but it's not the place you get to by starting with a notion to thumb your nose at Robert Taylor. If that was any part of it, the joke was on Vico, because the Don Juan *look* that haunted lobby posters throughout the summer of '34 did more than anything else to turn him into something like the classic matinee idol.

2. The *Strangler's Hands!* Slug

IT WAS THAT summer that the fan magazines picked him up. I don't know anybody in the business who admits to following them, but even I had heard the story that he was born in an attic where his mother kept a boa constrictor. Something too precise in his accent, the honing away of the "h" in *theory* and *throng*, these I suppose gave rise to the story that Vico came from some Baltic state accessible only by goatpath. How that was supposed to go with the Italian name is another story. It was generally accepted that his parents had been circus performers—the mother doing a dance with the snake that shared the baby's crib, the father a tightrope walker who one day on the high wire stopped and looked off as if he had heard a friend call his name, then stepped right onto the air. Vico's earliest memory, it was said, was not of his father's long drop, but of the gasp and moan of the crowd, a soundtrack cut all the deeper by the pressure of his mother's hand over his eyes. Was that, I wonder, his first insight into how to tease an audience?

The story went that he came to America on the run. To seduce the bride of a grizzled count, he posed as a nobleman, acted the part so well that the count called him out as if he were a gentleman. Vico planted a pistol ball in his shoulder and had to dash through a police cordon to the midnight train for Calais, or some such place. I once shared a sleeper car from California to Indiana with a corset salesman who claimed Vico went to public schools in Akron, Ohio, and his name was really Ernie something. He lived a block over from the Bijou Movie Palace and sneaked in the alley door for Saturday matinees.

Other stories were easier to shrug off. That shot, for example, of him lying asleep in a coffin some studio flack, it must have been, called his bed. Arnie Crossman in Publicity told me the coffin wasn't in his home but on the lot, a studio prop for a Lugosi film, and Vico'd been caught there snoozing between camera calls. The asylum rumors sounded more like truth, particularly if you recalled that seven-minute crack-up he did in *Price of Madness*, that ends with the camera pulling slowly away from him thumping his forehead against the baseboard. But that only proved what everyone knew, that Vico had the power to draw you into experiences you weren't anxious to share. If the slur had any checkable fact behind it, I don't recall it, and frankly wouldn't believe it. In this town there's nothing that can't be faked, and nothing they won't print.

But at first it was hard to see how they could have faked that shot every paper in the country ran, the one *Time* captioned "Strangler's Hands?" that catches his lips twisted in what seems like a snarl as he looks down on those long-fingered hands that seem to be dancing up an invisible piccolo or folding to pray. You had to look twice to see the chain strung between the wrists, and then, following it up to the cuff of his left sleeve, you made out the glint of popping flashbulbs on the iron bracelet.

That was shot in the spring of '36, just after they arrested him for the murder of Berenice. If you were in a movie theater later that week, along with ninety million other Americans, you saw the same shot on the Movietone News: the car nuzzling through the crowd to the curb, the wide-shouldered cops clearing a way through photographers and reporters and women—fans I guess—and when the door opens, the legs stay rigid a moment before they swing out, the black shoes grope the curb, and then that pale oval in the shadow of the cab looms into focus, and it's Vico—just like in the movies. You can see the big arm leap down from the upper right corner of the screen to grab him by the biceps. Then his lips curl around that sob and his hands go up to cover his face.

3. The Mask Slips

I SAW THAT newsreel not quite sober on the night before Berenice's funeral. By then Vico had been released, but wasn't answering his phone, and after I'd let it ring a long time I tucked a pint of whiskey in my sport-coat pocket and went to the movies. I had gone out thinking, He's not talking to you, won't see you; so put him out of your mind—and there he was on the screen. It hit me like a slap in the face.

That night I wouldn't let myself wonder why, only hunched in my seat and took a long pull from my bottle and watched the shadows on the screen swell and shrink until I fell asleep. It's taken me this long—nearly two years—to wonder why. From the time I saw it till a few minutes ago, that damn newsreel didn't cross my mind. My lungs still rattle, but a few days ago my fever was down enough so that I could get out of bed a few hours at a time, and I thought it might flush away the sour taste of all those fever dreams to write a memoir of Vico. Nothing else to do; this room I'm in is bare as a monk's cell. A couple times before I've come around after a bad drunk and found I'd checked in here at the Silver Palms. Why I don't know. Maybe because it's where I lived my first months in Hollywood. And where I came for a few weeks after Beth died.

Usually I stay on for another day or so, sorting things out. Then I go home. This time is different.

This time I've stayed on—first because I was too sick to go home, then because with Vico gone there's nothing I feel like aiming a lens at. Besides, I've got to do some thinking. I won't need money for a while yet, and I'll always have work when I want it. I'm that good.

My Vico memoir has been a good way to calm myself. Until tonight, that is, when the page under my hand dissolved into that newsreel of Vico getting out of the police car. Now that it's back, I can't get it out of my head. The voice-over's gone, but I keep running the shot over and over. Why did it bother me so, why does it still? Maybe because the shot is so much like one of Vico's own pictures, I can't believe it wasn't me behind the camera that day. At the core of every Vico picture is an unmasking, and it's the feel of one of those scenes that I get when I watch that frozen snarl from the newspaper stills melt to a sob.

Oh Christ, Vico, did you really feel that way about Berenice? It's as if I never knew you. And that scares me.

It's time I found out what I know.

CHAPTER
III

1. Over-the-Shoulder Shot

I KNOW THIS: Last week, early on the morning Vico disappeared, I was still in my apartment. I was asleep in my armchair, dreaming the rain was only in my dream. It was ticking against my window. I wanted to make it go away. All I had to do was open my eyes and for a long time I couldn't. When I did, what I saw beyond the glass was black. I might have been in a diving bell on the ocean floor, so deep no light could reach there, nothing could live. Then my eye caught a movement and I knew I was being watched. Out there in the black where nothing could be, something watched me. I leaned forward and it loomed. Through the glass that rippled and squeezed the features, it was the eyes I recognized. The face had the wide-open stare of a cameraman setting up a shot.

Old Spyhawk, I said, and the face in the window gave a muzzy leer. Welcome back, I said, because I swear that's the first I knew he was back.

Now I've got to think it through—if he showed himself, it must mean he knew I couldn't hurt him. What made him so cocky? If I can get back every detail, shot by shot, maybe it will tell me.

In the window Spyhawk swallowed. When his throat constricted, it forced down a thick bubble of pain. I swallowed again, trying to get the pain back. Why? Because with it—*it's coming:* with the pain, slipping away as it slid down my throat, was a memory. Something that would tell me what he'd done. (Where can this end? One dissolve fades to another.)

I closed my eyes. I put three fingers over each eyelid and waited. The dark behind my eyes danced awhile, then settled into another face—Bolger's. It was in a rage, eyes popping. I had to keep my fingers pressed over my eyes or it would slip away. Then it went anyhow. I thought if I could cut back to the last definite time I remembered, I might gradually pan forward till I got a sensible frame around Bolger's face. Then I might know why it was angry, why I could tell it was screaming curses at me even though I had apparently turned off the sound. My plan worked. I cut to the previous afternoon, right after Vico hit him. There was Bolger, not popping his eyes and spitting like a cat, but grinning. Grinning at me, even before he'd caught his breath from Vico's gut punch, shaking away Simmons's arm, saying, "Leggo, for chrissake—it'll take more than one punch from that little pipsqueak to put me down. C'mon, Farley, we're gonna celebrate."

I told him no, I was getting a cold and wanted to go home to bed. I had glimpsed Lisa gliding into the wings. I wanted to catch up with her before she got to Vico—was I even then, after what he'd just done, afraid she'd try to go to him? Bolger gripped my arm. "Hell, Farley, it's too early to go home. I'm going to buy you a hot toddy and watch you sweat that cold out your pores."

Get your paws off me, I told him, and I made for the door. If I took the path through the Petrified Forest, I figured I could cut her off before she reached Vico's trailer. That was the last time I thought of Bolger till I saw his red Nash parked outside the Penguin Club. When he saw me heading toward his table, Bolger's lip twitched into a snarl, but by the time I sat down the snarl was a good-humored leer.

"You run off to see could you snatch some of that nice tittie?"

Bolger is an Eastern college boy, but he cultivates blue denim and bad diction to be One with the Masses.

I raised my eyebrows and said, "I thought I might bring Vico back."

It was a tired lie. I wondered if Bolger had seen me in the parking lot skipping after Lisa. Sitting in my armchair staring at Spyhawk in the window, I swallowed again and my throat felt sour. I hadn't been lying when I told Bolger I was getting a cold. After two hot toddies I had pronounced the cold cured and begun matching martinis with Bolger. I ignored my tight chest, my leaking eyes and nose. Bolger was telling and retelling the scene with Vico as if I hadn't been there. My ears were plugging. His voice took on a harsh gargle like somebody talking underwater. It didn't matter—by that time I was underwater, too, swimming in dizzy circles. We were in that booth by the front window and I remembered looking out once and saying, "Christ, the water in the street is up to the hubcaps. We're going to have to swim home." Then I must have argued with Bolger, because there, sliding into its proper chronological setting across the table from me, was the Bolger face I had first remembered, flushed purple under the dim nightclub light, eyes bulging, spitting curses. Good horsey bones, I thought. Need a soft light along his cheek to bring them out. Von Stroheim would have given him the kind of full-screen close-up that shows you the pores on his nose.

Then I was alone at the table. The clock above the cash register read nine p.m. Still early enough for a good night's sleep. I came to my feet with that queasy lurch you feel when an elevator stops. Home for you, bud, I thought, before you get tipsy. Dissolve: I'm in the lobby of my apartment house shuffling the day's mail. That's when I must have opened the letter from Annie—I found it later in my jacket pocket along with the snapshot Beth's parents took at Christmas. In the picture she's wearing glasses that disguise her eyes—the one feature she got from Beth. From me she got the shapeless Farley nose, the heavy Farley jaw. The shot I keep on my bedside table I took when she was twelve, the last summer she stayed with me. The letter talked about a high school play she was in and said she would be spending Easter vacation with Beth's parents. I remember angling the page to get a better light on it—and that's when I should have known Spyhawk was back. I'd left the Penguin Club at nine and they don't dim the lobby lights in my building till eleven. There was time missing; something had slipped past in a blur, like brittle film that tears in the projector.

I took a step toward the light and my knee hit an ashtray—one of those metal tubes with a topheavy dish of sand. I grabbed for it and my letters fanned out and the ashtray clanged to the floor. All my letters and Annie's picture sprayed with sand and cigarette butts and a peach pit. The ashtray started rolling on its base and while I scrambled for it, I felt my hat leave my head and plop to the floor. I got the stand righted and looked around for my hat and found it under my foot. Shit, I thought, I'm good as Chaplin at this, and in the mirror by the stairs I did a jerky, teetery tramp walk. Then in slow motion I knelt to pick up my mail. Some time later I found myself touching drops of water I had noticed in the sand, wondering if they were rainwater or if I had been bawling among the spilled cigarette butts. I pressed sand onto my forefinger and brought it to my tongue and decided that tears would be more salty.

Still later I was reaching for the last envelope when I noticed the shadows of palm leaves sliding across the back of my hand. I pulled it back and put it out again, watching the shadows wrap over my knuckles. Hurry, honey, I'm starting to shiver. A good shot to try sometime. The plant I had crawled under was on a low stand in an orange clay pot you would need a two-armed hug to lift. The lower shoots drooped and their leaves were brown at the tips. A lazy swell and dip warped the ceiling and the light diffused over it like sunlight filtered through water. The light came from a pair of softly glowing globes hung on chains. Their bellies were dark with the husks of insects. Underwater shot, I decided. Shark's point of view. I picked up my last letter and my fedora, brushed sand from the crown back into the urn, and swam up the stairway. Once I got to my room I pulled a chair to the living-room window and shut my eyes. I opened them once to see Spyhawk staring in at me through the window, but after I remembered the argument with Bolger, I dropped off again.

A gust of rain at my window woke me. My teeth were clenched to keep from chattering. My suit felt heavy and damp. Earlier it must have been clinging wet. Stripping was like peeling off a skin. I put on my pajamas slowly to keep the cloth from rasping my flesh. My throat felt tight. My swallow pushed the pain down, but it bobbed right back and jammed my throat tight. I managed to get a couple aspirin past it and got in bed. The sheets were like sandpaper. I shivered and closed my eyes to lure back the dream. In the darkness behind my eyelids, I saw Spyhawk peering over the stern of my sailboat. He was waiting for something to surface—some fish or eel or squid that had never seen the light. When it swam up near enough, he would get behind his camera and start cranking. Get all the footage you can, Bolger had told him. You're in this too deep already. I realized I'd been wrong about the rain, it wasn't just in the dream, it was pocking the water so Spyhawk couldn't see down. Then it was all right because he had a fever and would have to go home to bed. He felt a smooth hand firm on his brow and saw the worried fold of flesh that raked my mother's eyelids as she shook down the thermometer and said, "Open," and laid it under his tongue. As soon as she took it out he would ask her to write a note excusing him from school, but then the playground bell rang and he knew he'd have to go anyway. I woke with the phone by my bed jangling.

When I picked up the receiver a voice said, "Christ, where you been, Farley?" and just for a moment, before a last wave from the dream washed it away, I thought I knew.

2. The Front-Office Fink

IT WAS THE voice that rattled me. Simmons has the kind of voice that can't ask "How was your weekend?" without sounding like he already knows the answer and expects you to lie about it. I've got to figure out how dangerous he can be and how much I gave him to work on.

It grinds my teeth to think he could be dangerous at all. Vico and I always smiled at his title in the credits—unit supervisor. We knew what he was: the front-office fink. He hangs around the set and has to be allowed to boss extras and keep lists nobody ever needs to see. That's a cover for his real job, spying for Krackenpov. He reports on cost overruns and schedule delays and which leading man breathes whiskey at his makeup call. On every picture we did where Simmons was underfoot, he also asked a lot of snide questions about who the leading lady was screwing. Vico and I could never decide whether that went into his report to Krackenpov or was a taste of Simmons's own.

When I heard his voice I could see him on the other end of the line. He would be standing at the table beside Bolger's camp chair. He would have his sunglasses pushed into his hair to make a little tiara that winks rhinestones under the klieg lights. That legal pad he carries on a clipboard would be held against his body in the crook of his arm and I could see his lowered eyelids and chubby hairless cheeks and that dimpled grin, that glaze of private pleasure you see on nursing mothers, that would come over his face while he was jotting his secrets on the pad. It's funny; looking at him, you'd be embarrassed to be afraid of him, but you could never quite forget that legal pad. A few of the people Simmons made notes about got yanked off a picture and didn't work again.

It was Vico who noticed that Simmons had a sense of caste that gave his voice perfect pitch. Late extras and gofers who didn't put enough sugar in his coffee got a rumbling bass. Set dressers, costumers, and gaffers, people roughly on the same scale as Simmons himself, were a middle-C tenor. A little ironic undertone in the chording, Vico explained, but lots of banter, lots of *glissando,* hmm, you guys? Then Vico did a few mi-mi-mis to find the note Simmons used with producers, directors whose last picture was a hit, and stars with six-figure salaries. What came out was a breathy falsetto full of what Vico called grace notes. When Simmons frowned and unfocused his eyes, Vico said, you knew a grace note was coming, and he would take a step closer to you and let you eavesdrop on a flutish murmur saying some sweet thing Simmons was too bashful to tell you out loud.

That's why, when Simmons's voice on the phone was an octave lower than usual, somewhere on his *chummy* scale, I knew there was trouble. Till that moment Simmons had come at me in a wide circle with a full front shot of the smile on his face that I could spot a long way off, and the question he would get around to after his preliminary bob and stammer would be full of if-you-woulds and do-you-think-you-mights. If he was treating me like one of the boys, something had made him think he could get away with it. Even half asleep, hung over, and in a fever, my first instinct was to show him he couldn't.

I was groping for a snarl that would make him put the Mister back in front of my name when I saw by my night-table clock that I was three hours late for the day's shooting. I blurted out, "I'll be—" and stopped. I finished in a croak: "I'll be right there."

"You sound awful," he said, "you sick or something?"

The voice was a little thinner, close to sympathy maybe, or maybe just disappointed. My own scalp and my right cheek felt clammy, as if huge blisters had collapsed there. I grabbed at Simmons's diagnosis.

"Yeah," I said. "Sick in bed." I tried to give the words a sour sickroom odor. "And you'd better have a damn good reason for not calling me till eleven o'clock."

That was good: Simmons let out a gratifying squeak.

"Gosh, Mister Farley, I'm really sorry, but..."

When I heard that, I decided the trouble couldn't be too serious and lost the next few words as I rolled back the covers and stood up. My skull felt thin and brittle and jammed with pain. As I stood reeling, before the backs of my legs touched the edge of the bed so I could sit down, the phone receiver was close enough for me to hear "...calling it murder, so I thought you..."

"What?" I said, "What murder? Who's calling what—oh,

hold on, Simmons. I'm very sick, I've got to lie down." I was stretching out slowly, calculating the way each change in elevation shifted the pain in my head, when I saw on the pillow a drying spill of vomit. Then I felt it on my cheek, matting my hair. I tried to find a clean place on the pillow. Simmons was saying, "...not official, of course, because they haven't found the body yet, but with these cops buzzing all over the set *grilling* people, we figure it's got to be at least a suicide, and when Bolger said, Do you think it might be a kidnapping, all this detective would say was at this point he couldn't rule it—"

I dragged my voice up to a croak and said, "For God's sake, Simmons, slow down. What is this murder-suicide stuff? Who's dead?"

The pause at the other end of the line might have been exasperated or puzzled. Simmons said, "Mister *Vico*, Mister Farley—like I told you."

The pain seemed to flood the inside of my skull with light. The only dark spot where I could look was a charred figure with the light burning through all around him, and I heard myself say—out loud and maybe clear enough for Simmons to hear: "Spyhawk—so you finally killed him."

Simmons was telling me the police detective who had been asking for me was waiting to take the phone.

So now it's in the light—the real story. This time it's more than just sorting out that's brought me to the Silver Palms. I'm on the run.

CHAPTER IV

1. A Slice of Ham

ALL RIGHT: What do I know about Spyhawk?

I went through high school never looking my mother in the eye, because it was my fault my big brother died. Every time I saw her polishing his humidor that she never gave away or looking out the kitchen window up the way he used to come, I'd think she must be wishing I'd never been born. One Saturday I tried to confess it to Father O'Brien, but I got so choked I couldn't talk and left the confessional without absolution. The night I graduated from high school I stayed out most of the night drinking and my friend Bern and I were standing on the bridge over Ten Mile Creek looking at the moon on the water when he asked me how my brother died and I told him my brother was a railroad signalman who got crushed between two boxcars on the Baltimore and Ohio line. It just came out, and once I'd said it I thought, If that's true, how could I have killed him? And it *was* true. Jimmy died three hundred miles from home and we got a Western Union telegram at suppertime, August 14, 1909. None of us could finish eating, but late that night I came downstairs in the dark and got the slice of ham I'd left on my plate out of the icebox, and ate it. Sometime between then and the next morning Spyhawk must have told me he'd killed Jimmy. Spyhawk was always a liar. It wasn't only for things he'd really done that he could convince me I was to blame.

But I could never be sure when he *wasn't* lying. And if he did kill Vico, I'm the one who's guilty. It sounds odd putting it that way, but how do you talk about someone you've got to be drunk to recognize in a mirror? If it weren't for the things he's cluttered around my room, I'd hardly know him at all. You wake up with a book by your pillow that you never bought and wouldn't read. You find a strange name and phone number in your wallet. How do I know what he might do?

2. The Coming of Spyhawk

HERE'S WHAT I know about Spyhawk's beginnings.

I was about eight years old when I started spending paper-route pennies in the Mooney Street Arcade, and when I woke from a dream, the last thing I'd remember would be looking down one of those eyepieces like a submarine periscope that they used to have on the old hand-crank Kinetoscope machines. That eyepiece would fit around your face like a pair of goggles and shut out everything around you, so the movie was private, for you alone, and even if it was a street shot of people gushing through a factory gate at closing time, watching it gave you an eye to a knothole in a fence and they never knew you were there. After the arcade tore out the Kinetoscopes and began throwing pictures up on a screen with a couple hundred people sitting in rows of chairs all seeing it with you, I almost lost interest in the movies. What pulled me back was that shot at the end of *The Great Train Robbery* where the cowboy levels his sixgun at the audience and fires. Even the first time I saw him point the gun, I wasn't one of those people who would shout and duck under the seat. Every time—and I either paid my money or snuck in through the alley door for a couple dozen shows—I sat very stiff with my fingers wrapped over the arm of the seat, and stared back at him. I couldn't figure out how it was that no matter where in the theater I sat, the cowboy would look out into that dark hall and aim straight at me.

Then for about a year all the dreams I had would end when one of the people I was watching would look up and see me. Whoever saw me would never do anything except look back, but I always woke up scared, sometimes in what my Grandpa

Simon with his little sneer would call a fit of the blubbers. Even when it got that bad I never stopped my detective work.

I had been reading Sherlock Holmes and I would shadow people around town and write up reports on where they went and what crimes I thought they were committing. If somebody I was shadowing stopped in front of Bender's Barber Shop to chat, I would try to get close enough to overhear him plotting. One of the people I shadowed was Mr. Kelsey, who lived across the alley and had a thick black mustache with twirled ends. Once I was watching his house through my bedroom window, something I often did on summer nights the year I was eleven. My father had a pair of binoculars he used on bird-watching hikes. I had sneaked them from the bottom drawer of his dresser. When the gas went up in the bedroom it was Mrs. Kelsey moving around inside. I used to feel sorry for Mrs. Kelsey, because I had decided she knew she was married to a ruthless criminal but couldn't do anything about it. She had hired me to mow their lawn and after I had finished, she would invite me inside to pay me. I would watch her move around the kitchen, chipping ice off the block in the icebox to give me a cold drink and talking about the heat and how if she could get Mr. Kelsey to oil that lawnmower, it wouldn't be nearly so hard to push next week, and whenever she mentioned him, her smile would twitch and her eyes shoot to the door as if she were afraid he was about to come in. That night while I watched her bright window floating in the back-alley dark, Mrs. Kelsey slipped off her dress. Underneath she wore a cotton chemise with a low neck that showed the cleft between her breasts. It wasn't as if she were undressing for the whole neighborhood to see. The backyards were full of thick elms and cottonwoods. She kept well back from the window. Nobody passing in the alley could have seen, only somebody at an upstairs window in my house, where no lights showed. She was out of sight for a minute and her shadow on the wall leaped and fell like a dark flame. When she came back inside the frame, she had unpinned her hair. It fell around her shoulders. She sat on the side of her bed, so I could see her only from the waist up. I thought she was kneading her thighs. She lifted her shoulders and rolled her head back and let it rock from one shoulder to the other and back. Then she looked out the window straight into my eyes.

I knew it, sure as I had known the cowboy with his pistol was aiming at me. Maybe a glint of light had caught the glass of my binoculars. It was the moment in my dream when the one I was watching looked up and saw me, only I couldn't break out of the dream. For a few moments Mrs. Kelsey sat absolutely still, looking back. My head was floating. A sizzle filled my ears, like what you hear when someone slaps a piece of meat into a hot greased pan. My chest heaved. Another fit of the blubbers, I thought. But I couldn't wake up. I couldn't look away and I couldn't wake up.

Then it was all right.

There was a boy kneeling at the window in the dark bedroom and he went on looking, but he wasn't me. He was the one who watched as Mrs. Kelsey lifted the back of her hand to smooth away a coil of hair that had fallen across her cheek, and then went right on with what she was doing. When she lowered her hand, it went below the edge of the windowsill and she tilted back her chin till her eyelids were slits, but the one she kept looking at was the boy in the window. Not me.

The next thing I remember was lying on my bed. I was back inside my body, but I knew I wasn't the only one who lived there. I had my fit of blubbers, quiet as I could, because I had sworn never again to let Grandpa Simon know I cried, and before I fell asleep I whispered, "Who are you? Who are you?"

3. Introduction in the Dark

THAT SATURDAY IN the confessional I told Father O'Brien I had accidentally seen a woman undressing. He asked how long I had gone on watching, and I said only a few moments, but... He waited. But I can't stop... thinking about it. He told me I must be firm. My soul was in mortal jeopardy, he said, and I must find activities to occupy my mind and avoid the occasions of sin. I said my penance kneeling at the communion rail in front of the altar of the Blessed Virgin. While my mind wandered through a second decade of Hail Marys, I found myself wondering if the creature I had discovered living inside my body was my soul.

After that I tried to stop playing detective. There was a park near my house and I spent a lot of time walking in the woods and on the golf course. Every few days I went to the library. I paid a ten-cent fine out of my lawn-mowing money so that I could finish *The Last of the Mohicans* before I took it back, and when I walked in the park woods, I carried a sapling I had twisted off at the root, where it curved like the stock of a deer rifle. I would stalk one foot in front of the other, Indian-style, not stepping on twigs, and whispering over my shoulder to Hawkeye, who was always behind me on the trail, and I would suddenly freeze and hold up one hand and then squint down the barrel of my stick at a squirrel on a branch. I was doing my best to believe that I had dreamed the boy who went on watching Mrs. Kelsey. He only tripped me up now and then when I would be whispering to Hawkeye and suddenly realize I was actually talking to that boy inside me. He frightened me, but I wanted to know more about him.

The only time I saw him was in dreams. One night I dreamed of watching him go from room to room inside the Kelsey house. The rooms extended like a telescope into turrets and hallways that got longer as I snuck along them, and just as he came to the door of Mrs. Kelsey's room the boy in the dream looked around and stared directly—not at me, since I wasn't in the dream except as the camera that saw it—but at the place where my eye hovered, invisible in the dark. Usually when I woke up I would try to get out of my mind the image of whoever it was staring back at me, especially if it was the boy. That night, though, I tried to get it back, because just before I opened my eyes, he had said something, a whisper. There was a sliver of light along the floor and another speck at the keyhole where he had been looking, and I was afraid they would hear him, but he looked at me and whispered again, louder, and the third time I heard him: *Spyhawk,* he said. The light through the bedroom keyhole shone on his face, I could see him grin, and he whispered, *Spyhawk.*

My parents named me Griswold after an uncle who died before I was born. At school it got twisted into Grizzly and Gristle and Greasy. When that boy inside me said his secret name was Spyhawk, I envied him. Who he was fit smooth as a layer of skin over what he did. One reason I get along with actors is because I know what it's like to feel that the person you are is never the one they see.

If I were an actor, I'd get wise-uncle parts. An uncle seasons slowly. In his twenties, while the glamour boys are playing leads, he's a now-and-then extra with a mug shot on file at Central Casting. Then, by his late thirties, say, the lines of envy and denial have cracked into what directors call character. He starts getting work. The credits roll by too fast for you to catch the name, but he turns up in every fifth picture. A bit of a stoop in the shoulders, absentminded-seeming, addicted to a prop cigar he revolves between his lips while he listens and nods. Soon he gets supporting roles, and they get more important. He's the wisecracking sidekick who makes bail for the hero and tells him to marry that gal before she gets away. He's the gunman turned sheep farmer who teaches the kid to handle a sixgun, popping whiskey bottles off the fencepost, and when he gets ambushed riding through the draw, his death speech is what puts that final glint of steel in the kid's eye. He's the uncle, the one the girl finds reading in the den when she comes there to cry alone, the lanky affectionate holiday houseguest who listens while she unpacks her heart, and tells her to marry that guy before he gets away. Oh, yes, he's the uncle, again and again, and when he happens on a lady with bad trouble trying to be brave, he puts on his uncle frown like a favorite smash-brim cap.

The uncle: It's easy to think that's what he is and all he is—until the day he wakes to find some stranger's drunk his liquor; there's a cigarette burn in his tweed sportcoat; a splashstain on the kitchen wall and a shattered glass on the floor below it; someone has soaped a filthy word on the bathroom mirror. Then he knows that Spyhawk's back. And Spyhawk is nobody's uncle.

By the time I was in my twenties Spyhawk was a part of me I'd learned to live with. It was a twist in the way I looked at things—seeing double. I could never tell when it would happen. I'd be in a bar talking with friends or in bed with a woman, and there would be a shadowy corner near the ceiling, sometimes a closet with the door open a crack, and I could sense it—an eye watching me. The next moment I'd be inside the eye and the one at the table or in bed would be Spyhawk. Sometimes it would stop there. Other times, the scary times, the eye would just go away—fade to black—and then Spyhawk would go on with whatever he did while I was away.

After high school I put myself through a couple years of college working in a camera shop. My boss, Mister Edmunds, was a thin-boned man who read Wells and Shaw and had a temper that made him weep. He had got fixed in his mind an idea of justice, the right way for things to be, and when people disappointed him he would wave his arms and shout. After a long day he would sit around the back-room table where the prints were packaged, talking politics with his son. The two of them were alike in everything except their ideas, and as they talked, their voices getting edgy, then husky with rage, each thing they said would be a slash at the other that punished the one who said it, too, and I would leave Spyhawk at the table counting prints and pricing envelopes while I watched from the curtained doorway to the darkroom, and when they had goaded each other past all stopping and filled the room with their shaky voices and their hot male smell, suddenly Mister Edmunds's eyes would go bright and blinking, and I would think: God, oh God—how they must love each other.

I knew from Spyhawk where to put a camera, but it was Mister Edmunds who taught me film speeds and light. I liked him. There's no telling how long I might have stayed with him if it hadn't been for Spyhawk. One day I was out front polishing the glass case where he kept the display cameras. It was the week we were rushing through the high school yearbook pictures, so Mister Edmunds was overworked and grim with worry about the world. A woman came in to complain about a studio portrait. It was Mrs. Kelsey, whom I hadn't seen since she and her husband left the house across the alley from us to move farther uptown. She recognized me. We talked a minute before she said she had to speak to Mister Edmunds. He had shot the portraits on a day when I had classes. I tried to tell her how busy he was developing the yearbook pictures, but she insisted. It just doesn't look like me, she told him. That's not my nose. You've got the smile all lopsided. Now the sizzle filled my ears. Mister Edmunds stayed calm and suggested that it was a very attractive smile. When Mrs. Kelsey said she was sorry but it wasn't and she didn't intend to pay for the print, Mister Edmunds told her maybe she should go home and look in a mirror. Then Mrs. Kelsey said she didn't like his tone and he said he couldn't do any more about his tone than he could about her face. By that time it was Spyhawk running a dustcloth over the shelves and I had become the eye, hovering somewhere above. The last thing I remember is Mister Edmunds, his voice thick and quivering, saying, "I've been in this business twenty years, madam, and there's one thing I know—the camera doesn't lie. You can't fool it and it doesn't lie. *That's your face.*" The next morning I woke knowing Spyhawk had been around and I was worried without knowing why. By the time I got off the streetcar a block from Edmunds's Camera Shop, I felt like vomiting, but I still didn't know why. I started to go behind the counter as usual, but Mister Edmunds said, "Hold it—that's for employees only. You step up this way." He motioned me down the counter on the customer side, across fiom where he was standing at the cash register. He punched the register and counted out eleven dollars and fifty cents. "That's all I owe you," he said. "Now get out of my store." I was shaking. "Are you firing me?" I said. "Firing you?" he said. "Aren't you the one who stood right here and *cursed* me? Aren't you the one who said you got nothing more to learn from me? The one who quit on me in the middle of the busiest week of my year?"

I left. All I could have said was no. No, I'm not the one.

That same week I quit school. The money I'd been saving for next semester's tuition bought me a train ticket to California. Till I began getting jobs at the studio I lived on the rest of it, along with some money my grandmother had given me to help with my education. For a while after I got married Spyhawk dropped out of my life. He didn't show up regularly again until Beth died. The day after the funeral I came home and he was waiting for me. He didn't show himself, but he was in every empty room, strong and sly. I had sense enough to tell my boss I'd have to take a few weeks off. I showed up for work five weeks later with only a hazy notion of where I'd been. Then I went to work for Vico and Spyhawk seemed to disappear for good. I would feel the eye watching on rare occasions—once while I was drinking, I recall, and again in that bad week when Vico was being held for Berenice's murder. Then not for another year, till we started work on *Loves of a Spy.* From the first there were things about the picture that made me uneasy. Even the title was a sly dig in the ribs, as if Vico knew or guessed something about my old problem. And I felt Spyhawk stir in his sleep.

CHAPTER V

1. The Private Eye

I'VE SLEPT A couple hours, and eaten. I called the desk and ordered two eggs over easy and toast with orange marmalade and a pot of coffee. When Mr. Pugh wheeled it in, I was in the bathroom. I opened the door to find him standing by his cart in the center of the room, but looking a bit breathless, as if he might have done a quick sprint from the desk where I do my writing. "Feeling better, aren't you?" he said. "Getting the old appetite back." I gathered up the papers and said I'd eat at the desk. I put the manuscript face down as he wheeled the cart over. He leered and said, "Doing some writing, I see."

"Fiction," I told him. "Thought I'd try to crack the pulp market. Detective story."

"Private eye, huh? Not much in it, I hear. Penny a word."

"That's okay. It's just a hobby. Something to do while my lungs get stronger."

I gave him two bits and he left. I don't think he had more than a glance. If his eye had caught Vico's name, the only way he could have avoided mentioning it would have been to hold his breath till he got through the door. But I've got to be more careful.

2. Crane Shot

IT'S POSSIBLE, of course, that all these precautions are ridiculous, that I'm hiding out for nothing. Spyhawk, as I've said, has lied to me before. My brother Jimmy died between two B&O boxcars. Whatever has happened to Vico (and the newspapers Mr. Pugh brings me morning and afternoon haven't mentioned his name for the past three days), maybe Spyhawk had nothing to do with it.

Maybe. But I don't know. All I *do* know is that there's a gap in my memory of the night Vico disappeared. After my argument with Bolger I left the Penguin Club. That was at about nine-thirty. The next thing I remember is stumbling over that sand urn in my apartment lobby, and the dim lights mean it must have been past eleven. I can't recall traffic noises from the street, so the chances are it was *long* past eleven. The silence was the three or four in the morning kind. The gap could have been as long as six hours. Then I nodded off sitting in my armchair and woke up thinking it was Spyhawk looking in at me through the window. And the next thing I knew Simmons was breathing down the phone at me.

All I've got to go on, then, is the knowledge that the instant Simmons told me the police suspected Vico had been murdered, I sang out Spyhawk's name like the next note in a tune I'd been humming for weeks.

But what kind of evidence is that? I can't even say for certain that the police suspect me. Only that I'd be a fool to assume they don't.

Simmons was such a rabbit I could look him in the eye through the phone. I'd made him stutter like an extra in the first take of a three-line bit with Gable. Then he passed the phone to the detective and the voice in my ear—all chewy and thick as if he was eating a caramel—brought back stock footage from an old nightmare. It was Hoensinger. Whom I knew. While he asked my address and why I hadn't called in sick and told me *A few questions* and *No, it can't wait* and *I'll be there in half an hour,* the caramel burr assured me that this was only routine, nothing I could say had not been heard before, nothing would not be understood.

I lay back in bed, tried to wet my lips. They felt jagged and brittle. Only my cheek was cool. It was the ninth take, and when Vico said, *What is it? What are you staring at?* his voice sank to a moan and I knew this would be the take we would use. I was shooting over his shoulder at the horrified nurse, scissors in her right hand, the bandages still dangling from the other as she drew back, while I panned with her till the cloth-draped mirror entered the shot. *Why is that mirror covered?* Rear shot of Vico entering the frame, yanking the cloth aside—close tight on the mirror, the acid-leached face of Vico's Don Juan. I lurched up onto my elbow and saw my pillow glistening with vomit. The police are coming, I thought.

In the bathroom while I was washing my face and hair, I sank to my knees, my hands clutched around the rim of the toilet bowl. I heaved. Whatever it was inside me that wanted out couldn't tear itself loose. I found myself wiping my mouth with the sleeve of my brown suit, which was lying on the floor. When I tried to stand, I discovered the floor was slowly spinning. Each step I took came down a couple inches to the left of where I expected. I wasn't drunk, not anymore. It was the fever. The floor spun away and I pitched into the doorjamb. I steadied myself, then slowly slid my grip down the jamb till I was on my knees. While I crawled over the bathroom floor and the bedroom, collecting my wet clothes, I was also watching from above, and Vico was with me. *Tilt down,* I heard him say. *Make him all legs and back. An easy shot,* I told him. *Like the one we did in* Doomed Cargo. *We'll need the crane,* Vico said. *Twenty feet up, looking down on him, he'll be— A beetle,* I said. Below us, Spyhawk wadded my sodden suit jacket under his arm. *Pushing his ball of dung,* Vico said. I was sweating and panting, but found I could stand again if I kept a hand on the wall. I dumped my clothes into the closet, ate a couple more aspirin and got back into bed to wait for Hoensinger.

A last thought stung my eyes with tears: No one, I said aloud, loved Vico more than Farley did.

3. The Spyhawk Pietà

I WAS ON the soundstage with Vico, setting up a shot. We had to get a take before the rain came. But rain was already rising up the walls of the soundstage. I spit water down my chin, choking, and opened my eyes. A pair of gray eyes watched me. I pretended not to know him. He had an arm under my head, supporting it while he held a glass of water to my lips. Rain still ticked on the windowpane, but it was no longer the black mirror where I had caught Spyhawk staring at me. The pale light it diffused through the room was moist and grainy. The gray eyes looked me over. The lines around them were fine as diamond scratches in glass and they said the man was ministering to a weakness he had never felt. I couldn't look away. I took a breath and dissolved out of myself and soared off to the window. Looking back, I saw a good fadeout shot: Spyhawk gulps the water and we know he's going to live. But letting Spyhawk have the scene was too risky. He could never get through it without me—someone cautious, someone crafty, someone scared—to cover his tracks. So when the fade to black began and I knew he would be left to manage alone, I fought my way back.

"How did you get in here?" I whispered. The face above me was less than two feet from my own. The arm held my head in a vise. I spat water down my chin and whispered, "That's enough." I was trying to wave the face back, but my whisper—all I could manage—drew it closer. He nudged the glass to my lips again, then set it on the table by my bed. The glass made a wet ring on the letter from Annie.

"You let me in," he said. I knew his voice.

"I've been asleep. How could I?"

"You buzzed the lock on the downstairs door. You told me to come up. You left your door unlocked. You got back into bed and fell asleep. Maybe you were never really awake."

The voice didn't quite match my whisper. As I listened, I saw myself doing what the voice described.

"More water?"

I nodded, then recalled the vomit-stained pillowcase soaking in the bathroom sink. He passed the open bathroom door without pausing and went into the living room, where the carpet absorbed the sound of his footsteps and I couldn't tell whether he lingered for a look around. I wondered what the living room could tell him. I did a quick pan over the pile of newspapers and back issues of *Life* beside the green sofa, the beer-glass rings on the radio cabinet, the portrait of Beth on the desk. I had framed her beneath a palm, low angle, intending the leaves to spray a protective canopy above her. It hadn't worked. The leaves shot like silver blades toward her bare shoulders. She had just come out of the ocean. *Hurry, honey,* she said, *I'm starting to shiver.* Heels clacked on the kitchen linoleum. The kitchen tap gushed. The footsteps clacked four times, then faded into the carpet, and I wondered how long his eye would linger over the breasts and hips of the woman in the bathing suit that had gone out of fashion sixteen years ago.

He appeared at my doorway promptly—a bulky man, thick in the neck and shoulders with a belt strapped high on a thick gut, not softly thick, not quivery but massive, crossing my bedroom with a stride that in somebody else, somebody it was possible to imagine preening, you might call mincing. But in him—with the lap wrinkles in his suit pants and the pocket bulge that might be the sandwich he would have for lunch—it was just a stride that seemed to reach for more than it got, as if he were reminding himself in the middle of each step not to come down hard.

"I know where we met," I said, "but I'm not good at names."

My first lie.

"Hoensinger. Detective Captain." He sat in a straight-back chair he had pulled to the bedside and put the water glass in another place on Annie's letter. "You talked to me half an hour ago on the phone." I propped myself on an elbow and drank water and put the glass back on a magazine. "Couple years ago," he said, "I worked out of Elaypeedee. Now I'm county."

I dropped back onto the pillow and winced.

"If you drank like this often," Hoensinger said, "you'd do it with more style."

"It's not just a hangover," I told him. "I've had a bad cold the last few days. It's gone into my chest. Fever, too."

That, I think, was where I became a suspect for him. It was

the wrong tone. He wasn't a doctor who needed a list of symptoms. I'd turned it into a snivel: Don't hurt me, I'm sick.

"I've got a couple questions," he said.

4. The Examination of Conscience

I'VE HAD THE same embarrassment when a doctor has told me to drop my pants. The intimacy doesn't leave you equally vulnerable. There followed a prodding and palping of tender places. Pulse counting silences.

Hoensinger began by saying he had heard there was some bad feeling between Vico and Bolger. The gray eyes waited while I blew my nose. A thin crust of mucus broke and crawled, exploring the caverns of my skull. The gray eyes still waited.

"Vico is used to directing his own scripts," I said. That had a proper balance—the reluctant citizen compelled to state the fact the staunch friend refuses to interpret. I can see Hoensinger: He raises his chin, his eyelids droop, hooding the eyes so that he seems to be peering a long distance. It was the staunch friend he was looking at, I knew. The staunch friend babbling about Vico's lovers and his lousy marriage and his incredible temper and his perfect casting for the role of wife murderer. The spy as staunch friend.

"You and Vico pretty good friends?" Hoensinger asked.

I knew it was useless to lie. My thawed mucus inched along, filling every hollow in my face. I looked straight at the slits where Hoensinger's eyes lay and said, "Vico's the best friend Farley's got."

The eyes remained slitted. Again I had said too much.

"Been with him since his second picture," I said, and blew my nose to remind Hoensinger it was my cold that made my eyes bright.

Hoensinger's next question edged closer to what he really wanted to know.

"What about those rumors in the paper—that Monty Druhl gossip column?"

I could see he wouldn't have any more mercy on the truth than on a lie. I tried to imagine what someone innocent and bewildered and feverish would say. Nothing came to me. It had always been Vico who wrote the dialogue. I decided to wait out Hoensinger's silence. When I breathed there was a merry commotion in my chest, like fizzing champagne. I concentrated on my breathing until I became aware of Hoensinger talking: "... couldn't seem to talk about hardly anything else," he was saying, "but every time I asked one of them, from the director on down to the stagehands, he'd mumble about this love-affair rumor in Druhl's column and say it *might* have been what upset Vico, so you know the natural next question is, who was playing around?"

The dreamy thick voice didn't fool me.

"I don't speculate about things like that," I whispered. I thought how fine that would sound in one of Vico's scripts. The slits winked away and the gray eyes came out full. I had forgotten: Hoensinger of all people knew how far I was willing to speculate. So I gave it to him. "Vico thought it was his wife."

"His wife and who?"

"Bolger."

"How do you know?"

"Monty Druhl says in that column of his that he hangs out in the Coconut Grove and the people that stop to talk give him his stories. A couple nights ago Vico called me. Wanted me to go there and keep an eye on Druhl. See if anybody from the unit sat with him."

"And did you?"

"I thought it would make Vico feel better."

"See anybody?"

"Lots. Agents, mostly. Starlets. Drugstore cowboys. Everybody come to polish the brass. Nobody from our unit."

Hoensinger pursed his lips and swallowed. If he had been looking for a place to catch me, this wasn't it. All I'd told him was true.

"Nobody from your unit? That doesn't prove much, though, does it?"

"What I said. I told Vico the same thing."

"Who do you think was feeding Druhl his stuff?"

I looked back at the level gray eyes and said, "I don't know. Ask Druhl." And Hoensinger said, "I did."

Then he waited. I did, too, while the pressure in my sinuses tried to crack the walls of my skull. At last I said, "Did you scare the truth out of him?"

"Not much," Hoensinger said. "Druhl would like nothing better than to get clapped in jail defending the First Amendment. He'd write his column from a cell and have more readers than Winchell."

His next question looped back.

"Was it Vico who thought Bolger was screwing his wife, or you?"

"I was talking about Vico."

"Maybe that ties in with something else," he said, and the gray eyes forgot me. They came back, and he said, "Everybody I talked to out at the studio says yesterday something pretty strange happened. Vico went berserk. First he rips his wife's gown. To the waist. Then he takes a punch at this Bolger guy and walks out. Is that pretty much how you remember it?"

I told him it was. Then he said I was Vico's best friend and asked if I had any idea what was in his mind when he did those things. His best friend.

"Who can tell what goes on in people's heads?" I said.

"That's not good enough, Mister Farley. There's got to be something. Some hint. Something he said, maybe."

I noticed a slight elevation in Hoensinger's voice, as if a part of him relished what he said: "There must have been fifty people on that set yesterday. A guy strips his wife to the waist in front of that mob—he must think he's got a reason."

"With a personality like Vico, reasons can get pretty complicated."

"Maybe not. Think of this jealousy angle. You could see it as a way to humiliate her. He yanks that gown—and what he's saying is this: You want to be a whore with this creep? Then do it now, right in front of everybody. How does that sound to you?"

"It sounds like you ought to be writing Monty Druhl's column," I said. It was a fine revenge, hearing that thick voice edged with excitement and letting him know I'd caught him skinny-dipping in one of Vico's fantasies, just like any fan. What he said bothered me because it sounded true. Maybe I didn't like to think he could know Vico as well as I did. I wanted to prove him wrong, wanted to tell him Vico's real intention was to give Lisa away; say to Bolger: Here she is—take her. But I'd spilled too much already. "Sorry," I said. "I guess there's no way to talk about it that *won't* sound like Druhl's column. It's just that—"

"Sure," said Hoensinger, "you're his friend." I couldn't tell whether he'd given that last word an extra shove. Then he said, "Does Vico have enemies—aside from Bolger?"

For a long time, it seemed, I had lain still. The surface of Hoensinger's gray eyes was still as a skin of ice, but when I glanced there, I could feel a current tugging underneath. The fluids inside my skull thickened. The pain pressed against the walls. I lay still holding it back. I squeezed my eyes shut and tried to focus on Hoensinger's question: Who were Vico's enemies? An image pulsed against my clenched eyelids, but all I could make out was a red flood. It pulsed once, twice, and I opened my eyes and said, "What kind of enemies?"

"The last few weeks Vico's had the jitters pretty bad. Part of it was Bolger. You aren't the only one who told me Vico didn't like Bolger directing this picture. I got it from Bolger, too. And if Vico thought Bolger was screwing his wife, that's another part of it, a big part. Human nature being what it is, both those things could come together by accident. But then you get that buzz in Monty Druhl's column. Makes it look like somebody's having lots of fun watching Vico squirm. So I guess I'm looking for somebody with a grudge." He waited. I was busy with the pain. "Okay," he said. "The monkey wrench in the works seems to be Bolger. How did he get there?

Vico always directs his own pictures, but not this time. Why?"

"Ask Krackenpov," I said.

"The studio head?"

"He's the one who saddled Vico with a director."

"Vico ever give him a hard time?"

"Always. Krackenpov wants a cheap picture, Vico wants a good one. They're natural enemies."

"Krackenpov is the boss. Why can't he just say, Do it my way or walk?"

"Actors have contracts," I said. "It costs money to fire one. Money and time—time to reshoot his scenes with another actor. That's more money. Try to replace your lead actor and your director both at once and you might as well flush your picture down the toilet."

"Sounds like a good reason to make sure somebody besides Vico directs Vico's pictures. Take away some of his power and you get a tame actor. The picture comes in on schedule, cheap. Box-office lines are just as long."

"It's a good theory. The risk is that your actor won't tame. Then you get what happened yesterday. Vico punches out Bolger and walks off the set. Your cast and crew sit around the stage playing pinochle and collect their paychecks. Nothing cheap about that."

"You and Vico knew that, too."

It was an accusation. The words had poured out just as smoothly, but with something, a flatness maybe, a slight tensing and clipping of consonants, that made you sure this was the tone he used when he said: "You're under arrest for the murder of..."

"What's that supposed to mean?" I asked.

Just before shooting began the previous day, Hoensinger told me, Vico and I had been overheard talking. *Loves of a Spy* was nearly two weeks past its wrap-up date and someone—he avoided saying who—had heard us getting a big kick out of how much that was costing Krackenpov. Even through the fever flush Hoensinger must have seen my color rise. Vico and I, caught like a couple of schoolboys whispering during choir practice. I was so shocked I admitted it. What shocked me was not the accusation, which wouldn't earn me a cell in Alcatraz, but the deliberate spying. There was no chance that the eavesdropping could have been accidental. During the conversation Vico and I had been alone—so we thought—at the dense heart of a forest. Not a real forest, but a set we had used a few weeks earlier, a twenty-five-yard stand of papier-mâché trees with paper leaves and a pump-fed brook winding through it. Constructing it had been difficult and expensive, and Krackenpov wanted it saved for a picture that would begin shooting the following month. Vico had gotten into the habit of following the dolly tracks down the path to the bank of the brook when he wanted to be alone between takes. He called it the Petrified Forest. I had known Simmons was Krackenpov's spy, but when I thought of him dodging along after us to hear what we said, I wanted to spit.

Hoensinger shrugged.

"The two of you weren't brokenhearted about the hole in Krackenpov's pocketbook," he said. "I don't give a damn about that. What it establishes is that Krackenpov might have had good reason to suppose that Vico enjoyed making him sweat."

I thought of the way Simmons must have drooled his daily report in the old man's ear, and said, "You can bet on it."

"But is that enough," he said, "to make Krackenpov hire a couple of goons to put the chill on one of the biggest actors in his stable? Just from the point of balancing books, the thing still doesn't make sense. Unless"—he paused and the words dripped out slowly—"unless there's another motive, something personal...."

With that much of a prod I told him about Vico's attempt to rescue Alice Brighton. One day about three weeks into shooting *Doomed Cargo* I was late to lunch. As I came through the commissary line I spotted Vico sitting with the new girl in the secretary pool who was Krackenpov's latest sweetheart. I was about to walk over when I felt a tug at my trouser leg. Bernie, the key grip, was cocking his head up at me with a grin that would have stretched the lips of an orangutan. "You better park yourself here today, Farley," he said. "They're playing a pretty intense scene over there." I parked and watched. Alice had her head bowed so that her short bob horse-blinkered her face. Vico, one hand on her shoulder, was offering her a handkerchief. He had tugged his chair around the corner of the table to put him close beside her. "How long has that been going on?" I asked. A minute after Vico had sat down with them, Bernie told me, he had stopped a fork halfway to his face and said, "Now why do you suppose that sweet little girl is crying in her soup?" He went over to find out. They were still sitting when Bernie and I left to get back on stage. Vico was half an hour late for his first scene and strolled in wearing a smug grin that he wouldn't let go of till it had ruined half his afternoon scenes. That night at the Penguin Club the smug grin crept back. He could hardly wait till the usual crowd emptied to let me chip the news out of him. It seemed Alice had won a hometown beauty contest and come to Hollywood on a six-month contract that hadn't been renewed. She knew she wasn't really an actress, but had let Krackenpov convince her that knowing how to act had nothing to do with being a star. After she had gone out with Krackenpov a couple of times, he had asked her to do something disgusting—"I'm not editing, Farley," Vico had said. "She wouldn't tell me, either"—and when she wouldn't, he had beat her up and she wished she were back home in Oswego. "So that's where she's bound, Farley, even as we speak," Vico said. "I grabbed a cab right at the studio gate and took her over to my bank and drew out two thousand bucks—enough to give her train fare home with a bit left over to live on while she finds another job."

Krackenpov always ate lunch in his private dining room, so a couple days later when he started across the crowded commissary floor, swinging his gut like a wrestler strutting down the aisle, the hush brought our heads up before he reached our table. He took a wide, flat-footed stance across from Vico, rooted a fist into his pocket, and came up with a fan of bills, which he peeled crisp as a cardsharp into the gravy on Vico's roast beef. He was puffing hard, but he got out his speech:

"There—little salad with your meat. Two thousand bucks' worth." Then, after a snort George Saunders would have envied, he hitched his trousers, sneered, "Sir *Galahad,*" and left. Standing by the hallway to his private dining room was Alice Brighton, waiting tiptoe on her spike heels and looking as if Krackenpov had just paid off the mortgage on the farm.

When Vico saw Alice with those my-hero eyes, he let out a bark of pure delight. Krackenpov's shoulders twitched up around his neck. He kept on walking. Vico kept on laughing.

After I had got the story out, Hoensinger passed me the water glass and I took a few more sips.

"So," he said, "there was something personal with Krackenpov. That's good to know." Then, as if he weren't changing the subject: "What time did you leave the Penguin Club last night?"

That's it, I thought: the question he's come all this way to ask; that he couldn't ask on the phone, because the answer he wants won't be in anything I say, but in my face.

I got as far as: "I left shortly after—" and froze.

"Shortly after you threw a drink in Bolger's face?"

My eyes were playing tricks like a rack focus shot that won't lock. A ghost of Hoensinger's face kept drifting off from the real one so that a bit to the right of his right eye another eye hovered. I could see through the ghost eye to a distant plane where Father O'Brien drew aside the panel and waited behind his black-draped grill for my *Bless me, Father.* I tightened my brow to make the ghost eye slip back inside the real one, and tried to focus on Hoensinger's question.

"I guess," I said, "I was pretty drunk."

"What got you riled?"

...*Father, for I have sinned,* sinned in a hissing whisper, and *My last confession was*...oh, how long, how long ago since I began sorting my sins from Spyhawk's and confessing only mine?

I told Hoensinger that I had tossed my drink in Bolger's face to cool him off. He was talking, I said, about Lisa Vico's body.

"Not much gentlemanly discretion, huh?"

"He said he'd have Lisa in bed within a week."

"Which means he hadn't yet?"

"Course not," I said. "She'd no sooner let that monkey touch her than—"

"But what do you suppose made Vico think she would?"

A sneeze was itching to blow a leak off the tip of my nose.

Hoensinger continued: "Vico was her *husband.* You sleep in the same bed with someone, brush your teeth with the same toothpaste, it seems you'd get a pretty good idea what that person might do and what she—"

"There's a side to themselves married people don't show," I said, the sneeze still feeling its way. "Not to each other. Not if they want the marriage to last."

"No need for lectures, Mister Farley. I been waking up beside the same woman twenty-seven years next month." He grunted and shook his head, as if to apologize for his testy boast. Then he said, "Tell me if I'm wrong. Didn't you get yourself twisted around? First you said Bolger wasn't screwing Lisa Vico. Then you said she was hiding it from her husband."

"That's not what I—hab!" My lungs were snatching air. "Not—hab!—what I said. I was talking—hab!—in general."

"Don't. Talk in particular. About Lisa Vico. Where you keep your handkerchiefs?"

I pinched my nose and the sneeze imploded. I felt hairline cracks of pain shoot along the plates of my skull. I shut my eyes to concentrate on being Farley, Farley shut them so tight I saw red. That's when I thought of Singleton, thought of Singleton's blood-covered face as they stretched him on the back seat, the shrieking head on Vico's lap. If anybody had a reason to kill Vico, it was Singleton.

Mark of Cain was Vico's gangster picture. He slips out of his gang's desert hideout and runs for the plane, leaving the others to die. The script called for his gang to tumble out of the cabin, popping revolvers and a machine gun at him as he sprints to the plane, climbs into the cockpit and taxis away. We had an ex-army gunner named Thornhill James firing bursts at the sand while Vico ran. Thorny said he was an expert and proved it by knocking tin cans into a spin at fifty yards. So long as Vico ran where he said he would, Thorny told us, he was safe as a baby hung on a tit. Simmons, fussing about what the insurance company and Krackenpov would say, tried to get Vico to let Singleton do the run. Vico wouldn't hear of it, not even when Singleton hinted that he needed the work. But the first time we ran a take, Vico stumbled in a crevice and sprained his ankle. That's why it was Singleton after all who made the run to the plane, Singleton who was about to climb into the cockpit when a slug from Thorny's machine gun ricocheted off a flat rock and drilled the plane's gas tank. The explosion knocked him twenty feet. A couple guys in the crew smothered the flames by wrapping him in a canvas we'd been using as a sunshield, but he'd taken a chunk of flying metal in his face. When I visited him in the hospital, he was in a cocoon of bandages. His face was an oval with a black slit mouth. There was a nostril slit, too, but no bump where the bandage would wrap over the bridge of a nose. Underneath the bandages there wasn't much left of his face. Being lip-stiff made him hard to understand, but he told me through the black slit that they were building him a new face, he would come out of it with a profile like Barrymore and play leading men. He always did enjoy feeding me wisecracks. That was after his fourth operation. I don't know how many more he had before they gave up on him. I heard that by the time he got out of the hospital, he'd gone simple in the head and was jabbering in bars about going back to the desert with a pick and a gold pan.

What must it have been like to live, to go on living, behind Singleton's smashed face? Who you are is the flesh of your face and the bone it's stretched on. Spoil the flesh with acid the way Vico did to his Don Juan; smash the skull, poor Singleton's skull; and you can't help, can you, but make another person underneath?

When Vico jumped onto the seat of that limo and made a lap for Singleton's head, I almost vomited. I was grateful when the doors slammed the screams inside the car, but in there with them was Vico, and Singleton's screams went on as if he'd been screaming like that since he was born and pain was the price he paid for every breath. Vico knew that trip would take hours. Yet he sat there—he sat there, Singleton bleeding in his lap, clawing at his shoulders. He sat and watched. Is there anything, I wonder, more chilling than the passion of an artist? Think of him, the great Vico, sucking up images—for what? Another film?

I lay there in bed with Hoensinger's chill gray eyes on me and decided to give him Singleton.

And that thought was my first hope. If it *had* been Singleton who killed Vico, then Spyhawk was taking credit for what he'd only wished, and never done. Still guilty, of course; Father O'Brien and I both knew you could burn in hell for bad thoughts.

Then the pain swallowed me, and when it recedes, I hear my voice discussing Lisa, explaining with patient care that she is a model who'd got tired of being stared at and Vico never should have put her in a movie. It is Spyhawk talking. I am watching from across the room.

5. Eavesdropping

THE MAN LYING in my bed is saying things to Hoensinger. Then Hoensinger is saying that he stopped off at the Penguin Club on his way to Farley's apartment.

"The bartender," he says, "tells me you and Bolger sit at that corner table pretty regular lately. That so?"

"I guess it is," Spyhawk says.

"First time he's had any roughhouse from you, though."

"I'm not usually a rowdy drunk. Not usually drunk at all."

"Tell me something. I thought you were Vico's friend. How come you spend so much time with Bolger?"

I wait for Spyhawk's answer. It doesn't come.

"You spying for Vico maybe?" Hoensinger asks. "He wanted you to check out Druhl. Maybe he asked you to keep an eye on Bolger, too."

"I do a lot of things for him that he doesn't ask. I get paid to think, not just follow orders."

Spyhawk sneezes and moans.

"So after Bolger left, what did you do?"

"Sat a few minutes. Finished my drink. Then went home."

"What time?"

"Ask the bartender. He probably remembers better than I do. I was pretty bombed."

"Take a guess."

"Nine-fifteen, nine-thirty."

"Check. Bartender says you left at ten after nine. A little wobbly, he says. You go home?"

"Yeah. First I took a walk."

"In the rain?"

"To cool off. It's not like me to blow up like that. I knew I was drunk and wanted to clear my head before I drove home."

"I put your suit on a hanger. It never would have dried clumped on the floor."

"You got a search warrant to go through my closets?"

"Movies," Hoensinger says. "Ever since Cagney it's classy to lip off at cops. Your closet door was wide open. I closed my eyes and *felt* for a hanger. How long did you walk?"

"Sorry. Half an hour. Maybe an hour."

"See anybody?"

"Not many people out. Too wet."

"Stop anywhere?"

"Just walked. Looked in store windows."

Hoensinger asks whether Spyhawk went straight home after his walk, and I am waiting for his answer. The phone in the living room rings. Hoensinger rises to answer it. While he is in the other room, I stare at Spyhawk. He knows I am looking. It's time for the fade to black. This time, though, he doesn't black me out. He's worried, maybe, not trusting himself to get through the scene alone. I was used to that. Vico would depend on me to tell him if a take was bad.

Hoensinger comes back into the room.

"So," he says. "You came straight home after your walk?"

"Yeah."

"That would bring you back here by, say, ten-thirty."

"That's right."

"Can anybody vouch for that?"

"I live alone."

Hoensinger sucks his lips against his teeth, then lifts a corner of his mouth in a lopsided grin till the suction breaks with a small liquid click. It is a punctuation mark, a close to his official interview. He rests his back against the straight back of the chair and says, "Vico get much fan mail?"

Spyhawk answers carefully: "A fair amount. Not so much lately. He hasn't made a picture in nearly two years."

"What kind of mail? He ever show it to you?"

"Not much. Once in a while, for a laugh. Some of it's pretty strange. After he did *Mark of Cain* a woman begged him to beat her—for her sins. I don't think he reads them all."

"How does he react?"

"That one bothered him. Maybe it *interested* him, I don't know. He read it to me. Very educated voice, elaborate buildup. Talked about how uncomfortable she felt intruding on a stranger, but he was the only one who could help her. Some complicated theory about St. Teresa and the stigmata. What it all came down to was a time and place when she would be most grateful if he would come over and whip the sin out of her."

"Why did he show this to you—for laughs?"

"Sure we laughed. But it was more than that. He enjoyed playing Sir Galahad. He had convinced himself he ought to do something and wasn't sure what. I told him to forget it."

"Did he?"

"A couple days later he asked me to read a letter he was sending her. He wanted to be sure there wasn't anything in it that could push her over the edge."

"What did it say?"

"Pretty harmless, really. He told her in the gentlest possible way that she needed professional help and he couldn't be the one to give it. 'I'm not who you think,' he told her."

Spyhawk is recalling something that I had more or less forgotten the day after it happened.

For a moment Hoensinger lets his gray eyes roll away, as if to hide some doubt or calculation. He pulls back and says, "Vico mention any letters this week?"

The end of Hoensinger's art was to drain himself of all desire and feeling so that as he asked his crucial question, his body would convey no hint of what answer he hoped or suspected to hear. So it was from nothing in Hoensinger's face, but from the common gossip of the next day's newspapers, that I learned that the phone call he took in my living room must have been his first knowledge of what the headlines called the "Kill-You-Annabelle Letters." Nothing in his face hinted at what place in his own calculations these letters had. Two letters, which in the following days inspired endless column inches of speculation that Vico had been kidnapped and killed by the crazed husband of one of his fans. Even the hack reporters paid Vico's art their tribute, knocking together an explanation of his death that sounded like a Vico film.

Spyhawk frowns, pretends to be drifting in his fever, then says no, Vico had not discussed any fan mail that week, and Hoensinger gets to his feet. At the door he says, "You do what I said. Take that Vicks and slather it on your chest and get some sleep."

On my bedside table is a years-old, half-used jar of Vicks he has found in my bathroom medicine chest.

I didn't hear him close the door. When I woke—it may have been only moments later—I was back inside my body. Spyhawk had left like a lover who slips out of bed while you sleep. No jotted goodbye slid under a placemat. Just a chill up my spine that said: *Run.*

I did—and never till now wondered why. What scared him? A dozen times today I read each word Hoensinger said, and each of my replies, and each thing Spyhawk said. At last I've found what he was hiding. It's this: Spyhawk didn't have to read a newspaper to know about the Kill-You-Annabelle Letters. The instant Hoensinger mentioned fan mail, Spyhawk thought of the Silver Palms Hotel.

CHAPTER VI

1. Getaway

IN THE FIRST moments after I realized Hoensinger was gone, I persuaded myself that for a little while, another hour at least, I could sink into my fever and sleep. With my eyes closed I found myself doing an inventory of all he'd seen. I saw my kitchen sink. A drip on the rim of the faucet fell. Another one gathered. I rolled on my side. A dusty wooden bird that would bob its orange beak for water stood by a tumbler I hadn't filled or washed in years. A Christmas present from Annie when she was eleven. I bunched my pillows and settled again, counting whiskey bottles in the grocery bag by the stove. I tried to stop it, concentrated on nothing. Nothing slowly faded to the glass of melted ice cubes on the arm of the living-room chair, the one facing the window where I had seen Spyhawk. It was only then—just as you need to catch yourself scratching to notice the rash—that I realized how the rooms where I lived had been defiled by Hoensinger's eyes. There was no corner that had been mine where his gray eyes had not probed or raked. No place where I could see anything of me but what he had been looking for.

Pulling my suitcases down from the closet shelf, I thought how many times I had filmed Vico in this scene. It was in every picture, that panic when he learns he's been found out; when the burrow where we've seen him plan his raids and gloat over booty and brood at the mahogany chessboard and spread on the table a map of the city's sewer tunnels becomes the trap he must escape.

Think of that shot in *Mark of Cain* when I look over his shoulder as he stares through the rain-streaked window. The police car undulates up the drive. He swings his face to the camera, straining to swallow the room through his eyes. The eyes harden. Quick cuts: to the Cellini music box, the silver cruets shaped like leaping dolphins, then back to the eyes. Which treasure is small enough to pocket as he runs for the sliding panel, the winding stairway to the sewers?

I gathered my treasures, too. Along with my shirts I put into a suitcase the Bible where my mother had pressed a spray of buttercups and bedstraw. I folded into a sweater a pistol discovered after his funeral in the bottom of my father's trunk—my sole memento of that silent man. I collected my photos of Annie and Beth. And finally, a string-wrapped shoebox of letters that I read each August 24th, the date I last saw her alive.

While I was packing socks and handkerchiefs, the floor began to seethe like water about to boil. I tossed a last handful of underwear and grabbed the sides of my bureau drawer. In its yellowed newspaper lining Lindbergh on Wall Street waved through a tickertape storm. I scanned each face in the crowd for the one not cheering, the one who hated Lindy enough to steal his baby. I swallowed hard, fizzing in my lungs. I closed my eyes and prayed not to fall. As I pitched forward, my ears filled with the moan that greeted Vico striding through his teeming fans. I lay for a while with the bureau drawer tilted above my head, resting and thinking.

Later, each hand holding a suitcase, I was sitting on the back stairs of my apartment building. What am I doing here in my pajamas, I thought, and saw that I was wearing my brown suit. I was six steps from the first landing, where a window hung pale silver in the dark. I sat there: panting, sweating, waiting for a reason to move.

I stood up with my suitcases. I planned each step as if I were descending a cliff. When I got to the landing I set the suitcases under the window and sat on one. Against the light above the garage rain fell at a sharp angle. Always backlight a rainstorm, I thought. It had been early afternoon when I started packing. Somewhere along the hall a radio baritone listed streets under water, talked about mudslides in the canyons and a washed-out bridge. My world wasn't the only one spinning away. Then another voice talked about soapsuds. It was a bubbly voice, and as it bubbled along, soapsud noises bubbled and burped around it.

My watch had run down. I tried to fix the time by the radio, but in the middle of the soapsuds music it clicked off. I looked back the long way I'd come. I could only remember the last six steps. I kept on looking until somebody holding my two suitcases appeared at the top of the stairs. It wasn't that I *remembered* standing there, rocking, leaning my shoulder against the wall to keep from falling. And I didn't imagine it. What I saw was real as the image that floats on your retina after the flashbulbs pop. They ambush you just inside the door of the precinct house and the cop with his arm on your shoulder has learned to lower his hatbrim and look at his toes, so he can see fine while you throw your hands out—blind, stumbling, trying to stop—but he tugs you along to the interrogation room and you are still blinking white suns when the cop across the desk asks when you last saw Vico and how he got along with his wife.

If I squinted or coughed or even took a breath, the man at the top of the stairs would disappear.

Still shouldering the wall for support, he edged one foot forward and stepped down. He stepped again, leading with the same foot. But a few seconds later a faint unpleasant tingle lifted the hairs on my arms and neck. He had melted inside. He pressed my lips in that tight smile I had learned from the mirror. Spyhawk. My good old grinning grunting Spyhawk self, my better-man-than-I-am, who from time to time claimed squatter's rights in my body.

I felt unsteady perched on the edge of my suitcase, so I slid my backside down the wall. Seated on the floor beneath the window, I made conversation with Spyhawk. Oh, by the way, I said. Are you renting or? Planning to—to support me in the manner, manner to which, how do you propose?

Once I had got the two suitcases into my car and fitted

myself behind the wheel, I sat still, listening. We forgot something, he whispered. I got out of the car and climbed back upstairs without asking what. Later he would let the bellhop call it my sample case. Getting it downstairs took a long time. While I was resting on the same landing, Mrs. Blodgett came down the hall. She wore an ankle-length bathrobe and carried a bundle of garbage wrapped in newspaper. She passed me with a bird-quick glance and hugged her parcel under her arm as if I might try to snatch it. From a little corner of newsprint Vico's black-and-white eye peeked at me. It was a still from *Mark of Cain.* On her way back she edged closer to the stair railing, her robe clutched to her throat. A few steps above me, out of reach of a sudden leap, she stopped and looked back. "You all right?" she asked. Spyhawk told her we were just resting. "Resting!" she said. "You been out here bumping that thingamajig down the steps for an hour and a half. Don't you think it's time you stopped moaning to yourself and got to bed? Other people have to sleep if you don't."

After I got the thingamajig into the trunk and myself behind the wheel, I remember telling Spyhawk I didn't think I could drive.

2. Spying on the Spy

I HAVE A vague memory, Spyhawk's not mine, but he gave me a few peeks. Each hand holding a suitcase, he crosses the high-ceilinged lobby of the Silver Palms Hotel. His footsteps on the terrazzo echo moist and squeaky. He's soaked through, but when he confronts the desk clerk, that will disguise his fever sweats. His lungs rattle like an idling cat. Under the rim of his dripping fedora, he inventories the old furnishings. By the elevator, the same stone urn. Over the sofa, the same painting: sleepy passengers boarding a stagecoach. The cloakroom next to the elevator is still used as a bellhop station. The eyes peering over the lower half of the dutch door are new. They are clear as watered whiskey. They skim away like minnows.

The night clerk is a woman with thinning orange hair. Through it as she bends to write, Spyhawk sees her glossy scalp. Signing the register book with an alias, he recalls this same woman behind the desk when he stayed here last. He checks an urge to scratch through the name he's written. Her eyes rise from the page to his face. "Somethin' a matter?" she says. It's her slur that saves him. Her slur and the smell of breath mints. No need to worry. Twice when he'd come in late without his key, she'd demanded proof that he was a registered guest. "Nothing," he says, and finishes the false signature with a flourish, so cocky he asks for his old room and gets it.

The clerk taps a silver bell on the counter. The curly head just visible above the dutch door doesn't move. In a tone that gently wakes a sleeper the clerk calls, "Mr. Pugh." A voice from the cloakroom says, "I am aware, Mrs. Copely, that a guest has arrived. I'll be there in exactly one minute." The voice is a windy tenor that might have been blown over the lip of a beer bottle.

"Yes, Mr. Pugh," the woman says, and leans toward Spyhawk. "He's just had an *awful* night of it. The rain, ya know." Her whisper quivers with adoration.

The red second hand on the clock above the elevator travels from three to nine. Again the woman leans across the counter. "Used ta be a perfessor, ya know." She purses her lips tight, then lets her secret break the seal. "Some trouble about a female student. Knew *exackly* what she was doing, ya know. One of those that learns filth in the cradle. But it still—still *ruined* him. He's a ruined man." She sighs and bites her lip and frowns at her crossword puzzle.

Then Mr. Pugh is bouncing across the terrazzo with the vexed authority of someone called away from important business. At twenty feet his eyes dip to the bags at Spyhawk's feet, and when they come up they bring along a wide smile with a neat center part in the upper teeth. He puts enough oil in his "Good evening, sir" to make sure Spyhawk knows he doesn't greet everybody that way and hefts the bags as if he's been asked to guess how much they weigh. At the elevator he eases them to the floor. There is a brief wait while the buttons above the door count backward from six.

"I see you have a taste for fine leather," he says.

"What?"

"Your bags. Elegant craftsmanship. You can tell a gentleman by his taste in wines and by his luggage."

The bags had been a present from Beth. She'd felt guilty about not wanting to travel East with me for my father's funeral. Spyhawk glances over the dutch door. Same folding chair, same card table with a checkerboard top. A hubcap-size ashtray, well planted with snubnose butts. A scattering of true crime stories. On their covers women in torn dresses shrink from blue-jawed thugs. Also some more serious reading: a volume titled *The ABC of Law;* another called *State Your Case—A Layman's Guide to the Legal Labyrinth.* Last night coming back from the newsstand I passed him munching a thick cud of polysyllables under his breath. But his most constant pastime was stacking his change. Nickels were five to a stack, pennies and dimes ten, and quarters four. As the night wore on, each time he returned from an errand he added his tip to the stacks. Only last night coming back from the newsstand I passed his station. He had just completed a stack of nickels and I saw him promote it into the ranks of finished stacks. His fingers danced along the ranks, making fussy adjustments.

Once in the room Spyhawk asks him to go to the newsstand for papers. Alone, Spyhawk sits on the bed and works the wet knots in his shoelaces. He flops back on the mattress in his wet suit, his eyes closing. When a sheaf of newspapers slaps the night table, his eyes twitch and open again. Mr. Pugh wears a dripping slicker. The night-table lamp throws the shadow of his eyebrows onto his forehead. His face is square and ruddy, puffy at the edges, and when he pretends to glance around the room for something more to do, Spyhawk sees a muscle jerking in his cheek.

"Oh—you're awake. Your newspapers, sir."

The newspaper on top of the pile slides to the floor. Mr. Pugh squats to retrieve it. His hair reflects like a blacktop road on a rainy night. A curl springs free and drops a thin black sickle on his brow.

"And your change," he adds, counting four ones and some coins onto the pile of newspapers. "I believe you'll confirm that's the full amount." He looks solemnly down. "Extraordinarily wet out there."

Spyhawk at last gets the point of these attentions and puts two of the bills in Mr. Pugh's palm. With a gee-whiz shake of the head and a grin, Mr. Pugh pockets his tip and turns to go.

"In my car," Spyhawk says, "on the back seat. Another... suitcase. It's kind of heavy."

Only a faint ripple of the muscle. As he starts for the door, Mr. Pugh's hand lifts in a definite salute. A few minutes later he is back, puffing, jolly, spraying water like a dog.

"Gee, that's a heavy one," he says. "I gather you must be a salesman."

Spyhawk, dozing again, opens his eyes and says, "Huh?"

"I can always deduce a salesman," Mr. Pugh explains. "His sample case is approximately three times as heavy as the customary suitcase. That's no estimate either. That's the testimony of what the legal professionals call an expert witness."

"Uhh."

While Mr. Pugh talks, Spyhawk's eyes stray to the top newspaper on his table. Flood headlines. Under the banner headline—a separate story—he sees what he expected: "Vico Feared Lost in Torrent." And under that, in smaller type: "Sinister Fan Letters Found." The photo, folded under just below the eyes, is a studio portrait: hair combed flat, eyes on the birdie, blandly calm—not at all like Vico.

"I've got a brother in the legal profession," Mr. Pugh confesses. "I myself am an associate in the firm."

"Uhh."

Spyhawk resists the temptation to pick up the newspaper. He tells himself, I remember, that it's too early in any case for a hint to have surfaced that Griswold Farley, cinematographer and longtime associate of Vico, has also disappeared after his initial interview with Captain Hoensinger.

"This is in the nature of temporary employment for me," Mr. Pugh is saying. "Perhaps you've heard of my brother, Albert H. Pugh? He's a prominent..."

Tomorrow is the real test, Spyhawk is thinking. If they're after me, if they can tie me to the Kill-You-Annabelle Letters, the papers will have it tomorrow. He misses something Mr. Pugh is saying, something that disturbs him, but when he focuses his attention, all Mr. Pugh is saying is that he'd made use of that training (what training?) in his deduction that I was just conceivably—here he inserts a jury-tantalizing pause—"a sewing-machine representative." Again the gap-tooth grin. "It's the weight of your sample case," he explains.

"Uhh?"

"It's certainly heavy enough to be a sewing machine. I transported a sewing machine once for a gentleman, but this was even bigger than his, I'd estimate. Heavier, too."

Spyhawk at last waved a dollar bill at Mr. Pugh like a flag of surrender. Once he was alone he stripped off his clothes, got in bed, picked the first newspaper off the pile, and settled himself to read. The columns of newsprint quickly evolved into the script for a new picture and Vico was explaining that Farley could not be his cameraman anymore, because he was going to play the lead role. I'm not an actor, Farley said, but Vico insisted. To shut out his argument, Farley pretended to be asleep. With his eyes closed, he listened to Vico give directions about lighting and camera setups. Spyhawk cracked his eyelids a slit as he had a few minutes earlier just before the newspapers had slapped the table by his ear, and thought he saw—as he had seen then—Mr. Pugh looking down at him.

3. Sizzling Steak

THEN I SLEPT. When I opened my eyes, the jagged frame of light on my ceiling was empty, waiting for Beth. What's keeping her, I thought, and knew without getting out of bed that the light came from a theater marquee in the next block, and I was here again, in my old bedroom at the Silver Palms Hotel, the place where I'd holed up after Beth died. I didn't like it dark when I slept, so I had never closed the shade. Sometimes a breeze would ripple the gauze curtains and I would lie for hours at night watching their shadows on my ceiling dance inside the frame. I would fill the frame with incredible shots, shots and scenes and whole films I never knew I could make until I met Vico, and in each film, at the heart of it, would come the scene, no matter how I tried to keep it out, where Beth made her entrance, and from then on the camera would see nothing else until I had to get out of bed and read for a while and have a drink. That's how it is that Beth became my first memory in the place where I'd come to forget her.

When I'm asked about home I mentally shuffle half a dozen post cards: a certain creaky bed; a kidney-shaped stain on a kitchen wall; an airing deck view of garage roofs and chimneys; the house where a chained dog howled in the neighbor's yard. All different places, all places I've paid rent for. I produce one at random for whoever is asking. So I envied Spyhawk his certainty. He knew where home was, his home anyway, and had got us there and put us to bed. Trusty Spyhawk.

The window was closed. The shadows of the transparent curtains lay straight in shaded bars. My eyes closed again. When they opened, I was coughing deep in my chest. The rain was still falling and I felt the gurgles in the eaves trickling down my lungs. I put a sofa pillow under my bed pillow to keep my head out of the water, and slept again till night. Shadows of raindrops still tracked across my ceiling. The cough was worse.

I needed a doctor, but not my usual one. After four tries with the telephone directory, I phoned the switchboard and asked if they had somebody on call for their guests. I recognized the voice of the orange-haired woman. She told me that a house doctor wasn't one of the hotel's regular services. I said I knew it was hard to get a doctor, but it might be hard to get an undertaker, too. Then I heard that sizzling from someplace far away inside my head and knew Spyhawk wasn't ready yet to leave me alone. The sizzling is a warning, or would be if there were anything I could do to prevent what was about to happen.

As a kid I would dream I had shrunk in my bed to the size of a pea, like the pea in the fairy tale my mother read me, and the mattress all around me was an ocean I couldn't see the end of, and all through the dream I would hear the sizzling. I called it my sizzling-steak dream, because of the juicy crackle.

Whenever I told my mother I'd had my sizzling-steak dream, she took my temperature. It was always the first sign of fever and the next day, deep inside the fever, my body would fry in the sizzle but never burn up, only shrink and blacken and harden to a clean outline.

I was hearing the sizzle as I talked to the hotel switchboard. I could hardly hear my words the sizzle was so loud, but I seemed to be asking the woman with orange hair to consider how many days might go by before they discovered my corpse and how the stink might make my room unrentable for weeks. I went on like that, telling her how soon the flesh becomes cold to the touch, even when it's been in a warm bath, until I realized the line was dead. I lay back in bed a little frightened with myself, with Spyhawk. The sizzling gradually dropped away and became the distant rush of waves on the beach outside Vico's summer house, which I wasn't surprised to hear even though I was miles inland with my window closed. But it wasn't closed. I must have opened it in my sleep to make the curtain shadows dance. That's why I was shivering. Because I'd opened the window. I pulled the covers around my neck and switched off the bedlight so I could watch the ceiling. The knock on my door a while later was a doctor.

The doctor was a little man who strapped his belt high over his belly. All the while he was thumping my back and chest and peering down the holes in my head, he has talked about his wife's desire for a swimming pool, which he objected to on the grounds that they lived only two blocks from the ocean.

"Walking pneumonia," he said, and suggested a hospital. Hoensinger knew I was sick. If he was after me, he might check hospitals. I said no. The doctor blinked sadly over his spectacles. He sighed, put his stethoscope in his bag, snapped its clasp.

"I got a warm bed, Mr. Fantomese," he said, and I learned for the first time what name Spyhawk had signed in the hotel register. "I got a warm bed and you hauled me out of it at eleven-thirty at night because my advice was so important it couldn't wait. So all you got to say to my important advice is no thank you?"

"I'm sorry," I told him. "It's a question of money. I can pay you, but a hospital... Isn't there a pill you can prescribe?"

"Your best pill is aspirin," he said, and told me to drink lots of fluids to thin the fluids clogging my lungs. "And when you cough," he said, "cough it up, don't swallow it down."

For the next few days it got only worse. I coughed and spat, coughing deeper, tearing my lungs and making my ribs ache, and spat into handkerchiefs, then into a ripped pillowcase I used while the handkerchiefs I'd washed in the sink dried on the shower curtain rod and the rim of the bathtub. I coughed and spat as if I were trying to spit up a soul. Inside my head, in the sizzle always with me loud as the sound of my breathing, I tried to get Spyhawk to talk to me. "Why did you bring me here?" I asked him. "Is it everybody you hate, or just me? Who are you?" All the days I lay coughing and spitting he was there, undeniable as an itch. But he stayed out of sight. After a week, still sick but starting again to pay attention to things around me, I told him, "Maybe I can't get a look at you, but there's somebody else trying awful hard."

My projector, the big case Mr. Pugh had called my sewing machine, was open on the floor, the front end propped with books so I could throw an image on the wall. I had been about to thread on it one of the reels I'd stolen, the one that would show the last shots I'd made of Vico and Lisa. All the silence of the room gathered in Spyhawk's sizzling whisper. "Yes," he whispered. "He's still looking."

Spyhawk had heard it, too: the faint grunt, deliberately shallow breathing. On the other side of the hall door, Mr. Pugh had his eye to the keyhole.

CHAPTER VII

1. The *Life* Version

I'VE BEEN HERE three weeks now. Today Vico's face made the cover of *Life.* The photo was a still from *Loves of a Spy,* one of the prison scenes, with the shadows of bars crossing his cheek and brow. The story inside is titled "On the Set of Vico's Last Film." It's illustrated with stills from the film and rehearsal shots. In one I've identified my own silhouette, partly detaching itself from the square bulk of the camera, my right arm extended like the arm of Michelangelo's Creator. There is a "candid" shot of Lisa on a backstage couch, her ankles tucked against her thigh. She stares off, musing, the cutline claims, on the quirks of fortune that have catapulted her from the heady world of New York's top fashion models into marriage with an eccentric Hollywood genius, and stardom in his latest film. Does she already suspect, the *Life* writer wonders, that tragedy lurks in the wings?

The story claims she is still too distraught to be interviewed. No need, really. Bolger has given them all the copy they need: the day-by-day progress of Vico's deterioration—his tension on the set, the endless retakes, his irritation over the harmless innuendos in the Monty Druhl column. "All this," Bolger says, "is the air we breathe in Hollywood. It wouldn't distract a pro like Vico. Not unless"—and his voice drops to what *Life* calls an ominous tone—"there was something else on his mind." Bolger gives a detailed account of the last day on the set, when the berserk actor assaulted his own wife and tossed a vicious punch the director easily sidestepped. The last shot of all looks up at Lisa on the sundeck of the beach house, her palms cradling her elbows as if the wind were chill, staring out to sea. It has the grainy look you get with a telephoto lens. The photographer must have staked out the brush leading down the steep hill to the ocean.

According to *Life,* three theories dominate the continuing investigation. Most probable is the suicide theory. Police are still refusing to release the text of the Kill-You-Annabelle Letters, but a source close to the investigation describes them as "the letters of a deranged fan promising to emulate his hero by murdering his wife." In Vico's troubled state, the unnamed source speculates, these letters may have been enough to "push him over the edge." Supporting the suicide scenario are the blood in the beach-house bathroom (crime-lab investigator kneeling over blood-soaked towel) and the footprint leading to the sea (crime-lab investigator kneeling over plaster cast of footprint). After first attempting to cut his wrists, the actor—his flair for the dramatic vivid to the last—"may have lurched out into the storm, stumbled down this path, and plunged into the churning waters of the Pacific."

The kidnapping theory had lost ground as the days went by without any ransom note turning up at the studio gatehouse. There still existed, however, the possibility of a "revenge slaying." The blood in the bathroom might result from Vico's frantic struggle to fight off his abductors, who had carried him away, probably unconscious, murdered him, and hidden the body where it might never be found.

This last scenario is the only one which seems to have a role in it for Spyhawk. But nowhere in the article was there any mention of Vico's cameraman, Griswold Farley, who had dropped out of sight the day after Vico himself. If Captain Hoensinger had any interest in Farley's whereabouts, he wasn't telling *Life.* Another thing, too, seems to take Spyhawk off the hook. The role doesn't quite fit. I can't imagine him locked in a life-and-death struggle with Vico in his bathroom. If he killed Vico, he must have done it in a way more like who he is.

But I stink of guilt. It's like a sweat I can't wash off. If Spyhawk's not guilty, what made me say, "You finally killed him," the moment Simmons told me the cops thought Vico was dead? If he's not guilty, why did he seem to know something I don't about the Kill-You-Annabelle Letters?

The evidence against him is all subjective. That's why it's hard to ignore.

One more question, maybe the one that includes all the others: If Spyhawk is the "revenge slayer," what is he avenging?

A scary question. As soon as I ask it, I think of another. I wonder—does it ever cross his mind what his films would have been with any cameraman but me?

2. Shakespeare's Home Life

SOMETIMES on the set the only thing between us was the lens. After seven years that makes for a kind of intimacy that ought to know at least as much as a ten-month bride.

I knew him outside and in. I knew that on close-ups his gray eyes would bounce back so much light from the arcs they would burn through the print like a white hole unless I made them swallow some darkness. I'd rigged a black velvet frame to fit around the camera. I knew when he was faking a scene with his actor's bagful of twitches and squints, and when he had slipped into a trance so deep that for a few minutes after the camera stopped running he would just look fuzzy and walk away if you said his name. A damn sight more than most reviewers could spot. And all through *Loves of a Spy,* I was just as certain that every time he stepped up to a chalk mark, he was standing not just in the right spot for the camera, but on the brink of some cliff only he could see. I knew nothing would keep him from looking over the edge and that all I could do was go on calculating how to keep him tottering there till we made the last shot.

Call that cold-blooded if you want, but the loyalty Vico counted on from me was to the artist, not the man. One day a couple years ago while we were shooting he was blowing lines all through rehearsal. I knew he'd been having a rough time with Berenice, so I called him aside and said, "Look, we can shoot that engine-room sequence today if you want to take the afternoon off." And he said, "Farley, nobody cares shit about whether Shakespeare had a good marriage while he was writing *Lear.* Four hundred years from now the only thing that will matter about me is how I did the work. Let's take a twenty-minute break and then shoot it." Shakespeare, for God's sake, I thought, but when he came back on the set we shot that scene where he starts bawling while he explains to Marian Dunn why he has to kill her, and he did it in one take. So I knew what Vico wanted from me was what he wanted from himself—a finished piece of work. And to get it I calculated his moods the way I calculate the angle of a shadow or the candlepower of a lamp.

Maybe "calculate" is a bad word for that instant, instinctive response you make to chance and circumstance. When he thought he was ready for a take, he'd squint into the lights, looking for me, and I'd give him a nod or shake my head. When it was bad and he didn't seem to know it, I'd say, "Larraine stepped into a shadow. Could we run that again?" And all the time I was translating his every blink and stammer to decide whether he needed the kind of crack that would goose him through a scene or whether any word I said would start him frothing. Nothing I did wasn't for his good, I'd swear to that. But working that close to him, living off his private juices, was like being plugged into a current that could short you out.

Think of it this way. The year before I went to work for him I was doing a shoestring western for Republic. We were weeks late on the schedule and without a cent for another can of film, and I was in a field waiting for a deer to break cover and run. If I set up too deep into the clearing, I would catch only a scampering dot. What I could get with a telephoto wouldn't match our close-ups. So I was at the mouth of a chicken-wire funnel stretching fifty yards into the woods. Rabbits and coons dribbled through. Finally one of the beaters jogged out to tell me they were driving a ten-point buck. It was in the funnel, but would it break right or left or straight at my blind? First there was a crackle like twigs in a bonfire and that cued me, so I was shooting the instant it broke clear and just as the hind hooves touched the tracks the forefeet were leaving, I caught a ripple in its flank that led my eye with its spring so I was there, shooting, tilting with the arc as it sailed a stump, and I got the whole jagged five-second dash till it dropped below a hill locked inside my frame. I never felt more free. Shooting Vico's films I had that same feeling, that breathless surge you get when each instant cues the next and you're there with it, not chasing it but inside.

I'm back to the same question: How could Spyhawk kill the man who gave me that?

When I wrote that question, it was sometime after nine p.m. For a while I paced around the room, then took the stairway down so I could slip past Mr. Pugh and go out for a walk. I drank a few beers in a bar, then walked some more, walked a lot. I decided it was no good trying to focus on Spyhawk. He was too quick for me. The only way to catch him in the light would be to track Vico, keep him locked inside my frame just like that buck. There must have been a balance between what Vico took from me and what he gave. I was looking for what he'd done to upset it. I stopped for another beer, then walked again. All the time I walked, I played a montage game, freezing on a single frame—the path to the ocean, water draining from Vico's footprint—and splicing next to it some image from the past, any little scrap we'd had, anything he might have said or done, that I might have shrugged off where Spyhawk wouldn't.

Moments that had seemed the center of focus—Vico's brooding over that nasty hint in Monty Druhl's column, the shouting match with Bolger—I replayed, concentrating on what happened beyond the spill of the lights. Each image seemed to reach deeper into the past.

Too many moments, one image breeding another, and when I tried to discard some, what was left speeded up into a jerky blur from a Keystone Kops chase. Vico's habit of working out every shot in his head before the actors got their scripts had spoiled me. He seldom suggested a shot I couldn't improve, but without his script I didn't know where to aim the camera.

There was only one fact I could fix that wouldn't blur away. Nothing in the *Life* article, nothing I've seen in print anywhere, has made the connection between Vico's troubles on the set of *Loves of a Spy* and the murder of Berenice, his first wife. It's something I could no more mistake than I would a smoldering arc light. So I'll try to get at the secret he never told me, something about the way he must have felt when he saw Berenice lying in the closet, her tongue squeezed out purple as a skinned grape. There must have been hints of it even before the murder, but afterward the signs were unmistakable. Something had invaded his life that made him alien to me.

THE SECOND PART:

WHAT HE SEES

If man will strike, strike through the mask!

—MELVILLE,
through the mask of Ahab

CHAPTER VIII

1. Victim in Purple

ALL RIGHT, THEN. Slow dissolve—to the foyer of a downtown restaurant. It's early February, 1930, and I'm standing behind a velvet rope, panning along the palm-shadowed tables, looking for a face I've seen only in black and white. I spot him, and with him a woman, her hand over his forearm. My first thought is: I *know* that woman. But the memory is blurred, something in the background of a shallow focus shot. No matter how many times I blink, it won't sharpen.

It must have been the pose I recognized, since her profile was curtained by a black fall of hair. She cut it in the kind of bob still worn only by a few aging flappers. She's leaning over the table, trying to make Vico look at her eyes. Her left hand is nuzzled under his right arm and hooked over the crook of his elbow. Her right hand pins his forearm to the table.

She seems to be in charge, but her strength is intensity, not bulk. She's long-boned but reedy, fragile, her head and large hands drooping. If you shift your angle she doesn't seem in charge at all, but only a rather awkward bird—a crane, say—clinging to her perch in a high wind.

Vico is hunched over the table. When the woman squeezes his arm or tugs on it, his big head nods, but he never looks at her. He stares at his glass and twists it as if he's waiting for tumblers to click.

The hostess prances over and asks whether I have a reservation. I tell her I'm joining Mister Vico. "This way, please," she says, and marches ahead as if I might lose the way. As we cross the floor, the woman at Vico's table sits up straight, gives that horse-blinkering hair a toss, and looks away. Nothing has drawn her attention. The look is a statement. She doesn't notice me coming. I have a second to study her face. I've seen it before, I'd swear.

As I stand over them, I know the instant before she glances up that her eyes will have liver-colored gouges under them. I know she won't look higher than the knot in my tie.

"Mister Farley, meet my wife, Berenice," Vico says. He doesn't try to stand. He waves me a chair with his free hand. The chair is on Berenice's right, wedging her between us. I've come to talk business, but we chatter like strangers at a party. Meanwhile the conversation I've interrupted continues in a private language of glances I'm not meant to catch and pauses before words that seem harmless.

One line of hers strikes me. Vico has just told the waiter to bring him another martini. "Remember," she says, and her voice has an I-don't-care lilt. "It's a question of who's in control." In this town lots of wives nag their husbands about drinking, but not in quite that language. Vico exhales through his nose, says he thinks the strip steak might be good, and cancels his drink. A demonstration of control, I gather, but from where I sit the one in control seems to be Berenice. While they brood over the menu, I puzzle about what, besides that two-handed grip, keeps Vico with her. Love? What kind of love is a hundred-and-ten-pound weight clamped to your right arm? In our last conversation before she died, the only time he ever spoke about his marriage, he said, "She's a saint, Farley." He said it in a boozy, hopeless monotone. "She knows everything about me, every nasty secret, and there's nothing she can't love." Maybe an audience like that is what an actor needs, but all I could think of was a pair of rubber boots I own, so tight they made my feet sweat.

Some people hang out a sign that says *Victim for Hire.* Berenice wrote it that clearly. The dress she wore peeled away from her arms and shoulders like a flayed skin.

Where the silky purple material reflects on her bare arm, it makes you think of bruises. Her biceps hangs flaccid, puffed at the elbows like a sack of water, and when she presses out a cigarette in the ashtray, the sack jiggles. I look at her knobby collarbone, the washboard ripple of her breastbone, and decide she's lost a lot of weight. She wears a sunset rouge and pancake to fill the creases in her eye corners. She remembers not to crack when she gives me a pressed-lip smile. The arithmetic of it was that Vico was barely thirty and this woman, nearly as I could judge, was forty-five trying with her decade-old schoolgirl bob and scoopneck dress to look twenty.

As we are about to order, she tightens her grip on Vico's arm and says, "Couldn't we go to Ciro's? I hate it here, oh *please,* darling?" Vico pats the hand resting over his arm and says, "Next time." Her voice is the only part of her she forgets to make girlish. It has a throb of elegant sensuality that gives my imagination something to play with.

Food is nothing to me but energy and shit. I don't dwell on it. While they studied the menu I studied Berenice. Every time she sipped her drink or shaped her cigarette ash to a point or slid her fingers into the hair at the base of her skull to massage a headache, I felt a sly tickle, as if she were doing a strip tease with my memory of her, and even now I think if I could recall where I'd seen her before that first meeting, I'd understand some essential secret about her hold on Vico.

If I could have kept my eyes that night on her alone, I might have seen her peel right down to the secret, but after eight years—I don't know what chance I've got. My mind had been mostly not on her at all, but on Vico. I'd just seen *The Whisperer* and being no dummy, knew damn well it was to somebody who was going to teach every director in town some new tricks that I was saying the seafood here was always dry, but the cook knew what to do with a slab of meat.

2. The Bouncing Ball

TRYING TO GET a clear shot of Berenice seems as much a dead end as tracking Spyhawk. Tonight I'm back with the idea that another way to approach the secret is through Vico's films—that if I can focus tight on them, I'll discover something I never saw while we shot them. Maybe *The Whisperer* is a good place to begin. Since it's his one picture that I didn't shoot, when I run it in my mind I'll be seeing pure Vico.

Vico had gotten notices full of exclamation marks in a silent called *Sad Smile of a Strangler,* but it came out just when every movie house in the country was getting wired for sound, and didn't get much play. So *The Whisperer* was his real debut—and some debut. It was his first starring role, his first time out as scriptwriter *and* director. Somebody important must have had a lot of confidence in him. I was always curious about that. It was one of the things we didn't discuss.

Word about *The Whisperer* got around town fast, but nobody quite knew how to describe it. Reviewers groped for the usual clichés, but the clichés to talk about what Vico was doing hadn't been invented yet. I was busy with a picture, so it wasn't until the night before that first meeting with Vico and Berenice that I got in line at the box office—and there was a line, six weeks after the premiere. I sat through two shows and only noticed when I came out onto the street that my jaw was aching. The gap between what Vico wanted and what his cameraman could deliver made me clench my teeth.

As I had him sized up, Vico was an ironist. He would jam into a shot everything it could hold and frame little counterpoint stories inside the main action. One of them came in the confession scene after the fire. He's flat on his back, handcuffed to the infirmary bed. He tells Margo about the orphanage where he grew up, how the priest used to strap him spread-eagled to a tabletop for "discipline"—ah! already a pattern begins to emerge: the title of his fourth film was *Discipline,* and I never before made the connection. Something about the window beside the bed bothered me the first time around, so in the second screening I watched it. Vico's cameraman, Bobby Sandford, used the window only to get a backlight rimming Vico's profile, but if you look *through* the window, you see a blur moving outside and a shadow like a flitting bird, except that a bird would be crossing the window instead of leaping and falling. Suddenly I thought back to that brief establishing shot of Margo walking through the court to the infirmary. In the court, bouncing a rubber ball against the wall, there had been a little boy in short pants. And it hit me: The *boy* is the blur, his ball is the shadow, and that irregular thumping thud that punctuates Vico's monologue is the kid's solitary game.

A week after I saw the picture I was talking about that scene with Herman Mayo, one of those directors who specializes in close-ups of heroines blinking tears. "Shit, he tossed away the best shot in the scene," Mayo said. "Remember that last line? He turns his head away from Margo, *away* from the camera. For no *reason.*" Now any cameraman worth his pay would have had a deep focus on that window, so we could *see* the kid outside. Even if it had been focused, Mayo would have noticed it only the way the princess notices the pea. New ideas disturbed his sleep. When Vico turns away from the camera—throws away his last line, according to Mayo—he's saying, "At night... after they untied me... I used to dream of swimming, swimming in air... long glides... through the clouds." His eyes are on the boy and his ball.

Mayo and Bobby Sandford deserved each other.

How Vico got saddled with Sandford I don't know. Sandford is what's known in the business as a "glamour" photographer. He mounts a key light directly above his camera to chase shadows from under the star's nose. Shooting everybody with a halo backlight and a focus so soft he must be smearing his lens with Vaseline is his idea of style. I could see Vico needed a cameraman who could give him a deep frame and a sharp line and throw a shadow that didn't look as if it came from fairyland. He needed me. Vico knew it, too. Later he told me it was when he'd realized what Sandford had done to him—in that scene and a dozen others—that he'd called me.

Finding Berenice at the table with him as I walked in had annoyed me. I'd thought we were there to talk business. That must have been Vico's idea, too—at first. So I agreed to shoot his next picture, but with half a notion that it might not come to more. I didn't have much patience with amateurs, no matter how *brilliant* the reviews said they were, and there's a strong whiff of the amateur in a man who makes a woman his motive. He won't hold an intention pure.

3. The Talkie Problem

WHATEVER WAS GOING on in Vico's personal life, I couldn't have been more wrong about him as a director. He had learned fast from Bobby Sandford's mistakes and wasn't letting anyone tell him what he couldn't do. When we sat down together to make the lighting plot for *City of Sapphires,* I remember saying, "In the banquet scene, we'll have to substitute something for this ice sculpture." Vico asked why. "The lights will melt the ice." Vico hooded his eyes and smiled that smile you see when the judge reads his death sentence in *Mark of Cain,* the one that cuts a scalpel-blade line in his cheek. When his eyes raised, they were frankly estimating how long I would be working for him. "We'll find a way," I said, and the result was that life-size frozen Venus the regiment salutes in its final toast. In the drinking contest that follows, with Count Boris and his cronies singing and sweating, we kept half a dozen of her sisters in a railroad refrigerator car wheeled right to the stage door, and when the lights melted one down, we tossed it out for the sun to finish and brought in another—pretty much the way we use live actors. For my money the most beautiful shot of the film comes when Boris passes out over the banquet table, staring up at the melting statue, and of course he's had the sculptor give her Lady Anna's face. I shot his face framed at the tilt of her head, looking down between her breasts. Then I cut to Venus, her blind eyes sweating, a pearl on the tip of her nose, cheeks streaming tears, chin dripping; and I pan down her breasts and belly, and on her belly the water ripples like a shiver and then oozes down between her thighs. The shell she stands in spills a busy drip-drip onto Vico's face. Slow fade to a rain-pocked street. Naturally the Hays office, brand-new that year, snipped everything between the lady's chin and ankles. But after that I figured Vico knew better than I did what I could find a way to get on a strip of celluloid.

—I've caught myself wandering. Is it Spyhawk, tugging at my sleeve, turning me down any alley that leads away from *The Whisperer*? What can there be in that picture that he doesn't want me to find?

When I think of *The Whisperer* today, nearly a decade later, it's hard to remember that in 1930 the biggest technical headache we had was sound. Actors had to clot around the hidden mike like iron filings on a magnet. If one of them strayed a yard away, the sound technician would call for a retake. The camera got nailed to the floor again, almost as bad as when they shot stage plays front row center. On the set during the long waits between takes I would have daydreams of Harry Lloyd six floors up the wall of a skyscraper or a carload of Keystone Kops sailing past a railroad crossing close enough to strike sparks from a cowcatcher.

Two minutes into the first reel of *The Whisperer* I realized that Vico had got the camera unstuck and the actors off their duffs. He had made a talkie that was also a movie. The trick was a voice-over monologue. In the middle of a scene the actors' voices would cut out and you would follow their movement as if it were a silent, while at the same time you overheard Vico's whisper, sometimes commenting on the action, sometimes deep inside his head, inside his own past.

Voice-overs are common enough today, but Vico told me the front office had been worried as hell that people wouldn't know what to make of it if they heard his voice when they couldn't see him move his lips.

Sometimes even a pro will shoot a scene thinking he knows what he's got, and only discover in the rushes a shadow he hadn't planned. That's how I feel now, when I think of my motives for going to work with Vico. It had nothing to do with technique—or at least, not nearly as much as I told myself.

It was the Whisperer's voice, telling me Vico knew my Spyhawk's heart.

But if I sensed even then—before our first meeting—that Spyhawk had a brother in Vico, what clues had I read in *The Whisperer*?

The opening montage showed Vico at a fairground, strolling arm in arm with a girl. Jenny Morris played the role. That year she married an ex-Broadway leading man named Barton Eagon. Then she married her agent. In her last picture she played the woman who gets run over so Joan Crawford can marry her husband. But that day the wind machine streamed a coil of honey hair across her eyes, and when Vico tucked it behind her ear, he let the backs of his fingers graze her cheek. Low-angle two-shot, the Ferris wheel behind them, the spokes turning from the exact center of the frame, slicing down behind her and whipping away past him. All in complete silence. Then you hear what might at first be a rumble. But the rumble is a moan, rising into the first words of that tense whisper, so close it might be inside my own head, saying: "No, oh no, nono." Then they're in the Ferris wheel, and as they reach the top of the arc, he slips a ring over her finger, their lips meet, and the voice on the soundtrack is moaning, "No, no, nonono, please no." And they drop away from the camera.

Another cut: as the rain begins to fall, they stop near a fence outside a large estate. They kiss. The voice is moaning, "Please, don't go, don't leave me, Marsha," while he smiles at her skipping away through the rain. She turns in the road to wave. A black limousine streaks through the gate. Cut to a head shot of Vico screaming, the sound for the first time synchronous. The frame goes dark. A light snaps on. Vico sits up in bed, his face swelling toward the edges of the frame. The only echo of the dream is a gasp and something in his eyes that fades as they come awake.

As each shot passed before my own eyes, I seemed to *remember* it. Was it Beth in my mind? We had never been on a Ferris wheel. It wasn't an auto that killed her.

Then Vico's voice, absolutely flat and deadly, says, "Marsha," and we cut to a shot of him at the same gate, entering by the road where the accident happened. At the door of the mansion he says to a footman, "You advertised for a valet." He's shown into the drawing room, and as Lady Geraldine lowers a teacup, the frame tightens around her like a noose.

In all his scenes with Lady Geraldine there are long takes of him staring at her without a word. She tips a perfume bottle, then with her finger brought to the hollow behind her ear, she stops, embarrassed, and says, "Why do you look at me like that? What are you thinking?"

Maybe that's where Spyhawk recognized himself.

There were other scenes he could have played, too. All those master-and-man scenes where the Whisperer is stalking Lord Carmody. Those shots of him holding Carmody's morning coat, flicking invisible specks of dust off the shoulder, while all the time the voice-over is talking about how the tuft of hair in Carmody's ear disgusts him.

That's crazy. I didn't even know Vico then.

There's one scene where Bobby Sandford's moondust lighting is right. She glides downstairs in her dressing gown. In her husband's place at the head of the table, Vico is drinking her husband's sherry by the light of a candelabra. "Giving ourselves airs, aren't we," she says, and plucks the bottle out of his reach. But we know by the hush of her voice she doesn't want him found out. Vico stares at his glass, twisting it between his fingers. Suddenly she is on her knees beside him, clutching his arm, pleading, "Oh, please, take me away, I hate it here, I hate him"—and this is

Oh Christ, that's *it.*

This is where I'd seen Berenice before.

One moment Lady Geraldine is on her knees saying, "Oh, please, I hate it here," and the next moment Berenice is tugging *with the same gesture* at her husband's arm, saying,

"Couldn't we go to Ciro's? Oh please, darling, I hate it here." It was such a smooth cut, you'd never know there'd been a splice.

And until you spot the splice, how can you know why you think what you think?

4. The Impediment

YESTERDAY'S SHOCK LEFT me a bit stunned. Stunned and puzzled. Having a clue in your hands doesn't mean you know how to read it.

My first thought is that the whole thing might have been a joke, that Berenice had been parodying one of Lady Geraldine's lines. But all her eyes told was pain and yearning. The parody, if there was one, had been Vico's. Had he, I wonder, heard that line often, and been aware of the source when he wrote it into his script? I try to imagine him indulging a sly twist of malice as he prepared Denise for the scene: "Now when you kneel beside me, slip one hand under my arm and put the other one like this over my forearm...." No—it wouldn't be a conscious thing, though the resemblance was too precise to be accidental. It must have been simply a question of him saying, "Do it like this," because that was the most natural gesture he could suppose a woman making.

Now that I recognize it, the resemblance to Berenice takes on detail, as if I were watching a layout sketch fill out under Vico's pencil. Denise Holston had the same Slavic breadth of nose and brow, the same foxnose point to her chin, the same thick black hair and a trick of fondling and coaxing it. On stage Vico always treated her like a queen, but one night after she'd wasted nearly an hour of shooting time with the hairdresser, he told me, "That hair's what she's got instead of a lapdog. Next she'll be feeding it bonbons and calling it Snookywookums." That line, even at the time, made me think of Berenice's toy poodle. But the strongest mirror of Berenice was in the way Denise used her voice. That sensual throb of hers was a perfect echo. Vico found a role for her in nearly every picture.

I'm getting closer. I think I know enough for a hypothesis, and it's this: I'll find clues to Vico's relationship with Berenice in every role he wrote for Denise Holston. A quick rundown. In *City of Sapphires* she played the boardinghouse landlady who snoops in Count Boris's dresser, discovers the stolen necklace. In *The Mask of Don Juan* she was the dance-hall madame who had him kicked downstairs; then, after the surgeon has given his face its mysterious fascination, she's the one at the Mardi Gras ball who taunts him, demands that he unmask at midnight along with the others. Finally, in *Doomed Cargo,* the film we were finishing when Berenice was murdered, Denise played poor Ivy Sprawn, the flirty widow who fumbles with her keys in the passageway so Vico will have to squeeze past her. She's the one who discovers the unfastened lock on the door into the sealed-off hold where Captain Fantomese is holding Marian Dunn captive.

It becomes clear to me now. Denise was always cast as the Impediment. From the moment she enters the film, any lawless dream is doomed. If the ideal of Vico's fantasy was Mirian Dunn, then Denise was the real woman—the one with pillow creases on her cheek and a cigarette breath who jabs you awake.

I never put my feelings about Berenice into words, never thought that much about her, but from the time of that first meeting she was always—like Denise Holston—the Impediment.

When the corpse of Mrs. Sprawn is found in the galley meat locker, Vico, as Captain Fantomese, says to the horrified passengers, "I think this was a woman who found out something dangerous, who knew too much for somebody's comfort." Only a week after we shot that scene, the *Tablet* ran a photo of Berenice, crumpled on the closet floor like a coat. Just as Vico found her that night. When he did, when he opened the closet door, I wonder was it pity came first to his mind, or joy?

5. Questions of Taste

I'VE SPENT A long time staring at the last sentence I wrote, trying to decide whether it makes me some kind of ghoul. No. I've got to keep hold of myself. It's not the *question* that raises hairs on the back of my neck. It's the answer I have to give.

Only one thing ever blocked Vico, cut him off from the source that kept filling the screen with dreams. Halfway through my second picture with him I'd figured out that any time his pace was half a second off, there was another feud with Berenice behind it. The tipoff wasn't obvious or melodramatic. I never saw bruises or scratched cheeks, never heard shrill voices behind the dressing-room door. Berenice's visits to the set were rare, so that didn't prove much. But there were days when Vico would come in with what he would call a new idea for a scene. I could spot a new-idea day by the way he stepped onto a set. Usually in the morning he was on stage shortly after I got there, an hour before the rest of the cast. He had a fetish about doing his own makeup, which meant he'd been up a good hour and a half before me, probably since four o'clock. He would stride around taking possession, rehearsing speeches in a monotone, flopping onto a couch fifty times so that when he did it for the camera it would look natural. Sometimes even checking setups and fixing shadows as if he wanted to put me out of a job. But on the new-idea days he would be sluggish, broody.

I would be on the end of a ladder changing a filter, and I'd look down and see him, only his feet in the light spill. The set might have been under a charm, and he didn't know the magic word that would let him set foot on it. Then he would say my name as if I were standing beside him at an open grave. I would climb down the ladder.

"Farley, I've got . . . a new idea."

And the mourning voice would shovel dirt into the scene we'd planned to shoot and prop over it a stone slab: something that shuffled actors from one arty pose to another and sliced the meat out of their lines. He usually had a reason for the change. I would argue against it and sometimes win. But I soon learned that I might as well have lost. He would drag through the original scene looking as if I'd siphoned off a couple quarts of his blood. Sometimes he would insist on the change and give no reason. When I argued, he would walk away.

Once during *Mark of Cain* we had planned a scene that had Sylvia Randolph begging him not to open the drawer where she keeps her scrapbooks, and he flips her shawl over her head, douses her like a candle. That morning Vico shuffled along the rim of the set and threw a sour look at the sun arc I had placed outside the bedroom window. It was shining through curtains, casting fretwork shadows on the floor. He rumbled something. I asked him to repeat.

"I said that's a three-p.m. bar of sunlight on the floor and this scene comes right after breakfast. You should check the script before you start making things pretty."

I told him the sun hit my own living-room floor at exactly that angle at exactly eight-thirty a.m. After a pause that lasted till I thought I'd won the point, he said, "Well, I want bare windows here anyway. Tell Minny to get rid of these curtains." I reminded him the curtains had been in every shot for the past three days and asked if he wanted to reshoot the whole sequence. He shrugged, walked off toward the tenement street as if he were meeting someone by the barber pole. At the corner he put one foot on a wood firepump and looked back.

"By the way," he said, "we're cutting the shawl business," and started away down a dim row of brownstone fronts and pawnshop windows. I'd had enough.

"Why, God damn it?" I shouted. "Why?"

In the time it would take to blink he was in front of me, so close I could hear the breath hissing through his nose.

"If you want lacy shadows weaving on the floor," he said, "go ask Krackenpov for a picture of your own. But this is my picture. I wrote it, I'm directing it. I'll make any damn change I please in it. I'm in control."

Control again. The word had come up more than once since

Berenice used it to talk him out of a martini. But I was not quite mad enough to tell him I knew who was pulling his strings.

"Maybe I will get my own picture," I said. "All you want is someone who knows when you need a new reel in the box. I asked for a reason about the shawl and what you said is no reason. Take away the shawl business and she just stands back and lets him open the drawer as if she *wants* him to find the letter. The shawl caps the scene and if you're cutting it, I want to know why."

"Because," he said, and a ripple in his chin was fighting back the words, "it's tasteless."

"Tasteless! You're playing a psychopath, for Christ's sake. Sometimes they ain't got good manners."

"Berenice says it's tasteless."

When he turned away that time, I let him go. You don't make a man with tears in his eyes face you. Talk about control.

After that day I didn't ask why. I shot the scene and waited for him to squirm over the rushes. A day or two later I might hint at a new bit that would make it worth reshooting. If he had swung out of his sulks, he might come up with an idea better than what we'd junked.

6. Ice and Lava

IT WAS LATE March of 1936 when we started shooting *Doomed Cargo.* By August 13 we were six weeks overdue, facing our fourth day trying to get in the can Wilson's death struggle with Captain Fantomese. I had decided Berenice must figure the whole picture was tasteless.

The pressure she put on Vico was doubled by Krackenpov. Two weeks earlier he had raided us like a T-man sniffing for bathtub gin. Tired of bland reports from his spies, I suppose. Frantic over costs. He came to find an excuse for a rage. With him—trailing him as if they were there to hold his train off the floor—were half a dozen guys with inkstains on their middle fingers, lawyers maybe, accountants, squinting into the arcs and stumbling over cables. In a *sotto voce* that drifted clearly up to my catwalk, Vico told Krackenpov that visitors on the set made him so ill he would probably have to drop out of the picture if Krackenpov stuck around. Krackenpov owned Vico's script and he could always get a new director. But reshooting all Vico's scenes with another actor, even if he hadn't been playing a double role, would have been a financial disaster. Krackenpov went back to his office where all the faces he had made famous beamed at him from the wall. For the next year and eight months he sat there thinking up a way to destroy Vico that wouldn't cost him half a million dollars.

Sometimes I try to tell myself, if Vico had only known how to grin and look sheepish when Krackenpov read him cost per day and contract obligations, *Loves of a Spy* would be in the can today and Vico and I would be planning another picture. Then I think of Lisa Vico's lower lip and hazel eyes, that remind me of Beth. Krackenpov couldn't hurt Vico, not really. Only Spyhawk knew enough to bring him down.

Part of the *Doomed Cargo* problem was the double role. For years Vico had prepared his roles like a miner tapping into a volcano. What gushed out was the kind of stuff most people are too civilized to uncork. He funneled it, gave it a shape I could get on film. At the core of each film he made was an eruption: Count Boris sobbing as he whips his orderly; the soaring shriek of Don Juan as his fingers lose their grip on the parapet. In *Doomed Cargo* the volcano was Captain Fantomese. The second day at sea, that dinner at the captain's table—all the polite faces freeze at the uncanny scream from somewhere in the ship's bowels. The captain goes on chewing his beef. "I heard nothing," he insists, and when the back of his hand spills wine from the goblet, he blames the choppy weather. But we know. I track in for a close shot of his sliding eyes, that muscle in his cheek jerking. We know that before the last fade we'll hear another scream, prying apart that insolent sneer. The eruption. Vico's specialty.

But this time playing Mount Vesuvius wasn't enough for

him. He had to cast himself also as Wilson, the timid scholar who stumbles into the secret passage to Melody's cage and makes up his mind to rescue her.

I think that meant a lot to him—being two different people. When I asked why, he muttered something about needing to extend his range, and did one of his famous discussion-ending walkaways.

He extended his range all right. Wilson blinking over his specs, so busy explaining symbolism in the Grail quest that he's the only one at the captain's table who agrees with Fantomese that there was no scream; Wilson greeting Ivy Sprawn with a quote from Milton; and later, when he discovers her corpse, that eager frown he buckles on to tackle a problem in logic. It was a beautiful character, and one Vico had never done before. The only problem was that to get Wilson he had to quarry ice, and the ice had turned his volcano into the kind of tepid soup you send back to the kitchen.

He would get Fantomese, too, in the end, but it was taking him about twice as long as usual and costing him a kind of agony I'd never seen before. Every time we were scheduled to shoot a Fantomese scene, he would come on the set with that graveside voice, telling me how he had to rip the guts out of his best lines. All his reasons came back to one: tasteless. Why, I wondered, did he keep showing his scripts to Berenice, letting her pick over each line? Once I even asked him. "She knows when something's rotten," he said. "And she never lies." End of discussion.

One thing seems clear. Berenice had finally wrapped him up. Wilson was just the kind of fuzzy lovable teddy bear she could cuddle with, and in order to turn himself into what she wanted, Vico was smothering all the Fantomese in him, putting a permanent chill on the volcano.

I would go along with whatever he said. Then at night looking at the rushes he would know they were bad. "Christ, Farley, what can I do?" he would say—and that was something new. Usually he was glad to let me touch up an idea after he'd laid it out, but he didn't need any brainstormers mucking with the source. I'd take him out for a drink, buck him up. Tomorrow we'll shoot it over, he would say, and put back a few of the cut lines. But the next day he would come in just like before, and I would think, Here goes another mile of celluloid. Here goes another twenty thousand dollars. But halfway through the last rehearsal before a take, he would get white-knuckled. The script girl would step in and mop sweat off his brow. Then his eyes would bulge and behind them you would feel the volcano churning and on his next line the voice would be the one you remembered from *The Whisperer,* that touched the base of your skull like a woman's hand, and if the scene didn't call for it you would have to trim it away in the cutting room, but from then on your eye would be alive, following every move because you didn't know which way he would spring, free as that buck in my dreams, bounding away down the ravine. Afterward, though, Vico would be pale, shaking. What he'd done terrified him. After we shot the scene where he twists Melody's arm to make her sing, he walked off the set and vomited into a wastebasket.

7. In the Cage

BY THAT AUGUST 14, a Friday, we had come to the climax of the film and the limit of Vico's endurance. Most of the problem scenes were in the can. We had found a patch of clumsy exposition—unusual for one of Vico's scripts—and shot and rejected two or three ways of showing how Wilson guesses that Ivy Sprawn's been murdered on her midnight prowl through the ship's innards. Vico hit on the idea of having Wilson find outside the engine-room door that tuft of fur from her stole. Then we had to reshoot Denise wearing the stole during her last conversation with Wilson. He thinks she's just making another pass when she tells about the noises she's heard through her stateroom floor: "Not an animal," she says. "It's something human making animal cries." It's also in that scene that she plucks off Wilson's glasses and teases him about his resemblance to Captain Fantomese. "You could almost be twins," she murmurs, "if you were more of a brute." We planned to dub in a voice-over of that line in the shot of him slipping into the captain's stateroom to borrow his uniform jacket and cap.

Then we did that crane shot of Wilson exploring the cargo hold. He closes the door behind him, closes off the furnace-room roar, the thumping pistons. He hears a whimper. Dust motes tumble in a bar of sunlight. He starts down the aisle. I crane up and back. As his figure shrinks, crates and barrels enter the frame, closing around him. At the height of the arc the crane shot holds—only Wilson's footsteps and that whimper on the track—then the crane starts down, Wilson slipping out of the frame as I close on a particular crate. I draw level with the iron bars, see the straw floor, the whimper closer now, intimate. She's huddled in the far corner, a strip of light on her bare calf, her face still shadowed. Only her eyes throw back a glimmer—until the footsteps stop outside the cage and she throws herself at the bars, her face bursting into the light. "Oh, please, don't hurt me again. I'll do anything."

Quite a shot, that. On hands and knees, eyes and nose running like a heroin junkie's, was Marian Dunn, the most elegant beauty on the lot. That's another reason why Krackenpov hated Vico. We had saved Marian's scenes for last and bribed people to give us a closed screening of the rushes. Vico knew that if Krackenpov saw how we were photographing Marian while there was still time to yank her, we would lose all the shock value of playing her cool sophistication against type. He was right to be cautious. When Krackenpov saw the rough cut, he screamed as if we'd raped her. Which in a way we had. Why Marian consented to it was a mystery. I remember Vico preening himself the day he announced we'd signed her. He never told me how he'd done the persuading. Maybe she agreed to it just for the chance to work with a genius. That was reason enough for me. I should have known, though, why Vico wanted her. My first hint ought to have come when I heard her voice in rehearsals. And there was another hint, too. One night we were watching rushes, and came to a good profile of her. Vico told the projectionist to back up and run it again. No particular reason, I thought. He just wanted to see it again. But each of her features subtly echoed Berenice Vico. She might have been a younger sister of Denise Holston. Can you judge an artist by the tenacity of his obsessions?

After we got the shot of Marian drooling through the cage bars, we reversed it, shooting through the bars at Wilson's look of horrified surprise. Or at least that's how Vico had scripted it. When we tried to shoot it, the face he offered my lens always seemed to have more in it of Captain Fantomese than Wilson. That was disastrous. He was disguised in the captain's uniform, and if the audience didn't know in a glance that it was Wilson they were looking at and not Fantomese, the point of the scene was lost. It was odd for Vico to have trouble with a simple reaction shot. But the trouble only began there. In the scene that follows he tries to convince Melody that he's not Fantomese. But Vico had lost his grip on Wilson. Two or three lines into the scene he would slide into Fantomese. It was perverse—all the Fantomese menace that he'd had to work so hard to pump up rose into his Wilson like a blush.

For a couple days we dodged the problem by shooting the fight scene, Wilson jumping on Fantomese as he's about to open Melody's cage. The key flies into the air. Fantomese and Wilson fall to the floor grappling for a knife. Wilson slams Fantomese's wrist against a crate. The knife slides across the floor. Melody grabs it and when Wilson and Fantomese somersault close, she stabs Fantomese in the back. Vico, as Fantomese, did a lovely gasp and sprawl. I was on my belly shooting from the floor, the fallen key in the lower right corner of my frame. Fantomese drops into the upper right corner, spitting blood. He pulls himself down to the center of the shot. Collapses. Then, with the wide-angle lens, I shot him reaching for the key. The hand that closes around it is as big as his head. The eyes glaze, the skull thumps the floor, but the fist stays tight. Cut it and print.

Then we went back to the Melody-Wilson scene with Vico wearing Fantomese's uniform. We sweated out a yard a day of usable film. By August 14 we had everything but the scene where Wilson pries open Fantomese's hand and unlocks Melody's cage. He kept insisting there was something awkward about the shot where he lifts her to her feet, helps her to stand. At about three p.m. a problem with a transformer made an excuse to break early and I asked Vico if he wanted to join our Friday-afternoon bash at the Penguin Club.

About half the time he would decline the invitation, and when he did, he always took a beat or two before he said, "No ... I'd better get home." Sometimes when he did say yes and we were waiting for the final round before closing time, I could see him tensing, getting ready for the buzz saw when he got home, and I would tell myself I was glad to be a carefree widower with only my mirror to face. So I knew his drinking with me was something Berenice disliked. But I knew he enjoyed it, too, and I figured he was a big boy and could decide for himself how much *control* he needed. But the fact remains: It was the booze on Vico's breath that started his last fight with Berenice, and that fight was what sent her out looking for someone to kill her. If Vico thought that made *him* guilty—and he did—then he must have blamed me, too. How much of that guilt could Spyhawk bear?

CHAPTER IX

1. The Merry Widower

THE ONLY TIME Vico ever unpacked his petty gripes against Berenice was that day—the day she died.

At the Penguin Club a pair of ceiling fans with blades big as airplane props stirred the smoke. Every Friday afternoon I stood the first round for my camera crew and whoever else tagged along. A good way to blow off the week's gripes. The slow-circling fans folded our talk in a sleepy hum and rolled it away on the smoke. During *Doomed Cargo* Vico had joined us more often than usual. Sometimes he glanced at his watch and only gulped a quick scotch. Sometimes he talked shop and pounded the table till just the two of us, glum and a little drunk, had filled the ashtray with butts and swizzle sticks, waiting to see who would call it a night. I was a widower and knew why I didn't want to go home, but sometimes I wondered about Vico.

What surprised me that Friday was not that Vico went home after one drink, but that an hour later he was back. By then the party had dwindled to Rimers and Curtiss and me. My back was to the door, so it was their dropped jaws I saw first, then Vico scraping up a chair. He was breathless, his cheeks blotchy. Berenice has walked out and good riddance, he announced. He bought a round to celebrate. He was jovial in a way that dampened everybody's spirits. When he ordered another round fifteen minutes after the first, Curtiss and Rimers decided it wasn't going to be their kind of party. They were both good family men who made it home while the steam was still rising from the roast. After they left, Vico stopped gulping his drink. Each sip became a separate decision. An hour later he said, "Let's get away from here," and that's how he wound up spending the night Berenice died on board a twenty-foot cuddy the papers never let us forget was called *The Merry Widower.*

The irony had originally been my own, intended only for myself, with a nod to von Stroheim's masterpiece. Fifteen years earlier I had bought the boat with money left in my wife's bank account. In '23, six years before the crash, it seemed wrong to dribble away the odd thousand left after the funeral on rent and liquor. The boat with its name was a way to use the money without forgetting how I got it.

I had known Vico a long time before we started drinking together after work. When we did, the boat got a new name. Vico never went to star traps like the Brown Derby or Ciro's unless he was with Berenice. He always felt more comfortable in places like the Penguin Club or the little corner bars out in West Hollywood, the kind with a moosehead over the cash register and billiard balls clicking in the back room. Sometimes even in those places people would point and nudge each other, and when somebody looked like he was getting up the nerve to introduce himself, Vico would say, "Let's get away from here." After that we usually went to the marina where I docked my boat. It happened often enough to give us a joke about painting over *The Merry Widower* and lettering *Away from Here* on her stern.

2. Lizard in the Sun

SOMETIMES WE WOULD beat a few miles up the coast. The night Berenice died we're on deck, passing a bottle back and forth. I am lying face up, watching the mast trace an arc between stars, trying to rock my head so that the tip of the mast will exactly block a particular star at each extreme of the arc. In a lazy, mind-doodling way it occurs to me that even if the tip of the mast swings exactly between those two stars every time, one of them is probably billions of miles deeper in space than the other. Vico is mind-doodling, too. He straddles the bow, his legs dangling over the side, dipping a line in the black water, lifting it to shake a spray at the moon, then dipping again.

"What you fishing for?" I ask.

If I were to twist my neck around, I could only see the back of his head, but I feel him smiling. It shapes his words.

"That's my cue," he says, "to say something pretentious and metaphysical." And he puts on a thick Charles Boyer bass: "I am feeshing, my fran', for the meaning of mai laife."

"Is everything metaphysical also pretentious?"

He thinks awhile, dipping and spraying.

"There might be something metaphysical about a good orgasm or a cup of coffee," he says, "but anything you might say about a good orgasm or a cup of coffee is probably pretentious. Including what I just said."

"You cover yourself, don't you."

"It's a habit. Like fighting with my wife."

A few hours earlier, when he came into the Penguin saying Berenice had left, was the first time in six years I'd heard him say a word about his marriage. Twice in a night he was inviting me to make his troubles with her part of what he could talk about. The actor in him couldn't wait for a role. He needed right now to act it, needed it so badly he was willing to do it without a mask. I wonder if I was a select preview audience, or would anyone, that night, have done as well. Shit. If he'd been alone, he would have mugged it for a mirror. But it didn't matter. I was hungry to be trusted.

"Is she gone for good?" I ask.

That was all it needed. First he told me about the fight, what she'd said and what he'd said. It was ugly enough. Then he told me that last year he'd thought hard about having an affair. Berenice didn't know about it, he said. I wondered about that. He seemed to think it would be news to me, too, the long lunch breaks he spent with Tess Frye. In the end, he said, he broke it off before it came to much because you can't love two women at once. With Vico's kind of innocence, you've got to be a genius to survive. The twist, he said, is loving Berenice, but not wanting what she wanted.

"She's older, you know," he says. I hold my breath, make no move to break the mood. Since the day I saw her at that table clutching his arm, I've been stalking this moment. "When I was twenty-eight," he says, "I'd been in Hollywood six years. I was what you call a cattle-pen extra. Every morning I'd go down to the yard for day work. Sometimes I'd work two, three days in a row. Want to know my first picture? I'm in the mob outside Notre Dame, hollering for the hunchback's blood. God, Chaney was beautiful. He could swing up those walls like a monkey. I wrote a script for him. An early draft of *The Whisperer.* Not my style, he said. You do it, kid. At the time I thought he was joking. A pretty mean joke, too. But he meant it. He could see what I didn't know yet—that I'd really written it for myself."

When he couldn't get work, he told me, he took odd jobs. He got to know a second-unit man for Griffith. A guy named Henchard. Sometimes Henchard let him hang around as a kind of assistant camp-chair bearer. Henchard was drinking so much Vico wound up shooting half his scenes. "That didn't matter," Vico is saying. "He had me typed as a fetch-and-carry boy. One day he said a friend of his needed extras to serve drinks at a party. 'Go to costumes,' he tells me. 'Get fitted for a tux.' You know, I almost didn't go. Told him I was an actor, not a goddam servant. 'Look,' he says. 'I owe this lady a favor. You owe me a favor. Doing favors is what makes this business run. You don't like it? Get somebody to owe *you* favors.' Talk about favors. There were days he was so fuzzy he didn't know which end of a viewfinder to stick in his eye. I almost told him right then how many times I'd saved his bacon with Griffith. Once I was standing next to him when Griffith came up and said, 'Damn fine work on that skirmish yesterday, Hench. You've got a good eye.' Good eye, for Christ's sake. While I shot that stuff, he was stone blind. Not so blind he couldn't remember who shot it for him, though. I'm no choirboy, Farley. I didn't expect him to tell Griffith. I did expect he'd say something to me besides 'You owe me a favor.'"

Vico takes a pull from the bottle, while I wonder if he's forgotten what he started to say about Berenice. A fishing boat rattles past, nosing toward its slot. Small waves slap our hull, the hollow knock like someone below wanting out. The boat bobs and so does Vico's heavy head, and the first few smacks throw a snag in his voice. "I was ti-ired," he says, "of bu-eeing hu-ungry." We both laugh.

So at five o'clock that afternoon he was in a tux trying to hitch a ride out Sunset. "Funny thing, Farley," he says. "People will pick up a bum before they pick up a guy in a tux." Hench had written the address on the back of a napkin and when Vico saw the place, he had to check the napkin to believe it. Iron fence, ten feet high, spike tips. So many trees, from the road he could hardly see the house. He walked up the drive and rang. Told the butler he was there for the party. The butler showed him into the drawing room. One moment please, he said. "Farley, I'd never seen ceilings that high. Outside a museum I'd never seen walls with oil paintings, never seen mirrors that would hold your whole body."

When she came in, he was looking at a Chinese vase. She told him she was afraid there'd been a mistake. The party wasn't till seven. By this time, very quietly, I've rolled onto my side and stretched myself, head in hand, along the bow; not too close, not close enough to let him notice how close, but close enough to see his faint smile in profile as he says: "I knew what the mistake was. I remembered Hench had told me to go around to the back door. Maybe it hadn't even slipped my mind." It wasn't hard for him to act embarrassed, to say, "God, I'm sorry. Your invitation got lost, but I was sure it said come at five." And she said, "Don't worry. Come talk to me while I dress." He followed her upstairs and they talked.

They talked, he told me, about movies, though I can't get back many details, and maybe I'm splicing together their conversation that first night with one he had told me about earlier, when it came out that Berenice thought von Stroheim, too, was tasteless. All that polish, she said. All that light bouncing off the jackboots and the buttons and the monocle. All that swagger. And the swords, the walking sticks, the swagger sticks—how much does it take to remind him he's a man? Vico argued that von Stroheim himself had punctured all that swagger, and brought up the scene in *Foolish Wives* where we see him getting strapped into a corset before putting on that officer's uniform with its medals and epaulets. Berenice, as I recall, wasn't impressed. "*Foolish Wives,*" she said, and shrugged. "You know," he told her, "von Stroheim did a picture called *Blind Husbands* as well as *Foolish Wives.*" "Yes," she said, but it wasn't the husband that he played in either one."

She'd told him, he says, she could see what *he* liked in von Stroheim, but for her it was different. It's a nice mirror, she'd said. But what if you'd looked in the mirror, hoping to see yourself, and all that looked back at you was silly Mrs. Hughes, lured out in the rain to be seduced?

How odd: That night I never thought of this, but now, as I write, I have a sudden image of Berenice in her purple dress, Berenice as victim, and I wonder how much she did to fight that impulse in her. Was she always the woman who invites bruises, or did she get that way because it was the only role Vico had for her?

Vico says he had to admit he couldn't recall much about Mrs. Hughes, but what, he asked, about the Maude George character? She was certainly more than a cut-out doll. "Oh, yes," Berenice said. "The one way von Stroheim can make a woman interesting is to make her a whore."

All this, of course, would have been a lure impossible for Vico to resist: the beautiful woman's contempt for what he loved—and how he did love von Stroheim, and played Count Boris in *City of Sapphires* as much to honor that ascetic lecher as to twist some truth out of his pose. But it wasn't just that he wanted to convince her she was wrong. Because I asked him: If their first conversation had turned into an argument, what kept him interested? And his answer told me he'd known that first night that he would marry her. "Art," he said, and I've got the words exact, "is a constant tension... between want and *must*. I knew she would never let me forget that. Never let me go over completely to one or the other." And after a moment, with just enough light on his profile for me to make out the slow, curling half of his smile, he said, "Besides. We weren't really arguing."

She had a copy of *The Waste Land* on her table and asked if he liked Eliot. He couldn't be sure, but it sounded like she was calling his bluff. He told her he read Eliot and Pound to follow their way of cutting from image to image. "Oh," she said, "you must be a director," and he said, "Yes—a director."

At seven o'clock they went downstairs together to greet the guests.

By this time I'm laughing. "Really?" I say. "You're not kidding me?"

"Why should I do that?" Vico says, which is not an answer.

"What did you suppose would happen when Hench walked in?" I ask, and he says, "I didn't have the slightest idea," and I ask what did happen, and Vico says, "She took my arm and walked right up to him and said, 'Mr. Henchard, I'd like you to meet a friend of mine. Emile Vico.' Before he could get his jaw off his Adam's apple, I said, 'Oh, Hench and I are old pals,' and shook his hand."

"What did he say?" I ask, and Vico tells me all he said was one word: "Vico?" He was so scared, Vico says, he swallowed air and started hiccuping. "I think he figured it was him I'd been fooling all along. I must have been a spy for Griffith, getting the goods on his boozing. Now all of a sudden here was this guy in a tux called Vico." And I say, "You mean he didn't know you as Vico?" and Vico gently swallows a belch and says, "Neither did I till that night."

Berenice had gone behind a screen to dress, he explains, and while they talked he was roaming through her bookshelves. Vico was the name on the spine of the book he was holding when she said, "Oh, by the way, who are you?"

I ask him, "Where did Emile come from?" and he says, "Out

of my head. It made a nice chime with Vico." "But what about Berenice?" I ask. "You couldn't keep it a secret forever." And he tells me that as the party was breaking up, he took Berenice aside. "There's something I have to tell you," he said. After everybody was gone, they went into the den. She was at the sideboard pouring them a Drambuie. "Before you give me that drink," he said, "you'd better know I'm not a director with Universal. I'm a tech assistant and a cattle-pen actor. I was sent here by Henchard to hold a trayful of martinis for you." There in the dark with his feet dangling over the bow of *The Merry Widower* and the water chuckling along the hull, he's blocking it out for me as if it's a scene we'll shoot tomorrow. "She had the glasses in her hands. She looked at them. It was the longest look in my life. Then, still not looking up, she said, 'And all our talk about Pound and Eliot? Was that lies, too?' I didn't know what to say. 'And the script you told me about,' she said. 'The one you said you showed to Chaney. Was that a lie?' 'The only lie,' I told her, 'was that I don't have the two hundred thousand dollars I need to produce it.' She looked up at me and handed me the glass and said, 'You didn't really think I was going to ask you to empty ashtrays, did you?'"

Waiting for a shot, you spend the time staring at a ledge on the face of a cliff. You watch the shadows shrink, watch light fill up the mouth of a crevice. Then something deep inside the cool rock feels the sun and scrapes a few pebbles. One moment the crevice is empty. The next, something has wriggled into the light. You press the shutter, a strip of celluloid uncoils past your eye and coils again, and you've got it: a lizard blinking in the light, the deep rock dew still on the scales and pinpoint horns it grew in secret in the dark.

If you can wait long enough, you'll always get the shot you want.

Since that first day, staring at the two of them from behind a velvet rope, I had waited to see where Berenice had hooked him. That night on *The Merry Widower* I spied it. I spied it the moment I asked myself how an actor who'd never shared a scene with less than twenty people got the backing to star in and direct a film from his own script. Long after he stopped being in love, I decided, Vico was still paying back favors.

Vico took a last pull from our bottle and threw it at the moon. We broke a few eggs for a late supper and he left at about eleven p.m. He went home to discover his wife's corpse and I spent the weekend on the water, restless and lonely without knowing why.

One more shot comes in front of my eyes. Just before he steps onto the dock, Vico turns back to me. "I wouldn't have opened my mouth about this stuff," he says, "unless I knew it would never go any further." I nod. I'm even, I seem to recall, a little disappointed that he feels he's got to mention it. "Of course," I say.

That night, alone on the water, I stumbled over a wet towel he'd left on the cabin floor. I looked around at the egg-caked dishes on the table, the paper napkin he'd shredded while he talked. "Damn you, Vico," I said. "You always leave me to mop up."

He had trusted me. Instead of feeling satisfied, I was hungry for something more. Or something else. As I chugged into the harbor Sunday evening, a man in a gray suit strolled onto the dock to admire the sunset. He had his hand out for the mooring line and flashed his badge before I could begin collecting my gear. Within a few hours I would be sorry I had been trusted.

It's only now, writing this, that I find myself wondering whether he had trusted me at all. That story of him bluffing his way into Berenice's mansion sounds like some of the lines he fed the fan mags. Or like a scene from *Loves of a Spy.* Of course that's no proof it didn't happen just the way he told it.

3. Just Another Judas

I'VE COME TO what I can't forgive. What I wish I could scrape out of my skull.

The thirty pieces of silver must have been just an excuse,

a reason Judas had to give to explain why he did it. How can you ever explain? It was just something that happened, like when you wake up after a party and don't want to think about what you said the night before. *Why* think about it, when there's no way to change it and nothing to say but the punch line to a joke I can't recall: "I'da been faithful forever, darlin', if I'd never got tempted." But what tempted me? Should I say I sold Vico's soul because he didn't offer to wipe the dishes?

Maybe I should say I was scared for my own skin.

I *was* scared, but only at first; maybe especially scared because the guy they sent to pull me in—the detective who met me at the dock—was a piece of bad casting. It was as if you were being fitted for a hangman's noose by Buster Keaton in a porkpie hat.

He was young and shy with a nose like a wad of bubble gum, but nobody was going to push him. He had a way of peeking under every card before he answered questions like "Who the hell are you?" and "What do the cops want with me?" His name was Sergeant Felix, he said, and grinned as if he thought I figured I had got him to admit something. Felix, I thought. A smart-aleck cat from the cartoons. His voice was *chirpy* and he used it the way some people who don't have children talk to children. All he would say about why I was wanted was that somebody named Hoensinger had a few questions for me. He walked me to the parking lot. He skipped a step ahead to make sure I knew who was being led. It left him slightly breathless, which pleased me. I had seen the badge, but still half thought I was being ribbed until we got to my car. I fished in my pockets for my keys.

"We'll take my car, Mister Farley," said Felix.

"How the hell will I get home? Look, it's late and I'm tired and I've got to work tomorrow. Are you sure all this is necessary?"

"It's pretty important, Mister Farley," he said. He let the button on his gray suit slip open. A leather strap crossed his chest from shoulder to armpit, where the flat steel butt of an automatic hung. I am always fascinated by the tools of an odd trade, but this gave me a different feeling. He tucked a thumb in his belt to give me a good look. The gesture was silly and repulsive—like some idiot in a public toilet flashing his prick. The whole thing was nightmare slapstick.

Felix held the passenger door of his car for me, something the doorman at Ciro's does to make you feel important, and sealed it after me. Sliding behind the wheel, he brought the mike of a two-way radio to his mouth and said, "Felix here, I got him. We're coming in." The receiver made a staticky squawk. I had spent the weekend under the sky, in control. My own kind of control. One hand on the tiller, the other on the line. You can scoop up that big dumb muscle of wind and make it take you anywhere. But there was no way to snatch the muscle out of Felix. I found myself sweating and rolling down the window.

As he drove I tried again to find out what they wanted. Felix kneaded his nose as if he were shaping a blob of clown putty and thought about what to tell me. "Captain Hoensinger says he'll tell you what's what," he said. I got the idea that Felix spent more time than he liked telling people Captain Hoensinger did the talking. On the last stretch of road before we hit the town lights, night fell and my vision closed down to the narrow funnel of Felix's headlights. I knew I hadn't done anything that could make trouble for me, but that just made it more difficult to guess which direction they would strike from. If I needed an alibi for the weekend, I was in trouble. I hadn't seen anybody since Friday night when Vico left. Once we slowed for city streets, I could feel the heat again. Walking up the station steps, Felix crowded my elbow. It wasn't a felon's escort, no handcuffs, no beefy clutch under the armpit. It was a nudge, gentle enough, but alert to any balk. Ahead in the hallway half a dozen men with suitcoats over their arms and shirtsleeves rolled to the elbow leaned along the wall. As we passed, I caught from the corner of my eye a scuttle and stoop, and when a voice barked, "Hey!" I saw three or four guys with cameras thrown up to their faces just before the flashes blinded me.

Felix had got the treatment before and knew enough to shut his eyes. I broke stride, blinking, dark suns drifting wherever I looked. He took my arm and marched me along. Behind us echoes tumbled and bounced. "Who is it, Felix, what you got?" "Hey, bud, you kill that broad?" Slapstick. It wasn't meringue pies in the puss, but I'd been ambushed. They had snatched my face, my private face. And I knew how the shot would come out in the papers: furtive suspect's over-the-shoulder glance, pop-eyed, gape-jawed, guilty.

In fact, none of the papers printed it. When the story broke, it was Vico's face they wanted, hungry for the secret lines of shock and shame. Which I might have expected.

4. Sun and Wind

NOW IT'S COMING, the moment Spyhawk gives him up, and it's all a Marx Brothers whirl.

Here is Felix, leaning across me to open the door. Then a whoosh and a rattle of paper and he steers me up to a desk, the chair behind it empty, and from inside the desk, it seems, a voice patiently curses the bake-oven room and says it has better things to worry about than getting an ashtray on every goddam piece of loose paper. The door shuts, wind from a fan grazes my face, and the backs of my calves touch the seat of a chair.

Four thick fingers clutch the far edge of the desk, then someone lurches up and settles in the chair. The drifting suns hover between his shoulders. A voice from behind the suns tells me its name is Captain Hoensinger and asks me to state mine. The fan ruffles my hair, then moves away. Since I am not looking at the desk, I can see it, see the fountain pen poised above the pad. I don't want my name on it. Again something mine is being taken.

"G. R. Farley," I say, and the voice says, "Give me the names, please."

"Griswold," I tell it. "Griswold Rufus Farley." I hate my

given names, both from ancestors I never knew. When I was a boy, I filched other names, secret names. That's one reason, I suppose, why I thought I understood Vico.

The triple suns are fading now—the cores blacken, the auras grow bloody.

"Mister Farley," Hoensinger says, "you're a hard man to lay hands on. Where you been all weekend?"

Behind him is a file cabinet where the fan looks down, slowly moving its head back and forth between us, whining nnooo-nnooo-nnooo to everything that's said.

Suddenly the door I entered by flies open. A gust of wind gets under the papers on Hoensinger's desk and skids them along toward the edge till his flat palm smacks them, and he bellows, "God damn it, I said *knock.*" In walks Groucho Marx, a uniformed officer with dark-rimmed glasses and a black mustache. "Sorry, cap'n," he says. "I figured you oughta hear this," and points his nose at Hoensinger's ear. While he whispers he tips the ash from his cigar at the wastebasket beside the desk. The ash lands on the floor. Hoensinger's hand on the papers relaxes as he listens, but his jaw sets hard. "You tell him," he said, "there wasn't a horse named Diaper Rash *in* that race. I don't think there's a horse named Diaper Rash in the *world.* You tell him to send you down here when he's got a *confession.*"

On his way past Felix the mustached officer winks. I watch for him to wiggle his cigar, but he doesn't. The papers under Hoensinger's hand rattle till the door closes.

"So where have you been?" he says to me.

I ask him if I'm under arrest. He says no and repeats his question. Being relieved makes me angry, but I'm still frightened and I know as soon as I let go my anger the fear will show, and I say, "Sergeant Felix here knew right where to look for me. My guess is somebody's already told you where I was." Hoensinger lets out a patient breath and says, "I been sitting at this desk a lot of years, Mister Farley. *Most* of the questions I ask I already know the answers to. But I still gotta ask."

"On the water," I tell him. "Up past Malibu."

"You disappear like this every weekend?" he asks.

"Most," I say. But I can't leave it at that. Suddenly I'm jabbering: "Unless you put yourself out of touch, any producer on the lot can call you in Sunday afternoon. I've got better things to do than shoot test shots for some front-office jerk's new girlfriend."

Hoensinger asks if I have a radio on my boat.

"What's that got to do with anything?" I ask.

"I'm trying to get an idea of how much you know about why you're here," he says. "If you've got a radio on board, you've heard the news."

"So," I say. "Whatever we're talking about isn't a parking ticket. What news?" Hoensinger doesn't answer. "Sure, I've got a radio," I say. "I need it for weather reports. Storm warnings and such. Now and then I pick up the tail end of a news broadcast." He doesn't say anything. "Hitler wants Czechoslovakia, what else is new?"

Then Hoensinger asked if I got an early start Saturday and I tell him I left Friday night and he asks what time. No special inflection, no meaningful glance to Felix, and when I tell him, "About eleven-thirty. Before midnight, anyhow," he seems hardly to have waited for the answer, he's there with the next question, and he's given no sign that I could read at the time or remember now that would have told me this was the single crucial question.

"You always sail at night?"

"I was late starting."

"Before that, were you alone?" I remember Felix snapping his gum, I remember the fan turning its face away from me, and then I say, "Something's happened to Vico. What is it?"

The instant I realized—with a nasty buoyant skip of the heart—that all Hoensinger's probes were aimed not at me but at Vico, I guessed the scenario. Vico reeling home; Berenice at her most tastefully sarcastic, goading and goading till he gets his hands around her throat. I saw it just as if I had wound up a little Vico doll and pointed it home to throttle its wife.

That's a cheap thing to say. Spyhawk didn't plan what happened. All he did was to very faintly sneer at Berenice's notions of good taste. Then he sat back and watched Vico writhe. Writhe and wish she were dead.

All right. I wished it, too.

That's guilt enough to make you burn in hell, but not in the electric chair.

"What happened to Vico?" I ask, as if the possibility of something happening to Berenice were more than I could imagine.

The door opens again, and a man with curly blond hair leans his head around it and raises his eyebrows. "Pastrami," Hoensinger says. "With *hot* mustard, this time. There's mustard and *hot* mustard." The head disappears. Harpo. In the next few minutes the door opens two or three times more. I'm watching for Chico, but he doesn't show. Felix goes on smacking his gum, the fan still shakes its weary head. But now the world narrows to Hoensinger's eyes; and his voice, though at times I can hardly separate it from the moan of the fan, his voice is all I have to answer to.

Three times Hoensinger takes me through a Friday-evening itinerary, clocking each step. We quit shooting at three-thirty, I tell him. By four we were at the Penguin drinking. Vico left at four-thirty, was back within the hour saying Berenice had left him. I let him work for that a bit: "Well, he seemed... upset.... It's not my business to wash his dirty lin—ah, if I don't tell you, you'll get it from Curtiss or Rimers...." After they left, I tell him, Vico and I sat and drank till about eight-thirty, then drove down to *The Merry Widower:* Got there around nine, maybe a little after. "Still there at ten-thirty?" Hoensinger asks. If I'd noticed how careful he was about that time, I might have salvaged a bit of my soul.

But I have decided that if a jury can be convinced Vico was too drunk to know what he was doing, he may get a light sentence, so I am preparing the ground for his defense. I hear myself saying: "...by that time, I guess we'd decided to go below and fix supper. Vico was pretty far gone. We broke a few eggs. I usually keep enough food on board for a three-day run. Took our coffee up on deck. Vico was about talked dry. The night was clear, a fair breeze. I asked if he wanted to run up to Laughton's Mouth—a little cove about twelve miles up the coast.... No, I didn't think he would. It was mostly a hint that I wanted to be on my way.... Yes, positive—he couldn't have left before eleven-twenty...."

I scc Hocnsinger calculating how long it would take for Berenice to fan Vico's rage to a blaze. I see his sliding glance to Felix, their silent agreement, sealing Vico's guilt.

I saw it all right—and never gave a thought to the laws of my craft. A Russian named Kuleshov filmed an old man, the corners of his lips jerked up. Then he cut from that smile to a steaming bowl of soup. The audience saw a starving man. Now he trims off the soup. Splices in a mother standing at a Vermeer window, stroking light beams in her daughter's hair. See the sweet twinkle he's put in the old man's eye? Now he scissors out the mother and child. Cuts to a woman undressing. See the old lecher leer? That's Kuleshov's law of montage: Meaning belongs not to what you see, but to you. And nobody sees the rushes uncut.

So what good does it do me to wonder what was really in Hoensinger's head? Why he wasn't content with my timetable? It either proved that Vico had time to kill Berenice, or that he didn't. If he didn't, the interrogation should have ended there. Before I had time to say more. But Hoensinger's pause, the look he exchanged with Felix, was followed by just the line you would have expected if he had established Vico's opportunity. His next question probed for a motive.

"Mister Farley," he says, "after Curtiss and Rimers went home, did Vico say any more about his argument with his wife?"

It was while I lay on deck watching the tip of the mast tilt back and forth, tracing the arc it made between stars. Vico was dipping a line from the bow and spraying water drops at the sky. They rose among the stars and the shore lights turned their bellies a starry silver, and just for a second, just long enough for you to make out strange new constellations, they hovered there, and when they dropped back it was stars rushing down the sky, the end of the world, till they fell ticking in the bay.

That moment was real; the one it happened to was Farley. But—I'm trying now to tell the strict truth—Vico and Farley had not been alone. Huddled below *The Merry Widower*'s waterline, in that inch of bilge you can never pump dry, was Spyhawk. Later in Hoensinger's office it was Spyhawk, not Farley, who looked straight into Hoensinger's eyes and gave it all away. Farley heard every word but couldn't stop him.

"Vico said she told him," Spyhawk begins, "not to be there when she got back."

"Did he tell you how he felt about that?"

"I imagine he felt pretty lousy, don't you?"

"What did he say about it?"

"He told her not to worry, he wouldn't be there. And she said, I'll count on that, and slammed out."

"Did he have any idea where she intended to go?"

"Sure. She told him. What he said was that she told him she was going out to get a man."

"What man?" Hoensinger is saying. "What man was she going to get?"

And Spyhawk says, "Any man. She was going to bring him home, she said, and let him fuck her in Vico's bed."

That's what Vico made me promise not to tell—that and the way it took him. Poor drunk Vico on a ten-minute crying jag, snorting and sobbing.

"That's what he told me," Spyhawk says. "Now for Christ's sake, what's going on?"

Hoensinger offers the most slender smile. It's only now I can see it for what it was—the half-smile of the starved, beauty-loving old lecher in Kuleshov's famous lesson.

"Why would she want to do that?" Hoensinger asks.

"Maybe to prove she can."

"Is that Vico's opinion?"

"Probably. It's mine. Sometimes it's been hard to keep Vico interested. She's fifteen years older than he is."

"She was, Mister Farley," he says, coming to his feet. "He started catching up Friday night."

He knew when I was wrung dry. Felix held open the door. I walked toward it. Hoensinger stopped me, told me later he would need a formal statement. A dozen reporters had gathered in the hall. Some were drifting over when a door down the hall opened. A gang of men marched out, someone I couldn't see in the middle. The reporters forgot me. There were shouts, popping flashbulbs. As the crowd surged past I glimpsed Vico, the iron cuffs pinning his hands over his crotch. His head was swinging around as if he had seen me first and looked away. A cop steered him through another door and the reporters followed, leaving me to find my way out alone.

5. Reverse-Angle Shot

THEY HELD HIM two days, then—from late Friday night when he called them and met them at the door in a daze till that Sunday night when I got back—before they had to admit he was only an actor whose wife had been strangled by somebody who probably never even machine-gunned a carload of detectives. Al McMahon, my friend on the *Tablet* city desk, told me about all the real detectives shuffling around like Mack Sennett lunkheads when they released him. By that time I'd gone home. Al covered the press conference Vico gave on the steps of the precinct house. He started out very polite, Al said, very patient, waiting for the jostling and shouts to die. He read from a little card in his palm a legally phrased profession of his innocence and abhorrence of the crime, ending with a hint that the county of Los Angeles might soon be dealing with a false-arrest suit. Then of course he wanted to leave—just as if *Price of Madness* weren't box-office bonanza all over the country. That's when things got ugly.

The cops that fought his path to the street weren't really out of line, Al said, just jolts and bruises stuff, and Dusty's camera breaking was an accident, but the sleeve of Vico's jacket was ripped away from the shoulder by the time he got down to the pavement and found cagey Al planted smack in front of the door of the studio limousine. "I put on my best smile," Al said, "and said, 'How does it feel to be a free man, Mister Vico?' 'My wife is dead, punk,' he says, 'How would you feel?' and then he rakes his shoe all down my shin." Al told me he hadn't thought of it that way, but the line was good copy and he used it in his lead.

6. Control

GOOD AS IT WAS, that line was not quite Vico's final statement of his feelings for Berenice. To get that I have to cut back to the last scene of *Doomed Cargo*, the one we'd interrupted in midafternoon so Vico could go home to his last conversation with Berenice. It was the big fight scene between Wilson and Fantomese, that ends with Melody knifing Fantomese and Wilson getting the key and letting her out of the cage. I had thought it was going fine, but Vico said there was something wrong. Vico was hurting bad, not wanting to see anybody or be seen—I know because I'd tried a dozen times to phone him, and went out to the house and banged on his door Monday night till he came and stood on the other side of it, not even opening it, and said, "Not now, Farley. Not now," and walked away and wouldn't talk anymore. But with only a minute or two more of film to get in the can before he could wrap the picture, not even Berenice's murder would make him walk away from that last scene. Two days after the funeral he called in the crew to finish it. He had a new ending, he said.

I hadn't seen him since the funeral. He had stood by the open grave with his wife's gray-cheeked mother, the only one there who didn't sweat. The sun that day had been blinding white. Stepping out of the car I had placed my foot in a piece of chocolate melting on the pavement. When I stepped away angry flies buzzed back to the feast, and I walked up the hill to shake his hand and say how sorry I was. I watched his chin stiffen when they lowered the coffin into the ground and all I thought about was who would bring chocolates to a funeral. He had looked back at me when I shook his hand, but when we met on the set he was all business. I murmured something silly like "You've had quite a time," and he told me to set up a shot as if I were a second-unit assistant.

We started with a two-shot, close framing. Wilson is sprawled on the deck panting after his struggle with Fantomese, his head against the bars of Melody's cage. She's at his shoulder saying, "The key... get the key...." We shot it in one take. The change came in the next shot, the final setup. Before, we'd planned to have him walk over, staggering but on his feet, and the camera shooting from under. Now he wanted a crane shot ten feet up. I had been curious to see how Vico's art—that tension between want and must that he said Berenice never let him forget—would be affected by her death. But this seemed like plain bad judgment.

"You're taking away his triumph," I said. "He'll look small." He gave me a don't-argue look and I set it up. No rehearsal. He whispered a few words to the extra playing Fantomese's corpse and called for a take. When she says, "Get the key," he goes after it, but crawling, dragging one leg. From the crane I shot down on him: pulling himself along on his arms, breathless with pain. It was like shooting a wounded crab. Vico's instructions had been precise. "When he gets to the corpse"—we had already shot a close-up of Vico as Fantomese with the key in his fist—"dip till you're under his nose and tighten on the face, the hand. Then pull back a little when he stands, and follow him."

"If you want a head shot," I had asked, "how am I going to fit in the hands, too?"

"I think I know a way," he had said. When I craned down on him, I saw one of his hands was stiff. Makeup had made a raw scrape over the knuckles, as if during the fight it had been stepped on. He tried to open the dead man's fist, and grimaced. He pinned Fantomese's arm under his own and pried with his good hand. He seemed weak, clumsy. Fantomese had a grip even death couldn't open. "When should I close for the head shot?" I had asked. "You'll know when," he said. I did. Wilson, stretched out beside the corpse, resting on his elbow like a Roman emperor, lifts the dead hand to his mouth and sinks his teeth into the closed fist. It might have been a chicken leg. When the key drops to the floor, he palms it and stands, staggers, stoops to scoop up Fantomese's captain's hat. Then, with a slow Vico smile at Melody, he adjusts the cap on his head, slips the key into his pocket, and says, "All right, Farley, cut it." For the final setup I tracked past him into a close shot of Melody's face, her fingers tight around the bars. I froze just before the scream.

I think the reason he didn't rehearse it, not on the set at least, was that I was his audience. He didn't want me just to photograph it, he wanted me to *see* it. He wanted somebody to know that—two days after we'd shoveled his wife under—he was celebrating a rather terrible liberation.

We shot the whole sequence in a day and Krackenpov was furious till he got word that preview audiences loved it.

CHAPTER
X

1. Type Casting

THAT SUNDAY NIGHT after Hoensinger released me I hadn't hung around to see Vico. Later, catching up on the papers I'd missed during my lonely weekend on *The Merry Widower,* I realized I had saved him. I had been his alibi for the time Berenice died and I had steered the cops toward another suspect—the man she had told Vico she would bring back to the house. Vico himself never told Hoensinger about that. I wondered how much Hoensinger had told him of what I said. That story of an unknown pickup was the last argument Hoensinger needed in order to make holding Vico any longer seem foolish. I could pretend that was all I ever intended.

One night a couple months later I sat over a final brandy with Al McMahon and he explained the logic of the case against Vico I had destroyed. Hoensinger was a smart cop, he said, who had made detective by keeping things tidy. His solution to the murder was tidy as mathematics. It was a statistical fact that most people were murdered by friends or relatives. Murder was intimate, a family affair, and when Hoensinger clapped the bracelets on Vico, he was doing what all his years on the force told him made sense.

"You're underestimating the power of type casting," I said. "Even cops see movies. They know how dangerous he is."

But McMahon held firm: "You're supposed to be some kind of an artist, ain't you? Hoensinger's got an aesthetic sense, too. And what he had was *tidy.*"

McMahon explained how Hoensinger went hunting for a tidy relation between cause and effect. When he discovered a lady with a wrung neck, the first thing he did was ask people on either side of her apartment whether the husband had been smashing flower pots against the wall.

"That's how he met Mr. Terhoost," he said. "Retired jeweler, lived on the other side of Vico's bedroom wall. Started out as a watchmaker and ended owning a string of stores. Kind of guy who can time the tick in your sleeve and say your watch needs cleaning. He's the one told Hoensinger about the squabbles. Every few weeks they would break out, he says, but on that Thursday night there was a dilly. Turned off the radio, he says. The voices coming through the wall were a better show. Then Friday afternoon, more shouting, just for a couple minutes around five p.m. Then everything's quiet till about ten-thirty. When the voices start again, it sounds at first as if they've patched it up. It's a murmur so low he can't make out words, even with the radio off, till suddenly she yells, 'Get out, get out of here!' Then there's a crash like a lamp pitching over, and a scream. He thought she must have screamed herself hoarse, Terhoost says, because for a minute he can hear something like coughing. Then everything's quiet, so he turns the radio back on.

"You can see how it fits, Farley. Thursday-night fight, Friday-night corpse, murder charge for the husband. As far as Hoensinger's concerned, it's the shortest distance between two points. Especially when the husband answers the door with enough booze on his breath to make an L.A. patrolman take two steps back. And the first words he says are, and I quote: 'This way, officer. I'm the one who killed her.' (Here I tried to interject a *but,* which McMahon shrugged away.) So he cancels it later. His lawyer says he was *distraught*—lovely word, ain't it. Means he's delirious with grief, doesn't know what he's saying. But that's not the kind of line you can scoop up like a bad solitaire hand."

I reminded him that if there was one thing certain about the Berenice Vico strangling, it was that Vico couldn't have done it.

"Sure, we can see that now," McMahon said. "The confession was play-acting—the big star grabbing the juiciest role in the script. But at the time, to Hoensinger, it looked like a perfect forty straight off the rack."

That's one of the things I liked about McMahon. He made things simple. Vico was an actor. Strangler was a role. He never had to ask for another reason why Vico would confess to a murder he didn't commit. If I'd brought up my own idea, he would have hooted. My idea was that Vico confessed because, one way or another, not literally, not legally, but *some* way, he was guilty.

2. The Pond in Winter

MCMAHON AND I date back nearly sixteen years. I met him here in the Siver Palms. For a while the year my wife died, I couldn't stand to go home. Beth's parents had taken Annie. She hadn't even been in the house long enough for me to miss her. But without Beth the place was empty. My eyes would light on something that had been hers and three hours later I would shake myself as if I had fallen asleep on my feet or sitting on the edge of the bed, and there in my hand would be a shoe or a book or a dress and I would have an awful headache from crying. Yet I couldn't bear to sell the place. Finally I took a room here, this room, just because the hotel was on a streetcar line to the studio, and I'd stayed here a few months after I first came to Hollywood.

When I got home in the evening I would pull up a chair to the open window and prop my feet on the radiator pipes. Sometimes I would try to read. Sometimes I would look at pigeons strutting on the rooftops and listen to traffic noises in the street. I was three floors up. The second night I noticed prostitutes on the sidewalk opposite the hotel, but it wasn't till the next week that I realized that now and then they brought their clients to rooms on my floor. I would open the hall door on the smell of perfume. That didn't bother me too much. Beth never used it. Then one night coming home late I was fumbling for my key in the hall. Behind the door of the room next to mine I heard someone moaning. It was a lovely luxurious moan. I started trembling, half sure I recognized the voice. In my apartment I heard her through the wall. By that time I knew by sight most of the girls who used the hotel, and wondered who it could be. There was one who had a faint cleft in her chin that I couldn't look away from. It was Beth's chin, horrible because she wasn't Beth, but fascinating, too. I thought about it: If I cracked my door when he left, I might call her into my own room. But I knew the lovely moaning she would make would please me only if I could forget I had already heard it through the wall. And forget about Beth watching. Sometimes in the night I would still let myself talk to her as if her head were beside mine on the pillow. But I had been in Hollywood long enough to see a few people get swallowed. I wanted my own fantasies clearly labeled. I tuned my radio to a music program and thought of a pond I'd skated as a kid, that people said had no bottom. I dreamed of lying stretched on an ice-covered pond, trying to see the bottom. The next day I decided I would have to move again.

That night, though, I stepped into the elevator with a fat man reading a book. In his right hand was a half-peeled orange that he was gnawing and sucking. He had quivery bulldog jowls and a wide mouth moist at the corners. As he ripped at the orange, a fat drop smacked the page of his book. It was a gold-bordered page, custard-smooth, and where the drop fell the paper puckered. Looking over his shoulder, I saw that the pucker defaced the end rhyme of a couplet from Pope's *Essay on Man.* The little fat man chortled and looked around at me.

"Wicked man, Pope," he said. "Wicked, bigoted man. Nasty little hunchback who never got laid. But God, he could slice and zip."

I invited him in for a cup of coffee and we talked.

3. The Reasonable Man

MCMAHON HAD TWO passions: heroic couplets and the scholarly study of sensational crime. As a police reporter, he spent his day drooling over the various ways people run amok.

He enjoyed his work. Once he turned down a city-reporter slot in order to go on chasing sirens. He would tell me stories about the things he read in the police reports every morning on Hoensinger's desk, things the papers would never print. He told them with tears of laughter running down his cheeks. What made it all hilarious was that this was the kind of silly trouble people got into when they stopped being *reasonable.* That's where the heroic couplets came in. Dryden and Pope, the masters of satiric wit, took all the unreasonable vices of mankind and made them march to an iambic beat and every ten beats they slapped down a rhyme that shot the joke home. When he read out a passage from *MacFlecknoe,* the one where Shadwell, crown prince of Dull Verse, gets dumped from his throne into a sea of shit, his right foot beat time. At the end of the passage he clapped shut the book and cackled with the mirth of reason triumphant. It was the same laugh he had for police-blotter stories of suburban matrons caught shoplifting and movie stars who gulped pills by the handful to sleep away an unrequited love, and drunk teenagers found yards from their smashed cars, blown barefoot and shirtless by the crash. The only satisfaction for a truly reasonable man was to be a student of human folly, and that's why McMahon studied crime.

Over the years I acquired more information than I could use on the symptoms of strychnine poison, the wood grain in the ladder placed to the Lindbergh baby's window, and contradictions in the Slater trial testimony. One night Al met me with a sash weight he said had been the centerpiece of a party he had attended at the home of a former county prosecutor. The party was to celebrate the anniversary of the gassing of a couple who had murdered the woman's husband with the sash weight. The lovers had tried every subtle scheme they knew, Al had explained, but their poison only made the poor husband complain that his chop had been undercooked, and after the lover had badly shocked himself they gave up trying to wire the husband's favorite armchair, and simply brained him with the sash weight. The police, Al explained, had taken barely half an hour to evaporate the sash-weight-wielding-burglar story.

When I saw him wiping laugh tears with his necktie, I realized that for Al the blood, the splitting skull, had no part in it. In the solved cases it was the slapstick assault of passion on the vast sanity of moral law that delighted him, and in the unsolved ones, over which he fondly brooded, his fascination was with that sanity threatened, under attack, perhaps outwitted. When I joined him in our favorite Chinese restaurant he would rise from his chair like an eighteenth-century courtier and stick out his hand, and as he squeezed mine, he'd beam and say, "It's nice to be vertical, ain't it?" Staying alive was a singular accomplishment enjoyed by people who were reasonable.

That first night we talked I mentioned something about my dead wife. He guessed my whole problem and gave me a reasonable lecture on how to deal with it. He was an authority, it turned out, since he was living in the hotel for the same reason I was, to get away from his wife, though in his case the wife was still living.

I stayed on in the hotel, meeting McMahon every night after work. He boomed out couplets full of reasonable malicious wisdom. We laughed and drank like a pair of bachelors until his wife gave in and called him back home. I met him in the lobby with his suitcase. "See you, kid," he said. "Home is where the nooky is." By that time he had laughed me and reasoned me out of brooding over Beth's death. You die of a broken heart, he promised, and I'm gonna laugh myself sick at your wake. I did the reasonable thing—sold the house we had lived in together, moved into the apartment where I lived till a few weeks ago. Now and then I even picked up a woman, but nothing permanent. I had managed with McMahon's help to shrink the throb Beth left me down to one sore place, like a cracked rib or a bad liver. Usually I could ignore it, but whenever a woman had been around long enough to press the sore spot, I squirmed out and made myself double busy on a picture. What I had instead of Pope and gory murders, in which

I took only an amateur interest, was my camera. Sometimes behind the lens, watching Vico let an emotion tear at him, I would smile McMahon's sweet smile of Reason.

4. The Vico File

IN THE MONTHS after Berenice died, the carbon copy of the homicide report kept getting new paragraphs clipped to it as the police went through a string of interviews. For the first week, each morning when Al sat down at five a.m. behind Captain Hoensinger's desk in the precinct station, he would find the Vico report on top of the pile of overnight business, as if before Hoensinger finally lifted his feet out of the file drawer that was his footstool and fisted the cardboard coffee cup to pitch over his shoulder, sometimes even hitting the wastebasket, the Vico case had been the last one he gave up on. Then Al began finding it under more recent stuff. Once in a while Hoensinger would get a tip from a drugged-up extra with a grudge and a new interview would bob the report back to the top for a day.

Meanwhile somebody at the studio had remembered that *The Whisperer* wasn't Vico's first film role. While he was editing *The Whisperer* he'd done a role in a second-bill nail biter. It had been ten days' work and supporting-player billing, something to give the studio a chance to *launch* him as a personality—"As if I were a ship," Vico once told me. "I expected them to break a bottle of champagne over my head." It was released two months before *The Whisperer.* He appeared only in the third reel, but more than one review singled him out. Once *The Whisperer* made him a star, nobody gave it much thought. Not until six years later, after Berenice's murder, when somebody, people said it was Krackenpov himself, remembered that Vico's debut had been in a picture called *Sad Smile of a Strangler.*

It was scheduled for rerelease and actually booked as a coming attraction in West Coast theaters before, as rumor had it,

Vico one afternoon elbowed past the main-office receptionist and entered the private sanctum of Papa Krackenpov. Till that moment only Krackenpov himself had ever slammed that door. The shouts that came from behind it informed people in the waiting room that the actor who did *The Whisperer* could project without a mike. *Sad Smile of a Strangler* stayed in the studio archives.

Vico couldn't do anything about the tabloids, though, and whenever they had a bad week, with no star smashing his car or falling out of somebody's bed, they would dust off the old zinc plate with the "Strangler's Hands?" caption, and the other one, too—the one that showed the most thigh of the woman curled in the clothes closet. What Vico thought of that, I can't say. He had dropped out of sight.

After six months the edges of the Vico file's top page were showing their threads and Al knew all the thumbprints and coffee spills as well as he did the testimony. One day he realized he hadn't seen it for a while, and asked Hoensinger where it had got to. "Over there," Hoensinger grunted, waving Al to the "Unsolved" cabinet. People don't stop killing each other just because a movie star's wife gets choked, Al told me. Vico's lawsuit never came either. The next time you saw his name in the columns, it was to trumpet his wedding to a New York model named Lisa Schoen. The announcement a few months later that he had signed to do a picture called *Loves of a Spy* was an item only in the trade papers.

CHAPTER XI

1. The Bait

SO WE WOULD make another film. The week before, I'd got the word from Krackenpov. That's why the phone call didn't surprise me, the old Vico voice: the way it would squeeze sideways into a joke, then scoot off—hand on hat and coattails stretched out flat behind as he rounds the corner—and before you catch your breath to laugh, he's waddling past the cop on the beat, prim as a penguin. Swinging his cane. Oh, he was smooth. You'd hardly guess it had been a year and a half since the last shot of *Doomed Cargo,* when he'd said, "Cut it, Farley," and walked off the set before Rimers could hit the dimmer switch. A year and a half since he'd buried Berenice. It might never have happened. It was just Vico calling, the same call I'd got so many times before, saying, "Come out to the beach house, I've got a new picture." Except word gets around. In the commissary dining room everybody knew he'd been back in town six weeks already. Calling me was strictly business.

Before I start on what happened that night, I need one thing fixed in my mind: That whole week, since Krackenpov's message, I'd been telling myself it would be okay. All Hoensinger had needed from me was the time—the exact time I'd said goodnight to Vico. Why should he bother telling Vico I'd given him anything more? I'd told myself that. It made sense. I believed it. When you've been on a binge, a few aspirin take away the headache and you swallow down your sour throat and get something on your stomach again. That's how I felt about Spyhawk. What he'd done bothered me, disgusted me, but I didn't brood. It was Spyhawk, after all, and I knew in a way he was me, but only in a way.

Vico always called at sunset. I aimed the nose of my old black Packard down the streets that got me quickest out from under the streetcar cables that sliced up the sky, and north onto the Coast Highway. Like always. And like always, he'd dangled his bait to make me hurry. Imagine a master criminal, he'd said once. His disguise is a mask of his own face. And another time: Can we make a liquid mirror, Farley? Something that drains anybody who looks back at it? When he said things like that to me, they got inside my head while I was driving, as if somewhere down the road he was projecting shots from the new film onto the clouds, and I would watch some heavy slow-motion Vico close-up till the wind pulled away the nose or the jaw and it loomed and closed the sky above me.

I'd taken the bait for *Loves of a Spy*, but even while I felt it tugging me down the road, I couldn't quite tell where the hook had bit. "This time, Farley, we'll see how good you really are. We're going to balance a whole picture on a single glance, a five-second shot of a beautiful woman looking absolutely blank. Then we turn that glance inside out." The idea made me a little uneasy, as if there were a joke in it that I didn't get. I was glad that night there were no clouds. Once the sun was gone, the light bled fast and the sky was an empty screen. It was easy to think only of the bad news I had to deliver.

2. Deep Focus

WHEN VICO ANSWERED my knock, he was leaner, his eyes sunk a bit deeper in their

No. I've caught Spyhawk snipping again. If I'm not careful he deals a sequence of shots smooth as a cardsharp. First he lays down a shot of Farley's old Packard pouring along the coast road; then the dark jagged near horizon streaming past his left front fender peels away like a diagonal wipe as the road tugs seaward; then—just as the car turns up the long dirt road to the beach house—cut to Vico answering my knock, leaner, his eyes deeper in their sockets.

Nobody wants to watch you park the car, walk up the path to the door, raise your hand to knock. It's a natural cut: snip-snip-splice. The blink of an eye. But it's *then,* while you're in the dark, that Spyhawk palms the ace. I have to watch every second.

I'll park the car. In slow motion.

It's only where a ten-foot spill of firm gravel meets the highway that you would call Vico's private drive a road. Beyond that point the gravel dribbles away to a pair of tire ruts. They snake up through weeds strong enough to tickle a car's belly and the scrub oak closes around you and for a dozen yards you bump along with branches scraping your fenders. That's how Vico liked it, to keep out tourists. When you come to the clearing, the slope gets steeper and you see a hill with a knob like a humpback whale's backbone, and behind it the roof and attic windows of the house. The concrete apron behind the house leaves barely enough room for a turnaround and it's on the edge of a dropoff to the ocean, so I never used it. Halfway up the slope is a copse of pines where my car can nuzzle under the branches into a weedless patch of level ground. The night of Vico's disappearance Lisa could have driven past that copse and never seen a car, if a car had been there.

I cut the motor and step out. There's another fifty yards up to Vico's door, but I stand under the pines a few minutes. I always do. First, from over the hill, comes the clamor of waves, surging and surging again. A mob at a premiere.

With the waves come gull cries. The gull's out of sight too, but I only need that sharp, ugly squeal to see it. Hungry. Pan down on the gull as it flaps inland. Track it over the beach, over the roof of the isolated house, then let the gull slip off the top of the frame as you glide down, dolly in on the man at the edge of the pines, looking up at the house.

It's been minutes since the last tick of the Packard's cooling motor. Now all I've interrupted stops holding its breath: from the swampy brush beyond the pines, cricket chirps. Above the field swallows in the last light skim insects out of the air. And I, my back against a pine trunk, absolutely still, have become invisible. That's how you get the best shots.

I wait till I think he must have thought he'd imagined the sound of a car. Then I start up the flagstone path to the house. Always before, within ten yards of the door I would glimpse behind the living-room window a sliding shadow. The opening door would release a gust of stale pipesmoke that hit me like a breath from a tomb. "Open some more windows," I would say. "How can you live in this heat?" Sometimes he would be naked except for a pair of shorts, the hair on his chest basted in swirls, and always more gaunt than I remembered, as if the new film had been rendered from his flesh. In a whisper, his voice gone rusty, he would say, "The heat helps me think," and slip an arm around my shoulder as he led me back to the study where he worked.

But this time Vico doesn't meet me at the door. He doesn't answer my knock. I wait, knock louder. I peer in the living-room window. The curtains make a narrow vertical frame, enough for me to see the back of a stuffed chair, a sketchpad and pencil resting on its lcft arm. On the pad is a nude study: a woman before a mirror, unpinning her hair. Suddenly the waves arc crashing inside my head. The line of her white back and her white upraised arm throbs. The waves inside my head throb. Her fingers sink in churning coils of hair. One coil drops along her white shoulder like the blade of a knife.

The one who walks down the porch steps isn't me.

He backs away from the house till he can see over the porch roof. No light in the upstairs windows. He'd have noticed it coming up the path, but he's double-checking, acting puzzled, all very proper if someone is looking. He feels under someone's eye, someone with a long lens. He walks around the side of the house. It's like switching to deep focus—his horizon leaps out to the farthest swell of the ocean, the earth's curve.

Digging his heels to keep balance, he steps downhill to Vico's driveway, a ledge above the long hill down to the beach. I think he intended to see if Vico's car was gone, try the back door. Vico's study was far from the front door; he might have fallen asleep on the couch there and not heard my knock. A cry floats up from the beach. Maybe a gull. Spyhawk walks to the edge of the driveway and looks down the path. For about ten yards it drops through waist-high weeds, then coils behind a boulder. The boulder always made me think of von Stroheim. An over-the-shoulder shot of a bull-neck bald Prussian head. Where its neck sprouted from the ground, the roots of a stunted cypress had sunk like talons. Spyhawk leaps into a patch of high weeds, then scuttles down to the boulder. Breathless, the waves throbbing in his ears, he raises his head above the tossing weeds.

The two of them stand at the foot of the path. Vico seems to be gripping her wrists. She breaks away and lopes up the frame to the water. Vico watches. She wears a bathing suit, but stops where the farthest spill of the waves can only tickle her ankles. Vico shouts something into the crash of a wave, and as the water recedes, the woman throws back a cry. One word: No. Nooooo, with all her breath. Then she turns again to the ocean.

Looking at her, Spyhawk doesn't see Vico disappear. He must be out of sight on the path, coming toward him. Spyhawk scrambles up, keeping the rock and cypress between them, grabbing fists of grass. A couple yards from the crest of the hill, he raises his head above the grass. The surf is curling around her thighs. Vico's head is bobbing up the hill. Spyhawk crests the hill on his belly to keep below the grassline and crawls till he's put the house between him and the place where Vico will emerge onto the driveway. Then he stands up and runs a wide arc to the front of the house, intersecting the flagstone path halfway up the hill from his car. He takes the walk up the path slowly. By the time he gets to Vico's door he's wiped his brow and fought his breathing steady. The house is still dark. I knock and Vico answers.

He was leaner. His eyes sunk deeper than I'd recalled.

3. The Unholy Three

BY THE TIME I knocked on Vico's door, my mind had emptied of everything Spyhawk had done. The Farley that Vico saw was the only one I knew about. Under Vico's eyes I became all surface, like those aerial shots of the flooded Santa Ana, where the twists of the channel disappear under a spreading glassy lake.

Until just now, when I wrote it, I didn't know what had happened. From sentence to sentence, I didn't know. I would have an image in front of my eyes, and as I turned it into words, the words would pull me along to the next moment of what happened, and the next. It's not at all like a memory, where even when you want to think only about the day you first kissed her, you can't help knowing how white her skin will look the day you find her dead in the bathtub. Everything that happened is inside me, feeding in my guts, and I can only get at it by dragging it second by second, segment by segment, into the light.

What's in my eyes now, this moment, is Vico gripping my hand, meeting my eyes to prove that he can, leading me back to the study where he works. It's a dim room, high-ceilinged, ribbed with dark beams. Windows open, inhaling a breeze from the ocean. Loose papers, the pages of open books are slightly aflutter, like the curtains, the spare shirt hung from a closet door. Those few times when I arrived while the sun was still above the water, the plaster would have a crimson glow. This evening, though, he goes ahead of me into the shadows and pulls the chain on the desk lamp.

There is another lamp in a corner, its neck bent over the shoulder of a couch. I see the couch with its balding velvet nap and lumpy cushion. The blanket that usually hung over its back along with a pair of pajamas is gone. I glance at the floor on the lamp side for the book that's always there—most often some mystery, sometimes an odd choice, like Darwin's *Voyage of the Beagle* open to a passage on lizards. That's gone, too. Without its cozy burrow signs, the couch looks forgotten. Why should a man with a new wife sleep on a couch alone?

"You've cleaned house," I say. "Tidy. New Year's resolution?"

He shrugs, pulls up to the desk the sturdy captain's chair, its armrests grooved to the grip of a three-fingered man.

"Every snake," he says, "sheds a skin now and then."

So much for Berenice.

Which is not to say the markings of the new skin will be unlike the old. All about the room, shelves and walls and tabletops bristle with artifacts from his trips to Africa. Each year since 1932, when he signed a contract that gave him two hundred grand a picture, he had spent the month preceding work on a new script roaming the Congo or the Cameroons. Precisely where or with whom I never knew. Letters to the hotel at Léopoldville, where his ship docked, would return unopened. The first year Berenice went along, but never again. Once, in '35 I think it was, I asked if he would like me to pack a camera and join him. His face stiffened. "It's not like that," he said. "I don't want anything to do with cameras out there." I must have looked disappointed, because he softened his don't-touch-me voice and tried, reluctantly, to explain. "I use a camera to get inside my head. Out there I'm trying to see inside God's head." I thought of the year he'd come back with an insect bite the size of a Ping-Pong ball under his ear, and I'd said, "Damned unpleasant God you've got." "Horrible," he said and gave a shudder. "You've got to shake tarantulas out of your shoes. Once I got up to piss and found an adder in the chamber pot." But when I asked, as I did more than once, why he kept going back, he would mumble that next year he might try the desert instead, or choose that moment to discover on the desk top his new trophy, as if a ceremonial necklace or a carved bone scraping tool were explanation enough. One year he brought back half a dozen spears, some polished and hung with feathers, others clearly usable tools. They clustered in an urn by the french doors leading onto the sundeck. I imagined him grabbing one up for a moonlit run on the beach. The next year on the fireplace mantel he had propped a huge voodoo mask, its lips peeled back in a riptooth grin. Part of our ritual would be his explanation of how he'd come by it—the mask or juju rattle or whatever—and I'd always get a story of a five-day hike, a young hunter met on the trail, or a toothless crone in a straw hut. For all I know he bought his trinkets in a Léopoldville tourist shop. The year before Berenice died he had led me to the mantel and introduced me to a pair of black wrinkled heads the size of fists, their eyelids sewn to the cheeks as if before they'd gone to sleep they'd said, Don't wake me ever.

"I call this guy Comedy," Vico said, holding a skull with a grip like a Red Sox pitcher. "And here's Tragedy." I said I couldn't tell them apart and we had a good laugh.

But now the familiar room doesn't put me at ease.

"Any new artifacts for me to fondle?" I ask.

"Not this year," he says. "Iced tea or coffee?"

That part of the ritual was still intact.

He had someone in once a week to change the sheets, but couldn't stand servants in the house. He goes to the kitchen, leaving me by his desk. It's drawn up flush to the windows. A strip of beach shows below, but the woman he was with isn't there. A stone fertility goddess, all breasts and belly and buttocks, like stone bubbles blown from a pipe, squats over his manuscript. Also on his desk, along with a collection of carved wood warriors with skinny legs and long jaws, is his greatest vanity—a glass-framed 11-by-14 glossy of himself, arm in arm with Lon Chaney on the set of *The Unholy Three.* Chaney completed that film the year of his death. His smile at the young actor who has just made his debut in *The Whisperer* has a wary squint. Between them is the ventriloquist's dummy Chaney used in that picture. The men are shaking hands, not with each other, but with the dummy's crossed arms. Its onion-bulb nose reflects the flashbulb. It cocks a quizzical leer at Vico.

I stroll to the fireplace. On the mantel where Comedy and Tragedy used to nuzzle cheek to cheek there is a bare space.

It crosses my mind that maybe the new Mrs. Vico is squeamish. Always before he had worked up his scripts in isolation, driving to town only on weekends to be with Berenice.

When he returns with the tea tray, I give him a chance to be candid.

"I understand congratulations are in order," I say.

"Lisa's out for a walk on the beach," he says. "She'll be along soon."

Quite an actor. He never missed a beat.

It occurs to me now, as I write, that a neat splice from my handshake and murmur at Berenice's graveside to my congratulations on Vico's marriage would leave no gap in the continuity of my life. In eighteen months Vico had grieved and remarried. Fifteen, nearly sixteen years after burying my own wife, I still think of myself as a widower. The last time she touched my face, it was smooth as her own. Each year now, as my sideburns gray and the rays at the corners of my eyes sink deeper and my skin dries toward the leather cheeks of Vico's shrunken heads, I grow more strange. I become someone she would no longer recognize. All that's young in me is what I remember of her.

Vico and I take our accustomed places at his desk. He lifts the bulbous rock from the manuscript. As usual, it's not just dialogue. His master script is always full of diagrams and sketches—a camera script. I am the invisible character in every film, the one who sees everything and never has a line.

"Well, here it is," he says, and as I sip my iced tea, he slides across to me sketch after sketch, filling my head with pictures. I nod and coo and suck an ice cube, waiting for the right time to slip him my bad news.

4. Distraction

IN THE BACKGROUND as he talked, for us both though he didn't know it, was the woman on the beach. When I raised my eyes from his sketch, I had a clear shot through the window: between the trunks of a pair of palms that leaned head to head above the roof; past von Stroheim's skull and the vulture-cypress pecking at his ear; beyond the place where a rib of rock that ran along the hill beneath the weeds broke and spilled rocks to the shore. The banks at the crest of that wash cupped a V-shaped wedge of sand; cupped more broadly and finally not at all the silver undulant skin of the sea. If she crossed that wedge of sand, a thumbnail at arm's length would block her from view. But we couldn't keep our eyes away.

It occurs to me now that I'm describing a classic Vico scene. You can trace it as far back as *The Whisperer:* Vico in the foreground explaining one of his dreams, while outside, framed by the window, a boy bounces his ball, a woman walks on the beach. This time it will get shot right. None of Bobby Sandford's fuzzy backgrounds. I've got a long lens on that wedge of sand.

For all I knew then, she could be his heart's dear or a new whore. To me she was something else, something I'd needed only two quick shots to invent. The first shot was that sketch on Vico's living-room chair—a nude at her mirror unpinning her hair. The second shot had told me even less. With the light all but gone as she ran from Vico to the water, she'd been no more than a woman-shaped hole in the glaze on the sea. There was no face in either shot. Still, that run of hers had a loose-hipped lilt that made me grunt, made me risk Vico spotting my head above the grass.

Why?

I see it now: I had told her to wait while I set my camera, but she darted away down the beach for a quick dip and later when she said, "Hurry, honey, I'm starting to shiver," I told her, "That's why I wanted you to wait." The faint tightness that locked around her smile in the photo on my desk was what I hadn't wanted Hoensinger to see.

It was that smile I'd always wanted her for; it promised all kinds of secrets, but not quite yet. She was still shivering when we got back up to the house, and that night she slipped into a hot bath and slit mouths in her wrists to tell me secrets I'd never cared to hear.

When I got back, the water was cold, but pink—an ocean sunset just begun to fade. Fine setting for an ivory cameo, breasts and shoulders drained, so white I couldn't believe they'd ever been warm, and lips gray as old ice. I never told Vico, not even when his own wife died. Grief is just another dance.

I have to admire his concentration. The woman he'd left on the beach might have been years away, long dead. Over the first few sketches he stammered, trying to recall why the shadow of the venetian blind should ladder up the counterpane and when to track in on the cigarette lighter. His eyes would flick to the window, groping for a thought, then back to the sketch. While I stole my own glance. She was there. The ocean was gray now, and the farthest thrust of it tongued around her ankles. As it slid back down the beach, her shadow seemed to squat; maybe something, a shell or an odd stone, had rolled to her feet. I looked back at Vico and asked a tough question about the setup of a shot. He raised his eyes, pretending to consider it in the unfocused distance, then frowned as if at a twinge or cramp, and answered me. He was elaborate, precise, and convincing. When I looked up again, beach and ocean made a seamless plane of darkness. Vico had at last lost himself in his own story, and so did I.

5. Raw Material

THE SHOOTING SCRIPT for *Loves of a Spy* may be the only map I've got through the maze. From that first camera call to the day of his disappearance Vico was charting a maze. The script he wrote for Lisa will tell me how he loved her, if he did. It will show at least the web he thought would trap her, and who he thought he was in the last dream he dreamed of himself. Maybe it will even point to where his body lies.

Before he let me see the first page, he held a hand over the script and explained that it was based on fact. An odd point, I thought even then, since he knew as well as I that whether or not it would work had nothing to do with where he'd got it.

The summer he'd met Lisa in New York, he told me, she had friends among a knot of Jewish refugees from Germany. One of them was a journalist named Knopper. Vico had asked him what he knew about the Klamstadt case. A few months earlier an Englishwoman named Klamstadt, the wife of a wealthy German contractor who had made his fortune building Hitler's autobahns, had caused a brief volley of headlines in England and America. She claimed to an English newspaper that the Nazis had murdered her son. One of her husband's work crews, she said, had discovered a beaten and shot body in a roadside ditch. A member of the crew had known their son two years earlier when he spent a university vacation working on a road gang. The authorities had ignored him when he said he recognized the corpse. That night he came to Herr Klamstadt. At first the Klamstadts were incredulous. Their son had graduated from Oxford with a first in classics and so far as they knew had spent the three years since then in England touring with a minor theatrical company. They'd had a postcard from him not three weeks ago. Frau Klamstadt, however, was unsettled enough to wish to view the body, and when the authorities showed reluctance, she was stubborn enough to insist. She confirmed the identification. Herr Klamstadt publicly demanded an investigation. It came out that Hermann Klamstadt had left the theatrical company nearly a year before. Within two months he was back in Germany under another name, weeding flower beds on the grounds of a government minister, one of von Ribbentrop's personal aides. At last the Klamstadts were visited by a police official, who told them that their son had been suspected of espionage. He had been shot at while making an escape, and had apparently died on the roadside of his wounds. The official, Frau Klamstadt said, had expected that explanation to silence her husband's demands for an investigation. It did, but not her own. That night she called a friend in the Berlin office of the *Times*, ending her account with the information that the bullet wounds her son had suffered while successfully eluding the police consisted of a single bullet hole entering his left temple and exiting the right. The day after the wire services picked up this story there was another, saying that Frau Klamstadt had been admitted to a private sanitarium suffering from nervous strain. That's the last she was heard from.

Vico's conversation with Knopper, the Jewish newspaperman who had just squeezed out of Germany, put together the pieces of the Klamstadt story. Most of Knopper's information was rumor, locked into focus by a single conversation with a Nazi prison guard. Knopper had met the guard in a beer hall, almost by chance, and kept his glass full by design. "Even drunk," I asked, "why would a Nazi blab to a reporter, especially a Jewish reporter?" Vico smiled. "Knopper is a blue-eyed blond," he told me. Even so, Vico had asked the same question. What Knopper had said was: "Otto's conscience itched. And I was there to scratch."

Otto told Knopper that Klamstadt *was* a spy, that he had been caught in the minister's study photographing sensitive papers. They had him cold, but had taken a slow month breaking several of his bones to find out how he had discovered the secret cupboard where the minister kept his papers. Finally Klamstadt confessed that he had been making love to the minister's wife, and they shot him. The wife's death from "heart failure" was reported on the obituary page. Knopper's theory was that it was out of tact for the minister's delicate feelings that the trial and executions had not been public.

That was Vico's preamble, his account of the source of *Loves of a Spy*. The first thing that occurs to me is that he'd never before bothered to account for a script's source at all. Why was he doing it now? Why was he making the story's origins outside his own secretions a kind of boast? I can recall him giving me the precise lilt of Knopper's self-mocking shrugs. It was more than just an actor's habit. He had been working hard to make it *Knopper's* story. Was it that he didn't want me to see how much it was his own, see the welds where something in his own past had linked him to Klamstadt? Yet at the same time he couldn't resist revealing the welds, those details that took on meaning simply because the script had suppressed them. Vico had pared away Knopper, for example, the eyes of the story. Aesthetically that made sense. The only eyes he needed were mine, eyes that could be sensed without being seen. But he'd also pared away all of Klamstadt's past, particularly his past as an actor, which he'd gone to some trouble to find out. He'd written the English company Klamstadt had acted with, and asked them to type out for him reviews that had mentioned Klamstadt. Why, I asked. Vico looked surprised. "Whether he was a good actor or a bad one," he said, "has a lot to do with how I play the role." So how good was he, I asked. "He played melancholy old men," Vico said. "And melancholy poets. Once a melancholy child murderer. Not much range, they said, but depth."

Vico had pared all that away, and all the grief of Klamstadt's parents. Pared them away—or maybe buried them so deep they could shape the play of a scene without being mentioned. Like the gossip he never quite confirmed of his own snake charmer mother, his father's plunge from a high wire. In fact, all that Vico used was the kernel of Knopper's story: the spy in bed with the minister's wife. For Vico's imagination, what could be more familiar, more cozy? He had traveled across a continent to find a story he could have pulled out of a back drawer in his own mind. Hadn't he known that? It's like asking whether he could recognize his reflection in a mirror.

6. The Arrest

AS USUAL THE sketches Vico passed to me were laid out in panels, a newspaper comic page with wide margins. The margins gave him room to scribble blocking diagrams, notes about shot length, lens size. The first page, headed "The Arrest," showed Vico as Klamstadt. He's in gardener's overalls, prowling an elegant bedroom. He pulls open dresser drawers, checking for false backs. Feels underneath them for something that must be flat. His fingers spiderwalk along a high shelf of books, not grazing their spines as if he were checking titles, but probing, probing behind their uneven horizon, probing for something small and important. (Was it a name, Vico? This was the first scene in the first film you would make after Berenice's death. Maybe it was a way to enshrine the moment you met her. Is that it, Vico? Were you thinking of the woman behind the screen, tossing silk stockings and chatter about von Stroheim across the rim while you scan her library shelves for someone to be when she asks your name?)

"From the instant he appears," Vico was telling me, "they've got to know this is not his room. He's an intruder, this is a theft. Mostly that's my job, but you, Farley, you're the accomplice. That's why so many subjective shots. His hand sliding under the shirts. The camera scanning bookshelves."

In the back shelf of a liquor cabinet his fingers pause, explore. Cut to his face, an alert stillness. The hand withdraws, and held—even in the sketch held delicately, as a woman might hold a cigarette—held between forefinger and middle finger is a key. (Vico told me more than once that the key to a role is a name, so his mind is here still translating that scene with Berenice.) Quick takes, the marginal notes read: "7 secs., 5 secs., 6 secs., 4 secs." A file cabinet, the key slides in its lock, Klamstadt removes a folder, deals the papers onto the counterpane, and pulls the bedside lamp switch. No light. Pulls it twice more, checks the plug at the baseboard. Strides to the window. The venetian blinds clatter up, continue rising *in reverse angle,* silently, seen through the twin overlapping irises of a pair of film binoculars. A voice says, "Captain, I owe you an apology. Your burned-out bulb has done its work." Another voice, with a chuckle: "It's as I said, Herr Stauffer. He needs strong light to photograph the documents."

The next sketch should have been a simple two-shot with one of the men lowering binoculars from his eyes. Nothing complicated about the angle. It might have been a hasty cartoon. But Vico had got lost in it, lost in the eyes of Herr Stauffer. He'd shaded them like whirlpools, sucking everything toward them. When we shot that scene, I remember, he made Scottie Fielding do a couple dozen takes. "That's not it, Scottie," he kept saying, and nothing clicked until he said, "Make it look as if he's just taken off a blindfold—catch him blinking in the light," and on the next take Scottie was perfect. "And also," Herr Stauffer says, "for what you ...suggested about my wife—an apology." "We shouldn't decide that yet," the police captain says. "Perhaps he found a way to get inside without her help. But we must move quickly."

I never knew whether Berenice had a husband when she met Vico. Was he out there somewhere, shuffling in the silver light along a row of ankles and knees, bumping empty popcorn cartons and saying *Excuse me* when he steps on someone's toes—a sad little cuckold come to stare up at shadow pictures of the man who stole his wife?

The camera tightens on a cigarette lighter raised to Klamstadt's eye. The design along its narrow edge is an Egyptian ankh and a sun disk. When he spins the flint wheel, an aperture behind the sun snaps open and shut. Bending over the papers he's strewn on the bed, Klamstadt moves down the rows, snapping pictures. From outside the shot a woman's voice whispers, "Hermann." Urgent. He lowers the camera. I track in on his face.

Vico often didn't know who would play certain roles. In the sketches they would be a blur, just detailed enough to throw the right shadow. But roles he had cast would bear a likeness. He had an eye like Toulouse-Lautrec for the quick, grotesque line that made a dewlap or a dimple the shape of his victim's most cherished vanity. But on self-portraits—there he would linger. They showed intimate study, mirror-staring study. He knew all the moods of his face. Oh, for a few hundred feet of him, sketchpad in hand, grimacing at his shaving glass. Not that it would tell me anything new. Beside him in a dark projection room I would sometimes slide my eyes away from the light-and-shadow Vico swelling and shrinking on the screen, and study his rapt profile.

"Through all this, Farley, no music. Heartbeats. Heartbeats and breathing. Even during Stauffer's dialogue I want heartbeats and breathing on the track. I want to see if I can make an audience breathe in sync with me, pump its blood in sync." (Every artist's modest request of the world.) "Until she calls his name—and for three seconds his heart stops, his breath stops. Silence! Farley, on the soundtrack it will be a thunderclap."

In the next shot he is looking down the hall. A woman at the head of the stairs says, "He's coming. Two men with him. They're at the door." Close-up of her, the voice of Klamstadt saying, "If he suspects, say nothing. You hear me—say *nothing*, and you're safe."

And where I had expected a precise cartoon of Denise Holston, Vico's surrogate for Berenice, there was a new face. Not the usual vague oval with a question-mark squiggle for a nose, that signaled an uncast role, but a particular face. More than a cartoon. A study. She was young, but the expression, particularly around the eyes, seemed aware of things you need a decade or two of adulthood to absorb. I wondered if Vico had been cheating a bit, slipping behind the girl's face to look out with his own eyes.

I interrupted him: "But isn't Bere—isn't Denise available for this picture?"

Vico gave me a curious glance. I remember his exact words.

"This is a romantic lead, Farley. We need a much younger woman."

Just like that. A younger woman, please, and on your way just order a dozen roses, will you, for Berenice's grave.

Track shot: Klamstadt racing back to the bed, scooping documents. Cut to what she sees: at the bottom of the stairs, just entering, her husband Stauffer. Behind him bob the heads of two policemen, one with a drawn gun. She sweeps down the stairs, her arms out. "Darling, what is it? Who are these—" Two-shot of Herr Stauffer slapping her. "Up those stairs and to the left," he says. Pan the two cops galloping up right off the edge of the screen. Cut to Klamstadt still snatching papers from the bed, stuffing the folder. As the cops burst in, he grabs the bedside phone, twirls the receiver over his head like a lariat. The cops fall back. Then the one who chuckled over the burned-out bulb cocks the hammer of his pistol and grins.

"Cut to Klamstadt," Vico said. "The spinning line goes limp. Fade to a prison corridor."

7. The Interrogation

IT'S HARD TO escape who you are. Vico had told me this picture would give him a new style, full of hard angles and slangy talk, fresh as a newspaper exposé. The news from Nazi Germany, he called it. But in the sketches Klamstadt's prison was a medieval fortress. The walls were rough-cut blocks, the windows two feet deep with pointed arches, the halls caverns where dripping water echoed. About as newsy as a Gothic monastery. Vico's imagination had squirmed off the hook and splashed right back into the stagnant pools where it swam best. I thought of telling him the prison could just as well be smooth concrete with two-tone walls, and then thought again. That reminded me too much of the room where Hoensinger had put me through his grilling.

Vico showed me a sketch. Long shot, camera angled down on Klamstadt. A standing lamp spotlights him in a stiff-back chair. Jackbooted thugs stand around with only their jackboots in the light. A thug behind Klamstadt has a fistful of hair. He tilts Klamstadt's face to the light. As if you ever had to ask Vico twice to hit his mark.

"Knopper says they beat him every day," Vico said. "Every day for a month. He never opened his mouth. Except to scream." Then he looked at me. "What do you suppose gives a man that kind of will?" he asked.

It was that look he had in *Discipline* while he's toying with the paper cutter on his desk, and he says, "You have one last chance, Pilcher, to give me a complete account of Weller's whereabouts after curfew," and the reflection of the paper cutter wraps along Pilcher's throat like a silver gash and I cut from Pilcher just starting to blubber to a tight shot of the contempt in Vico's eyes.

I'd ignored his question, but he wouldn't let it go.

"Where does he get it, Farley—that kind of will? From a woman? From God?"

I stayed silent. It was then, I think, that I realized Hoensinger must have told him everything I'd said. The new film wasn't about Berenice at all. He wasn't interested in flesh that couldn't wince when he poked. But how had I betrayed him? I'd been his alibi. I'd saved him a few nights in jail, maybe even saved him a trial for murder. But I'd blabbed about his lousy marriage, said things he'd never have told even me if he'd been sober. And this was my punishment: He'd worked up a neat parallel for my grilling in Hoensinger's office and found a way to make it frame the entire picture.

"Every time one of those thugs asks a question," Vico said, "it will cue a flashback. What we'll show in the flashbacks is all the things he'll never tell them."

There it was. Vico as Hamlet and I his whining Claudius. Was I expected to break into a sweat? I didn't sweat. I gave his plot my keen admiration.

"Oh, that's going to be fine," I said. "That will work fine."

Vico blinked and got back to the script. He always treated praise like a social blunder, something to be ignored. The next sketch was a close-up of the officer in charge of the interrogation. It was a rough sketch, a role he hadn't cast yet, but he'd put in the eyes a chilly Hoensinger stare. "In this shot," Vico was saying, "Hoensinger"—(he gave him another name)—"is saying, 'We know you had help from Frau Stauffer. We need you to tell us whether she is simply a foolish wife or a traitor.'"

And Vico by now is deep in his dream, gasping, moaning as he rehearses how Klamstadt will say it: "Never," he says. "I never spoke to her." And he jerks as if he's been kicked. "Once.

One day. To ask if she, if she wanted me to—to trim the apple tree."

Cut to a flashback of Klamstadt fixing an apple blossom on his lover's shoulder. Cut back to the prison, where Hoensinger is saying, "We want the name of your employer, specific details of your orders." A thug is twisting Klamstadt's arm behind his back and Klamstadt is shaking his head and moaning, "No employer, no orders," when we hear a bone snap. Vico gasps as if in mild surprise and drops his head to simulate a faint. That's how it's done, he seemed to be telling me. It's easy to look into Hoensinger's eyes and deny everything. When it gets hard, you just faint.

As Klamstadt loses consciousness, with an echo voice-over repeating, "...specific details of your orders..." we lap-dissolve to the dingy office of his contact, a grandfatherly pipesmoker with a mouthful of oily principles. "The camera concealed in the cigarette lighter," he is explaining, "has a dual function. Its ultimate purpose, of course, is to photograph the minister's secret treaty documents. It can also, however, help solve the problem of how a gardener on the minister's estate can get his foot, so to speak, in the door."

"I don't understand," Klamstadt says. "You've told me that the way to get in the upstairs rooms was to make the minister's wife fall in love with me. I've done this."

"Not unpleasant work, I trust?"

Klamstadt ignores the remark, says, "I'm only waiting for a chance to be alone in the room."

"We've no more time to wait. We need the documents immediately. You must persuade the wife to cooperate."

"How?"

"Surely there are moments in your pleasant afternoons with Frau Stauffer when she is in a position only someone intimate, as you are, could share. When she is, let us say, lounging on a bed, unfastening a garter? And you are, not implausibly, fondling your cigarette lighter. If you were to confront her with photographs of a few such intimate moments, and suggest..."

"That they be shown to her husband."

"Precisely."

So that was Vico's notion of my art—the cameraman as Judas.

8. Snapshots

VICO WAS SAYING, "We're in the prison again. We've got a part for a comic jailer. Somebody who can look fat and stupid. That's for the shock, because Fritzi will be the one to break Klamstadt down." As Vico played him that night, Fritzi bubbled over with chuckles and leers, sinister but not at all stupid when he peered into Klamstadt's cell to say things like "Peek! There he sits, mouth shut tight to keep the pins from falling out. You know what you look like? My wife pinning the hem of a dress. Pinchmouth, I call her. *Pin*mouth. Ha-*hah*!" If Vico had cast himself in the roll, he would have ruined it. Too much imagination, too much vitality. The scenes we shot with Jack Wallace in the part were a disappointment to Vico, who could only see it the way he'd imagined it, but I think they would have been perfect. Wallace is a one-note actor. His pouch-eyed drawl wrapped around Vico's jazzy lines would have made him a star—if the picture had ever been released.

"I'll tell you something, Pinmouth," Vico chortled. "You can go your whole life with pins in your mouth. But if just once, with one person, you took the pins out to say something, we *get* you. Ah! I saw you blink. You did, didn't you? You trusted somebody! Who was it? It was her, wasn't it?" He cut from that line to a glance at me, a glance meant to sear like a blowtorch, then showed me a sketch of a loving head shot of Frau Stauffer. "Let me help," she was saying. "I'll never let you down."

"Dissolve from that," Vico said, "to this front shot of her."

Her head lay on a pillow, close-up, half in shadow like a new moon. It was a study, the same as his self-portraits, and the curve of light along the cheek kept me looking.

"She tells a lazy story," Vico said, talking not as if it were something he was making up, but something he remembered. "Childhood in a convent school, arranged marriage with a stranger, watching him change into something she can't stand to look at...." For a moment he trailed off, while I wondered whether he had after all found a place in the film for a little slice of Berenice. "As she speaks, Farley, you drift into a profile shot. The frame opens, takes in, first of all, this shot" (beyond her pillowed head the sketch showed a bedpost, and hung over it a man's shirt, a gardener's cap), "then this one, looking past her, deep focus—Rudi standing by the window, the venetian blinds drawn. Rudi—oh, yes, that's Klamstadt, that's the name she knows him by. Spies don't generally use their own names on the job. As he reaches for the cord to open the blinds, she's still talking—it's one of those times when a woman is more exciting than ever, just because she's forgotten that she's naked." For a second he seemed about to tell me something, then he went on. "She's still talking, but you let her slide left out of the frame, you're tracking in on Klamstadt. Make him loom, Farley. And as he opens the blinds, we hear her say, 'Oh, the sun! It blinds me, Rudi.' You're close enough now to see him raise the cigarette lighter, his thumb on the wheel, and we cut back to her, blinking, her dressing gown open, the sun on her thigh like molten silver. 'Please close them,' she says, and he says, 'I only want to see you. A flower should open in the sun.'"

I'd had enough. I said, "You think you'll get this past the Hays office?"

Vico never missed a beat.

"Look at *It Happened One Night,* Farley. Can you imagine what that bedtime strip looked like on *paper*? Gable and Claudette Colbert undressing with that sheet between them? What smuggles it through right under Will Hays's nose is *style.*"

"No, Vico," I told him. "It's jokes. They joke their way through it. You can even show a girl prancing past the window to run her bath so long as the one peeking is Harpo Marx. Will

Hays isn't afraid of anything he can laugh at. But this—this is steamy."

"Maybe. We'll see. Instead of jokes, we'll make him sweat. What Hays has got to be thinking about in this scene is not how far up her thigh the slit in her dressing gown goes, but whether Klamstadt will click the shutter on that camera."

He looked me in the eye. I didn't blink. My heart was pounding, but all he could see was the cinematographer discussing a shot. It's not just actors who can use masks.

9. The Unmasking

HE SEEMED TO be trying to find out how far I would let him push me.

In the next shot, Vico said, Klamstadt has his thumb on the wheel of the lighter, which is also the camera shutter. We hear the pipesmoking spymaster in a voice-over purr: "Not a gentlemanly tactic, I admit. But think how many people may die if you fail. Or would you rather think of the tears a rather impetuous woman weeps into her pillow?" Klamstadt flicks the wheel, strolls to another angle, closer. In the margin of his script Vico has diagrammed Klamstadt's approach to Frau Stauffer's bed. *My* approach, since I am his eyes here, tracking in on her. "She is sitting on the edge of the bed," Vico says, "like this." The sketch shows Frau Stauffer, the plunge of her dressing gown more reckless than anything we would be allowed to get on film. Looking up with a faintly wanton trust into the eyes of the man holding the camera. Obviously sketched from life.

She rises into a two-shot, lifting a flickering match to his cigarette. Ah, yes. Vico had not lost his touch. He was still able to make an audience skip a heartbeat in the pause while he thinks what to do. He puts his hand over hers and blows out the match. Then he presses a spring at the back of the lighter, breaks it open to pull out the raw film. It coils in his fist like a snake. That's the unmasking, the ritual scene in each Vico film.

"My real name is Hermann Klamstadt," he whispers. "My mission is to steal a copy of the treaty your husband has been drafting. This film would put you in my power. Now I am in yours."

Moments like that don't thrill me anymore. I know what Frau Stauffer doesn't. Vico never gives himself away.

The scene ends, of course, where it began: a soft-focus head shot of Frau Stauffer, closing toward my lens for the embrace. "Let me help," she begs. "I'll never let you down."

I had made no promises. Not one.

10. The Betrayal

"NEVER LET YOU DOWN," Vico repeated. "We'll have a voice-over echo of that line as we dissolve to Klamstadt's prison cell. We hear the fat jailer say, 'On your feet, traitor,' and Klamstadt sits up in his cot, blinking, rubbing his jaw. 'What's proper etiquette for a firing squad?' he says. 'Shall I shave, comb my cowlick down?'"

"Plucky to the last," I said. Vico barely smiled.

"And Fritzi says, 'Go right ahead. Look pretty for your girlie. They tell me she's been fussing with her hair today, too.' Then in this sketch we've got Klamstadt in close-up, lathering before a mirror while you look over his shoulder. It will be tricky, because I want Fritzi reflected too, breathing garlic or whatever while Klamstadt shaves. And Fritzi says, 'Shall I tell you about protocol for these affairs? We follow the custom of high society—ladies first.' The razor stroking Klamstadt's chin pauses. A sensitive mole? No, he continues the stroke down his neck. 'Ah, yes. While you wait your turn, you can watch your girlie's performance. Will she accept the blindfold? Will she blow you a last forgiving kiss?' Klamstadt's razor strokes his face smooth. He's reaching for a towel, and he says, 'For weeks your thugs have punched me around. I've got a headful of lumps, cracked ribs. I can't—'"

"What about that broken arm?" I said.

"What about it?"

"In this sketch you've got him holding a shaving mug in one hand and a razor in the other. He must heal fast."

Vico grunted and said he'd have to fix the scene where they break Klamstadt's arm. Maybe that could be where they cracked his ribs. Then he went back to Klamstadt's dialogue: "'I can't take a breath without pain. I've told you nothing. Today you decide to shoot me. That's fine. If you want to shoot the minister's wife along with me, that's fine, too. I still tell you nothing. She's a silly woman. I poured a little ketchup on my handkerchief and wrapped it around my thumb. Told her I'd cut myself with the garden shears. Antiseptic? Of course, she said. Silly woman. In the bathroom, she said. Right up those stairs. And once up the stairs, I slipped into the minister's bedroom—'

"And Fritzi says, 'You've told that story before.'

"'Under torture,' Klamstadt says, and Fritzi gives a little shrug, and says, 'Call it that if you like. I think you enjoy being beaten. The lady bruises more easily.'" I thought of Berenice the night I met her, wearing her purple dress, and wondered if she had been in Vico's mind, too.

Fritzi's next line is: "You might as well know: She gave us a full confession."

Close-up of Klamstadt adjusting his tie; and of Farley, his eyes not daring to rise from the script.

"A pity," Klamstadt says, and Vico gives the line an insolent drawl. "How you must have made her dance—and all for a lie you could make up yourself."

"Then Fritzi says, 'Stick out your wrists.' Klamstadt obeys. The bracelets click. Two guards clomp in. They lead him handcuffed from the cell." A classy prop. I might have bet money the next picture Vico made after his arrest would include a handcuff scene. He had a woman's eye for what jewelry suited him.

11. The Kuleshov Experiment

I NOTICED A PAUSE, brief as the pause of the razor on Klamstadt's cheek, before Vico laid down the next page of sketches. In the first shot, he explained, I would be tracking backward down the prison corridor, shooting Klamstadt as he is led to his execution. The second shot reversed the angle. The camera is Klamstadt's eyes as he is bustled down the corridor. The next sketch shows a dolly past doors with frosted-glass windows, bulletin boards papered with wanted posters, and suddenly I know where we are. It's the corridor of the precinct hall and Vico is being led from one interrogation to another, and in the next sketch a door is opening, there is someone in the doorway, and to show the camera is tracking, Vico has blurred the image so that all I can make out is the head turned back to someone inside, and Hoensinger was telling me not to leave town, I would be needed to sign a statement, and in the next sketch the blur is turning toward the hall but Vico has an arrow above the frame to show that the eye of the camera makes a sudden lurch away.

"This stinks," I said.

Vico's eyes were bland, mildly curious.

"What's the trouble, Farley?"

"It's all a bit too familiar, don't you think?"

I was ready to have it out, ready to tell him if that was how he felt about what I'd done, why didn't he get somebody else to shoot his goddam picture. But the look he gave me—he had eyes like my setter the day she wouldn't come when I called and I threw a crabapple that bounced off her nose. I couldn't be sure he was acting. I lost my nerve.

"You've made this film before," I said.

"When?"

"When? Try *The Whisperer* for a start. Look at the plot. Poor boy takes job on wealthy estate. In *The Whisperer* you're a manservant. Here, a gardener. Next—surprise!—you make love to the wife as a way to get at the husband. Avenging a sweetheart's death, stealing the minister's treaty, it's the same thing. And both films are an exact copy of—"

"Go on, Farley. A copy of what?"

But I stopped there. I couldn't quite bring myself to remind him of the bit player walking into Berenice's mansion a servant and tap dancing out with a rich wife to bankroll his first picture.

"Never mind," I said. "It's slipped my mind."

"Farley, what's eating you?" He was all patience. While I kept myself tongue-tied, not trusting what I might say, he went on, soothing and reasonable as he was in *Mark of Cain* when he tells Grip that it's his body the police will have to find in the empty shack. "Sure there are similarities. *The Wedding March* is similar to *Foolish Wives,* but I'd hate to flush one or the other down the toilet. The similarities in this picture—to *The Whisperer* or whatever else you can name—are the last thing in my head. That picture was all Ferris wheels and lightning flashes. This has a completely new look. I want to get the feel of making love while the sun comes through slits in the venetian blinds. I want dust floating in the sunbeams and afternoon traffic noises floating up from the street."

That's how he always got to me: filling my head with shots, making me think how to light them, what stock, what lens would give me that bedroom haze he wanted.

"But most of all, Farley," he went on, "this film is about the Kuleshov experiment. While I was in New York I went to a party where they showed a print of Barrymore in *Dinner at Eight.* It struck me how the stage had spoiled him for a screen actor. He keeps twisting up his face. He rolls his eyes, his eyebrows do calisthenics. It's ludicrous. Stand him next to Gary Cooper, next to Garbo. All Cooper has to do is *be* there, even with a face full of novocaine, and you've got a shot charged with feeling. And Kuleshov tells you why. The shot means nothing, it's the sequence that means. Now here's what I want you to do. You've been tracking down the corridor. We bump the camera now and then, give it the feel of Klamstadt hustled along between Fritzi and his goons. In this next shot the person in the doorway starts to turn around just as Klamstadt looks away, and I want the camera to swerve back and lock on her." (It was here that he laid on the desk the next page of sketches. I wonder now how I could have been so surprised to see in the doorway the face of Frau Stauffer rather than my own. Or had Vico, even in his earliest plans for the film, merged his images of Lisa and me?) "Klamstadt stops," Vico was saying. "Everybody stops. Fritzi says, 'Go ahead. No reason why you can't say goodbye.' She looks at him. He looks back. Now here's where Kuleshov comes in. Fritzi's just told him she's been tortured till she confessed, so what he sees in her face is the long ordeal. We cut to a shot of him thinking what they must have done to her, thinking about their hands on her skin. She lowers her eyes. And he takes a step to her, steps into a two-shot and grabs her hand, and whispers: 'It's all right, Madeline. You weren't the weak one, it was me. I had no right to ask it. Just remember—'"

The next sketch showed Frau Stauffer drawing back in what Vico called a "hiss of terror." In the *next* sketch, Fritzi's triumphant simper. Then Frau Stauffer's husband motions another pair of goons to take her away. As they drag her ahead of him down the hall, Klamstadt is screaming after her, begging to be forgiven.

"And the last thing he shouts at her," Vico said, "is going to be, 'Remember—I *love* you.' We'll make the echoes in the corridor come back in a babble."

An artist lives most of his time inside his head. He doesn't really need much from people. Maybe that's why an artist's revenge can be so ruthless. All your betrayal and shame twisted into something immortal.

I think Vico was describing the surge of music, the final dissolve, but my eyes were drawn past his shoulder to the woman who stood in the study doorway, her eyes staring into mine in a way that I knew at once.

12. The Look

THE PAST HALF hour I'd been aware of someone in the house. Two of Fritzi's thugs had been beating Klamstadt, I recall, when the screendoor snapped shut. Vico's moan had been answered by the jew's-harp twang of the screendoor spring, the door's sharp cough as it slapped the jamb. The door was directly below our window, but I hadn't heard her on the gravel drive. A shadow in the dark hall passed the study door to the stairs, leaving on the still air a faint sea-smelling musk. Above us, in a room where I'd never been, bare feet made old boards groan. Crossing, recrossing the ceiling, prowling as if she had no idea where to look for whatever she was hunting. Then Vico's design pulled me back to Klamstadt and she slipped from my mind.

The desk lamp cast a tight aureole that seemed to float us in the dark of the room. Each time I glanced up from a sketch, the dark would be full of currents—coils and whirlpools of darkness where dark things swam. When a light from the hall sliced a hole in the dark, the doorframe too seemed to float and she hovered on the threshold with the silk of her kimono drifting around her. The hall light pouring through the silk silhouetted her thighs.

How long was it—a second, half a minute—before Vico noticed me looking past him? For that long the look that passed from her to me and back was private. My sense of it was that she *recognized* me. At the corners of my eyes, where the lensman's squint had settled, I felt a tingling, as if her look were smoothing the creases away, remaking the man she'd known. That same intent look was how I'd seen Beth last, standing in her dressing gown at the bathroom door, steam from her bath rolling behind her, and she said, "When will you be back?" "When I'm damn well ready," I said, and walked out. Not a month, not a week since then that I haven't seen her there in a dream, and watched me walk away.

"Lisa," Vico said, looking up at last. "Come in. Meet Farley."

She was aware how little the kimono hid her body. She tried not to come in, said something about not being aware that Vico still had company, but Vico said, "Come on in. Farley's just folks and there's nothing he ain't seen—right, Farley?" Vico never had trouble knowing what kind of coax or prod would make an actor do what he wanted. She tossed up her chin and pranced across to me, and every step made the silk that hugged her breasts shudder. She offered me a pressed smile and a palm still ocean-cool. Vico had stepped back as if to watch us both. It was his scene, but for a moment, while we said our Pleased-to-meet-you's, her eyes locked mine in that private look.

Now, inside the desk lamp's circle, her lower lip was a shade full, the tilt of her nose not quite familiar. Only the eyes refused to admit the counterfeit, as if Beth peered at me through the holes in a living mask.

"Farley," Vico said, "meet the woman who's going to play Frau Stauffer."

Her head jerked toward him as if she had been slapped. A coil of driftwood-colored hair dropped from her shoulder and grazed the hollow of her cheek.

"I thought we were still discussing that," she said.

Vico waved a dismissing hand and strolled from the desk lamp's tight circle into the shadows. He flicked on the lamp over the couch, dissolving the circle.

"Do we really want to get into this in front of Farley?" he asked.

"You brought it up."

I knew I wouldn't get a better chance to see how he'd react to the bad news I was bringing from Krackenpov.

"In fact," I said, "it may be a little early to talk about casting."

I can't say what changed in Vico, maybe just his weight shifting to the balls of his feet. But he knew something was up.

"You'll play the lead," I said. "Just like always. But for the rest... we'll have to see what the director wants."

Whatever he'd been expecting from me, that wasn't it. It took a couple seconds before he could say, "Who?"

"Did you see *Gutter Princess*? It could be up for an Academy nomination. The guy's name is Bolger. That was his first picture. Krackenpov wants to give him another shot."

"On *my* script?" His voice rose higher than he'd expected. He leveled it and said, "Lisa, you'd better let me discuss this with Farley alone."

She started obediently toward the door, then stopped.

"If you're going to be working late," she said, "I'd like to drive to town and see a movie."

Vico said it was too late. Lisa said there was still time to make the last feature. Vico didn't want her going alone. She mentioned someone named Alice who would go with her. They could have a drink afterward, and talk. Vico didn't want her driving if she was going to drink. With a voice that could chip ice she promised she would spend the night at the town house and drive back the next day. Vico objected that he would need the car early in the morning. The other one was still in the shop. While they wrangled I looked at the sleek kimono clinging to her thighs and breasts, and realized that when she'd come to the door she'd had no intention of leaving the house that night.

"Look," Vico finally said, "why don't you just forget—" But her glare was round as a cat's. He dropped on the couch and said, "Farley, would you give my wife a ride back to town?"

"I'll be dressed in five minutes," she said, and strode out.

It had all happened so fast that none of us had time to think that it didn't make any sense. Lisa was going to town because Vico would be working late with me. But Vico had just asked me to drive his wife to town, which meant we wouldn't be working late. It's as if all they'd needed to set them off was an audience.

As soon as she was out of the room, Vico said, "Now what's all this shit? If Krackenpov's tossing something like this at me, why doesn't he tell me himself?"

"Don't look at me," I said. "He said you don't answer your phone. I was surprised, too."

"Who is this Bolger?"

"He's good. He's been around a year or so as a scriptwriter. He's also an arrogant bastard."

Vico stood up and paced over to the fireplace mantel. Then he went to the door and fingered the African hunting spears as if he were deciding which one to take with him to Krackenpov's office.

"What about Krackenpov?" he said. "What kind of bug's up his ass?"

"He was all smiles. I'm supposed to tell you he knows you've had a hard time. He wants to work you back in gradually. Light responsibilities. Then he gave me a cigar and a slap on the shoulder. Personally I think he wants to make trouble."

The understatement made Vico snort.

"Do I have to take this?" he said.

"You know your contract better than I do."

He was back at his desk now, his palm over the fertility goddess that weighed down his script.

"I wrote this for Lisa," he said. "Nobody else is going to play it. Nothing Krackenpov wants, nothing this Bolger fink wants is going to change that. No goddam suspension is going to change it."

He was full of fight. It would have been hard to predict that this was the picture that would break him down.

"That's what he can do, then?" I asked. "Suspend you?"

Vico shrugged.

"He can try. How tough is this Bolger? Can we work him? Huh, Farley?"

He whirled on me, dancing on his toes and feinting punches. I laughed and ducked and said I didn't know, I'd only met Bolger once.

"I think we can work him, Farley. We'll stand him in a corner and tell him to suck his thumb. You and I will make the picture, same as always. When this Bolger wanders into the sightlines, we'll just pick him up and carry him back to his corner. What do you say?"

I laughed again. I said it might be more complicated than

that, but we could give it a try. Then he thought of Lisa and got grim again, almost pleading. "You can see she's right for it, can't you, Farley?" I said yes, but there seemed to be some question about whether she wanted it.

Then she was standing in the door.

13. The Bride

READING OVER THE past few pages, it strikes me that Vico's dizzy plan to have me drive Lisa to town makes a kind of sense if he'd intended—knowing it or not—to push us together. Is that possible? With Vico it's hard to know when you're too subtle. But the way he had bullied her into the room wearing only that silk kimono—wasn't he asking me to look my fill? Why? Did it please him to watch her squirm under my eyes? Or was it part of *my* humiliation, like having me film my own betrayal? The more I think on it, the more the motives branch and weave, and no one of them really cancels another. Maybe after just six months between the sheets he was bored with her, needed my heat to rouse his own. Maybe it was a simple calculation that old Uncle Farley with the honey-drip voice would make her ashamed to be scared of the camera. That feels right, but still not quite in character for Vico, whose calculations were never cool. Put it this way: He was giving her a taste for his own choice erotic sweet, dangling me as a bait to teach her the same excitement he felt when *he* stripped for the camera.

Whatever his motive, that drive to town was the start of my next betrayal. On the dark path down to my car her heel wobbled and she slipped her hand inside my arm.

"I heard what you said," she told me, "about whether I wanted the part. Thanks for bringing it up."

"I wasn't taking sides," I said. "Just keeping all the facts of the problem in front of him. It's part of my job."

"Yes. He's told me how you work together. I think you're the only one in this town he trusts."

Holding the passenger door for her, I smiled in the dark. Ah, Vico, that was a nice touch. Telling her that.

Once we had turned onto the highway, I said, "You really don't want to do it, do you?"

"You sound as surprised as he is."

Wasn't it, I wanted to know, every girl's dream, breaking into pictures with the hottest director in town?

"Hollywood isn't the only town," she said. "In New York I spent three years modeling. The only people I saw were squinting through a viewfinder at me. Lift your chin, honey. Wet your lips. The day I met him I had a bus ticket back to Columbus in my purse."

"And Vico wants you to go through it all again," I said.

Hearing her tell how it was on the other end of the lens gave me that odd tingle I get when I know Spyhawk is watching, about to take over. When she first started modeling, she told me, photographers staring at her made her feel beautiful. You've got lovely bones, honey, they would say, and run the back of a hand along her cheek. "As if," she said, "my bones were something I had accomplished." She resettled herself in the seat with an impatient squirm. "But that's all they're interested in."

"What's all?" I asked.

"Bones. Complexion. The way you pose, the smile. All they see is a surface."

"That's not quite true, you know," I said. "A good cameraman can reach inside. He can probe every secret you've got."

Her laugh was a blend of bitter and apologetic.

"I forgot," she said, "you're a photographer, too. I'm sorry." After a minute she couldn't leave it alone. "I still think you're wrong, though. They talk a lot about soul, personality. Especially when they're trying to get you to bed. But the film sees nothing but good bones and clear skin."

"I'm not saying a photographer is some kind of missionary, but do you really think he doesn't give a damn about soul or whatever you want to call—"

"Not about mine. If my complexion, my bones, make him

feel good, he gets excited and talks about soul. He's looking at me, but what he's seeing are his own feelings. His own damn soul. That's not the same as caring about mine. All he thinks he knows about me he can find in a mirror."

Her talk was so intent that I realized she must be thinking of somebody in particular. I smiled again to think she'd picked up Vico on the rebound from a fashion photographer.

Before she got out of the car, she asked me to talk to Vico for her, convince him that it wasn't just what he called stage fright. She wasn't an actress and didn't want to be. She said Vico might believe me. He trusted me. She said she did, too. Maybe that's why I couldn't look at what was happening to her later without feeling responsible.

"It will be hard," I told her. "I think you're right for the part, too." She had started to get out of the car, and sat with one foot already on the running board, looking back at me. "You've got a certain quality," I said.

"Do you mean soul?" she said, and smiled, not the pressed model's smile I'd got before, that won't crease your skin, but a real friendly forgiving smile so broad at the corners it pulled away from her teeth. That's how Beth smiled.

Driving home I thought of Vico's sketch of her sitting on the bed, her dressing gown slit high up her thigh. I thought how we could light that shot.

There's one more thing, something I forgot. I wonder if she ever thought of it. Coming down the path, just after she'd put her hand in the crook of my arm, she asked me why I had parked so far down the hill. I like the walk, I told her. Behind the wheel of a car there are some things you never see. Like what, she wanted to know, and I told her about a hole under the dead oak tree at the edge of the clearing. "Once just after sunset I saw a streak of fur over there," I said. "Then something glittered, just enough to catch the light off the clouds. It was watching me from the shadow of the burrow." What could it be? she wondered. A fox? "I think they live in big families," I said. "You'd see the entire hillside honeycombed with escape routes if it were foxes. This was something solitary, waiting for me to go away so it could come out and hunt."

From the start, it seems, I was only a breath away from telling her everything.

CHAPTER
XII

1. Casting the Bluefly

VICO PLANNED HIS campaign against Krackenpov with the same heavy-breathing intensity he put into that scene where Klamstadt photographs the documents. Early next morning I got a call telling me to cancel whatever I had planned and meet him for lunch at the Coconut Grove. Since I had nothing planned, that was okay with me, but why the Coconut Grove, I wanted to know. Vico hated star traps. He explained that we were lunching with the town's most important legal talent to plan strategy for his court case against the studio. The idea was not just to lay out the strategy, but to be *seen* doing it at the Coconut Grove, to be seen with Milt Beach of Beach, Barton and Huskleson.

The question I didn't ask was why he wanted me along. Given the way he felt about me, it would have been natural for him to suspect I would tattle everything he said to Krackenpov. Maybe he guessed there were a few things I still wouldn't do, and maybe he just weighed the damage I could do against something more important to him. This was going to be a performance, and he'd got used to me being his eyes.

When I got to the Coconut Grove, Vico and Milt Beach had the ashtray and water glasses pushed to the edge of the table to make room for legal papers. To prove they were already buddies Vico had hiked his elbow onto the back of the seat and stretched his arm along it toward Milt Beach. Both Milt Beach's elbows hugged his ribs and both his blue-veined hands dangled over the documents. With the pages of his contract separated and spread before them like an ordnance map, Vico was playing general, his forefinger ranging from one clause to another to show where Milt Beach should lay down barrages against Krackenpov. As I slid into the booth Vico raised his hand to silence me while he finished his point, something about his right to oversee script changes. His introduction, when it came, was one of those pieces of magic he carried off so well, where a couple throwaway lines get transformed into a succulent *bit.* The tone he had decided on was curt flattery, the assumption that Beach and I knew each other well by reputation. "Milt, meet Farley," he growled. "People in this town know I don't lift a finger without Farley." Then he got back to the contract, and I spent the next hour and a half watching Milt Beach follow Vico's darting forefinger and noticing the way Milt Beach would twitch his nose or scratch behind his ear when Vico confused a legal point with a moral one. I wondered why Milt Beach was letting Vico do all the talking.

When we parted, Milt Beach said things looked good and he would work up a few strategies and contact Vico in a couple days. A couple days later Vico called me with the grim news that he was obliged to accept Thad Bolger as director of *Loves of a Spy.* The only concession Krackenpov had agreed to was casting Lisa. All the strategies Milt Beach had worked up, it seems, involved Vico's willingness to go on indefinite suspension to win his point. And since Vico wasn't willing at all to delay *Loves of a Spy,* he ran out of bluff fast.

After his eighteen-month vacation Vico wanted to hear clappers snapping again, wanted it bad. Maybe he was afraid he'd been out of the public eye so long that *Spy* already had too much the smell of a do-or-die comeback. Maybe he was afraid Lisa would go back on her promise to play Frau Stauffer. Maybe both those reasons are true, and another one, too—stronger than either. He was an artist.

His wife's death, his remarriage, and—judging by the script I'd seen—my blab session with Hoensinger had crammed his head with new shots, new angles. He didn't like Bolger, not even as a nominal director, but he was in a hurry.

Vico's first move was to make sure Bolger knew where he

stood. The film was scheduled to begin shooting January 14th. On the 13th a memo from Krackenpov informed us that Bolger was finishing location shots for another picture and wouldn't be available till the end of the week. Vico tossed me the memo and smiled. "That's fine," he said. "We start shooting tomorrow—as planned."

"Without a director?" I asked.

"Do you think we can manage?" Vico said.

"The question is, will Krackenpov stand for it."

"He should be grateful. He always bitches when we're a few days behind schedule. Stage Nine is empty and waiting and as far as I can see the memo doesn't say anything about postponing. It just says we'll get a few solid workdays before the boy wonder comes around to ask which end of the camera you point at the actor."

Her first day under the lights told me Lisa Schoen was no actress. The genuine article, someone like Vico himself, powers a performance from somewhere *under* the lines of a script. The lines are leaves on the surface of a pond. Scanning through them while you do the lighting plot for a script, you can feel the breeze blow, guess how the leaves will drift across the water. But an actor starts from underwater. He says the lines, word-perfect if the script is worth respecting, but sometimes he'll slide right past a word you'd think the whole speech was leaning on. Where he does lay the stress you notice an odd current stirring the leaves. Suddenly bubbles are churning up the surface and you think, Christ, there's something down there, something *alive.*

Lisa had a solid mellow mike voice and she read all the surface currents, everything that blew on the breeze, but there was nothing swimming down below. What saved her from looking silly was her complete lack of any desire to act. An ambitious amateur, pelting stones at the pond and slapping the water into a froth, would have been a disaster. She was too intelligent for that, too sure of her limits. She did what she could because Vico wanted it, but once he said, "Flip a little giggle onto the end of that line," and she said, "I can't do that," and didn't. The strange thing was that in the rushes that night her reserve translated into a smoldering subtext. It was not acting, never would be. It was personality, the kind that sustains more than one career in this town. And another thing: No matter which way she turned the light hung in a sheen on the fine straight bones of her face.

Here in my room at the Silver Palms, the marquee lights from the street throbbing on my ceiling and Vico gone nearly a month now, it occurs to me for the first time to wonder if there was a special significance in the scene he chose to get in the can before Bolger showed up. Something private between himself and Lisa that he wanted undefiled. In his shooting script he called it "The Pastoral."

2. "The Pastoral"

AT THE EDGE of the minister's estate, beyond the flower garden Klamstadt has been hired to weed, are a dozen or two acres of trees. Vico had found a shady woods on the studio back lot and had his flowers planted in a nearby clearing. Deep focus: Klamstadt huge in the foreground, pressing the dirt around a new-planted rosebush. Beyond him she approaches against the sky, her white dress swaying against her thighs, a forsythia swaying at the edge of the frame. Her shadow falls across his hands. "I like your touch with flowers," she says. He doesn't look up. Only the camera sees his smile. She drops to her knees, her face enters the frame. The wind machine floats her hair around her shoulders. Their two faces lean above the swaying stalk of a rose. Their eyes meet over the flower, and here was Vico's taste for the incongruous image that could rescue a scene just as it was veering toward cliché: her mouth opens, smiling. "Look," she whispers. "A rabbit."

"Okay, cut it," Vico says. "How was it that time, Farley?"

"Let's print it," I say, and I'm already thinking of watching the rushes, thinking how that moment, the moment when she raises her eyes to him and lifts her hand to draw that strand of hair through her fingers, is something I've got forever. What made me so smug? Did I really think that having it curled in a can in the studio vault would be the same as *having* it? All I've got is a memory, a little dimmer every day, like a proof that fades in sunlight, and pretty soon all I'll have will be the memory of thinking I had it, really had it, the moment itself.

Reverse angle. The background no longer sky, but the woods at the edge of the garden. Cut in close: A rabbit browses in high grass. "It's heading for the woods," Frau Stauffer says, and disappears into the trees. Vico follows.

The back-lot woods had a special meaning for Vico. The week before shooting started we cut short our lunch so he could show me a path he'd found leading to a brook. He planted himself on a mound at the bank. Hardly any light got through the trees. He stuck his head into a slender shaft of sun. "This is it, Farley," he said. "So long as he's in the minister's mansion, he's a trespasser, but out here... And this is where he takes her away from Herr Stauffer." He went on, telling me how we would shoot their first kiss with her leaning against a tree, him brushing a cobweb from her hair and then letting his hand linger on her cheek. Then the camera would crane up, admitting more and more of the woods into the frame. He wanted the trees closing a protective circle around the lovers. During the torture scenes, we would periodically cut back to some moment from this scene. "It will open the picture up, Farley. Every other set is filled with corners, walls, windows. It's the spy's world. But out here, he's planted in nature, what's between him and her is... solid."

"It's damn near impossible to make it through this brush on foot," I said. "How do you think we're going to get a crane in here?"

He had plotted out an approach that would only require cutting down about a dozen trees for the heavy crane truck. By the time we shot the scene, grips had made a wide avenue into the woods. We did a few easy shots of Klamstadt and Frau Stauffer strolling along the path, then set up on the bank of the brook. Grips with machetes had cleared all the brush from the bank and covered the bare ground with stage-grass mats. This tame clearing in the woods was where the chase after the rabbit ended. That finished the week's work.

The rushes elated Vico. He sat each night in the projection room, Lisa on his left, me on his right. Every time he saw a close-up of her I could feel the excitement run through his body. Beautiful, he would murmur. He wasn't talking to me, and the odd thing was, he wasn't talking to the woman by his side. It was as if she didn't exist, except as a shadow on the screen.

Friday night we all went out for a drink. I came inside with them for a nightcap as the phone was ringing. It was Alex, the projectionist. After we left Bolger had stopped in and seen the week's rushes. He was furious.

3. The Tender Stalk

THE NEXT DAY we were still in the garden with the rabbit. All morning we expected Bolger to make his entrance armed with dark glasses and a riding crop. Vico was strutting around, clearly looking forward to a scene that wasn't in the script. About noon we realized that Bolger wasn't going to show up. By that night guys in the unit were laying cautious bets that he had slipped his resignation under Krackenpov's door. Monday morning we reported to Stage Nine and saw how Bolger had spent his weekend.

We expected to find there the prison-cell set and the room where Klamstadt was tortured. The flats were there, all right, but stacked in a corner, unpainted. In their place was a forest, nearly an eighth of an acre of plaster trees with lamps throwing leaf shadows through the branches. Nobody'd seen anything like it since the set for *A Midsummer Night's Dream*. At the heart of the woods was the glade Vico had found on the back lot. The mound by the stream echoed when you kicked the grass and the stream rippled over plaster rocks.

Vico was too surprised to say much. He swore and kicked a plaster tree root into the water. He bellowed for Slim Mirkle, the art director, but it was early. The unit men were just arriving. The trees trapped his voice inside the woods. He turned on his heel and strode along the path. At the edge of the clearing, waiting for him to find his way out, was Thad Bolger, his tongue wetting the tip of a slender cigar. No sunglasses. No riding crop. Just a lean, hollow-chested cowboy with sleepy Lincoln eyes full of intelligent hate.

"Nice piece of work, ain't it?" he said.

"Nice and unnecessary," Vico said. "We shot this scene last week, while you were away."

Bolger gave a lovely performance. Vico was nearly six feet tall, but Bolger was enough taller so he could shift his weight onto one leg and lean at him with a patronizing slouch. He explained that the scenes in the forest were not what he had in mind. He wanted a lot more camerawork on the path leading to that clearing Vico had discovered. "Do you know," he said, "when I was a production assistant, I used to eat my lunch in that spot. It's a damn shame you boys had to hike into the woods and chop down all them trees." Bolger made sure to mention that he had cleared the construction of the indoor woods with Krackenpov. There was not a whole lot more Vico could say. We went to work for the new boss.

At first Bolger's blocking changes made no sense to me. He wanted me to follow the rabbit browsing lippety-lippety down the path through his papier-mâché woods. The rabbit was a good actor, but it didn't see the part the way Bolger did. As soon as we hit the lights it squeezed its eyes shut and laid back its ears and hunched down in a passable impression of a fur-covered rock. When Arnie Crossman goosed it with a coat hanger, it shot off down the trail quicker than Seabiscuit out of the gate and left us with a performance that totaled about three seconds film time. After several more streaks like that, the rabbit was tired enough to give Bolger the lippetylippeties he wanted. Then we shot Lisa following the rabbit along the trail and by this time we were cracking jokes between takes about how we ought to comb her hair out and get her white cotton stockings so that we could get it right if what we were after was *Alice in Wonderland*.

We shot her running along the path, slowing to a tiptoe walk when the rabbit stopped to nibble, then sprinting ahead when the rabbit did. We shot it with the camera sliding on dolly tracks past bushes and tree trunks so that she seemed to dart from behind one tree and disappear behind the next. Then we did it again. She chased the rabbit with me tracking behind her on the path, the branches and tree trunks looming and bleeding off the sides in fuzzy focus.

By that time it was midafternoon, and we'd only seen Vico at lunch. He'd spent the day in his dressing room waiting for a call. If he'd snuck into the soundstage for a quick peek, nobody'd seen him in the dark. When he got his call he came onto the set blinking, mole-blind and sluggish as he was only on his worst days, when he couldn't tap into the juice that gave him a sense of who he was. He took one glance at Lisa, limp and dull, with a long day under the lights already behind her, and turned away. I knew the signs and made up my mind that we wouldn't get anything worth using the rest of the day. Bolger told us that now he wanted me to track Vico chasing Lisa while she chased the rabbit. Vico leaned toward me and murmured, "How long's this been going on?"

So we did. I shot Vico running down the path, Lisa ahead of him, deep focus, drawing him on. I got a couple close-ups of him looking at her. They meant nothing—a blank face. I didn't know Vico had it in him. Then we got to the point where Lisa rounds a curve in the path, maybe twenty yards ahead of Vico, and Bolger told him to crash through the brush as if he were taking a short cut to catch up with her. Bolger had me jolt the camera over bumpy tracks, make the lens nose aside the branches. That only took a couple of minutes and once it was finished I noticed Vico's face was no longer blank. He was alert, tense, listening to sounds nobody else hears. The next I knew he had taken Bolger off to the side and the two of them were talking low with lots of arm waving and pointing toward the path. When they broke apart Bolger announced that we were going to retake Vico's shots. This time when Vico followed Lisa down the path, he looked like he knew why he was doing it. On the close-ups his face had an expression I couldn't read, but it left no doubt something was happening behind his eyes.

There were no rushes that night. Bolger told us that before he ran it for us he wanted to get together with his editor for a preliminary cut-and-paste session to see what they had. I had no idea what he had, or thought he had. The night after that we saw what amounted to a rough cut of the scene, and I finally got the point—the point Vico had picked up as soon as Bolger had given him his blocking. That, I think, was what made Bolger a canny man with actors. If he had *told* Vico what to think, all he'd have got in those shots was a more or less animated carcass trotting through the trees. But making Vico work out what it meant from the blocking clues—that turned a torch on Vico's brain so that when he got to Bolger's meaning it fused with what his own mind had invented.

At first, cutting from rabbit to Lisa to Vico, with the rabbit setting a strange lurch-and-pause, sneak-and-sprint pace, the scene was almost comic. Then we got to where Vico darts into the brush. With a few cheats here and there, Bolger was shooting Klamstadt's point of view. The cutting got quicker. The camera seemed anxious to keep her in sight. Branches whipping at his eyes. Gasping for breath. Bolger had turned the stroll through the woods into a stalk. Watching it, Vico was grim and still. When the lights came up, he raised his eyebrows at me—baffled, he seemed to say, as if he couldn't believe Bolger had got him to do what he'd done—and left without a word.

The next day we shot Lisa walking into the clearing by the brook. Bolger had played with every switch on the dimmer board to give a lazy afternoon slant to the sun arcs beating down through his plaster trees. All it needed was a butterfly flip-flopping around the paper violets on the bank. The only thing about it I didn't like was that I was the unit cameraman and I hadn't been the one to work out the lighting plot.

Bolger had Lisa come down to the water's edge, squat to pluck one of the violets, then stand and turn back to face the path.

"No, Farley, that ain't right," he says. "Let's do it again. Now honey," he says to Lisa, "when you bend down to get that violet, I want you to look as though you're about to pick it. Then sit down beside it instead."

After we shoot that he tells me I can set up on the mound to get Vico's approach down the path. But not with the tripod pulled all the way. Now eye level is Lisa *sitting* on the bank. When Vico comes into a waist shot, I'm shooting *up* at him. Bolger has also had me put on a wide-angle lens so that when Vico kneels before me into a close-up, the distortion makes me want to pull back. His face is all nose. I'm about to cut the shot, when Vico reaches a caressing hand to the barrel of the lens and says, "Hello, Alice. Don't you know it's dangerous to chase a rabbit down his hole?"

In the old days he might have ad-libbed the same line, but it would have been a piece of raunchy fun meant to crack the tension. We'd have a good laugh and shoot another take. But that day the words had poured out in a simmer that was obscene and not at all funny. Somewhere at the edge of my vision I saw Lisa wince. It's hard to figure what he intended. Was it a way to mock the twist Bolger had given his scene? Or, coming after the stalk through the woods when his response had been a kind of instinct, was this the moment he yielded to Bolger's intention?

He broke from the shot without waiting for Bolger to call the cut. Bolger stepped out from behind the camera, puffing hard.

"All right, Ay-meel," he said with a smile that twitched a bit at one corner. "That works. I think you're getting the idea here. Now I want to set up a reaction shot with Lisa."

That night in the projection room we saw Vico say the line, then heard the words again with the camera on Lisa's face, her eyelids trembling as Vico's fingertips trace the line of her cheek and jaw. Good bones. Lovely complexion. I wondered if Vico ever mentioned her soul.

CHAPTER XIII

1. Sleeping Beauty

THAT NIGHT AND from then on Lisa didn't attend the screening of the rushes. For a few days I saw her only under the lights, heard her say only lines Vico had written for her. One afternoon we had to shoot a couple dozen takes of a scene where she tells Klamstadt about her childhood in a convent school, and that night I found myself imagining her in my old grade school, where every room had a crucifix above the blackboard and the desks were nailed in rows on wooden runners so that with your ear to the top of your desk the creaks and ticks boomed along the runners and when Sister leaned above what you were writing, the black long sleeve of her habit falling across you like a wing wrapped you in the cozy smell of her body and the rosary beads at her waist made a busy, intimate clicking and her silver cross swung against your cheek. Then I had to laugh. The Catholic was Frau Stauffer, not Lisa. At least not necessarily Lisa. Since it was for her that Vico had written the part, you could never tell what he might have scrounged from what he knew of her. For all I knew everything she'd said, that he'd made her memorize and give Frau Stauffer, might have been taken from some sleepy, drifting murmur, her hair spread on the pillow by his cheek, his semen still working inside her.

Then one day I stood in the commissary doorway, my eye sliding past the table where Curtiss and Rimers drew lighting diagrams on a napkin, looking for where she would be huddled with Vico. When I didn't see them, I decided to eat my lunch alone. I got an apple and headed out to Vico's woods, the real woods. Along the wide track Vico had cleared for the camera, leaves on the felled trees hung faded and crisp. From far off, as soon as a movement winked under the oak where he'd shot their first kiss, I knew it would be Lisa, and knew she would be alone. She was sitting with her back to me, her shoes beside her in the grass, her feet in the stream. The arch of her back as she stirred the water with a stick had a grace I'd never seen while she waited for the cameras to roll, a grace you would always have to take by surprise.

Coming down the path behind her I saw myself as Klamstadt, as Vico being Klamstadt. What Bolger and Vico had done to the scene made me uneasy. I coughed to announce myself, and her shoulders hunched. She twisted around, squinting in the sun.

I put on a suave leer and said, "Come here often?" and sat beside her, facing back toward the studio hangars. The white walls shimmered in the sun.

"Not much the way it was, is it?" she said.

Could Vico have brought her there before we began shooting, some evening maybe, to show her what he had to ruin?

"None of us is," I said.

I asked where Vico was. When they didn't join the commissary rabble, they would lunch together in his trailer.

"He's got a scene to work on," she shrugged. "He needs to be alone, he says."

More and more as friction between Bolger and Vico grew, he would need his lunch hour alone, and my meetings with Lisa—there by the brook or in her dressing room where she would brew me a cup of tea—became a ritual unpacking of hearts. I told her everything—leaving out Spyhawk. Leaving out the days following Berenice's death. But I did mention that Beth had been a suicide, and that my walking out that night made me responsible. "Responsible?" she said, and her eyes were puzzled and pained. "That's a kind of insult to her, isn't it? Was she so pathetic she wasn't responsible for herself?" There was steel in her, a dagger wrapped in velvet. And she, too, unpacked her past—as much as she thought I ought to know. In Hollywood she had no other friends, no people who didn't see her first as Vico's wife. Maybe in the modeling world she came from, women were too often rivals and she'd got out of the habit of seeing them as friends. She spoke to me, not quite as if I were a woman, but as she would to—might as well say it: an uncle. And I—I couldn't say a line out of character. Marry that guy before he gets away: That was what she wanted from me, and even the day she told me she was thinking of leaving him, all I said was, "Sleep on it. Don't do anything you'll have trouble believing you could have wanted." She grabbed my hand and held it, her eyes brimming, and from somewhere—inside her wrist, the hollow of her neck—filled the air with a faint scent of jasmine.

There were other times, too, when I'd said the right thing just by asking why. Why do you feel he doesn't *see* you anymore? Why are you afraid to have children? Why worry what your father thinks if he's been dead six years?

"Think of what *you* want," I told her. "What do you want?"

She looked away. I'd been around so many frozen glamour queens that I was mildly dazzled at the sight of a beautiful woman putting the ball of her thumb between her teeth and biting as if it were a grape. When she let me see her eyes again, they were confused. What hit me was that maybe she'd never before been asked what she wanted, maybe never even asked herself.

"I want—" she said, and jammed her thumb back between her teeth. After what seemed a long time she started talking. Her voice had an odd mocking lilt, as if she were telling me a funny thing done by someone she didn't much like.

"The summer I was eighteen," she said, "my sister got married. All that spring we sat around the kitchen table and drank iced tea and planned the wedding. My father rented the ballroom of the biggest hotel downtown. A sit-down dinner. Caviar and champagne. My father never ate caviar in his life and at home he drank beer. And Cora: When my father led her down the aisle, when I saw her with her arm in Daddy's arm, and his eyes so bright, Cora was looking for *me*. She gave me the biggest *smile*, and squeezed Daddy's arm. She wasn't even beautiful. All she was was first. I smiled back. It's all right, I kept thinking. Wait till my turn comes. Then it was over. Cora was gone. My mother and father and I sat around listening to the radio. And I thought, Good. We'll have a quiet summer. And two days later, mowing the lawn—my father had his stroke."

She held a sip of tea on her tongue as if she'd felt a leaf she didn't want to swallow. Then her chin shot up, defiant, almost angry.

"I don't know what I want," she said. "I want a big wedding from my daddy. Since then I haven't wanted anything much at all." Then she raised both hands and pressed her fingers against her temples. "That's silly," she said. "Forget I said it."

I was silent. What do you do when people tell you more than they want you to know?

Finally I said, "But it's important. It was important to say it."

Her hands were still to her temples and when she shook her head, they seemed to fight the gesture.

"Just spite talk," she said. "Silly. It didn't deserve saying."

"If you hadn't said it," I told her, "you'd never have known it was silly."

She took my hand again. She told me that I was wise.

"But you know," I said, "you haven't really told me what you want. Your sister's wedding is a Cinderella story, but"—I said it tenderly as I could—"it's a story you would have told yourself and really believed only the year you were eighteen, and then I think only for a few months. There was something else, something you started to tell and couldn't finish. What is it you really want?"

She blinked and shook her head.

"Go ahead and say it," I said, and then, again very tenderly: "It can't be more silly than Cinderella, can it? And saying it aloud can help. It's what you can't say aloud that wakes you up in a sweat."

That much, it seems, I knew. My twisted partnership with

Spyhawk had condensed itself to a pure truth, something I could give away.

"I want," she said, and had to start again. "I used to want some kind of—greatness. Maybe it goes back to the gold stars the teacher would paste on your homework papers, wouldn't that be fine? Corrupted by a gold star. But I've always felt, always wanted—I want to be asked to do something extraordinary, something that needs—something heroic. When I was eight, I started ballet lessons. I always loved it, but around the time other girls were thinking of nothing but clothes and boys, dancing became an—a kind of obsession for me. I worked my body till it—it sang. Then I—"

But here I had to know more and I said, "Why did you love it so? Why did you let yourself become obsessed?"

She looked at me as if I ought to have known. Or as if I did know and was testing her.

"I loved how hard it was," she said. "The discipline made me—pure. When I'd practiced a piece till every movement came without thinking, I would reach—I would break through into a—a state of grace. I felt a gyroscope at the base of my spine, spinning and humming, and every movement spun out from that center and there was nothing I could do so long as the dance lasted that didn't have—that poise."

Watching her, I could feel excitement climb her spine. She turned her head away, regal and serene.

"Then I developed bursitis in my ankles. I couldn't go on point anymore. I had to give it up."

There was nothing to say. I kept still.

"In high school," she said, "all I could think of was chopping off my hair and leading armies. I practically memorized *Saint Joan* and when I'd read everything on Joan of Arc, I started on medieval history and then one day Daddy came into my room and said, 'You know, Lisa, you're not Joan of Arc. You're Daddy's little girl.'"

She seemed to think the story was over, that she'd explained everything.

"That's pretty blunt," I said. "I'm not sure I like your father."

"No, he was right," she said. "He wanted to protect me."

"From what?"

"From getting—obsessed again. From what happened to me after I had to give up ballet."

"So what did you do then?"

After that, it seems, she waited. She gave up being Joan of Arc, but kept on waiting to hear voices.

"I was waiting," she said, "to be asked. Asked for that—heroism. When all I heard was silence, I realized if I really had it—that kind of heroism, that greatness—I wouldn't need to be asked, would I? Whatever it was I had to do, I'd know it, recognize it. So I finally told myself: There's no greatness in me. Nothing. Just nice bones and clear skin. And when he came along, I said, All right. I'll give myself to the greatness in this man." She gave me a quick look. "He is great, you know," she said, and I said: "I know."

"He wants me to be a movie star and I try to give him that. But he's never asked me for—whatever it is I need to give. Until he does, until somebody does—I won't know what it is, or how to give it."

That talk was a liberation for me. From then on I knew that nothing Vico had given her—or asked her for—had been enough. She was a sleeping beauty. Whoever could wake her hadn't been found yet. Any kiss might be the one.

2. The Seal

TO ME LISA was the victim. Not like Berenice—she wouldn't look good in a bruise-purple dress. But because of Berenice, because I'd watched what Vico could do, thought what he might do again. It was type casting. But just now, looking at the street outside the Silver Palms, I was sifting my head for clues. Two-second cuts I could splice to other cuts. And I remembered something else Lisa said, something that didn't sound at all like a victim talking. It sounded like someone with a razor in her purse.

It was the first day shooting the bedroom scene, the first day she appeared on stage in that gold silk nightgown we'd been waiting to see since the costume tests. The day things went too far to go back. Vico was losing control of his rage against Bolger. He muffed lines. His temper rasped like a match on a brick.

After an hour under the lights the damp silk was wrapped against Lisa's thigh. In another minute costumes and makeup would grab her to fresh her up. I wanted another shot before she wilted. I came close with a light meter. The breeze when she moved her sleeve was a swampy heat. I held the meter to her face and asked her to lower her hand. She had it pressed in a loose fist against her forehead as if she were trying to remember exactly something that happened a long time ago. "Sorry, Lisa," I said, "your face is in shadow." She flashed me a bright, hopeless smile and waved her arm to erase what I'd seen. Later that morning I noticed it again: her hand raised, the back of her thumb pressed to her forehead. Then it went to her lips, where she seemed to kiss the thumb before letting it drop a moment to her breast. That finished it. The fist opened, the hand settled on her knee. Twice more before noon, she made the same gesture. The last time I half recognized it. We took our sandwiches to her trailer. I waited till she was at her makeup table, spreading rouge for the afternoon shooting. "Was I really?" she said. "I guess sometimes I do it without thinking."

"What's it mean?" I wanted to know. Her eyes in the mirror met mine, then went back to their own reflection and seemed to find something there they hadn't expected.

"It's a prayer," she said. A prayer the nuns taught her in grade school. (Ah, one of Vico's pickpocket jobs. It wasn't only Frau Stauffer who was Catholic.) She raised her fist, the thumb straight against the forefinger, and said, "You make the sign of the cross over your forehead, your lips, and your heart, and you say: Jesus be in my mind..." (and she signed her forehead) "...and on my lips..." (and she signed herself there) "...and in my heart..." (and her thumb touched the base of the V where the dressing gown crossed her breasts). She looked away then, not to my face in the mirror but to me, her jaw set for any punch, ready to spit if I laughed. "My secret charm," she said. "Wanna make somethin' of it?"

I shook my head.

"Everybody needs one," I said.

Of course then I knew where it came from, since I'd been taught the same prayer by Sister Angela Marie and said it for all of three weeks whenever I caught myself thinking of Mrs. Kelsey at her window looking back at me watching her. By the end of the third week I'd failed the prayer so many times I let it go.

I asked why she needed a charm. The first time she remembered saying it was the day she modeled a brassiere. She stood at the door of the dressing room trying to get up nerve to walk out into the studio. On the other side of the door were the photographer and a couple other men from the ad agency and a man from the company paying for the ad. "And I was supposed to walk out there in my underwear," she said. "I had one hand on the doorknob, and the other was making the sign of the cross, over and over. I took a deep breath and did it one more time: Jesus be in my mind. And on my lips. And in my heart. Then I took another deep breath and smiled at myself in the mirror and opened the door."

I asked what the sisters would think of the way she'd used their prayer.

"I know it sounds silly," she said, "but it helped. After that, they could look all they wanted, and not be taking anything I didn't want to give. It sealed me off from them."

I looked at me behind her in the mirror. Her use of the prayer was a mirror version of my own.

"So that's what you were doing this morning," I said. "Sealing yourself off." And suddenly I had to think hard about not letting my eyes stray to her breasts. At the same time I felt a blind urge to protect her from Vico. "Listen," I said, "if things out there get too bad for you—"

But she eased my hand from her shoulder. Her eyes had gone dull, like a skin of ice over a pond. "Don't worry, Farley," she said. "Not about me." She turned back to the mirror, powdered the blush on her cheeks, then looked my reflection in the eye. "I found out something else during my underwear-modeling days. In a situation like this I've got one hell of a lot more control over how hot things get than any man in the room."

It sounded to me like a wobbly boast.

"What do you mean?" I asked. "What do you mean?"

If I hadn't pressed for an answer, she'd never have said it. I'd never have suspected her.

"Nothing," she said. "Only if things get worse, if I feel things getting out of hand—I'll know what to do."

I didn't believe her, not then. But once that last week's shooting started Vico fell apart so quick it's not hard to imagine that someone who could get even closer to him than Spyhawk was pressing a nerve. And who could get closer than Spyhawk?

Oh, she's not a killer, I know that. But I wonder. If Vico was talking about a midnight swim in the storm, was she tough enough to shrug and look the other way? Tough enough to give him a nudge down the path?

He would always cut a scene that wasn't working. With his comeback film in ruins, his new wife turning, he thought, to someone else, wouldn't a fadeout before the long decline into bit parts in other people's films have tempted him? Especially if he could have imagined the shot in the *Tablet's* afternoon edition. The cutline credit went to Butch France, a guy I'd never met but heard Al McMahon call a hot dog, the kind of photographer who'll hang by his toes from a hotel fire escape to shoot inside a bedroom window. He had circled behind the police cordon at the beach house and hiked along the sand to the path. He climbed the path as far as von Stroheim's skull and laid his camera along that thick neck. What he got in the foreground was a pair of lab technicians trying to take a plaster cast of the one footprint the storm hadn't washed away. And above them on a jutting ledge: Captain Hoensinger, his hand on the arm of the grieving widow; and the widow—the wind blows wide the skirt of her raincoat, blows a strand of hair across her mouth. And the widow looks out to the sea.

What was it, Lisa? What might you have told him or done?

Or was it not on Vico that she worked, but Spyhawk? Is the guilty one still me? All I know is she's no victim. She's dangerous.

3. Dissecting the Monster

THE NIGHT of Vico's ad lib about Alice and the rabbit hole didn't end after we'd seen the rushes. Spyhawk is an easy partner. He'd like me to think there's nothing about Bolger I need to tell.

The rushes put Vico in a good humor. He said a jaunty good night and made for the door without a glance at Bolger. I didn't tag along and he knew too much about a good exit to look back. I waited. Bolger finished giving some notes to his assistant director, then huddled a minute with one of Krackenpov's spies, a nephew who showed up if the old man was too busy to see the rushes himself. Over the nephew's shoulder Bolger saw me sitting in the back. His eyebrows shot up far enough to let me know he was pretending he was surprised to see me. He went on nodding at the nephew, but lifted a hand in my direction. It was a traffic-cop gesture, slurred but accustomed to getting its way, meant to pin me to my seat. Even indoors he dug in his heels when he walked and he strode up the aisle as if he were pacing off acres. His long hand shot down to squeeze my knee.

"You're doing a great job, Farley boy," he said. "You're the best in the business." And I said, "That's what I want to talk to you about—my job." He cracked a listening grin and I said, "One of the things I do around here is plan the lighting. This is the second day in a row I've been shooting a set lit by somebody else."

His mouth dropped into a startled O. Then he sat on the arm of the seat in front of me, waving cigar smoke out of my face and rumbling about what a problem he'd had over the weekend getting the forest scene ready to be shot. He knew I'd put in a hard week and didn't want to get me out of bed Sunday morning, so he just set the forest lights himself along with a couple of guys who'd worked for him on his last picture.

"But for this job," he said, "I want the best. From now on it's your baby. We got one more day on this set and if you see anyplace where you can improve my job, you jump in and set it right."

I told him the lighting was good. That made him invite me out for a drink to explain where he'd learned to light a set. He slid after me into a booth at the Penguin Club and must have caught the way my teeth clenched when he said, "I'm really grateful to have you on this job, Farley," because he made a face at his cigar and I didn't have to hear that line again. Instead he propped it up. "You've worked with Vico," he said. "You know his style. I'll tell you frankly"—and he propped his elbows on the table and leaned across it, a frank face full of wide blue eyes—"it's not a style I swallow without a gag or two. But that's taste, ain't it?"

That was record time for starting in on Vico. The problem with Vico's pictures, Bolger explained, was that they were unearthly, and he pursed his lips and puffed a wispy cloud of cigar smoke through them and nodded for me to watch how it drifted away. Then he explained some more.

"Criminals don't talk like Oscar Wilde," he said. "People don't sleep in bedrooms long as a basketball court and full of statues. They don't claw strips in their faces because a broad won't hit the hay with them. Or keep secrets under torture like a goddam Boy Scout."

He summed it up by saying Vico seemed to think the movie

camera had been invented to make fairy tales. I didn't talk about how much of the material for Vico's fairy tales came from his life. And from mine.

"What was it invented for, then?" I asked. I knew Bolger's answer. The distinction of his first film was that it had all been shot on location. He had talked Krackenpov into buying a derelict building down near Gower Gulch. He shot garbage on the streets, rats nosing at melon rinds, drunks sprawled in the sun. He hid his camera in the back of a milk wagon and shot street scenes full of free extras. After the first week's rushes Krackenpov was ready to yank Bolger and send him back into stunt riding for cowboy pictures, where he'd started, so he claimed. "All that squalor," Krackenpov was growling. "Squalor don't sell tickets." The next day Bolger jumped a few pages in his schedule to shoot some of Mona Vance's scenes. She played the dance-hall girl who falls for the hoodlum snarling his way from tenement to penthouse. The dance hall was a real rented dance hall with a revolving chandelier and a floor that creaked and rippled. The bandleader dangled a cigarette and squinted smoke. The gang he conducted kept hooch under their chairs in brown paper bags. Drifting through the hall, gathering all the drifting light to the shimmering dress that threw off sparks from her breasts and belly, was Bolger's discovery, Mona Vance. Bolger had picked her up back East in a nightclub chorus line. When Krackenpov saw her in the rushes, he decided to give Bolger's squalor another chance. On condition.

Gutter King went through a couple all-night sessions with a team of Krackenpov's glibbest writers and came out *Gutter Princess,* a gangster picture with a woman's point of view. The ads billed Mona Vance as the biggest find since Joan Crawford and the picture was one of Krackenpov's biggest grossers that year. An Academy nomination for Bolger his first time at bat. With his second picture still in negotiations, nobody could yet say first time lucky. All he had lost was Mona Vance, who went under personal contract to Krackenpov, and the talk around town was that when her option came up Krackenpov would drop her back in the gutter.

I only gave half an ear, then, to Bolger's lecture on the camera. I'm bored by setups that hold for five minutes while grubby people wash their socks and flick earwax off their little fingers. Bolger called this stuff truth.

"If that's how you feel," I said, "why are you on a Vico picture?" Bolger pushed his cheeks into a squinty grin and glanced over his shoulder at the next booth to make sure Louella Parsons wasn't listening.

"I got an understanding," he said. "With Krackenpov."

Now it was my turn to raise eyebrows.

"You ever hear of a book called *Tin Bucket*?"

I said no.

"Novel by a guy who shipped on a tramp steamer. It's got everything. Mutiny on the high seas. Screwing tootsies in the ports. I had Krackenpov buy it for me." He leaned close enough to tip an ash in my drink and said in a stage whisper you could have heard on the street, "I get to make it—just as soon as I finish with Vico."

I thought I would string this out. I was Vico's ears, wasn't I, Vico's man?

"You know," I said, "when you couldn't get Cagney for *Gutter Princess,* you shoulda played the lead yourself. Watcha gonna do—take Vico for a ride? Rub him out?"

He leaned back and shrugged into a chuckle that showed long teeth and purple gums.

"Vico's finished," he said.

His chuckle ended on a flat note. The whole conversation was ringing flat to me. Bolger didn't know me well enough to talk that way.

"It doesn't make sense," I said. "Why would Krackenpov sink his own picture?"

Bolger had a theory. He asked if I remembered the little sweet-ass secretary who'd worked in Krackenpov's office a couple years back. I seem to recall, I told him. I thought of

Alice Brighton and the way Krackenpov had dealt into Vico's roast beef the two thousand dollars Vico had given her to get out from under Krackenpov's fat gut.

"Vico got to her first," Bolger said, and shook his head at the follies of men. "It's that simple."

"Did Krackenpov tell you that?"

"More or less," he said. "It slid in on the tail end of a long list. Something about how he didn't want his stars turning his little girls into sluts. Seems Vico wouldn't let this tootsie alone. Offered her two thousand dollars to keep house for him. One day old Papa Krackenpov finds her bawling into her carbon paper and hears the story. Lit into Vico something fierce, I hear. Told him off right in the commissary in front of the lunch crowd."

Bolger made sure I knew he didn't take what Krackenpov said without a grain of salt. He told me the punch line of the story was that once Krackenpov had rescued this tootsie from Vico's clutches, she'd put out for Krackenpov. "That's gratitude for you," he beamed. "Ain't women grand?" He also informed me that guys like Krackenpov, guys who paid salaries to a small army and owned half a dozen lawyers just to fiddle their income tax, didn't make any decision involving money for reasons that were only personal. "They can't afford it," he told me. "They wouldn't last *that* long," and he snapped his finger into a smoke ring. No, the real reason Vico was getting dumped was that he had his finger in too many pies. A star who got script credit—he could get snotty with you. And a star that directed, too—that was the limit. He could paper his sets with your money and be too important to fire—and goddam *know* he was too important.

"If it's your job to hogtie Vico," I said, "you're not earning your salary. That forest scene you reshot is better."

Bolger's grin squeezed his eyes into crescent slits.

"Couldn't help m'self." He shrugged. "Besides, if the picture makes money, it still proves Krackenpov doesn't need Vico as director. And there's me to think of, too. If my name's going on this picture, it can't look sloppy."

"And you did it on a soundstage," I said. "Remember all those thousands of miles of film shot in studios, that you said ought to be flushed down the toilet? I thought we were supposed to be out recording life."

"In this business, Farley," he said, talking like a much older man, "you gotta be a pragmatist. A Vico film you shoot on a soundstage, where it belongs. Take it outdoors and it wilts in the light. I'm surprised Vico didn't know that himself."

I wonder if he did. I'm thinking of Vico's insistence that *Spy* was about a *real* person. The clutter of facts about Hermann Klamstadt that seemed to be a necessary foundation for his script. For the first time I realize that Vico knew damn well what he *could* do. He was trying for something else, trying maybe without much success to gnaw his way out of an artistic cocoon.

"One thing bothers me," I said. "What makes you think I won't take this little conversation right back to Vico?"

"Would it matter if you did?" he asked, and his horsey grin showed his gums again. "The chance of him getting me fired off this picture is absolutely zero. And if he's the one to quit, that's fine. I can start shooting *Tin Bucket* next week."

"That's still no reason why you should spill all this to me."

Bolger was busy, sculpting his cigar ash against the rim of the ashtray. Not looking at me, he said, "There's one thing, Farley, that you'd better know," and his voice was faraway, meditative, the deep-sighing voice of a man talking about a disaster that won't affect him and that its victims probably deserve. "Vico's on the ropes. This picture puts him on the canvas. Full count, Farley. He's done. Whether you decide to go to the showers with him is your business."

At first I thought it was a threat. With the cigar in the middle of his mouth, Bolger's lips made rapid, smacking sucks. He poked the hot ash in my direction and said, "I been watching you, Farley. I think you're too smart to go down with him. You know why? I screened a few of Vico's old pictures."

I waited while he puffed and blew.

"Like Krackenpov says, actors are beef on the hoof." He

puffed. "It ain't Vico makes his pictures work." He puffed. "It's you."

I rattled ice cubes in my glass.

"I could argue with that," I said. "But only up to a point."

"You know," Bolger grinned, "when I start shooting *Tin Bucket,* I'm gonna want the best man I can get behind the camera."

I went on listening a long time, thinking at every moment that I was just picking his pocket. Thinking none of it made any difference, nothing I said and nothing I listened to, because as soon as I got home I would call Vico and tell him everything. And I wanted to, I had to fight myself, make myself not call. Only one thing kept me from calling, I swear it.

I had never liked Berenice, but I'd watched what Vico did to her. And I saw every day on the set what he was doing to Lisa. I knew he had to be stopped.

CHAPTER
XIV

1. Table Crumbs

THE FIRST HINT of trouble on the set of *Loves of a Spy* reached the public on the second of February, 1938. It surfaced in one of those columns that can be cut to fit the space not filled with movie ads in your morning paper. Vico might think he was Pygmalion, it said, but so far he hadn't brought his ravishing bride to life. Under the klieg lights fashion model Lisa Schoen was stiff as a statue.

A few days later came the first story of a feud between Vico and Thad Bolger, "the brilliant young director of *Gutter Princess*." More feud stories followed. On February 8 the column said, "Vico and Thad Bolger are still locking horns, but tinsel-town tourists will no longer get their ears blistered. Stage Nine on Herb Krackenpov's lot has been closed to visitors. Sealed off, is more like it." The next story, a few days later, said endless retakes had put *Spy* nearly two weeks behind schedule. Cost overruns had studio boss Krackenpov screaming. Vico's comeback flick had better bust more records than a July heat wave.

All these stories ran first under the byline of a *Tablet* reporter named Monty Druhl. They were all attributed to "a source close to the production." After the first week Parsons and Hopper started to scramble for rumors of the rumors, but it was pretty clear that the source close to the production was talking only to Monty Druhl. His column was called "Crumbs from a Corner Table." In it Monty Druhl claimed to occupy a corner table in a famous Hollywood restaurant. Each night "the stars and the starmakers" slid into a chair at Monty Druhl's corner table and dropped little crumbs of gossip.

What Monty Druhl claimed was more or less true. I had never met him myself, but Al McMahon, who had a desk next to Druhl's in the *Tablet* city room, told me that Druhl actually did hang out at a table in the Rumpus Room, where he sipped exactly one ounce of scotch per hour. Stars on the rise were often nudged by their agents or studio heads to drop in and chat him up, try to get the title of their next picture mentioned. Monty Druhl also employed an unknown number of runners whom his column never mentioned. They hung out at other restaurants, I guess. More likely, they took shorthand and brewed coffee at various studios. They brought Monty Druhl more crumbs for his table. He also accepted crumbs from amateurs, people who had a grudge or who stood to get a fat role if word got out that the actor on the verge of being signed for it had his first martini of the day before the sun hit his swimming pool.

As Druhl wrote more and more columns about the problems on the *Spy* set, we began gossiping about him. During lunch breaks in the commissary, cast and crew buzzed like blowflies on a carcass. Had somebody on the set stepped on Monty Druhl's toes? Had we turned down an extra who happened to be one of his girlfriends? Boyfriends, somebody far down the table corrected. One thing we rarely speculated about, though it was on everybody's mind, was the identity of the "source close to the production" who was feeding Monty Druhl his crumbs. Once or twice Nellie Nugent, with a little squeal of dismay to prove her own innocence, cried out, "Who could it *be*-eee?" Nobody tried to answer her. Most of the actors were new to us. Except for Bolger, however, the crew had been together on Vico's pictures for a long time. Nobody wanted to accuse anybody. There were coughs, shrugs, lowered eyes. Later, though, when we were back at work, you would catch people studying pals they'd closed bars with for years as if they'd remembered something said in an old argument.

2. Interruptions

THE BELLHOP HERE is getting more chummy than I like. Last week he got me calling him by his first name. "That Mr. Pugh stuff," he said, "it keeps the desk clerks from thinking I'm an errand boy. But between buddies, let's make it Sammy." He also stopped talking like a senator, except when he remembered his lawyer brother. Then he started on his life story, in daily installments. So far he hasn't mentioned the line he gave Millie, that he's an ex-college teacher. But what happened tonight's got me a little edgy.

An hour ago he brought me some iced tea and leered over my shoulder, trying for a peek at what I'm writing. His brother the lawyer is an expert on mystery stories, he said. He and his brother both read mysteries like fiends. He'd be glad to give me an expert opinion on who my most likely suspect is. Writing a mystery, he said, it's absolutely essential to know the twists. Did I know that one twist is to clear your most likely suspect and then make him turn up guilty?

Usually all I need to wind up one of Sammy Pugh's conversations is a quarter, but as I was fishing in my pocket for change, he said, "It's not just *reading* detective stories that makes me an expert, you know."

I glanced up. His upper lids had dropped flat across his eyeballs in a shrewd blue stare.

"Oh?"

"I'm a bit of a detective myself."

I tried to tell myself it was silly. If he was a cop, somebody sent by Hoensinger, why hadn't I been under arrest weeks ago?

"A detective?" I said. "You're a bellhop, aren't you?"

Unless Hoensinger had wanted me watched. That could be it. If he figured I might lead him to Vico. Only how could he have known where I would go in time to plant a spy?

"Sure," said Sammy Pugh. "I'm a bellhop." And the way he curled his smile let me know that if I was ready to believe that, it wasn't worth his trouble to stop me. My heart was thumping in my throat. Then he took pity on me. His tight smile spread to a grin and he squeezed the tip of his tongue against the gap between his teeth. He pulled a straight-back chair around and straddled it backwards, close enough to puff stale liquor at my face.

"And you," he grinned, "are a sewing-machine salesman. Right?"

I didn't say anything. I nodded my head. He shook his.

"Wrong," he said. "My original hypothesis about you was just slightly askew, wasn't it? That heavy suitcase I brought upstairs for you—it was no sewing machine."

"What tipped you off?"

Sammy Pugh let a long breath slide through the gap in his teeth and chuckled, bobbing his head. The rakehell sickle of hair he'd trained to drop onto his brow dropped there and twitched.

"For one thing," he said, "sewing-machine salesmen sell sewing machines. They don't spend three weeks holed up in a hotel room writing a detective story."

"I've been sick," I said. "You know that."

"You're better now. You've been better almost a week."

I coughed and said I was still sick.

Sammy Pugh shook his head, still grinning.

"You're well enough," he said. "If selling sewing machines is what you do to get food on the table, you'd have been out pounding the pavement last Monday. And what's more—I'll give you dollars to doughnuts that's no detective story you're writing."

He sat there with the tip of his tongue pushed tight against his teeth. Trying to hold back all that cleverness was about to choke him. But when he went on sitting, just being sly, I decided he was waiting for a confession, and that meant he'd used his last match.

"You're pretty smart," I said. "You've got it all figured, Mister Detective. I'm not selling sewing machines. I'm not writing a book. So who am I?"

Sammy Pugh's grin wavered, and he gulped.

"I'm stymied," he said. "Who?"

"Figure it out, Mister Detective. The suitcase. What might a guy carry in a suitcase that would make it heavier than a suitcase with just clothes in it ought to be?"

Sammy shook his head. His grin had bent down at the edges and the red tip of his tongue ducked back from the gap in his teeth.

"You see lots of movies, don't you?" I said.

He nodded.

"Bad idea. It gives you funny notions about the world. Take gangster movies, for instance. You get the idea any guy who's carrying hardware's gonna have it in a violin case. No good. What do you do if some wise guy asks you to play a tune? What?"

"I don't know," Sammy Pugh whispered.

"Now me... I don't know a violin from a tennis racket. And some bellhop detective comes along and figures out I've got a heavy suitcase. Figures out I'm not a sewing-machine salesman. Maybe I'm a hardware salesman. Wanna buy a wrench?"

"No, thanks," Sammy Pugh whispered.

"I didn't think so. Just as well. You know why? That heavy suitcase of mine hasn't got a single wrench in it. So maybe I'm not a hardware salesman after all, right?"

"Sure."

"So what am I, Mister Detective? Scratch sewing-machine salesman. Scratch hardware salesman—maybe. Scratch *Black Mask* crime-story writer. Now look at all those papers on my desk. If it's not a detective story, what is it? What?"

"I don't know."

"Take a guess."

"I don't know."

"Need some help?"

"Yeah."

Vico always told me if you gave the right kind of a hint, your audience would do most of the work for you.

"Maybe it's reports," I said. "Reports to my superiors."

Sammy Pugh's blue eyes flickered. Whatever thought was darting behind them he was straining hard to follow.

"So let's put together the clues, Mister Detective. What else do you know? What else you been turning over in your mind down in that little closet where you stack your quarters?"

Behind Sammy Pugh's eyes something locked into focus.

"You asked for this room special, didn't you?" he said.

The night I registered he had probably overheard my conversation with Millie Copely. Or she'd told him. So there was no point in denying it. But I didn't know where he could take it or how I could twist it.

"That's good," I said. "You're sharp. Maybe you really are a detective. Now why would I do that? Why would somebody who's not selling sewing machines or hardware or writing a mystery story want a room on the third floor of the Silver Palms Hotel? What do you think?"

Sammy Pugh's sly grin wanted to come back.

"My guess is," he said slowly, clearing his throat, "you've noticed something a little peculiar about this floor."

I looked at the carpet under his feet. He giggled at my joke.

"*Third* floor, I mean," he said. "You guys noticed all the traffic, huh?"

"Tell me about it," I said. I relaxed into the shadowy gang he'd made me part of.

"Sure," Sammy Pugh said. "I'm willing to cooperate. My brother's a lawyer. I know my duties as a citizen. But you see if they found out downstairs I told you this, my position would be seriously jeopardized, so if you could just—"

"Just tell me about it," I said. "Tell me what I noticed."

Sammy Pugh cleared his throat again.

"I guess you noticed Millie usually steers the regular guests away from the third floor. She mostly books it to transients. Or tenants who are gonna be glad for whatever they get. Actors, a couple actors. They don't hardly spend time on the floor anyway. They hang around the lobby phone waiting for calls from Central Casting."

"Good enough," I said. "And what else did I notice?"

"I guess you noticed the traffic, right?"

I looked wise.

"Tell me about it."

Sammy Pugh took a big gulp of air and his grin came back and between his teeth the little triangular wedge of tongue flicked again.

"I'd say," he said, "you noticed a lot of men in the halls, all arm in arm with—shall we say—snazzy broads in spike heels?"

I nodded. I remembered the prostitute who'd lived down the hall years ago, the one who'd made me think of Beth. At the back of Spyhawk's mind when he'd insisted on this room might have been the hope that she was still here. Sammy Pugh laughed again, a tumble of nervous hiccups.

"That's why Millie keeps away regulars," he said. "She says a regular might think all the traffic along the hall lowered the tone of the neighborhood."

I pictured Millie snapping her chewing gum and drawling through her nose about the tone of the neighborhood. I wondered whether she'd remembered that when I was here before my name hadn't been Fantomese. I wondered if she'd seen *Doomed Cargo.*

"You were an exception," Sammy Pugh was saying, "because you asked special. But she never figured you'd be here so long."

"So why do you suppose I *am* here so long?"

Sammy Pugh's face got worried again. He groped around.

"With all those reports and things?" he said, nodding at my desk. "I don't know. I guess you're some kind of undercover cop?"

"Go on," I said. "What would I be doing here?"

"Maybe you're planning to put the arm on those three *whoores* that work out of this floor," Sammy said. He didn't sound convinced, so I shook my head.

"Course not," Sammy Pugh said. "If that was it, you'da had 'em two weeks ago. So it's somebody else, right?"

"Maybe one of them has a friend," I said.

"Sure," he said, getting excited. "Maybe some gangster busted out of prison."

"And one of the girls who lives here—"

"—is his girl, right? It's gotta be Sally, 'cause the room you asked for is just across the hall from her. So you take a room here with your tommy gun in the suitcase, and all you gotta do is crossword puzzles until he shows!"

It was like a story conference with Vico.

"Bingo," I said.

Sammy Pugh beamed.

I decided it was time to get rid of him.

"All right, Mister Detective," I said. "You're good. You can go now. But first—one word. You might want to consult your lawyer brother to find out what the penalties are for obstructing an officer in the performance of his duty. I think you'll find they can be pretty stiff. So if it ever comes out that you've mentioned anything about this conversation to one of the girls. Or even to Millie—"

But Sammy Pugh was past scaring. My story had tapped into the world behind his eyes.

"Listen," he cried, hiccuping and grinning and waving off my threats. "Listen—you don't have to worry about *mee*! I can help! I really am a kind of detective. I mean, not like you, but—it's like this. You need somebody who can really keep an *eye* on these girls, right? And on anybody they see? That's *me*!"

Sammy explained how sometimes he could get an eyeful just by following a soft knock with a quick twist of the doorknob. "'Oops, 'scuse me folks,' I say. 'Here's your drinks.' And sometimes I catch 'em in one of those silky see-through robes like they wear in the movies. You know the kind?" I told him I did.

I asked if Sammy Pugh's sudden interruptions didn't annoy the girls. He waved his hand as if a fly were trying to land on his nose. The only one who took offense was Agatha down the hall in 309, who once threw an ashtray at him. "But she's a sow anyway," he told me, "with *mammary* glands down to her bellybutton." Sally, the one across the hall from me in case I ever wanted a quick one, didn't mind a bit, and Rosie in 301 would just laugh and say, "You do that once more,

Mister Pugh, and I'm gonna start charging you." Sammy threw back his head and his hiccup laugh danced his Adam's apple. "I've seen all kinds of things," he said. "You'd be surprised the... the preversions of *de*cency some guys want to enact."

Sammy's stale liquor breath was close enough to gag me.

"Why do you do it?" I asked.

He looked puzzled.

"Why?" he said.

"What's the kick in it?"

"Well, actually," he said with dignity. "It's not just for kicks. I got my *own* ways of getting *kicks.* The first time it happened by accident. This guy was running an extremely compromising hand up Agatha's thigh just as I breezed in with a pack of Luckies. The guy cussed a blue streak. I was worried I'd lose my job. But you know what happened? He left me a whopping *tip*!" Sammy Pugh was grinning again. "That's human nature for you. No matter how burned they are, I always get better tips from the ones I've caught *in flagrante delicto.*"

I was tired.

"It must be nice," I said, "getting paid for work you enjoy."

"You damn bet it is," Sammy Pugh said. His legal phrases, I'd noticed, came and went.

"And this," I said, "is what you call being a detective?"

"Oh, that's special stuff," Sammy Pugh said. "Stuff I do for my brother. Legal stuff. I can't go into much detail. You know how these things are. Say you're a lawyer doing divorce work. You get confidential information that your client's husband is a regular with one of the chippies at a local hotel. What do you do? One of your several options is to consult a discreet person with an inside job at the hotel. Not just anybody—somebody you trust. *Family.* And if that family member happens to also be a quick hand with a flash camera—"

"Okay," I said. "I get the point."

"So you see, I got just the experience you need. All you gotta do is tell me what he looks like, this guy you're after, and I can let you know the minute he turns up."

I gave Sammy Pugh a detailed description of Herb Krackenpov. As I was steering him to the door, I tried to slip him the usual quarter, but he didn't even see it. He knocked it to the carpet grabbing my hand. He pumped it three times in a tight damp handshake.

"So long, partner," he said.

3. More Interruptions

I GOT HIM out of the room and tried to sleep. In the dark I kept seeing Vico's face the last time he ever looked at me with something like the old weld between us, the old sense that the two of us were making together something that neither of us could do alone.

It was quitting time on—it must have been February 23rd. Vico had spent the afternoon teaching the extras who played Fritzi's thugs how to hit. "Look," he'd said. "You gotta learn to choreograph these punches or I'm gonna wind up with a broken jaw." It's the seventh take. For the seventh time his head jolts back, he spins against the prison wall and slides to the floor. I dolly in. He raises himself on an elbow, bites the blood capsule in his mouth, and looks into the camera lens. It's a perfect shot, one of the few that week. Fritzi enters the frame, his hand slapping his thigh with a riding crop. "Now this time," he says, "the truth. When did she become your lover? How long has she been your accomplice?" Cut. Then Vico, close-up, and he says: "You don't want the truth. I can't fill in a timetable..." (pause...wince...) "...for things..." (another wince...a groan, perfectly timed...) "...for things that only happen in your head." And Vico, not Klamstadt but Vico, shoots a lumpy grin up my lens.

It was a typical Vico tease, only in the old days he'd have given me time to think what he meant by it before we went on to the next shot. But Bolger was yelling, "Cut it, Farley, for chrissake, you think I got film to waste?" That wrapped it up for the day. Bolger said tomorrow we'd start with shot 189 and by God get through 221 if it took till midnight. Then he tucked a pencil behind his ear and said, "Tomorrow, props and crew on stage at eight sharp, and be damn sure that bedroom set is *dressed,* Agnes. If we can't find the right venetian blinds for those windows, we can't *shoot.*" Somebody on a catwalk above the wall where Vico lay breathed a long-held *Ahh.* Vico squinted up, but the culprit was safe behind a glaring bank of fresnels. Somebody besides me, then, had been thinking about the bedroom shots. Probably everybody who had been on stage the day we did costume tests of Lisa in that nightgown.

Her dressing gown was some translucent fluff that seemed to float even when she stood still. Beneath it a gold satin nightgown wrapped her tight as a seal's hide. When she moved, cool tongues of fire licked her body. To shoot her you would have to stoop way down, like shooting the sun through an icicle, or the light would burn your film white.

The day of the costume tests Vico had been standing by. Not standing, really—pacing. Strutting. Stepping in front of the still photographer to tilt her head, telling him to soften the shadow under her nose. Showing her off.

He wasn't cocky for long. Bolger had ideas of his own. Always in the past when something went wrong—a piece of blocking that covered the butcher knife, an actor who kept balking on the word *mirror*—always before, we had turned to Vico. He would stare hard at the prop or the actor, sucking his cheeks as if the solution were an elusive taste. Then, dangling the pauses between revelations, he would pronounce a verdict. "Instead of mirror—try saying *glass* . . . and as you say it . . . lay your forefinger like *this* against your nose." "When you cross . . . *pluck* the knife off the table and . . . let it . . . *lead* you to the door." During *Spy,* however, while his improvisions were still in their cheek-sucking stage, Bolger would elbow in and growl, "Do it like *this,* for chrissake." His ideas were hard to argue down. And every time the hostility between Bolger and Vico flashed into words, the next day Monty Druhl's column would carry another weather report about thunderclouds on the *Spy* set.

Once Vico's confidence in the awed silence of his audience cracked, so did his concentration. He could be okay—even good by average leading-man standards—but he never gave you one of those moments where he would take a phrase or a gesture and play it like a Tommy Dorsey solo. Nobody else seemed to spot what was missing. Maybe it took an eye like minc, that had studied his every twitch and blink through seven pictures. But I could tell. He was mugging, not feeling.

But shot 189 opened the bedroom scene, where Klamstadt is snapping his blackmail photos of Frau Stauffer with a hidden camera. Then he has to show the risk Klamstadt takes confessing to her. Unless the audience believes there's a good chance Frau Stauffer might holler rape rather than swoon in his arms, the scene loses its guts. He's got to be at her mercy, naked to her, and the way to play that was to feel it.

Bolger's jabs had closed him up tight. I was waiting to see if he could pry himself open. And what Bolger would do to him if he did.

4. Bolger Explains

AFTER BOLGER'S INSTRUCTIONS for the beginning of the bedroom scene I waited till Vico had left the set, then asked Bolger if he wanted to stop for a drink. Once we were settled—he had comfortably slipped into the booth in the Penguin Club that had been empty since Vico's marriage—he leaned back in a sprawl and said, "Well, Farley, who do *you* think Monty Druhl's spy is?"

"My bet is it's you," I said.

People at other tables looked over their shoulders at Bolger's cackle.

"I notice you're not denying it," I said.

His smile continued not denying it.

"Has it occurred to you, Farley," he said, "that Vico is too old for this role?"

I said it hadn't. He closed his eyes and nodded. He had expected as much.

"He's been playing the same damn role for eight years, Farley. Every picture he makes"—and here he slipped the band off one of his long cigars—"he's got to kill off Daddy so he can hump the old lady."

He pinched that thought into a knowing wink and waited for me to say wow. I didn't. He was tolerant, deciding the idea had been a bit much for me. He hunkered over the table and flicked a lighter to his smoke.

"You see, as an artist, he's *arrested* in an Oedipal stage of development. Let me tell you how I see it."

By the time we were on our third drink Bolger was rooting through *Doomed Cargo,* speculating on the "psychic confusion" between Sonny-Vico and Daddy-Vico. "Daddy-Vico? Why it's Captain Fantomese—*ob*-viously." With each drink his diction had gotten more precise and languorous, vowels rolling around the caverns of his skull like ball bearings in a pinball machine. "Now what's sig-*nif*-icant here is that the Oedipal daddy is played by Vico him*self*—and he's full of that dia-*bol*-ical energy that used to go into Sonny-Vico, the Oedipus figure, you see? Now what's the goddam psychic economy here? I'll tell you: It's the transfer of psychic energy from Sonny-Vico to Daddy-Vico. He's trying, in that picture, to pro-*ject* his *ee*-go"—his lips tightened against his teeth as if he were jamming his foot into a tight shoe—"pro-*ject* his *ee*-go," he repeated, loving the words, "into the old man role. At the end of the picture, you recall, he takes the captain's place, becomes his own father."

I had got the point and was tired of it. I tried to change the subject.

"So what's going on in *Loves of a Spy*?" I asked. "And what makes Vico too old for the part?"

"What I surmise," said Bolger, taking a long pause to gather his concentration for a new rush of brilliance, "and you may find this a bit *sub*-tle, but I think it's true nonetheless. What I surmise is—that Berenice's death *trau*-matized Vico.

Just when he was screwing up his nerve, getting set to step into Daddy's boots once and for all—*bam*-o: Berenice gets murdered. That scares him right back inside the Oedipus role, sneaking into Stauffer's bedroom. It's cozy in there, see. *Womb*-y, if you get my point."

"So what you're saying," I said, "is that Vico is now... thirty-eight."

"Yup," said Bolger, beaming at the quick pupil.

"Pretty long in the tooth for a boy wonder."

"Yup. And so far, too locked in on Oedipus to play any other role."

"Thad," I said, "just for no particular reason at all, tell me: How old are you?"

"I wondered how long that'd take you. I'm just thirty, Farley. Same age Vico was when he made *The Whisperer.* And that little sweetass wife of his, in case you hadn't figured it, is a whole thirteen years younger than him."

All day I'd noticed that whenever he stepped in with a blocking suggestion, Bolger had been paying Lisa courtly little attentions. The way he leaned down to her ear for a buzzy whisper was a lumpish kind of bow. He smiled a lot, kidded her with bashful compliments, loosened her up. Sometimes he would lay his hand for a moment on her shoulder.

Vico had noticed, too.

5. Dream Cave

AFTER BOLGER SHOVED off I stayed on over a last drink or two, losing a little time. I don't remember getting home, which happened more than once as I saw myself emerge in Vico's portrayal of Klamstadt. But I woke in my own bed. It's odd I could have been blacking out again and never thought Spyhawk might be sniffing around. A dream woke me early. Not a nightmare exactly. One of those dreams where you worry things through and wake *knowing* you know the solution, only when you look you realize a part of it didn't cross over with you, and you have to go back for it. I lay there, my eyes closed, breathing easy, trying to get it back, and it started coming. There had been a lizard, and the answer I wanted was somewhere in the face, the wary, patient hooded eyes, and I tried to get it back, run the dream backward like a reel of film on the editor till I could get a freeze on the lizard's face. It was no use. The more I clenched to make sleep come, the more my ears picked out the ticking of an auto idling at a traffic light under my window—

That's odd.

What I've been describing isn't the dream I had then, the night before we started the bedroom sequence. It's the dream I woke from just an hour ago, before I finally got out of bed and ordered a cup of coffee from Sammy Pugh and sat down here by my window to write.

Always before when I've been awake at night, restless, knowing sleep won't come anymore and not wanting to listen to those three-in-the-morning whispers in my head, I've dressed and driven down to the soundstage to work out problems in the next day's shooting. It's what I've had in place of the dream I couldn't get back. I can't go there now, but the night before we started the bedroom sequence, I did.

Mushrooms in a damp cellar, that's what movie dreams are. They grow away from the sun. The soundstage at three in the morning: windowless, soundproof, vast, dark. A few dim rehearsal lights throw up haloes, cut here and there by the black angle of a flat, but walls like that don't close you in. The real walls, the walls and ceilings that close you in, are too far away to see. You walk from prison set to forest glade, run your hand along the chalky bark of a tree, pluck a paper leaf and crumple it in your fist. At the edge of the forest where no birds nest and nothing scurries or burrows, nothing nibbles or hunts, you enter the dark again, stepping carefully among the cables. You come out of the woods near a three-walled bedroom lit by a single bulb. You sit on the bed where she will lie, smooth your hand on the pillow where she'll spread her hair. Beyond the wall that isn't there, the big sun arcs wait.

The camera, too, waited out there, aimed at the bed where I sat.

6. Smoke Rings

AT SEVEN-THIRTY that morning I heard a rumble like distant thunder and the huge warehouse door opened a long vertical bar in the darkness. Ed Nagle, the head grip, came in whistling "Bye Bye Blackbird" and started snapping switches in the light panel. From a grid high above a pale electric dawn spilled down. Walls shot up around me, the ceiling clamped down. My cozy chaos shrank to a drafty barn. By then I had smoothed the bedcovers and was busy polishing lenses. Some carpenters came in hooting and set up a bang and a rasp. Curtiss and Rimers, arguing the chances of a European war, pulled a couple camp chairs up to the unwalled side of the bedroom. Simmons was dipping and gliding from one set to another, a butterfly with a clipboard. An hour later most of us had joined Curtiss and Rimers in a ragged semicircle of chairs. Vico and Lisa were still in the makeup studio.

I can see that circle now, see myself among them. There's the camera on its dolly platform above my shoulder. On my left Curtiss peels an orange. Rimers, on my right, is sipping coffee from a red thermos cup, holding it under his mouth the way an asthmatic inhales steam. Bolger is two chairs farther down. He sucks one of his cigars and admires the roiling shapes in the smoke. Lots of lip action, tongue action. A Thaddeus Bolger production.

Simmons bustles over with another chair, plants it at Bolger's elbow, and hands him a newspaper folded to an inside page. He's panting, trying not to, trying to swallow his excitement and take a deep breath, but still panting—the eager retriever who's just dropped a spit-coated tennis ball at his master's feet. Rimers is asking Simmons to pass along the sports page when Bolger says, "Ho-o-o-ly Christ!" The paper rests on the swell of Bolger's stomach and hops with his silent chuckle. "Druhl's column," he says. "He's at it again."

"Read it to us, read it," says Simmons, who's already read it.

Bolger looks around the circle as if he were about to do just that, but frowns and passes the paper to the grip on his right. The grip scans the column and raises his eyebrows with a low whistle so we'll all know what he thinks of it. He passes it to the next man, I can't recall who, maybe Ed Nagle, who passes it to Curtiss, who sits next to me. Curtiss reads solemnly, his cheek bulged with orange, and hands the paper to me, spitting seeds into his palm.

It was as if someone had filled a gap in Monty Druhl's knowledge of the facts. As before, the item hung on the sinister mystery of the closed set. Without backing off from his previous explanation, that the closed set was to protect tourists from the periodic "blistering exchange of courtesies" between Vico and Bolger, Druhl now claimed that visitors had been barred because of a love scene "too hot for civilian eyes." The last sentence of the item read, "Word from our source close to the production has it that there is an off-screen love scene brewing that's even hotter."

I think I handed the paper to Rimers. I was off somewhere, just for a moment. When I looked around again, all eyes had either turned or conspicuously not turned toward Bolger, whose face took on a rosy bloated glow. Apparently I wasn't the only one he'd told about his plan to move in on Lisa. To squelch a titter that would have forced him to admit there was nothing to admit, he chose this moment to make an announcement.

"You're going to see a little flesh here today," he said. "Don't make a big thing of it. You got work to do—and so does the lady. She ain't gonna be able to remember lines with all you horny bastards feeling your pockets for change." He paused, let a wicked grin shoot monkey creases all over his face, and said, "So take your peeks on the sly."

Bolger knew damn well we weren't going to see anything

the Hays office wouldn't pass, but he knew how to get us cranked up. He was thinking how much fun it would be to watch Vico watching us all watch his wife. I thought of Lisa, catching the eyes just at the moment they saw her looking back and slid away from her body. Soon the conversation about her became pretty general and not much different from what you'd hear on a grade-school playground. The only one who didn't say anything was Simmons, who peered along the row of faces to see when to laugh. Simmons and me—I didn't say anything either. I got up and fussed with the camera, then stood beside it looking over their heads at the set.

Then came a thundery rumble, a bar of light split the darkness, and just for a moment before it narrowed again and erased the pavement like a vertical wipe, I glimpsed Vico and Lisa together in the morning sunlight.

CHAPTER XV

1. A Private Talk

THEY CAME TOWARD us together, picking their way over cables, around sawhorses. Vico was talking, unusual for him since he was more often silent, concentrating with a dreamy toneless hum on the fantasy he would live in front of the camera. He held Lisa's hand formally, pressed between his elbow and side as if they were guests arriving at a Grauman's premiere. They stepped into the island of light, into the three-walled bedroom, and said good morning. Lisa wore the floaty dressing gown, alive to her slightest breath or movement, over the costume we were waiting to see.

The newspaper had disappeared. I could tell within a few minutes that they had seen it. I was busy directing a camera rehearsal, but I noticed that Vico, who seldom smoked, was lighting a cigarette off the tail of his last one. He walked as if he were wading through ankle-deep water. When Bolger approached Lisa to ask if she had any problems with today's blocking, Vico locked a stare on the back of his neck. She sat on the edge of the bed, her back erect, ankles crossed. One hand cradled the other in her lap. Her eyes were half lidded, her face solemn. I hadn't seen a face so completely rigid since Vico played Don Juan. She might have been waiting for us all to leave so that she could go to sleep.

I was directing a couple of grips who would have to push the camera dolly along a set of tracks laid on a two-foot-high platform. They had to swing me around in a snailshell arc, starting on the platform and then down a curving ramp, smoothly, while I panned, keeping Vico inside my frame. Vico would be standing at the final twist of the snailshell.

"Let's run through it," Bolger said. Vico took his place at the core of the snailshell and Lisa went offstage. I got on the dolly platform beside Handy, my operator. During the take, he would be the one aiming the camera, but I wanted to know for sure what he was getting, so I was in the jockey seat. Bolger called for action. Lisa appeared in the doorway, the dressing-gown sash tight around her waist. Beneath it the satin hugged her body. Bolger cued the grips. As we tracked away, Lisa's figure shrinking, Vico ballooned into the shot, gliding along the bottom of the frame from left to right, briefly covering Lisa. Then Lisa disappeared off the edge of the frame and I was left with Vico alone, still looking down on him but closing into a level close-up while he spun the wheel of his cigarette lighter, the disguised camera. I spiraled in on his face. He looked over the cigarette lighter, directly into my lens. Something about his expression, I remember, made me uncomfortable, but I didn't have time to think about it long enough to know what.

Then we did a few dialogue rehearsals, trying to get Lisa to loosen up. It was understood by now that the one who gave her acting directions was Vico, and Bolger handled blocking. He would say, "Cross to the dresser on that line," and she would say, "Why?" and Vico would tell her. Then we shot it. Again and again. Between takes, while Bolger and Vico wrangled back and forth, trying to get at why the scene wasn't working without either of them confronting the other on his own ground—Vico, that is, saying nothing about blocking and Bolger nothing about acting—Lisa sat on the edge of the bed. She cupped an elbow in each palm and closed her eyes and gently rocked her body as if she heard a distant lullaby.

Bolger, finally, was the one to say it. After the ninth take he walked over with his monkey-wrinkle smile and said, "You've got to open up that dressing gown, honey." As if all a flat scene needed was a little more flesh. She raised her eyes and stared at him. Not at Vico. "Don't be shy," Bolger said. "It's just like on the beach. After a minute you don't even notice it."

She didn't look at Vico. "I know what it's like," she said. "I spent three years..."

There was a pause. Bolger chuckled nervously. "Well, then..."

Still not looking at Vico, her voice as barren of reproach as if she were telling a stranger the time of day, she said, "I thought I stopped all that when I got married."

Vico had strolled over to the sidelines for a sip of coffee. The coffee table had been set up a few feet from me. He was in shadow and I only saw him in profile, but I think his lips were curled in a faint smile. Without looking at me he said, "Take it, Farley," and as I looked for a place to put his cup, he strolled back into the light and sat down beside Lisa. Suddenly it was as if the three-walled room with a couple dozen people staring at it had become a real bedroom, a private place where two people did private things, had conversations they shared with nobody else. Vico put his hand in the small of her back and whispered in her ear. I watched her face. I couldn't see anything in it change. Only it became very still, and being still like that, with her eyes lowered, it made me think of one of those deathbed casts—her face, all right, but a shell she had withdrawn from. After a minute she nodded and stood up, not waiting for Vico to finish, and slipped the knot of her dressing gown, letting it fall open. Vico stood, kissed her cheek, and gave her a one-arm squeeze around the waist. His release pushed her toward the doorway from which she would make her entrance.

I set up the shot. The clapper clapped. The camera held on the doorway for a count of five, waiting. Then she was standing there. A light behind the wall shone through the nightgown, silhouetting her thighs. The nightgown was V-cut with shoestring shoulder straps, and the dressing gown, open now, hung from the slope of her breasts.

Her first line, standing in the doorway, was "That's not true, you know. It could end any moment—or it could go on forever." As the camera dollied back, as Vico swam into the shot, she continued, saying, "All I know is, I can't be the one to stop it," and as she said "stop" her body pivoted into profile and I tucked it all onto the reel, thinking: *This will be the shot we use.*

2. Afternoon Twilight

BY MIDAFTERNOON WE'VE shot less than half the number of setups Bolger has scheduled. Lisa sits on the edge of the bed, her legs crossed, her fingers spreading a stocking. Gazing at Vico standing by the window, she says mournfully for the seventeenth time, "Who was that man who painted birds and shot them to study their markings? They say he loved birds." For the seventeenth time Vico opens the venetian blinds, framing Lisa and the bedspread in white bars of light. There has been a long argument over whether the scene would pass the Hays office if the counterpane was turned down and rumpled rather than chastely tucked over the pillows. Chastity, represented by Bolger, prevailed. For the seventeenth time Vico spins the wheel on his lighter as Lisa raises her hand to shield her eyes, lets the pause carry a moment too long, and murmurs, "Oh ... the light." "It's annoying, isn't it," says Vico, says Klamstadt. "The flint is so worn I can't get a spark from it." She bends to draw the stocking over her toes. Sometimes the take is stopped here, because she has tangled a foot in the long folds of her dressing gown or pinned it down with the heel of her hand. This time the take is allowed to continue, and she says, "I meant the light from the window. It blinds me." And Vico, sometimes with a shade of petulance, which is wrong, which stops the take, says, "I'm tired of closed bedrooms, tired of whispers, drawn blinds. Tired of seeing you only in this afternoon twilight." And then, groping for it, taking his own corny line and making poetry of it by the way he shows us Klamstadt discovering the thought, he says, "You ... you're a flower ... In the sun ... flowers open their petals ... to the sun." If the scene has come this far, Vico's voice catches on the word "sun." A few times he blocks, can't find the word at all. This time, after "flowers open their petals," there is an agonized pause, as if a pain were building pressure inside his chest, and "in the *sun*" explodes in a harsh bark.

And Bolger stops the take. "Shit," he says. "Shit. Can't you just cut the goddam *acting* and say the line?"

Vico, his temper clenched between his teeth, says, "Look, the word is giving me trouble, I'm not acting."

"That's for damn sure," says Bolger, and while they dig at one another, Lisa draws the dressing gown over the stockinged leg, lowers her head and lowers her eyes, and bites her lower lip. After a minute or two she rises, walks to the door leading to the bathroom, then off into the dark beyond the lighted set. Vico and Bolger are still arguing, but I listen for her footsteps in the satin-toed mules she's worn all day. Once she stumbles over a cable, the heel of a mule clacks. Nobody hears but me. Nobody but me sees the darkness cut by a brief rectangle of sunny pavement. In the doorway, blinded, she turns back. I am the only one looking at her. Her hand raises, palm open, quick as the spread and flutter of a startled bird, then the fingers lose their tension, the hand drops back to her side, and she turns away.

There was a comic interlude of shouts and sputtered curses when Vico and Bolger were ready for another take and realized that the leading lady had gone home. That night over drinks at the Penguin Club, Bolger told me he was about ready to move in and that tomorrow he intended to get the goddam dressing gown off Lisa altogether.

3. Table Crumbs

I GOT HOME around half past eight and had just settled in my armchair and propped my feet on the radiator in front of the window when the phone rang. Vico, the old intimate Vico with a voice that could make you feel you were part of a conspiracy, needed a favor. He knew I'd had a long day (we'd spent the rest of the afternoon inventing ways to shoot around Lisa's scenes), but there was no one else he could ask. He would arrange to have the second-unit camera crew do some pickup shots the next day so that I could get an extra hour's sleep, so that tonight I could hang out at the Rumpus Room and try to spot whoever was leaking stories to Monty Druhl.

I reminded him that it was Bolger who fixed the shooting schedule. Leave that to me, he said. I warned him that a stake-out of the Rumpus Room would never plug all the pipes that fed Monty Druhl's cesspool. Give it a try, he told me.

I got to the Rumpus Room half an hour later and Monty Druhl arrived fifteen minutes after that. I was at the bar with a good view of his table. He was a little man with sparse blond hair and a mouse-whisker mustache. Horn-rim glasses made his eyes look bulgy. When he lifted them to pinch the bridge of his nose, his eyes squinted. He blinked around the room and waggled a couple of fingers at Humphrey Bogart, who looked the other way.

Early in the evening it was stars and contract players who slid into the booth beside Monty Druhl for brief, intense chats. Before the intense part there was always lots of bustle and laughing, big smiles and hugs, and no matter what the voices were saying it all sounded like, Wheee, ain't it fun being famous! After midnight, when all the actors went home to get ready for early-morning makeup calls, most of the people who came to Monty Druhl's table had faces hollowed by anger or jealousy and had to work up their courage to ask him if they could sit down. I recognized a costume mistress who'd gone to another lot and a makeup man who was getting a reputation as a lush. While Monty Druhl's confidants talked, he nodded and wrote notes on lavender letter paper. Sometimes he slipped a bill under the confidant's cocktail napkin. The confidant would palm the bill without looking at the size and wait a couple more minutes before getting up to leave. Just before they broke away from Monty Druhl's table, all his confidants had a moment when they raised their eyes and seemed to realize with a shock that there were other people in the room.

In the lulls between confidants Monty Druhl would suck ice cubes from his drink and scratch at his notes. After an item read the way he wanted it, he would give a little smirk that raised bristles on his mustache. The things Hollywood people did horrified him, I'd heard. He was a crusader. At midnight he signaled for a check. I followed him to the *Tablet* office, where he would type up his lavender notes for the next day's paper.

In a bar across the street I met Al McMahon, who had just got off work. He had hung around the police station till eleven-thirty to get a story on a murder confession. He had a tableful of drunk reporters whooping and roaring, telling how Sergeant Manfred kept coming out of the interrogation room saying, "'Any minute now he's gonna crack, any minute you'll get yer story.' But it was what we in the profession call 'a difficult labor.' A caesarean, in fact—in the end they hadda do a caesarean."

The table whooped and roared some more and somebody bought McMahon another boilermaker and I went home.

When I called Vico the phone rang a long time. His voice was a groggy slur. I hadn't seen anybody from *Loves of a Spy,* I told him, cast or crew. "Not Bolger?" Vico wanted to know. He sounded disappointed. I reminded him that my not seeing anybody didn't prove anything. There were lots of ways to slip Druhl the news, ways that we couldn't cover. A telephone call. A middleman I wouldn't recognize.

I asked Vico if he wanted me to continue the stakeout the next night. "We'll see," he said. "Maybe his stoolie didn't have anything for him tonight."

"Are you kidding?" I said. "After what happened today?" On the other end of the line I could hear Vico wince. "By the way," I said, "did you get things straightened out with Lisa?"

"Yeah," he told me. She would be on stage in the morning, ready to work. He cleared his throat and said, "But this is her last picture, Farley. She doesn't want to act." His voice was puzzled, wondering. "We've had a little trouble," he went on. "She'll finish this picture, but she's gone to live in the town house till it's over. She needs to think things out, she says."

I told him I was sorry.

Maybe he read something into the way I said it, because the tone of his next speech had that tense rational calm. "Look, Farley," he said, "I *had* to cast her. I *wrote* it for her. Doing it with somebody else would be... It was—like a wedding present."

Vico had made me one of the highest-paid cinematographers in town. One reason why is that I told him what other people were afraid to say.

"If she never wanted to do it," I asked him, "was the present really for her?"

After a minute he whispered, "I guess you're right, Farley. Even that night we first ran through the script, you knew she didn't want to do it. And you said so, even then."

After they finished shooting, he said, he was going to make it up to her. They would take a long vacation. He was going to stop working so hard. He deadpanned his way through the clichés as if they were lines in a bad script, a character he couldn't even pretend to get inside. I let him writhe. Then he said, "Farley?" I waited some more. "You know that business about a love affair? That little turd in Druhl's column?"

"Yeah?"

"You think there's anything in it?"

I waited again.

"I mean," he said, "you haven't seen anything going on, have you? While I was busy?"

At that moment, of course, I should have known exactly how desperate Vico was.

"Listen," I said. "When you're busy, I'm busy, too, at the other end of the camera. How am I supposed to know what goes on outside any given shot we shoot?"

He laughed and told me to forget he'd said anything. His laugh was brittle, as if he were trying to cough up splinters of glass.

4. Professional Rivalry

IN THE NEXT day's *Tablet* Monty Druhl reported that Lisa Schoen had fled the *Loves of a Spy* set in tears, bringing the day's shooting to an abrupt end. According to Monty Druhl's "informed source," her distress was over a costume that left her "as near raw" as the Hays office would allow.

On stage that day she seemed not just raw but flayed, every nerve exposed. If she'd been playing the mother of a kidnapped child, her jerky movements and grim jaw would have worked fine, but they didn't suggest a woman flushed with passion. Vico's mood matched hers. Not much that we shot was worth printing.

That ended the week, and I thought maybe with Sunday to rest and talk things out, they might be back together by Monday. It didn't happen, or if they did reach a truce, it didn't survive that morning's Monty Druhl column. "You wouldn't think Garbo-class fashion model Lisa Schoen would need much coaching to do a love scene with her own hubby—or would you? Our little birdie on Emile Vico's *Loves of a Spy* set tells us that the newlywed Vicos are no longer nuzzling noses between takes. In fact, they're no longer speaking!"

Which was a fact. Between camera calls his eyes would slide past hers and she would pretend to be drawn to some distant corner of the set.

On camera things were just as bad. Lisa was taking all the lyric touches Vico had laced through her dialogue—lines he could only have written on his honeymoon, after she'd taught him a woman is more than seductive or silly or shrewd, lines that blended her tender serenity with his own broody conviction that time eats love like an acid—she'd taken all that and strained it through a jaw clenched with resentment and rage. What else could she do? What could she ever have done? For her, wasn't the whole business a lie?

As for Vico—how could he have known? He needed the lines, the camera turning, needed to see his shadow on the screen to prove there was someone inside him solid enough to stop the light. And he had broken through as he always did into one of his creative spurts, so that watching him you felt he was not just an actor, not even a brilliant actor, but a demon, who could touch places in your soul you'd forgotten could feel. In close-up I read his face as he forced himself to aim the cigarette lighter's hidden lens and snap the shutter. What filled his eyes might have been remorse—a remorse that had no pity for himself.

But Lisa ruined every take. At quitting time when she stepped at last out of the light, he darted after her and I was on the other side of a flat close enough to hear part of it. "You could at least remember," he was saying, and he was in a cold fury, "that no matter how you feel personally, other people are depending on you." And she was saying, "What do you expect of me?" And he said, "Not just me, I mean. Everybody down to the grips and gofers has something riding on how well you do out there." And she, snapping it out, "It was your business to think of that when there was time," and then, after a sharp breath, as if sorry she'd let herself go: "What do you want, what more can I do, what can I be but who I am," until he, with a slap or a shake that made her gasp: "Just this. If you can't act like a wife to me, at least act like a professional with a job to do. Or can't you act at all?"

And his footsteps left her. For a minute she was alone, standing in the dark. Only the day before she'd told me if things got bad, she'd know what to do, she'd be in control. Maybe, I thought. Maybe with ordinary men. But when Vico was riding his demon, only the demon was in control. I heard sobs, rasping. Then her footsteps left, too.

Then I was alone.

5. A Talk in the Petrified Forest

MY MEMORY OF that final day—the day we shot Vico's most stunning performance—is printed so deep I can hardly tell where it splices into the film.

Just as on Monday, Vico arrived on the set alone, clearly vexed that the last and therefore most dramatic entrance would belong to Lisa. He sent Simmons over to makeup to see how much longer she would be.

Once Bolger saw he had Vico on the set, he discovered a problem with the lighting. I was busy for a while, getting the proper angle of sun through the venetian blinds. When we were all set up and still no Lisa on stage, I looked around for Vico. He wasn't on the set. A few minutes later I was on my way back from the bathroom, passing what we had taken to calling the Petrified Forest, when I heard a sound like a hiccup, just that abrupt anyway. The plaster trees and the bushes were so thick no light fell past the first couple yards, except along the dolly tracks. I found him stretched on his stomach beside the stream. He was on the grassy rise where, a few weeks earlier, Klamstadt had loomed over Frau Stauffer.

"You fishin'?" I asked. I hadn't thought he heard me come up behind him, but he didn't act startled. Propped on his elbows, he was staring into the stream. There wasn't enough light to see his reflection by. "Sorry," I said. "I heard a noise. You know me—always poking around." His hand flicked toward the stream as if he were releasing a dart. I heard the hiccup again as something broke water. Ripples spread on the stagnant stream. "You want me to leave you alone?"

"No reason," he said. "Pull up a chair." His voice was flat and uninviting, but I sat beside him on the bank. He turned away and I heard a chipping sound. I looked over his shoulder. He was chipping with a pocket knife at the plaster trunk of the willow tree. He took a few chips in his palm and tossed another one into the stream. The water was black. The ripples that circled from the splash caught a faint silver reflection. Something that he murmured got absorbed by a rasping bandsaw at the other end of the stage. "... no reason for it," he was saying when the saw stopped. "We could have done the scene just as well out on the back lot. That little woods I picked. That was where I wanted to do it." It sounded as if he'd been saying the same thing for a long time.

"Sure," I said. "But think how many trees we would have cut down to get those fancy tracking shots."

"I hate this warehouse," he said. "No air. No sun. Disconnect the pump and the stream turns into a puddle. And the trees—" He waved to the hole he had made in the trunk of the willow, where he had chipped the plaster down to its chicken-wire frame.

"You remember," I said, "when we went out in the desert for those shots in *Mark of Cain*? We all thought we were going to go von Stroheim one better. How long did it take? Three days in that heat? Did we go that long? Which of us said it first? We wished we'd never left the soundstage."

"It must have been you, Farley," he said. "I liked it out there. Even at a hundred and thirty degrees."

"That ain't the way I remember it."

"When I put my hand on a rock, it was a rock," he murmured. "Not a goddam—" He threw another plaster chip at the water.

"Put your hand on a rock out there and you'd get a blister," I said.

"I still liked it," he said. "I liked all of it, until..."

"Singleton?" I asked.

He nodded and a faint tremor—quick as a twitch on a horse's flank—gave him away. There was a pang for Singleton in that tremor, but something else, too. There was also Vico settling himself in the backseat of the studio limo with Singleton's head a screaming mask of blood in his lap; settling himself, his mind full of the juicy irony that it might have been himself and not his stunt double who had taken a chunk of the plane's exploding gas tank in the face; settling himself to gaze all through the long drive to the hospital into that pool of blood at his own reflection, and to learn from it whatever there was to know about the things pain can make you do. Vico didn't fool me—Singleton's agony was another part of what he had *liked* about the desert.

"You still keep in touch with him?" I asked.

He seemed to hesitate, then shook his head.

"After he left the hospital, he dropped out of sight. I think I know where to find him, though. I never should have made him do that run, Farley."

It was an easy remorse. But I remembered the pure glee in his face when he'd grabbed my arm as I was coming up the hospital steps to get the news, and I kept saying, "But where the hell are we going? What about Singleton?" while he dragged me along, saying, "Where's your car? Did you bring the film?" All he needed was one glance at the exploding-plane rushes to decide it was too good to scrap and all that night while Singleton was in surgery Vico was rewriting the end of the script.

Just for an instant, while I watched him flicking chips of a plaster tree into a dead stream, I almost pitied him enough to say what I thought.

"Don't punish yourself," I told him. "You didn't put a gun to Singleton's head. He wanted the pay. And if you hadn't sprained your ankle on the first take, it would have been you with the gas tank blowing up in your face."

"You know your trouble, Farley?" he said, and these are about the last words he ever spoke to me. "You always let me off too easy."

Then we heard Bolger bellowing and knew Lisa was on stage and we were ready to shoot. We joked about how much money Krackenpov was losing on overtime, and got up.

As we rounded a bend in the path, Nellie Nugent was standing with her back to us, facing the bed, her back rigid, her calves and heels close together. I had the odd impression that she was standing at attention. She seemed to be looking with more than usual interest at something on the bed. Then I noticed another odd thing. Of all the electricians and grips and set dressers who bustle around a movie set before the camera begins to turn, not one was at that moment occupied with any work. The stage had become an irregular wheel and all eyes were spokes turned toward the hub, which was the bed. Just then Nellie lunged forward and a froth of gold fluff splashed over her, floating down over her head, her shoulders and arms, and while she caught at it, clawed it down like a cobweb, she was stepping off to the sidelines, and beyond her was Bolger, standing over Lisa who sat with her legs tucked under her on the bed, and the flaming satin nightgown was all that Lisa wore.

CHAPTER XVI

1. Ice Cubes and Communion Bells

I'M STOPPED. I thought every breath she took that day would be mine whenever I wanted it—and it is, it's there, I can sense it. But when I reach for it, I come up empty. Something about these last moments on the set Spyhawk wants to bury. All the more reason why I've got to drag it into the light.

I can get an image. I can see Lisa on the bed, and Bolger leans over her, arranging her blocking as if what he wanted was not movement at all, but a flow from one still shot to another. She leans toward him, her body—

There must be a party on my floor tonight. This is the third time in an hour that Sammy Pugh has rattled that cart with the squeaky wheel down the hall past my door. Through these thin walls I can hear ice cubes jingle in the drinks as soon as he gets off the elevator, *jingle like that bell I used to carry when I served Mass at the convent on Parkside Boulevard. After Mass I walked ahead of the priest ringing the bell to warn the nuns along the hall to kneel as he passed, bringing Communion to the sick ones.*

She leans toward him, and through the nightgown I can see the swell of her nipples, and Bolger is saying, "Now as you put your hand on the pillow, let it..." And he rocks his hip to show her: "Let it take your weight for a moment, so you can bring your legs down to the floor...." And she does. "That's it, only try to shift so the nightgown rides just a little higher up your thigh, got it?" And she does. For the first time since we came on the set, Lisa is lost in concentration, doing everything Bolger asks.

Bolger notices Vico and me standing behind him. "Oh, here at last, huh," he says. "Thought you guys knew we had work to do today." He snaps his fingers at Nellie Nugent to bring back the dressing gown and gives Lisa a particular line that comes after Klamstadt's confession. That line is her cue to shrug the gown to the floor. He calls places, and before he walks back to the camp chair where he watches the action, he gives Lisa's shoulder a friendly pat. "You'll be all right, honey," he murmurs. "Just do everything like I told you."

We take the scene from where we'd broken off the day before, Vico raising the venetian blinds and fussing with his cigarette-lighter camera while Lisa picks a stocking off the floor and draws it onto her leg. Only first Bolger has to explain his new idea for the camera. Instead of making the stocking bit a two-shot, including both Lisa and Vico, he wants to break it down: one shot of Vico at the window with his lighter, another of Lisa sliding her legs off the bed, looking directly into the camera. "Now you remember what I said," Bolger is telling her, and sitting beside her on the bed, his instructions are intimate as a bedtime story, and he says—

One of the nuns had a tongue dry as parchment that I used to think would never dissolve the host. That was the only nun I'd ever seen without her wimple, and I thought looking at her straight chopped gray hair might be a sin. Her dry cough was like the one Sammy Pugh sometimes hears as he clatters down the hall toward my door, though I'm nearly better now and this writing and my sickness seem like a long preparation for something I don't yet understand, as if I were a caterpillar who didn't know what wings were for, *and one day we passed her door without knocking. When we got back to the sacristy, I asked the priest why. He came close and laid a hand over my shoulder to draw me closer. His hand was heavy and cool through my summer shirt, cool as the buttocks of a marble statue I had touched in the museum. He smelled of communion wine, sour and desolate and pure.* And Bolger says to Lisa, "Just remember, it ain't a camera you're looking at, it's your lover." And Lisa says, "Yes. I understand." She looks up and her eyes fall on me. *He smiled down on me and said the old nun had died, and to show me how he felt about it he raised his eyebrows like an old person opening a birthday present from a child. I smiled back.* I get behind the camera, ready to shoot. Early last month while I was so sick I couldn't write or even think, I would lie in bed imagining whenever I heard the squeaky wheel on Sammy Pugh's cart and the tinkle of ice cubes in his pitcher that I was that nun hearing the bell come down the hall.

Vico watched all Bolger did and never said a word. That heaviness, that sense of being so tired he could hardly move that I'd felt in everything he'd said in the Petrified Forest, comes back to me. He was feeling the defeat other people live their lives with. He seemed to have resigned. Up till now, whenever there was a setup where he wasn't on camera with Lisa, he would be hovering beside me, straining every muscle to coax a feeling out of her. But now he's resigned, and on the first take he's in a camp chair near the dimmer board, tossing his cue lines over his shoulder at her. But Lisa doesn't need coaxing today. She doesn't even notice he's not there. She's aiming everything right up my lens. I had thought her reserve was seductive, but it's nothing to what happens when she uses her eyes, really looks back at me. Her legs slide out from under her and touch the floor as if she knew just what Vico meant about how flowers open in the sun. When she leans forward to reach for the stocking, she doesn't have to be reminded to keep her chin level so as not to cover the shadowy cleft that opens between her breasts. As she draws on the stocking, she angles herself perfectly on the bed to profile her calf and thigh. The day before, we'd tried that movement a dozen times, and given up. Now we get it in a single take and I remember thinking, Either she was holding back yesterday or she's been practicing. Vico had spent the night alone in the beach house. I wondered if Lisa had been alone in town.

My thinking that bothered me, but I can't get it out of my

head. In one of my late-night booze talks with Al McMahon he said that you can tell by the flush on a woman's skin if she's been in bed with a man. Maybe it's time I set up the projector and see what's in the can of film Spyhawk managed to steal. Once when I was sick I tried to look at it, but Sammy Pugh popping in every ten minutes with more icewater scared me off. Since he's decided I'm an undercover cop, he's dropping in just about as often to keep me posted on who visits the girl across the hall.

But I can't wait longer. My memory needs help. If I keep the sound low, I'll be safe.

2. A Window of Light.

THESE PAST FEW weeks all I knew about the cans of film I found in my suitcase was that they had on them uncut rushes from *Loves of a Spy.* When I found myself day after day intending to screen them and not doing it, I realized there must be something on them Spyhawk is afraid to let me see. Why he wanted them along I can only guess. I'm not even sure how he got them. At first I decided he must have bribed Fogle, the lab man, to make him an extra print. Then a couple of weeks ago, when Vico's disappearance was still getting mentioned every other day in the press, I saw a story saying the cops wanted to see the rushes of Vico's last minutes on the set and had discovered the film had disappeared. I began to suspect I had got the film another way. I could see myself—see Spyhawk, I mean—walking down aisles of racks in the dark lab, my flashlight skimming along the rows of cans from the daily rushes till I got to ours, and I saw Spyhawk lifting them down. It could have happened that way. Years ago I'd borrowed a master key and copied it before I gave back the original, so if I stayed out of the night watchman's way there was nowhere in the studio I couldn't go. I tried to convince myself I'd made up that version, just as I'd made up bribing Fogle, but the more I think about it, the more I remember.

First there is the rain drumming on the lab's tin roof, so it must be the night Vico disappeared. Then I see Spyhawk sloshing through the dark, the flashlight beam flitting among crates, trees, stuffed panthers, the front wall of a bank. I still hear rain, but the roof seems far above. He's ankle-deep in water. Around him now are what seem like tree trunks, those shell-blasted, leafless trees you see on every no-man's-land set in a war movie, and the trunks pale as if the bark had been stripped. He stops to play the flash on them and they aren't trees but women, mannikins, all of them bald with smooth hairless bodies, all standing with the same cool smile and unpainted eyes that look back at me blind as Lot's wife.

That's how I know that to get from the lab to the parking lot, Spyhawk had cut through the prop warehouse. One of the hairless women has fallen face down in the water, her arm broken off at the elbow. With the flash he spots the hand and arm nearby, and the lapping waves make the hand seem to grope for something underwater. The lapping makes a constant whisper, so that I was glad to get out of there and wade through the flood to my car.

Remembering it that way explains where Spyhawk was between the time he left Bolger at the Penguin Club and the time he got home, and why my suit was wringing wet. Where he was part of that time, anyway—a trip to the studio wouldn't take long.

The first shot on the third reel was the one Vico had said he would build the entire film around: that close-up of Lisa when they meet in the prison corridor after he's been told she confessed under torture. It was his Kuleshov experiment. What fascinated him about it was that she never says a word. "He sees what he puts there," Vico explained, and the tip of his tongue flicked out to touch the tip of his upper lip. "Nobody could *make* him believe she would betray him if he didn't expect it, even want it—and if he did expect it, that was because of something in him, not what he knew about her." It was a cat-and-mouse thing to say. At the time all I could make of it was that he was trying to confuse me, trying to prove that I couldn't be sure he was on to me. If I couldn't be sure he knew that I'd told Hoensinger more about his life with Berenice than he could ever forgive, then I couldn't be sure that what he was making me watch was his revenge. But I *was* sure. The script for *Spy* had too many parallels to be accidental. And especially this scene, where he makes me cut from a shot of her face to a shot of his first response to it: that same drop of the eyes and wrenching away of the face that I'd seen as he was led down the hall past Hoensinger's office, when he had made up his mind to refuse to see me before I knew he was there.

By the day we shot it, I could shrug the whole thing off. I would do my job, worry about whether the shadow was rich enough to cup the hollow of her cheek.

3. The Unmasking

IT'S EARLY MORNING and all night I've been watching the rushes. By now, the third night, it's a ritual. The projector is set up by my bedside. I turn out the bed lamp. The marquee lights from the theater across the street still toss a square of light on my ceiling. I lower the shade. I sit on the bed, my back pillowed against the headboard, and snap the switch on the projector. Then I'm alone with Vico and Lisa, and things begin to come back.

The last day's work is spliced into the end of the reel, but I run through the whole thing again and again, and when it comes to the bedroom set, the shots we worked on those last few days, the first thing I see is the window, that coffin-shaped hole shot through horizontal bars of light from the venetian blinds, and her gliding toward it, her figure shrinking on my bedroom wall, and it's like going back in a dream to a house where you once lived. I forget the juicers and grips gawking from the catwalks; forget Bolger framing the shot from half a dozen angles before he'll admit I've set the camera in the only right place; forget Nellie Nugent keeping a half-step behind him, forget Vico in the shadows waiting for his cue. All I see is what the camera aims at. There is a woman alone in her bedroom window, which makes a hole of light in the wall of my room. And one person watching. For a moment I'm surprised to see that she's wearing the dressing gown Bolger had talked her into discarding, and I have to stop the projector for a couple minutes to remember that he had her put it back on—partly to avoid having to reshoot the scenes in which she was wearing it and partly to get on film the moment of her taking it off. When she raises the blinds, then, the sun leaps up the window, surrounding her, pouring through the thin dressing gown and the nightgown beneath. Her thumb slips the silk cord at her waist and the dressing gown parts, drops from her shoulders to the floor, and with her feet planted slightly apart the light from behind her rises between her thighs like the blade of a knife.

She comes downstage onto a line with Vico. His head floats in from the lower right corner. Once she steps beyond the strong backlight that makes her nightgown translucent, the spill of the bedside lamp wraps her in a sheen, a satin hug.

I stopped the projector there, a little breathless, and backed up to her standing at the window, back to the moment she says, "I'm not afraid of the light," and pulls the venetian blind cord. I ran it through again so I could see all the ways the light was dancing with her body, and I decided it was the best lighting job I'd ever done.

In life, a part of you is always aching because one moment slides into another before you want to let it go. On film you trap it all. You can let your eye wander. The sixth or seventh time through, taking it all in easy, it belongs to you.

Again and again I watch the last scene. I rewind to the shot of Vico, who has moved into Lisa's place by the venetian blinds. No, that was another take, I've got to keep it straight in my head: The blinds are drawn and he opens the slats; then later *she* will move into his place, pull the cord to raise them altogether, admit the light not between bars of shadow but altogether, so that the bars of shadow squeeze upward and disappear into a solid glare almost as white as before the exposed film begins feeding past the projector lens. I have to hold myself to watching Vico. It's Vico, not Lisa, who will give me the clue that will tell me what's become of him. This is where he snapped and somewhere here is what snapped him.

Standing, then, by the venetian blinds, he flicks the cigarette lighter, and says that flowers open in the sun. He crosses right and I follow. In the next shot Lisa is watching him from the bed. I come closer. She smiles up at me. She takes almost exactly the pose I recall from Vico's original sketch, the one I saw in his script book a little while before I looked up and found her standing in the door. Her face has the look of that sketch, the trust and intimacy she gave her husband floats on the wall of my bedroom. Her hand reaches to her bedside table for a pack of matches. And now the final setup. The moment of Vico's unmasking.

He continues flicking the wheel of the lighter. She enters the shot from the left. Her palm cups a lighted match. In the script, in rehearsal, he guides her hand to his lips and blows out the match, then cracks the lighter open, spills out of it the raw film that would have been used to blackmail her, exposes it to the light. He had rehearsed the scene four times. Four times he had said, "I am not—Madeline, not who you think. I am Hermann Klamstadt. My job, my mission—is to steal from your husband a copy of a secret treaty he's been working on. This film would have put you in my power. Now I am in yours."

This was the moment, I know, the secret core of each of Vico's films. Yet he murmured the lines as if the scene were a piece of exposition. Or—not quite. I seem to recall a certain breathlessness, even in rehearsals. A trick of isolating one word from another. Could he have been simply uncertain of the lines, groping for the next word? Or am I making this up?

Let me start again. I can't recall whether I noticed his hesitation during rehearsal. Maybe I didn't sense it until the first take. Maybe what I remember is not something I felt at the time, but what I've learned from running the takes again and again on my bedroom wall. It may be that what I see is only what the end of the scene has taught me to look for.

Vico is flicking the cigarette lighter, looking back at me from the wall of my room. For an instant his eyes range the room, then he finds me there on the bed. What are you telling me, Vico? What do you want? What could you ever have wanted of me? His shadow turns away from me, as if he's decided I can do him no good. His cheek picks up a blotchy crease from a place in my wall where the plaster swirls. The plaster birthmark glides into his ear as Lisa enters the shot, offering him a match. He stares at it.

On the soundtrack Bolger's voice calls for a cut. Lisa's body relaxes, she squints past the lights toward Bolger. Vico still stares at the match.

"That's taking too long," Bolger says. "Look at the goddam match, then say your goddam line." On the screen Vico is abruptly alone. A hand with a clapper enters the shot. Vico again flicks the lighter. Lisa again enters the shot, offering him the match, and it occurs to me that an endless repetition of moments leading to a disaster I foreknow and do nothing to prevent will be the form of my fitting particular hell. Again Vico stares at the match. "I am—" he stammers. "I am Hermann—" And for half a second, the space of a dozen frames, I think I see his face contort as if he is in pain. Why *pain*, why *there*—at the moment when Klamstadt is about to reveal his true identity?

Then Bolger's gigantic back lurches into the frame, covering them both, and he says, "Just a minute, we gotta get some juice into this scene." By the time he has finished saying this, he has shrunk to a size with Vico and Lisa. "Look," he says to her, "you remember how I told you to take off that dressing gown *after* he's told you who he is? Well, I got an idea we can..." And he grabs Lisa's elbow and walks her a few steps away. They are still inside the shot, still in focus, their backs to me, Vico looking toward them. Then, just before Bolger glances back at me and hollers, "Cut the goddam camera,"

Vico turns away from them, his mouth open as if he is gasping, his eyes flicking first to me, then it seems directly into the key light.

It's as if what he saw didn't punish him enough, he had to stare into the light in order to crack that stiff mask. For a few moments Bolger huddled over Lisa, one hand on her shoulder, the other sweeping an invisible baton. I saw her nodding. Then they came back and we began the last take.

Vico is flicking the lighter. Lisa enters the shot, but she doesn't have the match in her hand. Her face gliding on my wall, moving in and out of the dark swirl of plaster, tells me nothing at all. Instead of handing Klamstadt a match, she walks to the window, still in the shot, though I pan to keep her centered. She stands looking out between the slats of the venetian blinds, framed inside their horizontal slits of light. All day I've wondered whether what she says next is a line Bolger had invented for Frau Stauffer, or Lisa Vico speaking to her husband. "I'm not afraid of the light, you know," she says, and what can I read in her tone? Is it musing, playful, seductive? Despairing? "We'll have more light, if you want it." With that, she raises the venetian blinds and turns to face Vico, face the camera, face me. "I don't care who might be looking," she says, and she draws the dressing gown away from her shoulders and lets it drop to the floor. The light streaming through the window haloes her. She strolls downstage to the bedside table, strikes a match and swings it up to the cigarette dangling from Vico's lips, and with a wistful lascivious pout, she says, "I'm not afraid of fire either." The seductiveness is clumsy, embarrassed. Or is she mocking him? Has she perhaps entered a conspiracy with Bolger to mock him? Is *that* what he thought?

For a moment Vico might have been about to respond in character. He plucks the cigarette from his lips, holds it as if it were burning and he doesn't know where to find an ashtray, then throws it and the cigarette lighter to the floor. Outside the shot the lighter clatters to the floor as Vico turns toward—no, *past* the camera. Bolger was standing to the right of me.

It must have been Bolger he was looking for. Not me. On film, what it seems to be is two people talking intimately in a bedroom, then an abrupt break, a violation of privacy. No matter how many times I run the shot, as his glance turns outward I expect to see a cut to the door, someone entering, interrupting.

Sometimes I stop the projector on these next frames, hold it two seconds, three, till I know in another moment the lamp will burn the film, and still all I can see are the several moments of a blur. Vico is staring at Bolger—or maybe at me—and his lip curls back in a snarl. Whatever he is about to say is cut off by another thought, something so desolating that for an instant, for a dozen frames, a spasm leaps in his face. Then, with precise articulation, but *shrieking,* he says, "I. Am. NOT. Hermann—NOT—" And he breaks off, staring around the set as if he hears a voice calling. Suddenly his body jerks stiff, his mouth is wrenched open, waiting for what he will say, and he shrieks again, unintelligible this time, and his hand shoots out to the scooped neck of Lisa's nightgown. A vicious yank pops the shoestring straps and drags the gown to her waist. Then his face looms toward the camera, balloons off the right edge of the frame.

The soundtrack records Bolger's yelp, followed by a grunt as Vico's punch sinks into his belly. On screen Lisa, bare to the waist, stares after her husband with the stunned horror you see now and then in newsreels of people at a fire or an auto wreck—people who can still hear the screams.

As Vico disappears down the path through the Petrified Forest, making for the door, Lisa gives her nakedness a bewildered look and crosses her arms over her breasts.

That's when I remembered to stop the camera.

THE THIRD PART:

HOW HE REACTS

On whatever place a man have fallen
thereon he must lean
that he may rise.
—St. Augustine of Hippo

CHAPTER XVII

1. The Mask

—THERE'S BEEN ANOTHER CUT. Not a Spyhawk cut. It's later—a long time later. So much later that I'm no longer the person who shot that film. Or the one who watched it on the wall of his bedroom in the Silver Palms Hotel. Or wrote about it, thinking he could find there what he needed to know.

I've become—or I'm becoming—someone else.

When I saw his body stiffen, as if he'd taken a hot-wire jolt, I knew that I was witnessing a form of possession. Not that demon possession that sometimes took the actor in him farther than skill and discipline alone could go, not that. But a real possession, when somebody dead takes your body by force.

What he shrieked just before he yanked down Lisa's gown was not, in the end, unintelligible—not to me. I lowered the volume, braked the reel on the projector with the heel of my hand to slow the image into a series of puppet jerks, slow the voice to a drawl, and when Vico's shriek had slowed to an agonized gargle, what I heard, the word he cried, was *Tasteless!* and I knew in that instant he had been possessed by Berenice.

To make doubly certain of what I had heard, I had backed up the reel to run the crucial moment again, and that's why when Sammy Pugh flung open my door clutching a newspaper that was his excuse for bursting in on me, what met his eyes, flickering on the bedroom wall, was a shot of Lisa—the rag of her nightgown hung at her waist and her breasts still twitching from the violence of Vico's yank.

Sammy's first response was a reverently whispered, "Shee-it!" When he could take his eyes away, when the film ran out into white unexposed blank, he turned to me and said, "Detective, my ass. Millie told me when you were here before, you worked for the studios. But I never figured you did *this* kind of stuff."

For a while after I married Beth, I thought Spyhawk had gone for good. I didn't know he was back till I recognized in her eyes the look I used to see when I was a kid waiting for a glimpse of him in the mirror. Then I started looking at myself. After he had done something that frightened me, I would wait till Beth was asleep and roll out of bed cautious as a man going to meet his lover or his blackmailer, and blink my eyes dry in front of the bathroom mirror and say to him, "What do you want with me? Who are you?"

The closest I ever came to an answer was not from that face in the mirror, not from Spyhawk at all. It was from Vico. On the shot where we first see him spinning the wheel of that cigarette-lighter camera, I'd been puzzled by his insisting on that long spiral in on the close-up of his face. Now I know why he did it. With his thumb on the shutter of his secret camera, about to take his blackmail photos of Frau Stauffer, he was showing me the face I never saw, the one that could hide even in the mirror. The face he saw staring at him every day from behind the camera.

It was only an hour ago, reading over this manuscript that I haven't touched for so many months, that I recognized myself in that shot. Christ, I thought, he knew all about it, all about Spyhawk, even then. Or maybe not. I had to wonder if he was only setting traps for some Spyhawk of his own. Or if he had simply stolen the look from me. The way actors do.

You don't find the real Spyhawk till you feel in every breath the ache of being separated from him, till the ache is so bad the things you need to do to make it end don't terrify you as much as the thought of it going on forever. The first thing you need to do to get at your true face, your Spyhawk face, is sink your nails into the *mask* and tear it away.

For me, it was only when Sammy Pugh took one look at

Lisa's nakedness and hailed me as a brother that the ache of the mask became more than I could bear.

2. The Subtle Arts of Sammy

BROTHER SAMMY. It must have been the voices that got to him. Voices coming from a room where he would have sworn only one person lived, someone who never had visitors. The voices must have worked on him like an itch.

When I was too sick to get out of bed, I had got into the habit of leaving the door unlocked so that Sammy could bring in my icewater without disturbing me. By the time I was up scuffing around in slippers and spending most of my time writing, the habit was no longer necessary. But by then it was invisible. The only time I locked my door was when I went out at night to the bar on the corner where I used to drink beer in a shadowy booth and eat hard-boiled eggs and play with the shells while I thought about Vico and Lisa. But after I started using the projector, I kept my key in the lock and took to meeting Sammy at the door.

That last night he knocked with my pot of coffee at about seven p.m. I invited him inside—partly because he was the only person I'd exchanged a word with for the past five weeks, partly because I'd caught the way he was craning his neck the night before when I kept him outside, and I wanted to give him a good look around so I wouldn't have to worry about being bothered later when I pulled the projector back out of the closet. He spent fifteen minutes telling me about his lawyer brother, explaining his theory that lawyers have a more than usual streak of the bully in their natures and how when he was a kid his brother was always getting him in trouble and leaving him to take the blame, and that's why he grew up the kind of person nothing gets put over on. By the time he left I'd had as much company as I wanted for a long time and I didn't rise from my armchair to see him to the door. He pulled the door closed, but not quite to the point where the bolt snapped into the lock, and three hours later, when he heard the voices inside my room again, he scurried downstairs for the sports page he'd filched from my newspaper to give him an excuse for bursting in on me, and returned with it on tiptoe.

3. A Flawless Exit

I HAD BEEN LUCKY. When Vico ripped Lisa's nightgown to the waist, his back had been to the camera. He reeled away, pivoting to find Bolger as if stripping his wife and sinking his fist into Bolger's gut were two frames of a single motion, separate in time only when you held the film between your fingers up to the light. But as he rounded toward me, past me toward Bolger, he loomed out of focus, and all Sammy Pugh saw, streaking off the right edge of the frame into darkness, was a face wrapped in a caul of motion. Could he, even then, have made out the familiar matinee poster features? One of the cameraman's laws is that what moves draws the eye, and Vico was in motion. But with Sammy Pugh—and me too until I forced myself to look away—another more ruthless law held our eyes to Lisa's body.

Nothing he said suggested that he had even been aware of a man's image on the screen. After his first reverent exclamation he was all ababble, cawing and slapping me on the back, confessing in a rush that in the course of his work for his lawyer brother he had snapped a few "candid" photos that he would let me see, but that *movies* were a truly innovative idea, and we could go into business, him serving up the girls and me cranking the camera, and of course we would have to peddle our goods on the sly, exclusive clientele only, but he and his brother had some contacts downtown that would pay an easy five hundred bucks for ten steamy minutes.

His hat was off to me. As a fellow artist. His eyes glittered and his cheek pulled back from his eyetooth with a moist snap. He suggested refinements. My actress had a great body, but that look on her face was, if I didn't mind him saying so, a bit fish-eyed, not the right mood. I should have tickled her to make her smile, told her to dance around a little.

I darkened the screen. I backed him to the door. I promised I would think about it, discuss it the next day. The last thing he said was, "Okey, pardner, let's make it legal," and before he skipped off he pumped my hand in a tight, damp grip.

As soon as I was alone I went straight to the bathroom mirror. I still wouldn't believe I'd become the person he saw, but I knew I had to get away.

An hour later my suitcases were by the door. On the dresser I'd left an envelope stuffed with enough cash to satisfy a generous estimate of my bill, along with a huge, silence-buying tip for Sammy Pugh. When I heard him knock on the door across from mine I got ready, and after it had closed behind him I quietly lifted the suitcases into the hall, closed the door behind me, grabbed a suitcase in each hand, and walked down the hall to the stairwell. I put the suitcases on the landing and cracked the door just far enough to see that the hall was still clear. I had expected Sammy Pugh would linger a few minutes joking with Sally and her boyfriend. I was ten steps down the hall when the door opened and I sprinted on my toes back to the stairwell. While I waited, panting into the crook of my arm, Sammy Pugh knocked on my door. Clear down the hall I could hear his whisper. "Open up, Mister Fantomese," he said. "I've got a script idea that will make steam pour out of your ears." For a moment I thought he would use his passkey, but he must have left it downstairs. I heard him punch the elevator button, muttering to himself. The doors opened and closed, but he'd fooled me with that before. I waited, my foot keeping the stairwell door half an inch open. When I knew for certain he was gone, I opened the door, but I had waited too long. Halfway down the hall I heard the elevator clank. I ran back to the stairwell, swept up my suitcases and started down. The film canisters made the suitcase heavy, too heavy for a man who wanted to travel light, but at least Sammy Pugh had kept me from going back for the projector, and I would hang on to the film just long enough to burn it, because burning it was the only way I could be sure that ghost of Lisa's body would never again fall under his eyes.

Or mine.

4. Goodbye to All I Knew

ONCE YOU START leaving behind the things you thought you needed, it's hard to know what you can't do without. I was feeling reckless, light-headed, ready to do whatever came to mind and eager to see what it would be. Maybe the sudden exertion after so much lying around had brought back a touch of fever. My hand, I remember—fitting the car key in the ignition, it trembled.

My first stop was a barber shop, where I got my ears uncovered. A few minutes later I was sliding into my old booth in the Penguin Club, the one where Vico and I had spent so many nights, where I had sat with Bolger while the rain poured down the mountains and spilled up over the curbs the night Vico disappeared. Curly, the bartender, gave me a round slow look and brought my usual gin and tonic to the table himself.

"Mister Farley," he said, and nodded approval as if I had accomplished something difficult and whimsical, like building a three-level card house. "Long time no see."

"You're looking good, Curly," I said. "By the way, I seem to recall I was a bit preoccupied the last time I was here. I hope I didn't forget to settle my bill."

"You settled, Mister Farley, and left a handsome tip to boot."

"I guess I should apologize for—"

"You were the perfect gentleman. Even tossed Mister Bolger a hanky to mop up the drink you sloshed in his face." And then, leaning over the table far enough to breathe a whiff of chewing gum, "I never liked that bastard and he ain't been in here since. You done me a favor."

We both laughed and then he got serious and made the comment I'd been expecting: "Too bad about Mister Vico."

I looked solemn and nodded. "I don't suppose there's a chance—" I cut him off with a shrug. "What I figure," he said, leaning into a whisper, "if he was alive, he'd a turned up by now."

I agreed. I said things wouldn't be the same without him. Then Curly made the comment I hadn't been expecting.

"You know, there was a cop in here a couple weeks ago, asking about you."

I took it head on: "Yeah, I know who you mean. Heavy-set guy. Gray eyes, talks like he's got a cigarette cough."

"That's the one," Curly said. "Hoensinger, his name was." And then, with another confidential Chicklet breeze: "He asked me to give him a ring if I saw you."

"Never mind," I said. "I stopped in to see him myself this morning. These cops. Don't leave town, he says, and expects your life to freeze. I told him he'd do the same if his father had a stroke and left him with forty cows to milk."

"How 'bout that, Mister Farley. I didn't know you was a farmboy."

I wasn't, so I changed the subject, but it all went slick as ice on a skillet. I knew it couldn't last, but while it did it was like ordering the most expensive steak in the house without a dime in your pocket. You'd deal with the trouble on a full stomach. The way I was feeling, even if Hoensinger himself had walked in, I'd have had answers for everything. While I was working on my third gin and tonic a woman in the next booth told her boyfriend the story about Vico in the Tibetan monastery. It had grown since I'd heard it last, in another bar, told by somebody else. It wasn't just a face somebody had recognized in a tabloid photo. There was an eyewitness, somebody who'd actually talked to him, and he'd said he was doing penance for his sins. It's what I always said: There was nothing he couldn't make you believe.

As news, Vico had outlasted the flood that washed him away. In the barber chair paging through a dog-eared copy of *Life* I'd come across a photo spread I'd missed before: some Busby Berkeley chorus girls showing a little leg as they bedded down on studio cots the night all the bridges washed out. But that was weeks old. By now all the bodies had been pulled out of the mud and claimed, and suddenly the newspapers had realized that Vico hadn't been among them. In the last couple of days the gossip columns and features pages had broken into a babble of new speculation. The kidnap theory got another run. And the suicide theory: Somebody on the *Tablet* had goaded Lisa into denying that he was capable of killing himself. They'd got hold of a photo that looked like it came out of her modeling portfolio—glossy hair, studio shadows, and a store-dummy stare. If her name hadn't been in the cutline I'd never have known it was her, but I tore it out and put it in my wallet.

Later at another table I overheard a drunken gang of movie tech people deciding to crash a party at Thad Bolger's house. Among them was Mickey Strapler, a guy I knew. Five years ago he had talked about making it as an actor. Since then he'd grown a forty-pound gut and settled into boozy senility on a grip's steady salary. As they crowded toward the door, I jabbed him in the arm and said, "Hi, stranger, how's tricks?" He greeted me with a fuzzy smile.

"Hey, Farley, ain't seen you around lately."

I told him I'd been sick and offered to buy him a drink. By this time we were out on the sidewalk under a pink neon sign. He declined the drink as I knew he would, saying he was on his way to Bolger's party.

"Swell," I said. "I know Bolger, I'll tag along."

I squeezed into the backseat of somebody's convertible. The tires squealed and we lurched into the night traffic on Sunset. Next to me was a pretty brunette in a red sweater that matched her lipstick. She told me she was Jamie Something from Paterson and didn't always drink like this. In another five minutes I'd learned that she'd won a beauty contest in New Jersey and migrated to Hollywood on a six-month option. The studio had bought her dancing lessons and singing lessons and speech lessons and a hairdo that gave her headaches from sleeping in curlers. When she asked when they would use her in a picture, they put her in a gown safety-pinned up the back, stretched her on a divan that had been in Katharine Hepburn's living room in *Bill of Divorcement,* and filmed her being kissed by leading-man types. Two dozen in all. At the end of the day she had bruised lips and found out from the cameraman who'd asked her to dinner that it was the men they'd been testing. The cameraman bruised her lips some more and last week her six-month option was up and hadn't been renewed.

"What do *you* do?" she asked.

I told her I was a cameraman.

"Oh," she said, and turned away, and after that I laid the back of my neck on the car seat and watched the stars. I closed off every view but straight up and pretended the wind rushing in my ears and the gentle tug around the curves was soaring me through the sky and soon I could cut the motor among the white silent fires and just drift. Then a stretch of bumpy road made the stars bounce and double till I laughed. I had settled on a plan. My plan was to go to Bolger's party and see if I could hit him harder than Vico had. Thinking about hitting Bolger, I laughed and laughed and the pretty beauty-contest winner beside me said, "I wouldn't ask you for a screen test if you were the last cameraman on earth."

We left Sunset and wound high into the hills. After a while we drove through a gate in a spiky fence lined with trees. Past the trees the driveway broke uphill toward a house you could see a long way coming. Early cars had lined the drive. Latecomers got closer to the house by swinging onto the grassy downslope and parking side by side. Whoever was driving us did that. For a couple seconds after the brake was set I looked down on the city. The lines of all the streetlights seemed to converge toward a vanishing point somewhere out in the breathing black of the ocean. He's out there, I thought, his body wedged in some rocky grotto. By now the fish have nibbled his eyes away.

The car door slammed and somebody said, "Never mind, he's asleep," and Mickey Strapler said, "Hey, Farley, you coming?" I got out.

Bolger's house was a Spanish villa with a backlight that haloed the scalloped silhouette of its roof. Splashes of tinny shrieks came from the same place as the light. We ignored the door and walked around the house toward the noise. What had haloed Bolger's roof was the pool lights in his backyard. People were bobbing in the pool. Others around the pool and on the patio by the house bobbed to a clarinet lick. The band was on the patio steps. People in swimsuits were clustered with people in trousers and dresses. A couple doing a jitterbug lost the beat and stopped dancing, looking my way. Suddenly the chatter dropped to a hum. Christ, I thought, they've all noticed me. But the stares were passing through me. I caught their direction in time to see a woman on the high diving board unzip a gold-spangled evening dress and curl her shoulders to shrug it to her waist. The clarinet was frantic, but she let her hands drift down her body as if she were smoothing her slip, then slid her fingers inside the dress to ease it past the buttocks. It dropped. It surrounded her ankles like a pedestal. For an instant, an instant no camera was there to freeze, she was Aphrodite in a silk slip. Then a moan of approval from the crowd around the pool spoiled her poise. She glanced behind her along the narrow board she had dreamwalked out to her perch. From below a voice spread thick with patience called out, "The slip too, sweetie—nobody swims in a slip." Afloat on his back in the pool, legs sprawled like a dog that wants its belly scratched, was Bolger, a thin cigar clipped at a cocky tilt in his teeth. The woman above tried to smile, tried to step out of her dress. An armhole hooked her ankle. She was in midair before she kicked free and she hit the water still pedaling. She surfaced looking pretty miserable, ready to cry, and dogpaddled toward the edge of the pool. Then, either because she was postponing the time when she would have to climb out in her wet underwear or because the whistles and applause she was getting had made her think she was quite a performer after all, she pushed off from the side and tried a fancy stroke or two. Bolger had lifted his chin to keep the splash from putting out his cigar.

I still wanted to slug him, but not when he was already on his back. I picked a martini off the buffet table and drifted into the house. The more sedate members of the party were gathered in the game room. A few people leaning against a pool table were wrist-flicking balls off the cushions, counting the caroms. A bigger crowd was talking at the fireplace end of the room. Over the fireplace was a stuffed lion head. Somebody had hung around it a painted wooden collar in the shape of the MGM trademark. The lion, bare-fanged and scowling, didn't look amused.

At the center of the crowd was Nellie Nugent, explaining her theory that the spy on the set had been Vico sabotaging his own production because he was jealous of Bolger, and I was his accomplice. Somebody asked what evidence she had. She told how she had snuck after us into the Petrified Forest and squatted in the underbrush to overhear us plotting against Bolger. "Oh, come on, Nellie," somebody said. It was the level-headed one talking, the one that had spoken before. "You followed them in there? How did you know they would be *plotting*?" Well, she thought something was *fishy*. What were they *doing* in there, anyway? She did a detailed pantomime of how she had got tipped off to our fishy plotting by seeing Vico jerk his head at me, a high sign, she explained, directing me to the forest path. She reported tantalizing fragments of our conversation: "'... costing Krackenpov five grand a day.' That was *very* distinct, and then they both giggled like bad little boys, and they were squealing, 'Five grand a day, five grand a day!' And the next thing I heard just shocked me. I didn't know anybody could be so ... so *calculating*. It was Farley said it. He said, 'And Bolger will never work in this town again. That's certain.' The way he said, 'That's *certain*.' It just chilled my blood."

At that moment someone began coughing and nudging her, but she went on quite a while longer before she looked up and met my eyes.

"Go on, Nellie," I said. "Don't let me stop you. What did Vico say next? What did I say? And was his midnight swim through the six-foot waves all part of the plot?"

It's odd how a crisis brings out facets in people. Prim Nellie with her clipboard, so eager to fetch and flatter. Under the pressure of a little scandal and mystery, she had uncorked a talent for holding an audience. It had given her courage, too. In the old days if I forgot to smile when I asked for a cue, she would press her arms to her sides. That would squeeze her breasts forward as if she were reminding me she was a woman. At Bolger's party, though, she was the queen, the insider with the inside story. She wasn't about to step down just because one of the characters in her story didn't like her casting. She slitted her eyes at me, puffed out her chest without the aid of any squeezing arms, and said, "What do you know about six-foot waves? The body never washed up, did it? He might not even be dead."

With a dozen spectators swirling the olives in their martinis, I didn't want to argue with her. But that line got to me. What had she ever known about Vico alive, that she could be so sure he wasn't dead?

"If he's not dead," I said, "he's so changed from the man we used to know that he wouldn't recognize himself in a mirror."

If I meant something by that, I didn't know what. I wanted something that would leave them all gaping, and that's what came out. Maybe I was thinking of one of Vico's unmaskings, something like the moment in *Cain* when Sarah Merrill creeps down the cellar steps and her flashlight inches up the body of the man standing over a fresh-dug grave till it rests on the face of her dapper new husband.

I didn't know what I meant, but it worked. In the hush I turned on my heel, almost collided with a servant, and neatly added my glass to his tray as I made for the door.

5. Without Mirrors

THE SILENCE STREAMED away behind me. I laid my hand on the doorknob thinking how Vico would have envied my timing, how he would have been content to capture this suave grace after a dozen takes.

That's when Nellie Nugent found her voice.

"I'd walk fast, too," she said, "if the po*lice* had been asking questions about me."

I didn't hurry or slow down. I didn't let them know I'd heard. But once I'd closed them inside, once I'd got the stars above me again, I saw that I'd forgotten already what it felt like to soar. What had Hoensinger wanted to know, I wondered, and why? What did he already know about me that I didn't? I had thought that once I was out of Sammy Pugh's sight, I'd be a new man, but it wasn't that easy. My first mistake had been to fuel my soaring with booze. From the backyard I heard the bellow of one of Bolger's punch lines and his own bray leading the laughter. Christ, I'd already tossed a drink in his face. Was he worth more of my time than that? But that wasn't you threw the drink, I thought. It was Spyhawk. And then: No. It was me.

The line of cars nose to tail in Bolger's drive reminded me that I didn't have a ride back to town. My car was parked in a cinder lot next to the bar where I'd met Mickey Strapler. I climbed across the front bumper of a Nash and walked between a couple of other cars parked on the grass and on down the slope till I was far enough from the party hubbub to hear a cicada. The city lights right below me were speckled all over, but as they got farther away, they formed ranks and marched off into the sea. Standing there wondering how to get back to town, I had the old now-you-have-to-live-with-what-he's-done feeling, but it wasn't Spyhawk who'd done it. *I* was the one who'd wanted to punch Bolger. It made me queasy, as if I'd walked through a mirror and become my reflection. If that happened, there would be nobody to look at the one who looked back.

For the past five—no, nearly six weeks, the only one looking had been Sammy Pugh, who had ended by paying me the high compliment of assuming I was his fellow artist. Then there had been the stares of all the people Nellie Nugent had turned my way. But they had been easy to close a door on. You'd think I would have been feeling fine. There I was, the constellations of the city spread below me and the chaos of stars above—and me between them, invisible, with the widest angle on the world I could ever want, and instead of being my smug self, I felt that unless pretty soon somebody looked at me without seeing only the Farley I'd left behind, the one who was taking his place would disappear.

I started down hill to call Lisa.

CHAPTER XVIII

1. Gull Wing

IT'S ALMOST A week since I wrote the last lines. I've let the wind sift fine sand across the open notebook, where I've left "...I started down hill to call Lisa" hovering in the upper left corner of the blank page.

A while ago, to shame myself back to the job, I put my forefinger on the page and slashed a random mark in the grit. No more excuses, I said to myself. Even the dust is thick enough to write in. Then I saw the mark I'd made was a capital V. Like a forger, I'd mimicked the precise seagull-wing dip and arch from Vico's signature. It was Spyhawk, peeking through, letting me know that if I won't write it, he'll find a way. There's nothing Spyhawk makes me write that I won't have a chance to snip. I can cut, I can burn. But first I have to tell it. Everything I know—and since so much of what I know I learned that last night with Lisa, there's no way to leave her out of it. No way to pretend all I wanted was to help.

By now I ought to know: An eye can't help but look.

2. Retake

THE DAY VICO told me the man behind the camera is only an eye, we were on the set of the first picture we did together, *City of Sapphires.* It was one of those days when the idea you come on the set with just won't work and nothing you improvise strikes a spark. Vico called for a ten-minute break. He took a cup of coffee and climbed a steel ladder to the catwalk directly above the set. Five minutes past his ten-minute call, he was still there, brooding down on us. I went up after him. I knew that Simmons was probably already on his way to Krackenpov's office with the news that production was stalled because the director was in a funk. Later I knew he was no more in trouble during those silences than a cat perched by a mousehole, but at the time I thought it was funk myself, and I started offering suggestions.

His response to everything I said was so listless that when he rounded on me and snarled that I was only an eye to him, I had to grip the catwalk rail to keep from pitching over. I shut my eyes to fight it down. Vico never noticed. He had turned back to the set below us. If I had pitched over the rail and thudded onto the floor, my body would have held his attention about as long as any of the other images that his mind hooked and tossed back till it struck the one that would work.

But now, writing this, I can see him—elbows propped on the catwalk rail, shoulders heavy, deep in the dream I'd interrupted—and I hear him muttering as if I weren't there.

What was he saying?

"An eye," he whispered—and drew the word out in a sigh. "Yes, that's it. An eye."

And what I sometimes hear him say is not that the man behind the camera is *only* an eye, but—as if he were discovering it—the man behind the camera is an *eye*! Did I delete that word *only*—or add it? My focus on our whole eight years together blurs. What if Vico was not dismissing me, but discovering me?

I've said there were times when he jolted life into a scene by playing it to me. But I've never been sure, not really. Wouldn't he search out roughly the same shadow beyond the stagelights whether he was looking for the lens or for me standing behind it?

Only. I lived eight years with Vico's *only an eye* lodged like a piece of grit under my lid. If I can't be sure he ever said it, nothing I know about me stays the same. I thought I never blinked—except when Spyhawk blacked me out. Now I can't be sure.

I always thought no matter what I did, Lisa would be safe with me. I have to believe I would never have hurt her on purpose. I have to believe that what I called love was love.

3. Finding My Way Without Virgil

I CLOSE MY eyes and lie waiting. Black numbers splash inside a silver pool of light, counting down, and I count with them ...8...5...3...2...and there's the road outside Bolger's mansion.

I still hear party sounds, the little scree of Nellie Nugent's laugh, that came about six seconds after I shut the door, and behind the house, Bolger roaring orders from the pool. Far down the canyon the streetlights on Sunset and Hollywood Boulevard run side by side like sprocket holes. A car squeals away from a stop and gargles off downtown. But a block from Bolger's house the street I'm on becomes quiet and dark. It makes sidewinder curves down the face of the hill.

For a few minutes I follow it. Then I notice a pale gash against the black lawns, a flood gully slicing downhill, and I drop with the gully through empty lots and backyards. Most houses are dark. In one yard a big lazy collie trots out from the shadow of a porch with a warning rattle in his throat. I squat and coo and he licks my hand and lets me flow on down the gully. I pass a dark screen where the sleepy coaxing voice of a woman murmurs, "...if you could just manage to open that attic window..." And I flow on, circling wide past a house where the downstairs lights spill into the yard. In a few houses radios keep sleepless people company. Now a shrill female singer with a hiccup in her high notes tries to make me believe it's a sin to tell a lie. Farther down a solemn, scolding voice tells me I've ignored too long the rumors of war from Europe and had better arm now to meet the threat. Then I pass a little bungalow near the bottom of the hill, all dark but for the glow of a radio dial, while a thin Bible Belt lilt that crackles with static warns me that the jaws of the pit open for sinners. I come through a gas-station parking lot onto Franklin Avenue and spot a pink neon BURGER sign. Bugs circle the sign and crawl on it and on the plate-glass window and the sidewalk. Through the window I see a phone booth under a cola sign.

4. The Beach-House Phone

SOMETIMES AFTER THE bars close you find yourself coming out of a drunk in an all-night diner where people wish you'd gone someplace else. The waitress gives you a stare, scoops the nickel you bounced on the counter and goes back to her nail file. The guy at the nearest stool moves to an empty booth. Nobody wants your sloppy drunk troubles and the coffee's so thick the cream won't sink. When you stir it, grounds cling to your spoon.

I sat for a while deciding what I'd say. The pinhead reflected in the coffee urn tried to look sad and wise. I turned my back on him and took my coffee cup with me to the phone booth. The light didn't go on when I closed the door, but I knew the number without checking the book. As I dialed I caught myself bracing for Vico's voice. I hung up fast. What's wrong with me? I thought. It's Lisa I want to talk to. I sat there sorting it out, then dialed again. It rang a dozen times, two dozen. I had to make her answer. I dozed off for a minute. Her voice jerked my head up, but when I said *Lisa*? into the receiver it was still ringing. I hung up and was dialing for a cab when I thought of the beach house. After what had happened, I couldn't imagine her there alone. Also, I remembered the phone cord had been yanked out of the wall. But that was nearly six weeks ago. I got a ring, and then another, that I imagined floating through the dark halls to the attic, where there would be the same musty closeness now, but crickets and starlight instead of the drumming rain, and in the middle of the third ring, the receiver lifted. Silence. Then her voice said, "Who is it?" Not harsh, not brittle. A moonlit-night kind of voice. But a sentry's voice, one who's going to want a password before you can get closer.

5. The Special Friend

HALF AN HOUR later a gray Chrysler stopped at the curb outside the diner. From my table by the window I couldn't see a face, only pale knuckles wrapped over the steering wheel. When I leaned close to the glass, the knuckles opened into a palm that waved a quick hello and snapped back onto the wheel. As I slid into the passenger seat her eyes took a second longer than they might have to meet mine.

"You look tired," she said. "Are you sober?"

"Mostly," I said. Her voice had been a shock. I'd thought I knew its inflections by heart, but what I recalled was the soundtrack from the rushes. The real thing was softer and it had more places it might go than I could follow. I caught a faint breath of jasmine. I thought of the way she tossed her hair to dab perfume behind her ears, the way she raised her chin to touch it in the hollow of her throat. I wondered if it could be for me. Or if she'd hoped I would surprise her by pulling him out of my hat. Her dress was the somber purple of a woman not quite ready to declare herself a widow.

"Where's your car?" she said.

I told her. She put the Chrysler in gear and eased away from the curb. She listened to my chatter about Bolger's party. She didn't pretend that Nellie Nugent's version of my last talk with Vico in the Petrified Forest either shocked or amused her or made her curious to know what we'd really said. She drove without glancing away from the road.

On the phone, as soon as she heard my voice, she had said, "Have you found him, Farley?" I'd told her not yet, but maybe a talk with her would turn up a few missing pieces. "Yes," she'd said. "For me too."

At the parking lot next to the bar where I'd met Mickey

Strapler there were still plenty of cars, but she spotted mine and eased into a space beside it. She switched off the motor, then faced me along the seat. It was dark, but her eyes caught a glint from a bare bulb above the back entrance to a pawnshop. A dull silverfish glimmer that kept out any gaze that tried to see deeper.

"Where have you been, Farley?" she said.

"A long way off," I said. "Has Hoensinger been asking about me?"

"Yes."

I waited a second, then said, "What did you tell him?"

"What you told me. That you had a hunch you might know where my husband was. That you might be gone for a while."

She didn't volunteer anything more.

"Why are you living at the beach house?" I asked. "It's... isolated. Aren't you a little scared?"

"Why should I be frightened?" she said. Then she seemed to relax a little, take a breath. "In town the reporters won't let me alone. They've been to the beach house, too—more than once. But the long drive keeps some away." Then, after another pause: "Besides, if he comes back, if he can—it's the beach house he'll come to. I want to be there when he does."

"I thought you were finished with him. Have a change of heart?"

I was afraid of that, it was what I half expected, what I was ready to worry out of anything she might say next. That's why I wasn't listening to what she did say.

"There are things I need to know. Things I suspect, but I'm not sure of. Certain questions I have to ask."

"How do you know he's going to feel like talking?"

"He won't need to. The look in his eyes will be enough."

"Maybe it will," I said, but after all that had happened what I was hearing made me bitter and mean and tired of being gentle. "What if he's dead?" I thought that might jolt her, but she came back as if she'd already thought it through.

"That's why I want to talk to you, Farley. You were his friend. A special friend." And she repeated it, hissing softly in the dark: "Special. I can get what I need from you, too, can't I."

While I was groping for something to say, a noisy gang spilled out of the bar. There was a hot discussion about a prizefight. Three or four guys were throwing mock punches, shuffling on their toes in the cinder lot, while a squeaky voice that couldn't get anybody to listen kept saying, "Tunney coulda took him, Tunney coulda took him the best day he lived." Somebody lurched past us to the mouth of an alley and unzipped his trousers to piss.

"We can't talk here," I said.

My place was closc, but I couldn't be sure Hoensinger wasn't having it watched. I was glad when I didn't need to risk it.

"Come with me, Farley," she said. "Come to the beach house. You can take your car and follow me back."

All the way out Sunset's twisting run to the sea, she was sliding through traffic lights as if she wanted to shake me, but I stuck on her tail and once we got onto the coast road, out beyond the city, I held her in a steady beam of light while the dark rushed in at my back.

6. The Stranger

THE MOMENT I saw her I knew that she'd changed. It threw me off balance. I'd imagined she would be the same person I'd watched on the rushes. I'd watched it so often it had buried all the hints I'd got of the woman she would become, the one rounding the curve ahead of me. All through the long drive I tried to get them back.

I thought of the moment the camera stopped turning, her arms crossed over her breasts, the fingertips touching the front of her shoulders. That was the moment the change began. The crossed arms had a formal grace, a dignity she seemed aware of, that she wouldn't break even an instant to draw back the coil of hair dropped across one eye. It's more than modesty. The crossed arms are a kind of magic, a seal on her privacy.

And I remembered how she would protect herself from the photographers by that thumbnail sign of the cross over her brow, her lips, her breast. Jesus be in my mind and on my lips and in my heart. At the time I thought, This is all he's left her, the bastard. Only children's magic to keep off the stares.

Then she was gone, swallowed into the shadows beyond the bedroom set, and I thought, Now she will see him clear. Even then, with my mind on Vico and what he would find in his trailer, a part of me was thinking of her, and that was one of the reasons why I got away from Bolger so fast and ran to head her off—I wanted to be there, wanted to watch how it took her. Outside I expected the steady rain that had started the previous day. Instead it was more like a tropical storm. Too far, I thought, it's gone too far, and set off sprinting through the puddles. No joke anymore, and by the time I got to Vico's trailer I was soaked. I was pounding on the door, thinking, I'll tell him everything, it's gone too far, only there was no answer. All I could hear was rain on the trailer roof. "Let me in," I shouted. "It's a mistake, I can explain." But there was no answer, and suddenly I thought, If he hasn't been here yet, I might still head it off. I rattled the knob, then fumbled for my key. It was a risk. If he was inside not answering, he would learn I had a key. But it was no use anyhow. My key must have jumped from my pocket as I ran.

Lisa's trailer was parked next door, and I saw her coming, walking. I fought down my breath. She was wrapped in the dressing gown now, her hand clutching it to her throat. She held her arms stiff, as if the skin beneath had been scorched by my eyes.

"He's gone," I said, coming to meet her. "Either that or he's locked himself inside."

"That's all right, Farley," she said. "I don't want to see him," and even through the rain I should have noticed how her voice stripped what she said to a hard outline.

I waited while she got into her street clothes, then ran with her to the parking lot. Raindrops drummed on the cars. Vico's car was gone. I offered her a ride home. She got out on the sidewalk in front of the town house. There was a puddle in front of the porch stoop that she didn't bother stepping around. She was wearing those open-toed pumps she had on later at the beach house. I had the car door open and one foot on the ground, but by then she was up to the door and I saw she wasn't turning back.

That day there'd been too much on my mind for me to notice that the Lisa I knew was gone, and two days later, after I realized she'd been grilled all night by Hoensinger and decided I had to call her, I didn't notice it either. I never knew it, but I was talking to someone else, a stranger. What did I say that she might suspect? As soon as I heard her voice I began the speech I'd prepared.

"Listen, Lisa, I'm dropping out of sight for a while, and I just—"

But I never got that far.

"Eric," she'd said, "is that you?"

"Just a second," I told her, and covered the mouthpiece while I squatted on the wood seat of the phone booth with my head between my knees and gulped some air. I was in a high fever and I'd dressed and walked two blocks to a drugstore rather than call from the Silver Palms. I didn't want the call traced if she heard anything phony in my story. Vico had never, not even that night on *The Merry Widower,* told me his real name.

"It's Farley," I said.

"Oh," she said. "For a second you sounded..." And her voice was wary, not sure yet whether she was being fooled. "Why is your voice strange, Farley?"

I told her I had a ticklish throat. I was whispering to keep from coughing. Her mistake was an odd confirmation of something I thought I'd imagined. Hearing my own voice inside my head, the way you do when your sinuses are clogged, it had struck me that my loosened vocal cords perfectly mimicked one of Vico's voice-over monologues in *The Whisperer.*

I asked about Hoensinger's grilling. That's when she told me he'd tried to make her name some second-rate leading man to round out his cast for the classic tabloid crime of passion. The sizzle in her voice pleased me, but it blended with the sizzle in my ears.

"What I called for," I said. "What I want to say—I'm dropping out of sight for a while. Got to leave town, check a few hunches."

And she said, "You know where he is, don't you, Farley? Take me with you."

No, I told her, it was only a hunch and I couldn't take her along. She wanted me to explain my hunch.

"I can't," I said. "It might get us in trouble."

"Who?" she said. "You and Eric? What kind of trouble?"

I kept telling her I couldn't explain, it wasn't something I could involve her in, it was too ugly.

"All right," she said, "don't tell me. But from the sound of it, I think you'd better take it to the police."

I can't do that, I told her. She wanted to know why. That's when I thought I might get her to help me keep Hoensinger off my tail.

"Listen," I said. "Hoensinger told me not to leave town, and if he comes to you—what I need you to do is tell him I'm looking for Vico, just what I've told you. I can't explain it now, but if he drags me back before I have a chance—"

She cut me off.

"How can you ask me to do that," she said, "when you won't tell me why?"

I was more and more dizzy and sick, and finding it harder to invent what I needed, but I hinted that Vico might be involved in something illegal, in trouble with the mob, and the last thing he needed was for me to show up with a carload of cops. She didn't go for that story much. When she pressed me on it, I got panicky and put my finger on the receiver so it would seem we'd been cut off while I was talking. As soon as

I'd done it, I realized what a melodramatic trick it was, how Vico would have snorted and said, We can do better, Farley. Either she wouldn't believe it or she'd swallow it whole and call the cops. I called her right back.

"Sorry, Lisa," I said. "I just pulled the phone off the table. Look, I can't wait any longer. What I've got in mind is such a long shot I can't— Chances are the body will turn up on the beach in a day or two, and I'll turn around and drive home. But if I find anything, I'll call you right away."

Then I hung up. Maybe it was her wanting to go along that had given me the idea she might still go back to him if he was alive. Once I was back in my room and in bed again, coughing and tossing and swimming in and out of my fever dreams, I saw there was another way to figure it. Apart from anything she might feel for him—whatever feeling there could still be for a man who would do what he'd done—knowing whether he was dead or alive was important for *her.* If he was dead, after all, she was a widow. A rich widow. And free. If he was alive—

How could I tell what she'd do? Since that night I hadn't seen her. Only photographs. One of the first was in that batch of newspapers Sammy Pugh brought up to my room the night I checked in at the Silver Palms. There it was, her ghost in shaded dots. One wing of its raincoat collar at a jaunty tilt, the cup in its limp hand almost dangling, the coffee touching the low rim, touching so close that thinking how she wouldn't even notice when it spilled made me queasy. But her face, even through the shock and exhaustion, set in a stubborn refusal I couldn't figure out. All I knew, sure as if I'd been there, was that she'd just heard a voice call, "Hey lady, look here!" and not only didn't raise her eyes, but didn't need to fight off the impulse. She'd wet her lips and smiled at the lens for the last time.

Beyond that, what could I tell from a photograph? What was a photo, after all? Proof that once somewhere there'd been flesh enough to stop the light. I studied the photo for clues to how she felt about Vico, and learned only what you'd learn from the hollow in a pillow: She'd been there, but some other time.

Even at the pace she'd set I had nearly an hour's drive to mull things over, but as her headlights raked the attic windows of the beach house, I still had only the vaguest suspicion that the woman I'd followed out there was someone I didn't know at all.

CHAPTER XIX

1. The Empty Room

HALFWAY UP THE beach-house drive I pulled off into my usual spot in the grass, while Lisa continued over the hill and around the house to the garage. The car door slammed as I walked up the path. Framed by the living-room window, her silhouette crossed a light she'd left burning. Clouds drifting in from the ocean had fogged out most of the stars I'd seen at Bolger's. At the foot of the steep drop beyond the house the sea exhaled a raspy breath that broke with a cough. I remembered walking the beach with Vico years ago past a cliff where water had hollowed a cave. The echo when the waves broke high enough to slap the cave wall was the cough I heard. My pneumonia was almost gone, but the damp air snagged in my throat. She met me at the door.

I went to the kitchen with her and leaned against a counter while she made coffee. Neither of us wanted to say anything until we were settled, but the small talk drifted in currents we couldn't always predict.

"I never realized," I said, "how quiet it is out here."

"It doesn't bother me."

"Funny I never noticed it before." I'd come for the truth and was already weaving a lie to trap it. "Always too busy, I guess."

She scooped a spoonful of coffee from a bag and leveled it with a precise forefinger.

"Busy doing what?"

"Listening to... Eric." I went on quick. "Hearing him go through a new script. He could fill up a room even when you were alone with him."

"Yes. I know."

"He does all the parts. In different voices."

"I know."

We sat at the kitchen table to wait for the water to boil, watching each other across it, me toying with a saltshaker.

"It's never really quiet," she said. "There's always the ocean."

"I'm not used to it," I said. "Living in apartments, you've always got somebody the other side of the wall. Always somebody flushing or coughing or playing a radio. You learn a lot about people you never see."

On the beach, water in the rock cave coughed and slapped.

"Once last week," she said, "I was walking down the hall to the study. A few steps from the door I heard someone inside."

"You heard someone?"

"A creak in the floorboards. You know that board in front of the desk, the one that groans when he rests the leg of the chair on it?"

I did.

"My heart started pounding," she said. "I felt him in the room."

"What did you do?"

"I stopped outside the door and thought, What if it's a stranger? I was so scared I couldn't go inside."

"How long did you stand there?"

"Thirty seconds or so, I guess. It seemed longer."

"Then you got up your courage and peeked around the door."

"Yes."

"And you saw . . . an empty chair?"

She nodded.

"An empty room?"

Again.

Her hand lay flat along the table. Smoothly, nothing so rash as a pounce, I closed my hand over hers. "So you sat in the empty chair in the empty room," I said, "and cried awhile." Under my palm I felt the fingers curl, the knuckles prod.

She gave me a puzzled, almost hostile look.

"Well, not quite," she said. "In fact, I was furious."

The coffee had perked. Her hand slid out from under mine and she got up to get the cups.

"I went straight to that cabinet," she said, "the one where I made him put those damn shrunken heads of his. I never thought anything would make me touch them, but I grabbed one in each fist and took them out on the deck. I pitched them far as I could down the hill." Her laugh was a sharp bark. "Now every time I go down the path for a swim, I'm afraid I'll stumble over one of them." She stopped smiling. "And it didn't do any good. I still feel like someone's in the house with me. And I don't always suppose it's Eric."

"I don't like the sound of that," I said. "You should be in town, someplace with enough people around so you're not tempted to imagine things."

Again she looked puzzled, faintly annoyed.

"It's nothing I brood about for hours on end," she said. "Just a feeling."

We took our coffee into Vico's study. The window over his desk was open and the white gauzy curtains dipped and bellied across it. All his little African stone dolls were waiting, patient as the Lindbergh baby's teddy bear. The photo of Vico with Chaney was the only thing missing.

She put the cups on a low table in front of the couch where he used to flop after working all night on a script. When she went back to the kitchen for cream, I stayed by Vico's desk, thinking: I was sitting right here looking past his shoulder the night I first saw her, stopped in the doorway because she hadn't expected to find him with company, that floating nightgown almost a prophecy of the one Vico made her wear in—

And then she was standing just as she had that night, looking back at me with the look I recognized, that went through me the way Beth's look used to, only she had on the purple not-quite-mourning dress and held a tray with a cream pitcher and a sugar bowl.

"What are you staring at?" she said.

2. Trying Out a New Script

I WAS LIKE a fat man who can't stop sweating. I felt lies seeping down my armpits. I was thinking, I told her, what a smashing model she must have been. It was the wrong thing to say. She broke the pose with an impatient toss of the head that couldn't help being graceful. Even indoors, holding a bowl and pitcher on a tray, she had a model's long-legged stride.

"What's wrong?" I said.

She clapped the cream and sugar on the table with the coffee, then sat on the couch.

"I'm sorry," she said. "I'm just tense, tired of waiting." She started to reach for the cream pitcher, stopped herself and picked up her coffee instead. "And I don't like being stared at."

"It's not always easy to escape, is it?" I was laughing. She asked what was funny, a little prim. "I'm not laughing at you," I said. I was crossing behind her to turn on the standing lamp that looked over her shoulder. "It's me, too," I explained. "Maybe all of us, itching inside our skins. You get tired of being a model, tired of being photographed. You want to become another person." I sat at the other end of the couch. Her profile, lit from behind, was absolutely perfect, just a fraction longer than Garbo's, the same jaw, same high cheekbones. "So you marry a movie actor and wind up in front of a camera that shoots twenty-four frames a second."

"You're right," she said. She seemed apologetic, as if I had scolded her. The cup was perched on her knee. She bent over it as if she were studying her reflection in the coffee. Her hair fell forward, spoiled the line of her neck. "That's one of the things I've got to understand—how I let that happen."

But she seemed to know. Already, instinctively, her hand was tucking back the strand of hair, the chin coming up, the eyes coming around to me coy and sultry.

"Don't blame yourself," I said. "You can't help being beautiful. And you shouldn't resent it. It's part of what makes you fascinating."

"Not to me," she said. "To me it's just a bore."

She smiled and leaned back, ever so languidly, into a new pose. The fashion model's instincts die hard as any other. One reason why she lived at the beach house, I had decided, was to drape her grief along the kind of driftwood *Vogue* photographers think is arty.

And then, still smiling, she said, "Where is he, Farley?" Just as if I knew.

On the set when she looked out past the lights, I would feel her eyes groping toward me, groping past the glare of the spots into the dark where I stood by the camera. Now I was in the light along with her, no lens between us, nailed to the other end of the couch in Vico's study. I didn't look away. I looked back at her, just as I did in my room at the Silver Palms, as her eyes find the lens, staring soft and level from the wall, and her face comes to rest over a hairline crack in the plaster that creases her brow like a scar.

"You were gone six weeks, Farley. Did you see him? Where did you go?"

Her voice had a lemony pucker that expected the worst. It gave me my cue.

"I didn't see him," I said. "That's why I think he's dead. I can't think where else to look."

"Why couldn't you tell me where you were going? Why were you gone so long?"

These were the questions I'd been waiting for. I'd done some thinking about how I would answer them.

He'd disappeared once before, I told her. There had been a girl. Nobody special, just an extra. They hang around a few months, then go back to Montana or Pennsylvania, wherever it was they first fell in love with Gable's shadow. This one lived in Indiana, I said, a little town called Fairmount.

"Are you telling me," she asked, "that he did this... often?"

"No," I said. "I just thought if he did it once, he might do it again."

"How did you find out? Did he talk about that sort of thing?"

"It happened one day when we were between pictures," I

told her. "Berenice called me to ask if I knew where he was. I hadn't even known he was out of town. Then one night months later we were out on my boat. He was a little drunk, told me about the girl in Fairmount. I matched up the time he mentioned with Berenice's call. When he disappeared again, I thought of her. I drove there and looked her up."

She had never stopped looking at me, though whether her eyes were on my mouth or my eyes I couldn't say.

"I don't mean this to sound like a third degree," she said after a pause, "but you were gone six weeks. Did it take all that time to—"

I was ready for that one, too. The girl had turned out to be married, I said. I had a hard time finding her under her new name. She hadn't seen Vico. Then on the way back I'd had car trouble. I was holed up in an Iowa hotel for a few days, and started drinking. The few days had turned into a few weeks.

"After all," I said, "what was the rush? If they found him, I'd hear it on the radio. See it in the papers. I've had some vacation time coming anyhow, and I didn't feel like going to work on whatever Krackenpov threw my way. Besides, I had some thinking to do."

She must have caught the wobble in my voice. It made her look at her coffee. She lifted one hand and patted the air with it and murmured, "No need, no need. I forget. It hit you hard, too."

The wobble had been real. My story was tidy and uncheckable and I was hating every word. My old habits, a lifetime of disguises, kept slapping putty noses and spirit-gum sideburns over the face I wanted to expose. Beth was born in Fairmount. Once she left me, and I'd gone there to bring her back. The farm where her parents lived was flat in every direction. Standing on her front porch I'd talked her into taking a walk with me. I was shivering in my California clothes. There was brittle ice in the field ruts and no place within half a mile where we couldn't be seen from her father's kitchen window. She opened her coat to let me warm my hands against her body and let me bring her back out to the sunshine to die.

So I kept talking, making faces in the mirror to see if I could find one Lisa would like.

"The night I called you," I said, "just before I left, I couldn't tell you what was on my mind. That's why I made up that crazy story about Vico's mob connections—which don't exist. If I was wrong about the girl, there wasn't any need to let you think he might do something like that. If I was right, I'd have brought him back and never told you where I found him."

That's when I went dry.

Her wan smile might have been forgiving or full of contempt. "You boys stick together, don't you," she said.

3. Seductions

SHE LEANED BACK against the couch, eyes closed, lamplight wrapped along her throat. The front of the purple dress was a kind of elegant swaddling, the fabric crossing her breast from shoulder to hip. My eye fell on the low V between her breasts where one fold of the dress dove under the other. I wondered if my fingertips on that soft throat would startle her, thought how my hand might glide beneath the cleft of the dress and cup her breast. She seemed to know how long my thoughts could be left to stray on their own.

"The night after he disappeared," she said, "just before you called, in fact—I was lying in bed. Lying in the dark with my hand on the switch of my bed lamp. I wanted to think, but if something I couldn't handle came into my mind, I could turn on the light and make it go away. Does that sound crazy, Farley?"

"I lie awake in the dark, too," I said, "and think all sorts of things. It's the only way to make certain thoughts come."

"Just as the phone rang I was about to switch on the light.

The thought that had come to me was this: I'm not the crazy one. All these months it wasn't me. It was Eric."

"No need to switch on the light there," I said. "I can't see why you thought you were crazy, but deciding you're not—well, it shouldn't send you screaming into the night, should it?"

"I know," she said. "But it didn't work that way." How had I never before noticed that in profile the curve of her upper lip was the tender hint of a snarl? "What I'd been thinking, I guess, is that if I were the sick one, he would take care of me. I could do what he said and be cured. That's why I let him cast me as Frau Stauffer. He seemed so certain, and it was his world, wasn't it? What do I know about acting, about movies? About this town? But if he's the crazy one, nothing changes, you see. Because it's *still* his world. If we're lying in bed together and he whispers to me... whispers a plan, and I can see it's crazy, what can I do? Tell him? When you're an artist, he says, when you're trying to get at the truth... And then he whispers, Keep trying. Pretty soon you'll understand. And how can I tell him that's what scares me?"

I held my breath. Here was a Vico I'd never seen. All in a second I thought: *Stop her. You don't want to hear more. You're not some drooling fan.* And then, like a voluptuous whisper filling my skull: *Snatch that last mask of his away—and you'll know what Spyhawk knows. You'll know how Spyhawk trapped him.* And then, sharp as pain, quick as toothache when you bite: *What if he's alive?* A wave crashed on the beach below, spilled a lazy murmur up the sand. *Once she gives him away to you,* the murmur said, *she'll never take him back.* I let out my breath.

"You didn't have to go crazy at all," I said quietly. "You could do exactly what you did. Pack a bag and say you want a divorce."

"You can if you're sure," she said. "I wasn't, even when I left. And of course it's easier if you don't—"

"If you don't love him?"

That came out less gently than I'd expected. She took such

a long time peeling away each of Vico's masks. But I remembered how long it had taken me. You never quite stop loving the illusion, that moment when you think you've been singled out, not even when you can see his next disguise grinning beneath it. I told her Vico was a hard person to feel only one way about. She fixed me with a slanting look, like one of mine in a mirror, that tries to spy you sideways. "You can't love him," I said, "without wanting to kill him." And I raised my cup in a mock toast to prove I was kidding. My saying the worst would free her to think it, too, and that would ease her mind. But she was still staring sideways and I had to say more.

"This talk about Vico's crazy plans," I said, "I don't understand it. Unless you're going to tell me that what he whispered to you is that he planned to wait for the worst storm of the decade and then go for a swim in the Pacific."

She was still looking.

"Lisa," I said, "I've sat with him at that desk by the window through seven script sessions in as many years. I've listened to him frothing about shots he wants to get—a close-up of an eyeball with a pendulum swinging in the pupil; or a slow-motion shot of a woman falling from a tower, and he'll sit right there and tell you, Farley, as she turns in the air, I want to move in tight and catch her smiling as she falls. It *all* sounds crazy till you see it in the rushes."

Without quite knowing when, I had crossed to the desk by the window and was standing between it and Lisa as if there were something on it I didn't want her to see. I'd broken out of the circle of light. By the time I ended my little speech, I'd imagined I would be shouting across the room. But the air between us was thick as a whisper.

She was coming toward me, saying, "Did he ever tell you how he got ideas like that, Farley? Did you ever see him before he had a finished script?"

Outside the circle of light I could look away, fiddle with that breasty paperweight that had squatted on top of so many Vico scripts.

"He always went into hiding to work up a script," I said.

He was like some old miner. His last days in town, when he was already thinking about the new picture, you could almost see him looking over his shoulder to make sure he wouldn't be followed. Then for a while he'd be gone. The day he'd call me to start work, he'd meet me at the door smelling like earth, like some bedrock cave where he'd gone to chip away at his mother lode.

"When he got back," I said, "I'd be the first person he'd seen in six weeks. Sometimes on a weekend he might sneak into town to see Berenice, but she was never with him while he was writing."

"This year was different," she said. "I was with him every day. In the same rooms, anyway. A body beside his in bed. Sometimes."

I didn't have to ask what it was like. She leaned against the desk, looking out the window, down the tunnel of shadowy palms to the invisible wedge of beach where I'd first seen her, before I knew she'd be anything to me but another Berenice. What she said made me trust my instincts. It wasn't by accident that my little joke about Vico whispering wild plans in the dark had reminded me of the Kill-You-Annabelle Letters.

"Sometimes," she said, "I would look up from a book and see him staring at me, and wonder if he saw me. I'd say, Hi, honey, and he would go on staring. If I said it again, he'd blink and say he'd been thinking, and then without even looking away, he wouldn't be seeing me anymore."

I was disappointed. This was nothing more than a hard-working artist mildly neglecting his wife. A bride, of course, but a day comes in any honeymoon when you settle the hotel bill and go back to work. I told her so. A gentle scold, I thought, would prove I could take Vico's part and make it mean more when I didn't. It might also jar loose the real brutalities I knew she would hide till the last.

I could see my scolding had stung her. She was straining against the impulse to tell me everything. In the shadow by the desk her eyes and cheeks were hollowed as if the flesh behind her face were contracting with shock. The faint lines around her mouth had deepened into a glimpse of the permanent crease that would settle there in fifteen, twenty years. I knew how to wait. "You're wrong, Farley," she said, "it wasn't just during working hours." Her hand went halfway to her mouth. She wasn't hooked yet. If I forced it now, I'd get nothing. I shrugged. Not the we-boys-stick-together shrug that would have cut her off, but sympathetic. Sympathetic and puzzled. Then I took my risk.

"I've lost my taste for coffee," I said. "Do you think he would mind if I poured myself a glass of sherry?"

The liquor cabinet was against the far wall with a round African shield hung above it. If I'd had to leave the room, leave the thick shadows, the dim core of light by the couch, I'd never have taken the chance. The shadows absorbed her voice, gave it no more life in the world than it had inside her head. In the bright kitchen, bouncing off the angular walls, her voice would have startled her into silence. I squatted at the open liquor cabinet, my hand over the brandy bottle, hesitating. The brandy would be harsh. She would leave most of a glass untouched. Sherry goes down smooth. If I kept her glass full, she'd keep her mouth wet. I brought up the sherry and two glasses.

I didn't look at her until I turned and handed her the glass. She'd followed me over to the liquor cabinet. She glanced at the glass, her lower lip sucked between her teeth, then at me, eyes narrowed.

"Take a little," I said. "It's been a long night. More coffee will just keep you awake."

She took the glass.

"It wasn't just during working hours," she said.

I slipped my hand around her elbow and steered her back toward the couch, the circle of light. I brought the sherry bottle with me. "Here, be comfortable," I said, and moored her in her place on the couch. I put the bottle and my empty glass on the coffee table, then pulled a low wicker chair up close to her. Sitting side by side with her I only got her face when

I could lure her away from a profile. I wanted a front shot, full face. I poured some sherry and raised my glass. Her hand followed mine with her own glass, her lips touched the rim just as mine did. We drank.

Gently as I could I said, "Did you expect a nine-to-five job? Bankers' hours? That's not how it works."

"It's not that," she said. "Once the picture took hold of him"—she took another sip—"he was never with me. When he wasn't sketching or writing dialogue, he would be inventing little—" She gulped the words down.

"Tell me," I said. I was gentle. "I want to find him. Anything you say might be the clue I need."

"Inventing little scenes for me to play."

For a moment it was like opening a furnace door—a hot blast of fury and a hiss on the word "scenes" that made it writhe. That sounded like what I'd been dreading, some secret fascination that could hold her even while she hated it.

"Scenes for the film?" I asked. But the furnace door closed. She took a deep shivering swallow of sherry. I recognized the impulse, read it like my image in a mirror. It was slow coming, but she was giving him up to me. Just as he had given up Berenice that night on *The Merry Widower.* Just as I'd given him up to Hoensinger. Whichever way I looked, I saw a Judas looking back. A Judas—who longs to betray every trust. All that once was sweet to hear—the whispered secret, the final private self exposed—throbs like a festering tooth till we beg to have it drawn. It's only later, exploring the tender absence with our tongue, that we remember what we've lost along with the pain.

"Tell me," I said.

She took a sip of sherry, then put the glass on the coffee table as if there were only one right place for it to be.

"Did you know," she said, "we met at Lindy's?"

I filled her glass and sat back to let her talk.

"Did you?" she said.

"Did I what?"

"Did you know we met at Lindy's?"

I didn't know how to answer. Her look, for a single instant, had been a wide glare.

"I'm not sure," I said. I was stammering. "He might have mentioned—"

"Because I want to know, Farley." Her eyes were softer now, but still fixing mine, not letting me look anywhere but back at her. I wondered if I had imagined the glare. "I'll tell you about Lindy's, about the night we met," she said. "I'll tell you other things, too. But when I'm finished, I want your version. *His* version."

She didn't wait for me to protest or deny. She seemed determined not to let me say anything she would have to not believe. She started talking, telling me the story Monty Druhl and a hundred other reporters had been trying the last six weeks to pry out of her.

She never touched her glass again.

CHAPTER

XX

1. Secrets of a Marriage

"I KEEP GOING OVER IT," she said, "trying to figure out what it was I did that night, what I might have said that— I wasn't out to seduce him, I wasn't flirting, wasn't even paying much attention to the conversation. The only thing steady in my mind, the thing I kept coming back to, at first anyway, until he got my attention, was that bus ticket to Columbus. It was in my purse. Now and then I would rest the side of my hand against my purse, and I'd think, Tomorrow at eight twenty-seven I get on the bus. This time next week or next month or however long it takes to get a real job I'll be standing at a cash register at Woolworth's or taking orders in the Busy Bee Café and fussing with my mother about whether I ought to sign up for some college courses, and if I thought about him at all, at first, what I thought was that tomorrow I would get off the bus and say, 'Guess who I had dinner with my last night in New York?'"

It had been a blind date, she said, and Vico hadn't even been her date. The girl she shared an apartment with, another model, had arranged a double date with a couple actors in a new show. The party was one of those opening-night nail biters. I'd been to enough of them, the West Coast version, to know what it was like. The cast and director pull together four or five tables and drink till the newspapers hit the streets. Everybody rattles the ice in his glass and laughs too loud at jokes he hasn't caught. The gofer who brings in the papers has always peeked at the reviews before he hands them to the director and you can tell by his face whether the party will end in crows or groans. Vico once told me actors are people with no place to hide. As usual, I said, you're hamming it. An actor hides inside his mask.

At that party lots of masks must have developed new cracks in the smile lines. I remember the reviews. Gangster slang in blank verse, strikebreakers shaking hands with union men over the body of a mangled worker, then all marching off to bring the boss to his knees.

"Then there was my date," Lisa said. "During the show Cathy had nudged me and said, 'That's him,' but when we went backstage afterwards, I didn't recognize him until he picked the Andy Gump mustache off his dressing table and held it under his nose." Lisa's date had played an assembly-line worker who goes berserk and pours a bucket of bolts into the spinning gears of a steam turbine.

What Lisa couldn't figure out was precisely when or how he disappeared from the chair beside her and left Vico in his place. "Evaporated," she said. "As if he were a one-day extra Eric had hired to—" And she stopped, struggling to get it out. I knew the feeling. It was one of those thoughts that pour right through the words.

"Someone he hired?" I said. "Hired for what?"

"To bait the trap," she said.

There it was at last. To bait the trap. That was my first hint of how much he'd been in control: that she could imagine, maybe not out loud, but in one of those dreamy smothering suspicions, that Vico was somehow powerful enough, devious enough to have arranged her presence at the party before she'd even met him, maybe even arranged the party itself as a way to draw her in.

"One minute I was sitting next to my Andy Gump without his mustache," she said, "and the next time I looked it was Eric introducing himself just as if I didn't already know his face like my own fath—"

And that would have been part of it, too, part of the tension between them. He was a good thirteen years older. But that night, at that first meeting, his age was in his favor. It gave him authority. Not that he didn't have competition that night. Somebody in the cast must have had important connections. At the far end of the table John Barrymore was intoning obscene jokes in iambic pentameter. And at Lisa's left elbow was somebody who claimed to be Paul Muni, though Vico later told her he was an impostor, a third-rate ham who once had a role in a Muni film and imitated him at cocktail parties. The Muni impostor had just begun telling her something about how doing *Scarface* had brought out a strain of brutality in him that he'd been trying ever since to control and there were hazards to the actor's life that nobody knew about. "I just laughed at him," she said. "I should have listened." By that time Vico was at her other elbow, beginning a gentle tug-of-war for her attention.

The role in which he had cast himself was the broken-hearted widower mourning his fair young bride. He established his character with typical economy—a single tossaway line about how he'd come East to keep from thinking too much. He could count on her having seen the "Strangler's Hands?" shot in all the papers, and then the headlines about his release. Nobody knew better than Vico that the only sin in courtship or art was to be dull. He didn't let his mourning gloom stretch into pauses the Muni impostor might have filled. Film people on the make know their brightest lure is gossip. Over the first martini you tell a few grand-piano-dumped-in-the-swimming pool stories. By the next you're telling her what Gable said about Garbo and when your hand slips over her wrist, she thinks she's just been cast in *Grand Hotel.* But Vico was always Vico. He seduced his future bride with a passionate lecture on documentary movies. He talked a lot about Flaherty and said studios had to get off the soundstage and out in the sunshine. Look at *Greed,* he said. What makes it great is von Stroheim renting a city block in San Francisco, shooting his actors in rooms where people really lived. In her other ear the Muni impostor was murmuring a soliloquy: "Every time you shave, you face the brute head on. He looks back from the mirror and says, 'So. You know me. Now what?'" The best set designer in town,

Vico was saying, can't make a room look like a place where people have sweated and wept, counted their money, made love. What you had when von Stroheim was finished wasn't just a story, it was a slice of time. You read it in the plaster cracks, handprints on the walls. It all sounded like talks Vico'd had with me at the Penguin Club. What instinct, I wonder, had told him it would be more interesting than the Muni impostor's soul-baring?

"It wasn't what he said," Lisa explained. "It was that he cared so much about it and never bothered to wonder whether I did too."

I knew all about Vico's passion for von Stroheim. It was because von Stroheim had gone to Death Valley to shoot the last scenes of *Greed* that Vico took us there for the desert scenes in *Cain.* He loved the desert—right up to the day of the explosion that mutilated Singleton. Two days after the accident we went back for a few pickup shots. On the trip home he told me that morning he'd driven out alone so he could go for an early walk before shooting started. "I saw the sun come up, Farley," he told me. "I saw lizards, groundhogs, coyotes. There's a better picture out here than anything we've shot. Better than anything Von shot, too." And when we looked at the rushes, the shot he liked best was an accident—a whirlwind out on the dunes, weaving like a drunken top. He told her about that shot.

The Muni impostor sulked for a while, then said his goodnights and walked out with a chin-high stride Vico whispered to her the real Muni had stolen from Mussolini to use in *Scarface.* The last she'd heard from the impostor was a tender, wistful voice at her elbow asking, "Anyone ever spread-eagle you to the bedposts?"

Fade to black. Then a quick montage: Vico and his lady nestled in booths in various swing-band nightclubs, his lips seldom more than an inch from her ear, his voice close to a shout. And finally, after a week or so condensed to a few seconds of film, the two of them spun through a revolving door onto a city street, crowds and car horns, a momentary silence, and he says, "How about a drive in the country? A little peace and quiet." By this time the bus ticket to Ohio, still in her purse, was limp and frayed. The next day he called for her in a rented pigeon-gray Dusenberg. The country turned out to be Saratoga, where they stayed—in separate rooms, she specified—in a hotel with a lobby full of pier-glass mirrors and Victorian knickknacks and broadleaf plants that a maid spent a good deal of her morning polishing to a fine oily glow.

Her account told me how much time she had spent since then hauling each detail of that weekend out of her memory, holding it up to the light. As she put one fact beside another, sometimes starting a sentence, then dropping it, but later coming back, fitting the discarded idea next to another, her voice grim and patient, I saw that she was fitting together pieces of a puzzle, turning them over more for herself than for me, searching for clues to the pattern.

She remembered breakfast at the racetrack, watching morning workouts from the clubhouse porch, their table so close each gallop was a coming thunder, a rushing wind, mud clots tossed high off the hooves. She remembered a diamond-studded horseshoe ring on the hand of the maître d', who walked like a ballroom dancer and talked through a Bronx nose. She remembered peppermint-striped awnings and grandstand windowboxes planted with white petunias and red geraniums, and the loudspeaker baritone that rang out clear about one word in five. He loved to watch the horses run, she said, and told her anybody who needed money riding on their backs to get a thrill out of it would probably have had a bet down on how long it would take da Vinci to finish the *Mona Lisa*. Then he said it again, she told me: Lisa. Mona Lisa, and he ran his fingers along her cheek. She teased him about being afraid to bet, and he told her his father would sit over the supper table with him when he was six, matching pennies, and when all Eric's pennies were gone and he began to blubber, his mother would say, "He's just a kid, Ed, give him back his money," and his father would say, "That'll teach him not to gamble."

And it was only years later that his mother told him his father's father would sometimes bring home a paycheck on Friday night and sometimes just a long story about sure-thing hot tips, as if the proof that his judgment was sound and only dumb luck had robbed him could put potatoes on the table.

My daddy, he told her, didn't leave enough to buy his coffin when he went, but his gambling lesson was good as a legacy. When she saw a three-year-old called Be Merry dancing up to the starting gate, he shot her the bird-quick glance of a tout they had brushed off earlier and offered to bet her a kiss that it would win. "Yes, right there," she said. "That's when I should have been warned." And a flicker of satisfaction lifted her brow, and I saw she had fitted in place another piece of the puzzle. Just as the gong started, he said the stakes were too low. Why not make the prize a wedding ring? "Nothing romantic about it," she said. "Not after what he'd said about his father and gambling. There was a look in his eye—reckless, frightened maybe, hating something, hating me I think, or maybe himself." She walked away from him, broke into a run, got through the gate and out under the cool trees where the cars were parked before he managed to grab her, hug both her arms, hold them down to her sides, which was the only way he could stop her from twisting free, and with them both panting, their faces an inch apart, he said, "Will you stop a minute, will you listen?" until she said yes and he loosened his grip.

She had an old uncle, she said, who kept a canary, and when she came to visit he would ease his hand inside the cage and coax it onto his finger. Just like that, Vico lifted a tear from the end of her nose. "He was looking right into my eyes," she said, "and without even blinking, not thinking of anything except what he wanted to say to me, he put his finger in his mouth to taste the salt in my tear. What would it matter what he said after that? How could you say anything to him but yes?" That evening, sitting on the hotel piazza watching the promenade of society people from the spas and track fans in two-colored shoes with racing forms sticking out of their jacket pockets and a solitary black-clad, breast-length-black-bearded Hasidic Jew, they read in the newspaper that Be Merry had finished last in a field of eight.

"But—Christ!" she said. "Could it have been that simple? Did I give away my *life* because I liked the goofy way he dried my tears?"

"I don't know," I said. "He had a language that didn't need words. Sometimes I'd think a script on the page was pretty flat. Then he'd get in front of the camera. He'd slide up on a word and take a breath before he said it. He'd cut a line altogether, stick in a shrug, or twist his finger in his goddam ear—and it would say *more.* Sometimes just the second he'd pick to look away could... reach inside you."

"So in order to know what I was saying yes to," she said, "I have to translate the language. Figure out what he was saying, what he wanted from me. What did he want, Farley? Not a wife. Certainly not a wife."

"Maybe a muse," I said. "An inspiration, somebody who would—"

"Or a whore. More like a whore. Just look at the casting. It would have to be somebody he thought would *like* it when he stripped her in front of a couple dozen men."

"I'm not sure that's a fair way to see it."

"I wonder. That's how it ended, though, isn't it? So maybe thinking something like that might have been in his mind from the first isn't *completely* unfair. Especially when there are other hints along the way. But you wouldn't know about those, would you, Farley? Unless he told you? Did he? Did he tell you, Farley?"

Her questions were a hungry prodding, maybe random, maybe aimed someplace only Spyhawk would know was vulnerable. They were dangerous, and more dangerous because of the sweet throb in her voice that made me believe nothing I could say wouldn't be forgiven.

"Did he tell me what?" I said, and she said, "The way we lived."

I didn't really know how she'd been straining for an answer

till she gave it up, let the back of the couch take a little more the weight of her body. She let out a long breath, then dropped her eyes, seemed to release me, seemed to have decided maybe I didn't know after all what she suspected I knew, or if I did it was no use trying to make me tell. She raised her face to me again, but not her eyes, not all the way to mine, and smiled that pale, curled-at-the-ends smile that had made Vico say, Lisa, Mona Lisa.

"Maybe we're both right," she said. "Maybe for the kind of inspiration he wanted, a whore was just the right muse."

"Don't you think you're getting carried away?" I said. "Surely that day at the racetrack he wasn't planning—"

"No, I don't," she said. "That day in Saratoga was when *I* got carried away. Not now, not tonight. Tonight I'm asking the questions I should have been asking then." She was looking hard at me again, fixing me in place. "I think from the first night he saw me, what he wanted was that moment on the set when he reached out and grabbed the front of my nightgown. You didn't see the look in his eye, did you? His back was to the camera. Oh, Farley. It was pure *satisfaction*. That's how I read it anyway. Satisfaction and hate." I tried to interrupt, but there was no talking to her. "If it wasn't, if that wasn't what he wanted from me, then why haven't I seen him since?" She started to reach for her drink, then stopped herself, dropped her hand to her lap and covered it with the other. "It's just a question of translating the language, isn't it? If I could do that, I'd see that everything he said, everything he did, led up to it, promised it, should have warned me of it." She was talking barely above a whisper, almost to herself. "You're the one who called it a language, and you were right. But if that's so, if it was a language, without words but a language, and if I understood it, *knew* without words what he wanted—then what made me say yes?"

I tried to reason with her.

"It wasn't a plan, it was an impulse. You're giving it more—"

But she wasn't hearing.

"What was it in me that heard what he said, and said yes—yes, I like the music, and I'll dance."

I insisted that what had happened was an impulse. I made a case for it, talking about Vico's improvisations on the set, how he would sometimes go too far in order to loosen up some blocked place inside him. I could think of a dozen examples. I started telling her about when he opened the hand of Captain Fantomese with his teeth. I wasn't even thinking why I wanted to defend him. Maybe I knew the one I was really covering for was Spyhawk. But she cut me off.

"If it was impulse," she said, "then why wasn't I surprised?"

There was nothing I could say.

"I think I know why," she said. "I think maybe I was translating that silent language of his all along. Translating in my sleep, and then as soon as I got out of bed, erasing everything I knew. Because it sounded too much like a Vico movie to be true."

Ah! Her, too. I thought of that first read-through of *Loves of a Spy,* the moment I recognized that he was holding up to my face a funhouse-mirror shot of my blab session with Hoensinger. So: I wasn't the only one he'd gone after. He drained us all. First Berenice, till it killed her. Then me. And Lisa, which was what I'd feared all along.

"But I'm getting it back," she was saying. "Since he's been gone, I work it out, a little one day, more the next. Putting together all the little..." She held the word a long time. "...scenes." Like me, I thought, sweating in my room at the Silver Palms, writing my confession.

"Do you know, Farley," she said, "I think the first time there was really no excuse for me to have ignored it, to have not known it would all end in something very nasty and vicious, was just two days after the wedding."

I waited. She was giving him up.

"Tell me," I said.

"You'll appreciate it," she said. "It could have been one of his best scripts."

She was right. I could pick out his opening shot. She's

alone in their hotel suite, sitting on a couch, one leg tucked under her, reading a *Vogue* picture spread. "I expected him back any minute," she said. "We had a date to shop for luggage." She had been thinking not of the elegant clothes and driftwood-dappled beach, but of the sun. The glaring reflectors that doubled the heat, the torture of holding a pose. Then, a knock at the door. Two more knocks before she can cross the room. She opens the door. Over-the-shoulder shot: a round-shouldered man in steel-rimmed glasses. His eyebrows spring up stiff beyond the rims, his gray hair frizzles down over his ears. "Ahh!" he caws, and his arms fan out. "Since all the movies, it's been a curse. Headwaiters, hack drivers, they all spot the family mug." And his hands grab her shoulders, he drops a kiss on her left eyebrow, swings past her into the room and calls out, "Where's my baby brother?"

Before she can say a word, he's rummaging through kitchen cupboards, clattering glasses and ice cubes, cawing about his insurance business and his brother's sloppy housekeeping, and within a few minutes she finds herself at nine-thirty in the morning with a gin and tonic in her hand, perched on the edge of the couch while the little man prowls the room, saying, "Since you are embarking on a marriage to this wastrel brother of mine, there is one thing I must tell you. Watch for a lump at the foot of the bed. It's the jokes that signal his worst attacks. He doesn't mean them to be cruel, of course—scarcely means anything at all once an attack starts, and naturally during the sanitarium periods—generally about six weeks, by the way—he's just blotto: all lights out, phone off the hook. You know what I mean. But the jokes come first and I want to tell you, even today I can't slip under the covers without a shiver. Ugh! Warm your toes against a dead rat once, you don't forget it. Now when the attacks hit him, the number to call is—surely he's told you all this? Why, that *bas*tard, that *ly*ing *lun*atic, we always said that a man with his . . . *diff*iculties should never marry, but not even to warn his bride what she could—"

"Stop it," she'd said, and when she told me, she was trembling just as she must have been at the time. "Stop it, Eric."

Of course, when he saw her like that, blinking tears and her fingers pressed over her mouth, he grew two inches just by straightening his back and a quick pass sent the spectacles and gray wig flying, and he was holding her, stifling all but the faintest chuckle. By that night she had forgotten about it until she saw the lump under the covers at the foot of the bed, but it was only a slipper wrapped in a hand towel.

They spent the first part of their honeymoon watching movies in England and France. Why don't we ever get out into the sun, she said, and the next day he woke up insisting on a brief trip to Germany. Hitler was addressing a crowd that afternoon, the papers said, and he wanted to see firsthand the best actor in Europe. He had already bought train tickets before she convinced him he would have to go alone. He tore them up and said, "I'll catch it on the Movietone News."

Wherever they went he was at it: Working his trade, he called it. What trade, I wanted to know. "What would you call it?" she said. "Bumping into strangers and walking away with their souls—he was a kind of spiritual pickpocket." He would be ordering dinner, and suddenly she'd hear the reedy baritone of the diamond merchant who had wanted an autograph that morning in the elevator. Planning the day's itinerary she asks if he would prefer the British Museum or the Tower of London, and looks across the breakfast table at the loose-lipped scowl of the bellboy who had brought them tea rather than coffee.

"Did he think I had to be convinced he was an actor?" she said. "I'd seen his movies."

She wasn't stupid. She'd spotted the pattern. As on the day of his proposal, it was when a strong feeling surfaced that her husband turned into a stranger. "I kept telling myself it was nerves," she said. "He's scared as you are. Once he trusts you, he'll change. Thinking that way, you can get by for a while. You ignore a lot. You swallow a lot. Then one day something comes along that you can't swallow. Can't get it down."

They'd quarreled. She'd gone alone to the British Museum, he'd gone to a matinee of Laughton's *Henry VIII.* When she gets back, he meets her at the door. He's doing a forelock-tugging cockney, and he explains that while she was out, mum, there'd been a transatlantic cable and, well, mum, her sainted mother had passed to her reward. She's half ready to laugh and throw her arms around him, her usual sign that she's had enough, when she sees in his hand the yellow telegram slip.

"I felt," she said, "the way you do just before you vomit."

But when she burst into tears, he did, too, till she had to hold him and rock him and croon it was all right.

"He picked my pocket, too, didn't he?" she said. "My mother was dead and he walked off with the whole scene."

"Why didn't you leave him?" I asked. "Just get on a plane and go home to your mother's funeral and not come back?"

"I thought about it. I wasn't ready yet to call the rest of my life a failure."

"A failure?" I said.

"It's supposed to last a lifetime, isn't it?" she said. "Three weeks isn't much of a try. Besides—for a while I thought things might be different. I could feel him straining, trying to reach me. Being such a good actor made it hard. He would give up too soon, because there was always someplace to hide. But I thought—just a little longer, and..."

I envied her. How easy it was, at twenty-four, to promise a lifetime away.

They flew home to her mother's funeral and continued their honeymoon in New York City. The first night in town they met some friends for dinner. Among them was the refugee journalist, Knopper. Vico spent the night grilling him about the Klamstadt case in Germany. The next day she found him with a sketchbook, blocking out the prison set for *Loves of a Spy.* Soon he was littering the hotel suite with scraps of dialogue, sketches for scenes with notes on camera angles. No more taffy-stretched jaws or scowls and leers. His voice, she said, was always Eric's voice, only far away as a phrase on a stuck gramophone. At first she was relieved.

After a week the work stopped. He paced the suite, leaving food half-eaten, gouging pencil holes in his desk top. She asked what was the trouble. All he would say was, "The *man*, the *man*—I can't find the *man*." And he wandered off to a window as if the man might be waiting outside under a lamp post. That night when he came to bed she asked again, and this time he tried to explain. "I can get the story all right. Anybody with half a brain could spot the scenes, the dramatic turns. But I can't connect with what makes it *Klamstadt's* story. I can't find the *man*."

Which struck me as odd, since I'd always thought of Klamstadt as just a convenient skeleton for Vico's portrait of a Judas cameraman.

"Does it have to be Klamstadt's story?" she asked. "What if his family tries to sue you?"

"All the better," he told her. "I'm tired of making up lies."

She had that figured out, too. It was his way of doing penance. He was spilling over with fantasies, but they'd frightened her, repulsed her. So he was giving them up. Working from life.

At dinner, Lisa said, he would try out voices, gestures. Not the way he used to, like putting on a hat or a jeweled ring, but from the inside, as if he were someone with amnesia, puzzling out the names of his children and how many wives he'd had. Then he announced that he had to go home. He could only work at the beach house. That was the end of the honeymoon.

Once there, she said, he showed her where to sleep and where the bathroom was. Then, after a single morning with her on the beach, he disappeared into the study. For a week or ten days he would blink across the table at her as if he couldn't figure out how this strange woman came to be sitting with the spy, Klamstadt. "So there I was," she said. "Like a houseguest who doesn't know when to go home. We were together in bed, of course, and at meals. Except he'd told me if he was in the middle of something I should eat without him. The day he finished it was dinnertime, and I'd just started. I heard the study door open. His footsteps in the hall. Then I could *feel* him in the doorway, but he wouldn't come in till I looked up from my plate. It was an actor's entrance: He couldn't cross a room without an audience. So I looked up. He crossed the room. He slapped down in front of me this thick stack of pages. 'For you,' he said. 'The best female role of the decade.' Those were the words he used: best in a decade." She was looking at me calmly, her lips expressionless, daring me not to be outraged.

"But he'd remembered you, hadn't he?" I said. "Made you part of it. Brought you into the circle."

"Not *me*," she said. "It was never me he wanted. Not all of me. He'd just found a way to suck out what he could use and spit it into his damn script."

To be rid of him, to be really free, I knew she'd have to scrape raw every place in her he'd touched, hand over every memory. Asking for it would only make her protect him. So I found ways to defend him.

"But you know," I said, "in a sense I was right. You were a muse to him."

"Oh, yes, I'd forgotten. So I was. Shall I tell you what a muse is, Farley? If you were a *Tablet* reporter, I could give you an exclusive: A Day in the Life of a Hollywood Muse. First off, it's not something you *do*. There's no work involved, nothing to think about and sweat over and get better at and master. What you do being a muse is hang around. When the artist passes through on his way for a ham sandwich, you offer a suitable cheek for a kiss. When he frowns and says things are going badly, you sigh and give your eyes a few inspirational bats. But once he takes his ham sandwich and goes back into the study and closes the door—you mostly hang around. The muse takes her towel down to the beach and gets a nice tan. She reads a few books. And when she sees him at dinner, she says, 'Why don't you take a break tonight? We could drive into town and see a movie.' And he says, 'Not tonight,' because he's doing important work and things are going badly, which means you've not been a very good muse. But that doesn't bother the muse. All the muse *wants* is a night in town, away from the tough, demanding grind of being a muse, and she can hear the whine in her voice when she asks for it, and hates what she hears, but she keeps asking anyway, until he says yes.

"Then, the night he's promised is going to be hers, he goes back to his study after dinner. 'I'll just be a minute,' he says. So she changes her dress. She waits, tries to concentrate on a book. She never even goes to the door to see what's keeping him, because that morning he's told her things are going badly and he can't be disturbed, and when the man you're living with has had three Academy nominations in as many years, you don't just tell him a night in town is more important than his work. Finally she gets in the car and goes off alone. She stays out late, late enough to make him worry. When she gets back there's still a light in the study. She goes straight to the bedroom and goes to bed and waits half an hour till she can pretend not to notice when she hears him undressing in the dark. She feels him sit on the bed and he whispers, 'Lisa,' very tender, like a sigh, and she's thinking, *Here comes the apology—well, it's not going to be that easy*, when he says, 'It's time I told you the truth about our marriage.'"

That was Vico. Nobody ever took a scene from him.

"That's when the muse starts to tremble," Lisa said. "She tries to ask what he means, and chokes on it. The artist stretches out on the bed. He puts his hands under his neck as if he's completely alone in the room, thinking out loud. 'I don't know whether I really love you,' he says. He won't look at her. 'I'm ugly,' he says. 'I've known I was ugly since I was three years old. What if—what if I wanted to find out whether a woman like you, a *beautiful* woman like you'—and oh, how he croons when he says it—'would really live with me?' For a second all the muse can think of is a hotel wastebasket in Saratoga. That's where I threw my ticket home to Columbus. And then she says, 'What *if*? *Did* you? Don't you *know*?' And here's what the artist says: 'I'm not sure. Help me. Help me find out.' And he grabs her and buries his head against her warm muse belly and she feels him sobbing. After a minute his tears soak through the sheet. Artist's tears. First they're hot, artist's tears. Then they get clammy."

"Christ," I said. "Jesus Christ." I was shaking my head, but she went on talking.

"They talk till dawn," she said. "Dissecting what the artist *feels.* Finally they agree that he must love her. They're pretty sure about it, almost certain. And they agree that she loves him, too, and didn't marry him just because he was a movie star—yes, they got to that, too. Then he wants to make love, and when he's finished—when he's finished, he gets out of bed and starts dressing. And she—and the muse says, 'You've been up all night. Don't you want to sleep?' And he told me—he said he'd been working out a scene and had to go finish it, and thanks to me, he knew how it had to go. And I said, what did he mean, thanks to me? And he leaned over the bed and gave me a peck on the brow and said, 'I don't know what got into me. I always, *al*ways knew I loved you.'"

She looked at me. I waited for something to say.

"Is that what you meant, Farley," she said, "when you told me Eric married me to be his muse?"

She wanted an answer. Finally I said, "He made you his guinea pig."

"That's too easy," she said. "It's more complicated than that, isn't it, Farley?"

"You seem to think I know."

"Don't you?"

"I'm not sure," I said. "What makes you think so?"

"Do you need to ask? When he talked about his pictures, there was a *we* in everything he said. 'Then *we* set up the shot.' 'So *we* told Krackenpov he could this or that.' At first I thought *we* was the whole cast, the whole crew. But something came through in the way he said it—you couldn't feel that way about a gang. 'Who's *we*?' I said, and he shrugged as if I'd asked a riddle and the answer was so simple he couldn't quite believe there wasn't a trick to it. 'Farley,' he said. 'Me and Farley. He's my eyes.' You think I couldn't guess? Just seeing you together—even before that, hearing your voices from down the hall, that night you came to talk about the script—you think I couldn't guess what was between you? All the things that might get said? You were sitting over there at his desk, the two of you, making your plans. I stood in the doorway a long time, wondering. Whether I had any right to intrude. I'd lived with him a few months, woke with his body beside me in bed, felt him inside me—but there, under the light by the desk, talking across the coffee cups—there was the real marriage. You think I couldn't see it? I want to know what you talked *about*. Who he thought I *was* when he saw me standing there."

"We talked about the script," I said. She was veering close, not to Vico's secret but to mine, and I knew that whatever else I might confess, I could never tell her that the one *I'd* seen that night in the doorway with the backlight pouring through her dressing gown was Beth—my Beth, just as she'd been the last look I had of her. "Only about the script."

"Fine," she said. "Tell me about that. I want to know what part I was playing. Tell me, Farley. Knowing how I was used is the only way I can keep from being used again."

"You've seen the script. You memorized the lines. You know as much as I do."

"I think you know *more.* In seven years—seven years of *we,* on the set and in the bars and leaning over that desk with him—you picked up hints. You can guess where that script, that best female role in a decade, connects with things in me, things that he—couldn't get off his mind."

How could I tell what she was onto, how much he'd told

her? Maybe, for all I knew, the whole of what he'd learned from Hoensinger about how I'd blabbed.

"Why is it important?" I said. "He's gone. Dead. All you need is to forget him."

But she kept at me.

"Not yet," she said. "Not till I know who he thought I was. Tell me, Farley: When he looked at me—what would remind him of Berenice?"

"Nothing," I said. "You're nothing alike. Nothing at all."

"Something did. Because the *Loves of a Spy* script, the famous best female role in a decade, wasn't just for me. It was for her, too."

"What makes you think that?"

"He told me as much. We were arguing about whether I would play Madeline, and he said, 'Please, Lisa, you've got to help me get free of her,' and I said, 'Free of who?' 'Didn't you know?' he said. 'Madeline is Berenice.'"

I didn't know where the trap was, but I felt myself step into its shadow.

"All I know," I said, "is she didn't much like his pictures. The violence, the—strangeness. When she thought he'd gone too far, she would wheedle him to make changes, bleed out the highlights."

"Ah," she said, and I could tell she'd notched in place another piece of the puzzle. She even said it: "That fits. Maybe he recognized things in me I didn't know were there, cultivated them. If I'd gone on living with him, he might have turned me into her twin sister."

"What fits?" I said. "What did he do to you?"

"It slipped out during one of our fights. I was too angry to pay much attention. It's only this last few weeks I've wondered what he meant." She pulled a strand of hair across her cheek, made up her mind to tell me. "The night he kept me up all night deciding whether he loved me, getting ideas for his *scene*—it didn't end there. The next day while he was in town I sneaked into his study. I wanted to find out what kind of a *scene* he'd made me part of. I found his manuscript in the drawer. When he got home I was sitting in his chair, waiting. 'Do I get screen credit?' I said. 'It looks like I'm coauthor of this script.' 'That's private,' he said, and he took the manuscript off my lap. 'Private?' I said. 'It's going to be put on the screen and shown to millions of people. What's private is my *life.*' Farley, he'd taken things I said—things I told him with tears in my eyes, lying naked beside him after we'd made love—and put them word for word into his *script.*"

So: the Judas cameraman wasn't the only portrait from life in *Loves of a Spy.*

"I'd been trying," she said, "to explain why I got so crazy when he went days hardly noticing I was in the house. I told him about when I was in third grade and decided I didn't have a father. He was on the road so much he was like a guest in the house, and I made up my mind he was only *saying* he was my father. And there it was, like a page from my diary. Eric had got it all into one of Madeline's sweet little speeches. How little Madeline told all her friends at school and even her teacher that she didn't have a daddy, and the teacher called up her mother to inquire if there'd been a death in the family. It was a very touching speech. There were others, too. Things I thought he hadn't even heard."

"But he'd been listening all the time, then," I said. "He hadn't been ignoring you as much as you'd thought."

"That's what *he* said. 'It belongs to *me,*' I told him. 'I never said you could have it.' And he said, 'But I'm giving it *back* to you. I've told you—I want you to *play* Madeline.' And I said, 'You want me to say these lines as if they belong to a made-up character?' and he said, 'No—say them the way you said them to me last night.' And when I told him he had to take it out, he pointed to changes he'd made, talked about how the context gave what I'd said another meaning and it was really his speech now, I'd only *inspired* it. 'Take it out,' I said, and he said, 'I thought you'd be pleased. Using what you said was a secret between us, a way for me to tell you how I *love* you.' And I kept saying, 'Take it out.' And that's when he mentioned Berenice. 'You and Berenice,' he said. 'How do you think an artist works? You think I can sort out what's yours and mine? Sift every image, every snatch of dialogue to make sure I'm not remembering something you've told me?' And all I would say was, 'Take it out, it belongs to me.' That's when he seemed to get frantic, and he kept shrieking, 'You can't make me do this, you're trying to lock me out of my own mind.' And I said, 'It's *my* mind. My life. Take it out.' Sometimes while he was talking I would get the horrible feeling that he was *right,* that next to his film, a picture that might be a work of art, a masterpiece, my private self didn't mean much. But I—I kept thinking: If I give it up, what will I have that's me? What will be left? That terrified me. All I could say was 'Take it out.'"

"That speech of Madeline's," I said, "of yours, I mean. I recognize it. It was still in the final shooting script."

"Yes," she said. "I saw it, too. He promised he would take it out, but I guess—I guess he figured when we came to shoot it, he could coax me around. Convince me what a privilege it was to be an artist's muse. And all that talk about this being his last film was a good way to soften me up."

"Last film?" I said. "He never mentioned it to me."

"Exactly," she said. "Why should he? He wouldn't consciously lie, but it was something he only needed to believe when he was trying to convince me I was ruining his career, locking him out of his mind, as he called it. It was a threat, his way of begging permission to use every drop of me he could wring out."

She had given him up, I thought. He was more naked now than I'd ever seen him. My heart was knocking fast. I'd come to tell her the truth and I could tell it. He'd used her just as he had me, and she would know any defense against him had to be ruthless.

"I'd wondered," I said, "why you walked out on him during that last week of shooting. After what you've said, I guess I don't need to ask."

I was probing again, thinking of Vico's worry that she had a secret lover and testing whether she might reveal what had changed the way she responded to Bolger on the set. But I'd surprised her.

"At that point," she said, "leaving him never occurred to me."

"Have I been hearing you wrong?" I said. "This wasn't exactly the dream you'd had of what your married life would be."

"No. I try to remember what I *did* dream. I can't. The dream never stopped. I woke up inside *his* dream."

"Then why did you stay?"

"Why not?" she said with a wide smile. "Every day a new crisis. And he wasn't cocky anymore, not after he saw I wasn't going to let him fatten up his Madeline on choice morsels of my life. You see, he wanted not just to do it and not just for me to *let* him do it—he wanted me to *like* it. When I wouldn't, he treated me to a private performance: a Vico-going-crazy scene from a Vico movie. Moaning around the house, looking hollow-eyed, pounding his fist into walls. See that big cobwebby crack in the plaster? He couldn't hold a pen for three days after that. I had a giant jumping through hoops, Farley. It wasn't life, it wasn't a marriage, but it *was* fascinating." She stared at me, saying that—her teeth bared in a model's rictus smile. Then the rictus softened, her lips came together as if they'd exposed a deformity. "That's not true, that's not how I felt," she whispered quickly. "Maybe I wish it were. The fact is, until the last week on the set I was convinced that all he put me through was as much torture to him as to me, that if I once convinced him he could trust me, we could both wake up. That was what kept me in the dream—believing he needed me. On nights when he didn't close himself into his study again after supper, we would walk together on the beach. He could be... so tender ... so eager to ... 'Look at the gulls,' I'd say, 'the way the sun winks on their wings.' Or I'd pick up a piece of driftwood and say, 'Look how the wood splits along the grain.' And he'd say, 'Yes, *yes:* you give me eyes, you give me back my *eyes.*'"

Her voice was trembling, the beach below the study window was breathing as it had the night he'd said it, and I'd have sworn she never recalled, then or as he said it, that Vico had once called *me* his eyes.

"I might have stayed in his dream forever," she was saying, "if he hadn't—"

She faltered, clipped off a gasp, as if she'd caught herself falling into a doze at the wheel of a car.

I stayed quiet, hoping she'd drop back into the doze. Then, soft as I could and be heard, I said, "If he hadn't what? What did he do, Lisa, that finally made you leave?"

"One night," she said, "the night before we started shooting the bedroom scene, he left a little love note on my pillow. That's when I knew I had to get out."

I waited.

"Would you like to read it, Farley?" she said. "I'm sure he wouldn't mind. Let me get it. Maybe you can translate for me."

Before I could speak she was on her feet, had left the room. Her footsteps clacked on the bare wood floor of the hall, then disappeared into the living-room carpet. I heard the creak of a certain stair, then knew she was passing the door of the bathroom where the steam had come roiling out the night she discovered the overflowing bath, the blood-soaked towel, and then I could see by certain creakings near the ceiling above Vico's desk that she was in her bedroom, and a muffled sound showed me her yank at the bureau drawer by her bedroom window. She was back in little more than a minute, very slightly breathless.

"Here," she said. "Read it."

That's how I got my next-to-last portrait of Vico.

2. Secrets Exposed

HOW TO SET up the shot?

Start with a montage of self-revelations from the roles he played. The schoolmaster in *Discipline*—remember the funeral reception for the parents of the boy his torments drove to suicide? Think of the shot where he's passing the teacup to the mother with a tremor of barely suppressed hilarity. Cut to *The Mask of Don Juan,* the melancholy seducer fondling his lover's slipper, pressing it to his cheek like a fey Hamlet with Yorick's skull. Cut again, cut to the jewel thief in *Mark of Cain,* trapped between the glass wings of the jeweler's revolving door, cut to that close-up the moment he discovers that the wedged bulk preventing his escape is the corpse of his mistress, who bled to death while he ransacked the store, and his fists thump the glass as if what he is trying so desperately to shatter is the lens of my camera, which pulls back to show the crowd gathering on the street, the policeman pushing through. Now cut to this, a shot I never filmed: an empty bedroom in the beach house. Left foreground, a pillow. Beyond the counterpane, a door slowly opens. In comes a recently wedded actor, bearing a folded piece of paper. He leaves it on his wife's pillow and goes out.

It's easy to say what happens, but who—without Vico's genius—can say how to play it? Was there a hasty over-the-shoulder glance back to the door, nervous fingers fondling the paper? But it was after all his own house, his own bedroom as well as Lisa's. It's just as likely that he strolled in through an open door, flicked the note onto the pillow the way you sort a bill into a pile of other bills, and strolled out.

I think I can quote Vico's note word for word. I'm cursed, after all, with a photographic memory. It said: "You are going to try to give me your body. I am going to want it, want you so bad my prick stiffens when you enter a room. But I am going to turn away, try to turn away, so I can get something else instead. And we will have a fine tussle all alone to see which of us is stronger."

And that, I assumed, was when she got out. But I was wrong: She'd stayed one more night under his roof. It was hard, she stammered, imagining where she might go. And then, there was something else. She groped and couldn't find words. That night, neither could I. But now—distant from her, waked from my own dream of her—I think I know why.

The person she became after that last moment with Vico on the set had not yet been born. She was young, twenty-four just that spring, and hadn't learned how to judge yet, only how to watch. Like me, she was a watcher, and all a watcher thinks is, *So this is what it's like.*

She blinks in the glare of the arcs, her lips tighten, and when a man pulls a tape from the lens to her nose, and says, "All right, sweetie, here's your mark," she gives a little jump and says, "Yes, thank you," and you know she's been thinking, *So this is what it's like.* And when one night her husband drops on her pillow a twisted obscenity, she doesn't think, *I've married a madman,* but only *So this is what it's like.*

"At first," Lisa said, "I tried to believe it was a joke."

Her eyes stayed tight on my face, watching, it seemed, for some sign that I might think so, too.

"How did you know that it wasn't?" I said.

"Does it look to you like something he might think is funny?"

"No, it . . . I don't know what to make of it."

"I'm serious, Farley. You've known him for years. Was this his idea of a joke?"

"No. I just meant, how did he explain it? What did he say?"

"Nothing."

"He said nothing?"

"He'd arranged with Bolger to schedule the shots so we could leave at noon that day. Get away from town, out to the beach house. Something about the scene coming up next week bothered him. He was in the study doing a rewrite. I had come up from the beach about four o'clock. He knew

I always lay down with a book before dinner." She moved her shoulders uneasily. "It's hard not to sleep when there's nothing to do. And that's when I found it. I read it maybe half a dozen times, trying to figure it out. Then I went downstairs to ask him. His door was closed and I heard typing inside. I knocked. The typing didn't stop. I opened the door and started to say something, but he didn't even turn around. 'Not now,' he said. *'Please-not-now.'* I should have— but I didn't. I went away, like a good little muse. I waited for him at dinner. But it was one of the nights when he worked through dinner, and I ate alone. So I waited some more. The note wasn't always in my mind. When I couldn't invent any more ways to explain it to myself, I didn't think about it at all. I just waited. About ten that night I was reading in the living room. He went past in the hall. When he passed again, he was carrying a pillow and a blanket. I slammed shut my book and went after him to the study. He'd tossed the pillow and blanket onto the couch. 'What's this about?' I said. 'What's that note supposed to mean?' And he said, 'What note?' 'You know what note,' I said. He shook his head. I went into the bedroom. I had put the note in my jewel box. It wasn't there. When I got back to the study, he was busy at the desk, working out a sketch. I could see him, Farley, bending over the paper—the back of his neck, not his face. It stopped me. I wanted to curse him, shame him, but I couldn't make a sound. I was afraid. Suddenly it wasn't my husband sitting there. If he turned around, I'd see... somebody from a Vico movie. I didn't wait to be told, 'Not now.' I went to bed. I didn't see the note again till last week. I found it inside the box of rough-draft pages of the script."

Like the schoolmaster in *Discipline,* I thought, patiently explaining to young Siddons that he must either turn in his assignment or take a beating, while all the time a corner of the stolen paper pokes from beneath the master's desk blotter.

"How did you ever find it?" I asked.

"I was looking," she said. "There and everywhere. I had to prove I'd really seen it."

"To yourself?" I asked.

"To a divorce court."

"It doesn't look like that will be necessary."

"If it is," she said, "I'll be ready."

"Do you mean," I said, "that he never said another word about it, just moved his bed into the study?"

"Oh, he more or less admitted he wrote it. Next morning he came in to breakfast bright as a robin, said he'd fixed the script problem and it would play better than ever. That's when I exploded. I told him I hated his filthy jokes and wouldn't sleep with him if he'd written *Hamlet.* And he said, 'You can't help but play. You know I want you. If you don't play you'll never find out what it is I want more than I want your body.' I told him my curiosity on that subject was next to nothing at all. 'I won't play,' I told him. 'You hear? I won't play.' He just smiled. 'Let's go,' he said. 'It's a long drive and we've got to be in makeup by nine o'clock.'"

"Play," I said. "So it wasn't a joke. It was a *game.*"

"Not that either, Farley," she said. "I've had a long time to think about it. It was a role. His note was a script. It wasn't even me he had in his mind when he wrote it. It wasn't addressed to me by name, and it wasn't signed. He says he wants my body, but he's not sure whether to call me *you* or *it.* For all I know, he might have given the same *blocking instructions,* the same piece of paper, to—"

"What are you thinking?" I said. "Say it."

"To Berenice."

"Why does she keep coming into this?" I said. Suddenly I felt prickly, as if the shadows around us were filled with eyes. "You'd think she was a ghost in the house."

"Listen to me, Farley," she said. "He dropped a few hints, enough for me to know that his marriage to Berenice had ... some problems. But he lived with her seven years, Farley, and every year he made another film. It was only after she died that he ... well, for a long time he didn't work at all, couldn't even think about it. Then he married me. *Tried* to make another picture. But from the start it was—torture. A kind of terror. First the writing, then coming on the set—every day, just coming on the set was a terror. Sometimes in the morning getting ready to drive in for a makeup call, I'd hear him vomiting in the bathroom. You see: The real muse was Berenice."

"And that's why you wanted to know," I said, "what would remind him of her when he looked at you."

She nodded.

"Even before the note, he was trying to make me take her place," she said. "And when I wouldn't he got more and more desperate. I wouldn't let him put things I'd said into the script. He kept the lines in. I didn't want to act in it. He insisted. And once we got on the set, he refused to see that I couldn't give the performance he'd wanted."

"But you *were* giving it," I said. "You were, in spite of yourself."

"He could see the picture was in trouble, Farley. He talked to me about that, if not about ... other things. It baffled him. We'd come home after a day of shooting, and he'd say, 'Why are you being like this? You *know* that's not how to play it.' And I'd say, 'But I don't! I don't!' And he'd spend half the night drilling me on the next day's lines. Then, after he let me go to sleep, he'd stay up working on his own lines. He thought *his* role was in trouble, too. 'If you're not right,' he'd tell me, '*I* can't be right.' And nothing—*nothing* I could do was right and then came the note."

She was trembling. I saw her begin to reach for the drink on the coffee table. But again she stopped herself. She went on talking.

"The last night we spent together was ... I felt glad to get out alive. We had supper in town, got home about eight. We seemed to ... stalk each other. And the heat was ... the morning looked rainy so we'd closed all the windows, and all day the sun *baked* through the roof. He had the study. He left me the bedroom. When we met—in the kitchen, the living room, and never quite by accident—one of us would leave. I was so tense I couldn't hold a glass, couldn't focus on my lines. I went for a swim. When I went down to the beach, he was in the study. He might have seen me through the window. I was in the downstairs bathroom, toweling after my shower. I looked up. He was in the doorway. Maybe he hadn't seen me, didn't know I'd be there. He was hot, too, wearing just trousers. Maybe he only came down for a swim. But he stood there, looking. As soon as I saw him, I—I clutched the towel around me. As if he were a stranger. But he wasn't a stranger. He was—he was supposed to be my husband. I dropped the towel. Then I wished I hadn't."

My throat was dry. "What did he do?" I said.

"He went on looking. I felt like I was being raped. He took a long look. I held myself stiff. Any way I moved might be what he wanted. One second I wanted to do whatever he wanted. The next I was afraid that if I did, he'd hate me for it. And I'd hate myself. He took a long look. Then his breath came out in a... a kind of huff, as if he'd been holding it all that time. And he was gone. I stood still, listening to his footsteps. He went back to the study and closed the door.

"I'd planned to go to bed after my swim, so my dressing gown was there in the bathroom. I put it on and went upstairs. I went to my room. I thought it was over. But as soon as I was in my room, I felt stifled. I tried to settle down, but I couldn't breathe. I knew it wasn't over yet. When I opened his door, it was dark inside. Dark and hot. He wouldn't use a fan. He couldn't think with the noise. He was stretched out here, on the couch, naked, his script on the floor by his hand. He didn't move. I knew he wasn't, *couldn't* be asleep. I couldn't see his face, but I was standing in the doorway where..." She faltered, then said, "Where he could see me."

Oh, yes, I knew what she meant. She stood there, letting him look, giving him his own silent treatment.

"And he stirred on the couch," she said, "just turned his head, in the dark, and he said—Farley, he said, 'You know I love you.' I almost—I wanted to *run* to him, beg him to stop it, let me go." The look she flashed me dropped. "But I said, 'You love me? Then do something about it.' I went back to my room and got in bed. No, I didn't just get in bed. I *arranged* myself, waiting for him." She laughed at that, or tried to. "It went on that long, you see. It wasn't till I was lying there that I realized he'd got me playing his *role* after all. He'd given me a single peek at the script and there was nothing I could do but what he wanted."

I reached across and took her hand. She didn't seem to know I was holding it, but she gripped hard.

"I suppose I was a bit hysterical.... I didn't want to dress in my bedroom for fear he'd find me there. I got together some clothes in the dark. Before I could open the bedroom door, I had to dig a pair of sewing scissors out of a basket on the closet shelf. If I'd met him on the stairs, I'd have stabbed him, Farley, stabbed him to not let him touch me. I went downstairs to the kitchen. I got into my clothes standing by the back door. Then I had to go back upstairs, because I'd left my purse in the bedroom and that's where my car keys were. When I came back down, he was there, leaning against the sink, still in the dark. 'Let me by,' I said. 'You're voice is shaky,' he said. 'You're upset.' I told him, no, I wasn't. He was talking low, almost whispering, as if someone in the house might overhear. 'We've got an early call tomorrow,' he said. 'I'll be there,' I said. 'I'm an adult. I show up for work on time. I do my job. I just don't live here anymore. Now let me by.' I showed him the scissors. That made him smile. 'How do you expect me to get to work tomorrow?' he said. 'Call a cab,' I told him. I left."

Her grip on my hand shifted, tightened again, strong as a talon. Then she seemed to remember I was there.

"Farley," she said, "I dreamed last night I found that note on my pillow again, and all it said was *I love you.* No, it said *Lisa,* too. It said my name. *Lisa, I love you.* Is there any way to translate that sad note to make it say *I love you*?"

She looked at me as if that were a question I could answer. I eased myself from the wicker chair to the couch. She shifted her body toward me, tucked one ankle up between the cushion and her other thigh, and lay her arm across the back of the couch to offer me a place close beside her. But once I was settled, she circled around to the same old questions.

"Tell me, Farley, when he looked at me, who did he see? Was it Berenice? Was that note, that script he left on my pillow, something he'd acted out with Berenice? Who was she willing to be, that I *wouldn't* be? Or couldn't?"

"Berenice had nothing to do with it," I said. "He married her to bankroll his first picture. After that she was nothing to him but—"

"That *can't* be true. While she lived he could *work*. Whatever arrangement they had, however they might have twisted the idea of a marriage into some shape only they could live with, it let him work. Without her—"

"No," I said. "This is one thing I'm sure of. Berenice was never anything to him but an impediment. You want to know who Berenice was? Look at every role Denise Holston played in his pictures. Look at the floozy in *Doomed Cargo,* watch the way she hangs on his arm when he wants to explore the cargo hold. In rehearsals she wasn't getting it right, and he said, 'Don't just *touch* my arm, Denise, I want you to hang your weight there and *drag.*' That was Berenice. And when Fantomese strangles her, that's Vico putting Berenice out of the way. Why do you think he froze like a rabbit when they arrested him? They held him nearly two days on no evidence, and he couldn't convince them he was innocent. *I*—I had to do it. Did you think he was dumb with *grief*? He'd wanted her dead, he'd dreamed it a dozen different ways. He never knotted that stocking around her neck, but he was *guilty.*"

She was silent. I could see a thought struggling behind her eyes, but I wasn't sure whether she was trying to keep it back or set it free.

"What is it?"

"You just made sense of something he said," she told me. "It was the morning after his note, the first day I had to wear that nightgown with him taking those hidden camera pictures of me. Before we left the house, I'd been trying again to make him explain about the note. When he wouldn't talk, I clammed up too. We were driving the coast road on the way to the studio. Suddenly he said, 'Berenice would hate this scene. It's tasteless.'"

"Yes," I said. "That always came up when a scene had him scared. Tasteless."

"He hardly ever mentioned Berenice," she said. "It came out of the blue. I thought he meant *our* scene, the argument we'd been having. But that wasn't it at all. He was continuing where we'd left off—trying to answer my question."

"What kind of an answer was that?"

"It wasn't our fight he thought Berenice would hate. It was the scene we were going to shoot. So telling me Berenice would hate it is a way to *explain his note.*"

"I don't see how."

"Think of the wording. 'I'm going to want you, but I'm going to try to turn away so I can get something else instead.' What is it that he wants instead? What does he want more than my—more than me?"

"That morning, if I know Vico, the only thing on his mind was shooting that scene. But how does that explain a man refusing sex with his own wife?"

"It's funny," she said. "That note made sex the only thing between us. Alone in the house with him all I could think of was my body, mine and his, bodies and heat, till the heat just... melted us away, melted away—whatever else there was but sex." She took a quick breath and held it, pressed her lips tight, then let it out slowly. "Farley," she said, "could he have felt his marriage to me made him—unfaithful to Berenice?"

Her eyes were on mine, wide, waiting, but shrewd—ready to dart away if the answer sprang from somewhere else.

"Berenice was dead," I told her. "Dead."

"I wonder how much that matters," she said. "If you're right, that he had *wished* her dead, felt so guilty he couldn't shake it when they arrested him, then..."

"What?" I said. "What are you not saying?"

"That guilt of his," she said, "might have done a lot to keep her alive in his mind. It might account for the spooky feeling I sometimes got that he was looking through me at somebody else. Maybe the reason I felt like a ghost living with him is that she was more real to him dead than I was alive."

I said a quick no. "It's not that way," I told her. "You make it seem—" But she wanted reasons. "Look," I said, "if not having sex with you keeps him faithful to a dead Berenice, why does he ask you in the same breath to seduce him?"

"I thought," she said, "it was just for the fun of watching me chew my lip and beg before he went to bed alone. But you explained that, too, Farley. Berenice was the impediment. *Still* the impediment, even dead. What he wants is to break free—to make his film, to... maybe to not feel that she's in the room when he's alone with me. The way to get that is to *want* it, want it so bad he can stir up in himself whatever it takes to kill her for good. The way to get it is to want me."

"So he slams the two of you into a sexual pressure cooker in order to get his creative juices bubbling."

"That's what he lives for, isn't it?"

I could almost see her swooning toward him. She'd wanted to translate his pillow note into a love letter and she was doing it.

"Look," I said. "This is late-night talk. I can't prove what you say is wrong. But there's no way you can prove it's true. And whether it's true or not, I don't see how it matters. He's dead. Vico is dead."

"We can't prove that either," she said. "And if he is, I've still got things to figure out." She pressed the back of her fist against her lower lip, then shot me a look of reckless joy. "There might not be what you call proof," she said, "but at least there's more *evidence*."

"Where?" I said.

"In the film. In *Loves of a Spy*. We can translate the script the same way we did his note."

"Lisa," I said. "*Lisa*." I was shaking my head. "You want to go on some Boy Scout snipe hunt for Freudian motives. Vico used to love it, you know, catching the Freudians with their symbols showing. He'd drop a pattern of loaded images into a script and wait like a spider."

Lisa tried to mirror my smile, but her lips dropped to something close to a sneer.

"You were the one, Farley, who said Denise Holston played a disguised version of Berenice in every picture Eric made. Are you telling me now that there's no relation between what happens in his life and the kind of stories he invents?"

I felt her eyes on me, peering the way I used to study an aunt who painted thick makeup over a mole on her cheek. I knew damn well where Vico got the life model for *Loves of a Spy.* If Lisa began prowling the script for clues to Vico's life, sooner or later she'd stumble across a dead-center close-up of a Judas cameraman.

But I needn't have worried. The film she described wasn't much like the one I'd been shooting. It was a way to call Berenice back from the dead and give him a last chance to make her see things his way. The whole picture turned on the confession scene. Madeline was Berenice, according to Lisa, and that's why Vico had insisted on casting Lisa in the role. "I was standing in for her," she said. "The new wife for the old. Everything he makes me say, he really wants to hear from Berenice. It's as if he's going back to an old argument that broke off with her death. You told me she was the impediment, Farley, that she hated the kind of movies he made. Think of Klamstadt taking his cigarette-lighter snapshots of Madeline, pictures he knows she would hate, those nasty *tasteless* pictures, pictures that betray everything their love means. Now watch what happens. He can't go through with it, he loves her too much. He breaks open the camera, rips out the film. It's a complete surrender to her. Klamstadt's whole purpose, at least the purpose he started with, was to use that same camera as a spy, to photograph the minister's secret documents. Now he's given it up. That's Eric—telling me he's made his last film. He said it again, you know, just before we started shooting that day. He took me aside for a minute after the two of you came out of the Petrified Forest. 'I've decided,' he said. 'This is it. My last film.' He was ranting. He'd figured everything out. His entire life and his art had been wrong, all focused *in*ward, a search for some drunken *feeling,* when he should have been using his eyes, he said, *training* his eyes to see what was there. I cut him off. I said that was only what he thought I wanted to hear. 'Your last picture?' I said. 'Neither one of us believes that. Or wants it. Make all the movies you please—but no more with me.'"

Some things about Vico could still surprise me. What did he mean by it, I wondered, offering to sacrifice his career over a family squabble?

"Don't you see, Farley? What he wanted from me was the same thing Klamstadt gets from Madeline after he exposes the film and confesses that he's a spy. She *forgives* him. She *helps* him spy on her husband, shows him where to find the documents. He can go right on using his camera with his sweet meek muse at his side."

It made me smile. If she was right, Vico seemed to think just giving it up, ripping the film out of the camera, would be enough. Madeline would forget it ever happened. That wasn't how it worked.

"But then," she went on, "*I* became the impediment. He'd been looking for an ideal Berenice. He picked me out like a casting director—an actress for his new picture, a muse with no complicated notions about taste. Only I didn't work out. On screen or off, I can't act. And I kept insisting I was a *wife*—even if I didn't know much about *that* role either. I became the impediment all over again, worse than ever. Those lines he stole from me, Farley, do you remember where he put them? They're in the scene where he has Berenice—Madeline, I mean—convince him that she can forgive him. All that business about my father never home, and looking past me, over my head, and patting me off to bed, he's twisted it into the *reason* why Madeline can't despise him for using her like a whore. And then I yank the whole speech out of his hands, tell him it's mine and I won't let it go."

"He'd have had to fix that scene when we shot," I said. "It never rang true."

"That's not news to me, Farley. But just for a minute, think how he must have felt. I knew he was angry, bewildered more than angry, because he couldn't imagine how something that belonged to me didn't also belong to him. But I never guessed why it was so important. What the scene meant to him, what my not letting that speech go *meant*."

I waited, not sure where she would jump. I couldn't read her face, spitting with rage, sarcasm, but wrenched, ready any second to melt. When she spoke, she'd leveled the strain from her voice. It was calm, almost a whisper.

"It meant," she said, "he wasn't forgiven."

She was calm. Her eyes were glazed, no longer needing anything from me. She didn't need me to confirm it, not even to understand it.

"Assuming," I said, "that you were standing in for Berenice."

She nodded.

"And that," I said, "that's why he cracked in the confession scene? Because he knew in advance he wasn't forgiven?"

She nodded.

"Don't get too weepy about it," I said.

She raised her eyebrows, ready to listen but still calm, remote.

"He may have wanted some kind of forgiveness," I said. "After what he put Berenice through, I wouldn't be surprised. But he didn't need it."

"How can you know that, Farley?"

"Not having it didn't stop him, did it? Remember your *Baltimore Catechism*? To be forgiven you need to be contrite. To be contrite you need a firm purpose of amendment. What did Vico ever amend? Is *Spy* any less tasteless, in Berenice's terms, than his other films? Is there a single gesture *in his life* that corresponds to Klamstadt ripping the film out of his camera? You see? He makes a film about contrition, but it's the same old film, and he goes right on making it."

Her face was stiff, as if she'd been slapped.

"Yes," she said from far away. "He went right on making it. Up to the moment he ripped my gown. Then he stopped."

We looked at each other. Neither of us spoke. Her eyes blinked rapidly, but I couldn't see any special brightness there.

"Stripping you," I said at last, "that was pretty tasteless, too. In fact, it's Klamstadt's gesture, his grand renunciation, but in a funhouse mirror. Klamstadt exposing the film—that gesture hides his lover's body, protects her. But when Vico exposed *you,* Lisa, the crank was turning twenty-four frames a second. It was a take, and the whole crew watching." But I couldn't call her back. Her eyes had drifted past my shoulder to the window by his desk. A four-in-the-morning breeze grazed the back of my neck. It would be blowing the curtains in scallops, just the effect Vico wanted. "How you see it makes the difference," I said. "Do you know that double-take drawing of a lady at her dressing table? She's looking in her mirror. There's a dark nest of hair on her neck. You look close, and the hair echoes the oval mirror. Look closer, and suddenly you drop through the surface: the two ovals are the eyeholes of a skull. That's how Vico's last scene works. One way you look at it, he's admitting his atonement to Berenice stinks of hypocrisy—so he wrecks the picture. Yes, we'll have it your way, that's his gesture, his Klamstadt renunciation. But then look at the gesture itself: ripping you to the waist—" She was still looking past me. I had to make it strong. "All right, then. For Berenice. Out of guilt. But it's not atonement, nothing so noble. It's to be *rid* of her. 'But first,' he's saying, 'first I'll show the bitch what tasteless means.'"

"Yes," she whispered, and now I did see a tear, what was left of it—a glistening smear in the hollow beneath her eye. "Yes. Berenice wouldn't have approved."

She didn't move from where she sat, but she kept getting farther away, long shot, a sad Chaplin waddle down the road, a flip of the cane and iris out. How to stop her? My ears were roaring. The dark beyond the lamp was in a swarm, a dance of maggots eating the dark, swarming in shapes I'd put on film. I saw Vico smile and pocket the key to Melody's cage, saw him at the countess's door with strips of flesh hung down his cheeks, saw flames in his eyeballs wink and flash, while all around the drapes puff into pillars of fire and he calmly tells Lady Blanche why she has to die. In every film the same scene, the final seduction.

I saw how Vico would play it. Then I was watching myself.

CHAPTER XXI

1. The Confession

IT WAS TIME for my confession. In my room at the Silver Palms my fever sweats had transferred to the sheet and pillowcase a gray shadow in the shape of my upper body, while I tossed and moaned and planned all I would say to her. I had rehearsed it till I believed it, and I believed it with as much passion as Vico ever believed a line that made his audience gasp or weep. It's not hard acting when everything you say is true. Maybe that was Vico's secret.

Lisa had leaned forward, her head bowed over her knees, her loose long hair falling across her cheek like a widow's mourning veil. That will make it easier, I thought. Bless me, Father, I thought, for I have sinned. But I was so rusty at confessing I couldn't get started right. I had to work through all my lies to get at the truth.

"You know," I said, "you can't let him make you feel guilty."

A good start. Don't feel guilty. Oh, it was coming, I felt it coming. It was like passing a kidney stone.

But Lisa said, "Guilty about what?"

"About him dying," I said. "The *way* he died. It's what they want you to feel—guilty. And you have to remember it's an act. Any suicide acts his death, plays it to an audience. First Vico tried it like Beth, with a razor in the bath. But that was such a cliché. A few quarts of water in a tub? Not for him. He was Don Juan, remember? Always the romantic. An ocean. The biggest storm of the decade. All his mourners gathered on the beach to watch the body wash ashore. Just his style."

"But there's been no body," she said.

"Sure," I said. "Some things you can't arrange. I was surprised, you know, when he wanted to shoot that *Alice in Wonderland* scene out on the back lot. The sun doesn't always light the corner where you want a shot. He felt more comfortable on a soundstage. If he wanted sun, he told me. I gave him sun. Bright as he could stand it. Any angle, as many takes as he needed to get the shot. I could stop the sun in the sky for him. It was only things he couldn't control that scared him. That's why he wasn't content just to act. He had to direct, too. Write his own scripts."

"Farley," she said, "I know—I mean, I don't *know,* but something tells me: Eric's not really dead."

"For a while," I said, "it's natural to feel exactly what they wanted you to feel—that it's your fault."

"Farley," she said, as if I'd fallen asleep. "He's not dead. I know anyway he didn't commit suicide. On the phone that night, when he was raving about sunbursts and Gila monsters. There was something in his voice. Something like excitement. He wasn't depressed, he wasn't wanting to die. If you'd heard him, Farley, you couldn't believe that."

How odd, I thought. How odd she should think that. But I had to be gentle.

"You lived with him long enough," I told her, "to know he had more than one way of casting people for the roles he wanted to see them play. I'll tell you something I've known a long time, Lisa. Vico was a genius, yes, and in a way I loved him. But when he got what he wanted from you, he wrote you out of the script. He wrote out Berenice the day he got his hands on the money to produce *The Whisperer.* After that she was right where he'd been when he started—in the cattle pen. An extra you gave a day's work now and then for old times' sake. The night she died, she begged him to stay home, and you know where he was? Out in Newport Harbor getting drunk. I was with him. I don't know how he felt about having a murder on his conscience, but I feel rotten."

I had got up. I was over by the desk, as if that smarmy picture of him with Chaney could be ripped apart again. She didn't move or get up.

"Except," I said, "I *do* know how he felt. Nobody knows him like I do—like I did. Not even you. I know him because I've watched him. We're almost the same person. Sixteen years ago, and she said, 'Please, don't leave me alone,' and I'll remember her looking at me till—"

I was a little breathless. She was on her feet now, but far enough away so I could say it. I felt it coming.

"But you can't let yourself feel guilty," I said. "You have to remember it's an act. They plan it like a surprise party. No crepe paper strung from the chandelier, no cake on the table. But when you flick on the light, there's the body, white as chalk. And a little smile that says *Surprise!*"

She was looking. I wanted her looking.

"With me," I said, "there was always the body, that I couldn't not remember. White in the red water. And the lips: a kind of purple stain, a grape-juice purple. And the razor blade, she left it..."

I had finally reached her. She came over and put her arms around me. The ocean turned lazily over, churning Vico's corpse, but her hair smelled sweet as lilacs. Somewhere above us, after fifty-odd years with its shoulder braced to its mate, a beam yielded a fractional tick. Lisa heard it, too. I felt her back muscles tense.

"There it is again," she said.

It was only wood, I told her. It swells in the rain and the sun shrinks it.

"Whenever I hear it, I think there's someone up there. The night of the storm I heard it in the attic and thought it was Eric hiding from me. But I was afraid to go upstairs to find out."

I wasn't surprised. As soon as she'd opened the door for me I had remembered, just as if I'd always known, that the night Vico disappeared Spyhawk had paid him a visit. She raised her head from my shoulder. Maybe she had felt my attention flicker. Her eyes were green as sunlight through maple leaves. They were questioning or appraising or inviting or simply looking back at my look. Thoughtless as a camera.

My right hand slid to the swell of her buttock, the other hand locked on my wrist and tightened the circle. I leaned against the desk with her inclined along my body, and kissed her. Above us, holding his breath, Spyhawk lay bellied on the floor, peering through some crack in the boards. I thought when I left the Silver Palms I shook him off for good, but it seems we only swapped places. His head stirred like a drugged sleeper rousing, and I wondered if it was because she had felt me stiffen that she pulled away.

She went back to the couch, not in a hurry but not strolling, walking as if she had something on her mind and were alone in the house. She sat prim, the kind of prim you see on girls in the waiting room outside Krackenpov's office—back straight, knees and ankles parallel and touching, eyes in a middle-distance glaze. I looked away. Out the window. Through the gap in the trees. It was still night, but the stars were gone and the sky was sooty pale. The night's last black had gathered in the trees. Their heavy shadows were emerging like a contact print in the developer bath, before you can tell what the image will be. I looked back into the room. The standing lamp behind the couch made a fishbowl of yellow light that held us both, kept our voices pitched for whispers, for secrets. I knew I had to say what I came to tell her before the sun dissolved our mood.

I sat beside her on the couch and slid an arm over her shoulders, another across her lap. She went rigid, maybe not sure what I wanted. What to say: Listen, kid, I'm not some Harold Teen in a rumble seat? I murmured it was all right and drew her in. My arms closed around her. First her cheek dropped to my shoulder, teary hot. Then her head burrowed against my chest.

I had what I'd come for, it seemed—the living woman tight in my arms. Before tonight even the lovely rusty rose of her nipples had blackened in my mind and it wasn't the living flesh at all that I remembered, but only its black-and-white ghost sliding across the plaster cracks of my wall in the Silver Palms. I might have stayed there forever, watching shadows on the wall, dreaming my pale dream. But Sammy Pugh calling me brother shook me awake. I woke up hungry, starved for the living woman, ready to risk even Spyhawk to get her. If I closed my eyes, I knew I'd see him spying, luring me, willing to let me be the spy.

I was fighting it, feeling the weight of the living woman, feeling her breath on my chest. Her breath came steady now, but shallow. Scarce enough rise and fall to shift light on the fold of her dress. Then her voice, squeezed between my chest and her shoulder, said, "Why did you do it, Farley?" No grand accusation, almost a tossaway line, but it said all my secrets were known. She must have felt me suck a breath and hold it. She lifted her head, eye sockets pouchy, one cheek mascara-tracked, the other, the one that had pressed against my chest, printed with a fiery blush.

"Why did I what?" I said.

"You were the spy, weren't you, Farley? You fed Monty Druhl all those stories about a love affair on the set."

2. The Sincere Flattery of a Fan

LIGHT WAS SEEPING through the window above Vico's desk. A few minutes more and the lamplit circle that had kept us huddled close through the night would dissolve.

I heard my voice say the word: I. And I felt Spyhawk struggle to break free, but I said it again: I. And he was there. Trapped inside. Part of me.

"Yes," I said. "I was the spy. I had a friend on the *Tablet*. Al McMahon, police beat. I gave things to him and he passed them to Monty Druhl. Have you guessed why, too?"

She spoke slowly, planning where each word should go.

"Only hints from what you said. Making Eric jealous, you said. That was the way to fight him. The way I fought him, you said. That's what made me think you could have— But why? Why did you want to fight him?"

"If it had been only me," I said, "only what he was doing

to me, maybe I never would have. But six years. Six years I watched him with Berenice. When I saw him start on you, too, I—" I didn't know how to go on. It came out a whisper. "I swore I wouldn't let him." I'd been breathing hard. It got my cough going for a minute. When it stopped I said: "I never meant him to—go over the edge. I never believed anything could break him, that's why I— He seemed to think on a soundstage anything he did was in a dream. Whatever he brought through the door with him—whatever he'd managed to squeeze out of you—he owned, he could use any way he liked. It was all *art,* see, and because he could twist you into something beautiful, it didn't matter how much the twisting hurt. He seemed to think it all stayed just where it was—in the dark, in the dream, on the screen—and nothing he did there made anything happen outside. I had to show him he was wrong. Being Vico didn't give him the right."

She nodded as if she understood.

"Farley," she said, "if I hadn't asked you, would you have told me?"

"I think so. It's what I came to do."

She wanted to know why.

"You know why," I said.

"Why? I don't know why. Why?"

"So you'd know how I felt," I said. "About you. And because I want the one who does what I do to be me. I want one person in control—one. That means there can't be anything so horrible I can't admit I did it."

She looked at me. I didn't mind. I wasn't going anywhere. There was no Spyhawk anymore. There was only me.

"And because," I said, "I was afraid you might feel the way I did about Beth. That you pushed him over the edge. You had to know it wasn't just you. I had to let you know how far I'd gone."

"How far did you go, Farley?"

The window breeze had given her goose flesh. "I'll tell you," I said, and stood up and peeled off my sport coat. "I've told you everything," I said, tucking the coat around her. "I can tell you this, too." I took from my wallet a folded square of papers, the papers I'd never destroyed, even when the risk of Hoensinger finding them made me retch. Even while he was snooping through my house I was planning how it would have to be if I wanted to get rid of Spyhawk, I was setting up this scene with Lisa, rehearsing the little Vico smile I gave her as I dropped the papers in her lap.

"What's this?" she said.

"My draft copies of the Kill-You-Annabelle Letters."

I saw in her eyes the person she looked at become someone else.

Every few nights Sammy Pugh would ask if I wanted him to throw away the old newspapers I was hoarding and when I said no, he always snarled around like a hornet bouncing off the windowpanes, pretending to plump the chair cushion and hanging my robe in the closet till he'd tidied his way back to my door.

But I wouldn't be bullied. If I let him take the papers he would find out I was hoarding every word printed about Vico. After he was gone I would sit up in bed and deal my Vico clippings on the spread around me as if I were laying out a tarot reading. I had a separate pile for stories that featured the Kill-You-Annabelle Letters. I read them the way Vico read reviews.

For the first few days the letters were a mystery. All the reporters could get out of Hoensinger was that he had found on Vico's makeup table a couple of fan letters that "could have been disturbing to someone who'd been under mental strain." Both the *Times* and the *Tablet* had the same idea to fill the vacuum. They interviewed half a dozen stars about their fan mail, and headlined the ones who admitted, hedgingly, careful not to offend their loyal worshipers, that now and again a fan seemed to be disturbed or irrational. More than one quotation from their letters credited the actor with deeds real only to the camera. I came across phrases like "after you saved that girl from drowning" and "I know just how you felt watching your house burn to the ground because last year..." I remembered the night at the Penguin Club we had spent arguing about Vico's fans. He had a batch of letters that had been passed around the table and got beer-stained and hooted over. In them people offered to punch his teeth out or have sex with him or save him from hellfire. Vico insisted these people were harmless, talking in their sleep to him because he had put their nightmares on film. "It's not just dreams," I told him. "You invent possibilities they never would have without you." He laughed and said, "Farley, you give me too much credit. I'm not that unusual." But I could tell a few of the letters bothered him. He had a secretary answer most of them with a form letter that he would sign, but a few he wrote personally. The ones who made him angry or frightened or who sounded as though the most intimate contact they'd had in the past year was writing to a movie star. "Why in hell can't I get Bob Taylor's mail?" he said. "The women who write him want to get married or spend a month on Santa Catalina. Mine all want me to tie them up and hurt them." "It's because Taylor is Taylor and you are you," I told him. "No, Farley," he said, "it's not because I'm who I am. It's because of the films I make," and I said, "What's the difference? You think Bob Taylor could make your films?" He wasn't laughing by then, and he said, "There's still a difference between them and me." I gave the guys at the table a we-know-better grin and said, "Tell that to your fans."

Writing the letters I had thought like Vico himself, inventing characters, inventing voices for them, worries and habits, inventing their story. I went through a number of drafts getting the language right. Then I bought some new pink stationery and wrote Annabelle's letter left-handed with a narrow-nib fountain pen in purple ink. I gave Annabelle lots of flourishes. I decided she was the kind of person who dots her *i*'s with a perfect circle like a comic-page fish bubble. At first my left-handed curlicues struck me as clumsy, out of character, and I tried to smooth them out. Then I decided her jagged capitals were Annabelle's pathetic claim to elegance, and her whole personality blossomed for me so that I had to redraft her letter in her new voice. The final touches came to me as soon as I realized she was sitting in her breakfast nook while she wrote, listening to radio soap operas and eating chocolates. She had buttocks that smothered the edges of her kitchen chair and a bosom so huge and pushed up and squeezed together that there were wrinkles in the cleft. There were big flowers, water lilies, splashed all over her dresses and she wore three-inch heels to the grocery store and horn-rim glasses set with rhinestones. Sometimes the glasses sat on her onion-bulb nose and sometimes they hung from a black string and lay on her bosom like a necklace. Her hair was cut in flat black bangs and thick Shirley Temple curls that bounced when she walked. By the time I finished I could hardly believe she didn't exist.

I ransacked my memory to place her, turned up a strict aunt with prickly flower beds, the high school teacher who'd flunked me in math, and the librarian who'd refused to let me borrow an art book with Toulouse-Lautrec nudes. None of them was my Annabelle. The only feature I could connect with any woman I'd ever known was the black hair, which had a coppery tint I must have stolen from Berenice Vico. But if Annabelle was Berenice, she was a Berenice who could never rewrite your script or call it tasteless. When I finished her letter I damped it with dimestore perfume till the thick smell gagged me.

It read like this:

Dear Mr. Vico,

My husband did an impression of you at a party and now he does you all the time even when nobodys laughing. He lays in bed at night in his bed because he dosnt sleep with me in the big one anymore he kept saying I would ~~kick~~ keep him awake and he lays there saying Annabelle and he waits till I say what and then says Annabelle, I'm going to kiiiill yooooou, and its your voice. I tell him its not funny, Arnold, not at all, and he just does your voice again, You here me Annabelle, I am going to kiiiill yoooou, and its just like you talking ever since we saw you in Price of madness. I keep telling Arnold hes just an actor, hes not really like that at all are you? But you cant tell Arnold anything hes always just a mule even his mother used to say, so what I want to ask is I know hes writing to you since after all that chuckling and covering the envelope with his hand he left it out on the table when he was in the bathroom before he went out for his walk with Tuffy, thats our chow, to mail it. So what I want to ask and I know this is a sincere favor Im asking such a busy star, is will you please tell him to stop your just an actor? Even if you did wind up in jail over your ex-wife in that closet with the stocking around her neck? You think about that, Annabelle, he tells me, and I keep saying but they let him go, he didnt do it did you? And all Arnold says is you just keep that in mind. Please dont get me wrong I like you very much I'm sure if I ever was fortunate to meet you, but your voice in the dark is to much to bare every night. I try to understand a man needs some jokes but all I can do is lay there shaking and he doesnt even seem to here me when I tell him, please Arnold, dont I love you enouf.

Yours very sincerly,
Annabelle Katchemire

Sometimes when Vico had been neglecting to check his mail bin a secretary would give his letters to the cleaning woman on her way to do his trailer. It wouldn't surprise him to arrive there for his solitary makeup ritual—an invariable habit, no matter how the studio makeup artists grumbled—and find a handful of letters leaning against his dressing-table mirror.

When a scene was giving Vico problems, he was a fan-mail dipsomaniac, craving endless proofs that he'd convinced people someone with a genuine postal address lived beneath the mask. To make sure he'd be unable to resist it, I'd marked Annabelle Katchemire's envelope with the word "Urgent," twice underscored, and placed it against his mirror at the front of the stack.

That's where it is that last morning as Vico passes the studio gate in a predawn mist. That's where it is as he gropes for the trailer key he never knew I'd copied. That's where it is when he switches on the light, when he sits before the mirror, laying on the table his script open to the day's scene so he can glance at lines while he prepares a face for the camera, prepares himself for the moment of his confession to Frau Stauffer, his confession to Lisa. I think he doesn't see the letter right away. He dabs cold cream on his face, rubs it in, the old ritual, always soothing, always erasing the last memory of the night's dreams. Now he wipes his face with a tissue, reaches into his makeup case for the tube of number-five base that he will smear over his face up to the hairline and blend back to his ears and down his neck. He pauses, blinks, his concentration snagged. His makeup tube isn't in the case. Ah—he spots it there on the table, just in front of the fan mail left by the maid. He reaches for it, perhaps he has already squeezed some of the makeup onto his fingers, made a three-finger streak across his brow, his left cheek, then his right—before he sees the "Urgent" on Annabelle's letter. He wipes his fingers with a tissue before reaching for it.

As he reads: close-up of Vico's profile, drifting into a full-face shot in the mirror.

Once he's read Annabelle's letter he sorts the pile for Arnold's. There is no other Katchemire among the return addresses, but one envelope has no return address at all. He sees his name in a barely legible hand that reads like the jagged squiggles of a police polygraph test. It is unlike my own hand and unlike the one I'd invented for Annabelle. Quite a feat. Labor of love.

What he reads inside is this:

Vico, *mon semblable, mon frère,*

You recall that scene in *Price of Madness* where Celeste tosses in her bed with your face haunting her dream and that echo voice eternally repeating, I'm going to kill you, Celeste? A brilliant moment, I thought, one of your most *potent,* if you comprehend me, and it was that—absurd as it may seem—which gave me the idea. Call it, if you will, the *obsession,* since I now contemplate little else. I intend—as you shall observe for yourself if I've piqued your curiosity, stimulated you to accept my invitation to a little private party in the not too distant future—to reenact in very truth the scene you so artfully composed for the cinema camera. As I too am an artist—though my medium is flesh rather than film—I've devised for your delectation a few refinements of my own. I shall always be grateful to you, however, for delineating with such unsurpassed artistic clarity the precise conditions for the satisfaction we both crave. I've seen you often in person, as I reside here in Los Angeles also and have strolled past your house one of these nights.

Most appreciatively,
Arnold C. Katchemire

For the first few days after Vico's disappearance the press focused on the clues that made the most photogenic copy: the torn photo, the blood-soaked towel, the footprint on the path, the police interrogation of everyone who had witnessed Vico's sensationally choreographed exit from the soundstage. It wasn't until the eighth of March that keeping Vico on page one drove them to sniff out the station-house rumors of strange fan mail. The one who got the story first was my old pal, Al McMahon. That made me laugh. Creating Katchemire's personality, I had imagined what sort of letter McMahon might write if his taste had run to Vico films rather than heroic couplets.

McMahon's report came from "a source close to the investigation." Could the source, I wondered, have been Hoensinger himself? I couldn't imagine Hoensinger with the ice-gray eyes in a chatty mood, but I knew McMahon had a knack for coaxing confidences. Even so, he got only a taste of the story's meat. He wasn't permitted to quote the letters at length or give the authors' last names. "VICO FAN DRIVES ACTOR TO SUICIDE?" the headline read—and the story preserved the fine tension between the claim and the question. It evoked a demented mimic crooning death threats to his wife. It traced a distraught Vico from the dressing room where he'd left the opened letters to the soundstage, the papier-mâché forest, where Nellie Nugent overheard him talking with his cameraman—a conversation now characterized not as a conspiracy against Krackenpov and Bolger but as a despondent monologue, Vico brooding over his sick art and the fans it had created. The story went on to speculate about the missing hours between his flight from the soundstage and the late-night call to his wife, purportedly from the beach house—but who, McMahon ominously wondered, could say for sure? One person who had been asked, a paragraph near the story's end said, was the cameraman Griswold Farley, reputedly Vico's best friend. In a police interview the day after the Vico story broke, Farley had been unable to shed light on his disappearance, but he had since dropped out of sight himself, after telling Lisa Schoen he had an idea where her husband might be found. As the weeks went by, McMahon lifted the minor mystery of the missing cameraman higher and higher into his Vico stories, till I almost shared the spotlight with Vico. So much for friendship. That came later, though, when he was even more hard up for a fresh angle. For the moment, things were breaking fast as his typewriter carriage could skim down to the bell. Early editions the next day shouted: "KILL-YOU-ANNABELLE LETTERS A HOAX." In the first afternoon edition that headline had been pushed aside by further discoveries: "HOAX VICTIM LAST TO SEE VICO ALIVE."

Yes. They'd finally got to the real Arnold Katchemire.

Vico had taught me that when you want your audience to believe something incredible, you make the details true.

The Arnold Katchemire that Al McMahon had lifted into the public glare was a night-shift studio guard, a squat, pulpy man with gray skin and his shirt always tight and damp against his back. He was somebody who would have stumbled across Vico three or four times a month, somebody who would have flashed a light briefly in Vico's face, let out a mild wow at how late he stayed in the cutting room or how early he'd arrived, then shuffled off, chinking the key on his time clock. Not somebody Vico would know well enough to judge whether he might be a wife-killing loony, but somebody he knew existed.

The story Al McMahon and the others pieced together while I was sleeping off my fever in the Silver Palms Hotel was that less than an hour after he fled the set of *Loves of a Spy* Vico had driven out past Gower Gulch and visited the stucco bungalow of Arnold Katchemire. What came next, I told Lisa, wasn't something I'd planned. It had started, I said, as a joke—a joke with a point, a joke with a moral, but a joke. And even then I'd worried I might be going too far. I'd slipped the letters into the inside pocket of my sport coat, then never seemed to remember I had them when I was passing a mailbox. One night in a bar I felt something crinkle in my coat and drew them out, surprised to find I had mail addressed to Vico in my pocket till the perfume on Annabelle's letter brought back what I'd done. I covered the envelopes with my palm and slid them back into my pocket. Bolger, who was buying a drink, said, "Hey, whatcha got there?" "Just bills," I said. "Bills, bull!" he said. "If I saw you cover a poker draw that quick, I'd fold a straight flush." Without giving it much thought, I told Lisa, I'd made up my mind not to mail them. "I forgot all about them," I said. "Then a few days later I put half a dozen bill payments into the same pocket and mailed the letters with the bills."

That was true. All I kept back from Lisa, because of her eyes, because as I talked they seemed to be melting my face like candle tallow, was that once I realized the letters were gone I went to Vico's mail bin—it was the afternoon before his crack-up on the set—and picked them up along with his other mail. It would have been easy for me to drop off Vico's mail at his trailer and simply keep the Kill-You-Annabelle Letters in my pocket. I didn't. I took the day's mail home.

That night I was awake, thinking not about the letters at

all, thinking about Lisa and the next day's shots. At about three-thirty in the morning I thought I would go down to the stage and play with a couple light combinations. The sport coat I put on was the one that had Vico's mail in the pocket. This time not just the two letters I'd written. More than a dozen envelopes that I'd snatched along with them. A thick bulge, not easy to ignore, not possible to forget you had. The canceled stamps on the Annabelle Letters made them seem like all the others—Vico's property.

When I got to the studio it wasn't yet four a.m., and the big double gates you could drive through were still locked. I parked on a side street and used my pass key to get in by the pedestrian gate. I took a shortcut along the row of storefronts and brownstones where we'd shot the *Cain* street scenes, but it was still a long walk to Vico's trailer. I stepped along as if I were trying to stay ahead of somebody, cut across the lawn of the Southern plantation house. The shade trees there were full of bird squabbles—hunger cries and rage cries and cries of mine! mine! mine! On the street between the double rows of stages I broke into a sprint, then stopped, afraid a night guard, maybe Katchemire himself, would take me for a burglar and empty his service revolver at me. I thought of Katchemire rolling over my corpse to see what he'd bagged and spotting the return address with his wife's name on it. There were garbage cans on the corners and whenever I passed one I thought of ripping the letters across and closing them inside. But no place seemed safe. I turned into the alley between Stage Eight and Stage Nine sweating and breathless, watching for places where Katchemire might throw a light in my face, the way he'd done one night when I was working late, and when Katchemire would say, "Let's see yer pass," I saw myself handing him the letters. By the time I got to the shady knoll behind the stage where Vico's trailer was parked, I was convinced the only place for the letters that wouldn't bring Katchemire down on me was right where I put them, propped against the makeup-table mirror in front of his tube of number-five base.

It wasn't till I got to my car that I calmed down. I thought of going back inside to work with the lighting, the way I'd planned. I didn't want to. What I came for, it seemed, was what I'd done. And it hadn't been Katchemire that made my heart thump. I'd been afraid Vico might come early and catch me leaving his trailer.

Katchemire had been around that night, but he hadn't seen me. He got off work at seven a.m., so later that morning when he answered the door he was in his pajamas, squinting in the unaccustomed sun. He was, he told Hoensinger—and later a gang of reporters at a press conference—groggy with sleep. He could tell Vico had a hair tickling his nose about something, he said, but he couldn't tell what. It took a couple minutes to get through to Katchemire that Vico was inquiring about the health of his wife. Katchemire said you couldn't blame him for not having much patience with questions like that. Vico was "talking crazy," he said, "as if I was responsible, as if it was all my fault. He kept on at me. 'You're causing that woman lots of grief,' he kept telling me, and it's no wonder I lost my temper, is it? Wouldn't you of said the same to him?" And here Katchemire, who had at first seemed to duck his head against the pelting questions, aimed his big gray sensitive mole nose above the ring of men as if he were trying to sniff a better air beyond them, and looking directly into the newsreel camera, said, "Wouldn't you—if it had been your wife? You git off my porch, I told him. I never caused her no grief atall. She wanted to die, and all I said was, You go ahead then. And I never said I'd kill her. All I said was I would if I could." And Arnold Katchemire's chin and tender nose twitched.

Six days earlier, it came out, Katchemire had buried his wife after nursing her through a long year of cancer surgery, wasting debts, and pain. A crucial question, one that it took several tries to make Katchemire respond to coherently, was whether Vico had understood *how* Katchemire's wife had died—that on Katchemire's last visit to the hospital, as she whispered that the pain was awful and she wished he could please just for three minutes, Arnie, please just hold a pillow over my face and it will be over, he had held her hand and said over and over till they told him visiting time was up, I would if I could, sweetie, I would if I could. But before Arnold Katchemire could say all that, even if he would have said it to Vico or anyone if the hollering reporters hadn't broken him down, Vico had heard him say I'd kill her if I could, and backed away off the porch and lurched into a stumbling run across Katchemire's lawn to his car.

I never met Katchemire's wife. I never was told her name. I chose Arnold Katchemire for the reasons I said—because Vico knew he existed but nothing about him. And I don't read obituaries, ever. But somehow, maybe as I was flipping pages on my way to the latest Monty Druhl column, my eye must have grazed the black-bordered death notice that read "Annabelle Katchemire, 54."

For years Vico drained Berenice to a shadow, danced her soul on the screen. For years I watched her writhing in the light—as the Impediment, Denise Holston in all her boozy, flirty, interfering incarnations; and in other disguises I might not have recognized, but that Berenice, sitting beside him in the dark, hung with the garish emeralds she wore to each premiere, would know in an instant.

The Kill-You-Annabelle Letters would tell Vico he couldn't start with Lisa where he left off with Berenice. They'd tell him she was made of flesh, not light.

3. The Muffed Line

THAT'S HOW I said it: I wouldn't let him make her another Berenice. She seemed to understand. I asked if she did and she bowed her head and raised it, and raised her eyes to mine. The look that frightened me, that blistered my cheeks, was gone. No more that simple trust either—she'd seared away my Uncle Farley face for good. What she found beneath it gave her eyes a hungry awe, the look you give someone who makes his own rules. A look I'd caught in the eyes of Vico's fans when they saw him on the street. I'd always wondered if it was the constant stare of my lens that made it so easy for him to ignore that awe, even while he never stopped preening. Under Lisa's gaze I found it was an easy trick, one I liked. There seemed no need to ask if she'd forgive me.

Then, almost to herself, she said, "So that's it at last."

I wasn't sure whether what she'd said was a question. Her eyes had drifted away, noticed my sport coat still tucked around her shoulders. She seemed to flinch inside it.

"There's still one more, isn't there, Farley?" she said. "One letter you haven't told me about."

"Is there?" I said. Suddenly I wasn't sure.

And she said, "Weren't you the Faceless Man, Farley?"

I asked what she meant.

"You're not likely to forget, are you?" she said. "Whatever you said, it made a powerful impression on Eric."

I wondered if she was mocking me, then decided that if she was, I'd no right to anything else. I'd come to tell her everything and hadn't mentioned Spyhawk.

"I might," I said. "I might forget. I'm like that sometimes—when I've been drinking. Show me the letter. If I did it, I'll know when I see it."

Her hand, inside my jacket, pulled it away from her throat. She got to her feet. "Yes," she said, and went to Vico's desk. I followed her, stood at her side as she rummaged in drawers.

"He didn't let me read it," she said, and her voice seemed too cheerful, too much a voice jamming the silence with static. "But I'd know if it's here. It was written in pencil. Yellow paper with blue lines, like a school tablet." She glanced up to see if I recognized her description. "And sand," she said.

"Sand?"

She found the mail drawer and snapped off the rubber band that bound a bundle of letters. She sorted quickly to the bottom of the pile. Her nervous shuffling surprised me.

"Not here," she said.

"Tell me about it," I said. "When did it come?"

"Near the end," she said. "About a week before that last day."

"Tell me," I said. I kept my voice steady. "Tell me about the sand."

"We were having a late supper in the kitchen," she said. She was still nervous, but careful now, not babbling. She spoke as if it were something she'd memorized, and I might be angry if she got a word wrong. "When he slit the envelope, sand sprinkled out on the table. 'Riviera sand or plain old Malibu sand?' I asked him. He pretended not to hear me. I said it again. 'Sure,' he said. 'Monte Carlo. Suntan lotion. Cocktails at five on the marina terrace. It's an invitation. Want to go?'" She shrugged. "That's all I know about sand," she said.

I nodded toward the desk.

"Maybe it's in another drawer," I said.

She turned back to the desk, humoring me. One drawer had bank statements mixed with old scripts, scraps of dialogue, sketches for camera setups. Another was full of snapshots, including one I never guessed he would have kept. Somebody'd taken it the night we finished shooting *Price of Madness*. I was raising my glass for a toast, wearing the uniform jacket and monocle Vico had used in the picture. I was sneering at Vico, who had my viewfinder around his neck, the eyepiece to his eye. He was waving me farther back—stiff-legged, stiff-backed, bent sharp as a T-square so that his ass stuck out like a Keystone Kop about to get pushed into a mud puddle.

"It's not here," Lisa said.

"Keep looking."

She didn't ask why. I never touched anything of Vico's, but I watched her go through all the drawers. It wasn't there.

"Tell me about it," I said. "He didn't say who it was from?"

She stood with her back to the desk, the open window behind her.

"He didn't want to tell me," she said. "But I wouldn't let it go. I could see it made him—tense. Excited. The way you get before a cloudburst. You'd think he smelled it coming, the storm, a week away. I kept hounding him—who was it? What did he want? Finally he said it was just one more person he'd used. 'Like I'm using you,' he said." She lowered her eyes. "By that time," she said, "I'd been pretty candid about how I felt acting in *Loves of a Spy.* 'What does he want?' I asked him. 'This person you've been using?' And he said: 'More than I can pay.' Surely, I said, if it was a money problem—and then I saw he'd spilled his wine. It was a scene from one of his pictures. The glass rolling on its bowl, wine dripping onto the floor—and him glaring at me. 'My debt,' he said, 'what I owe'—and he was talking in that whispery voice he uses when he's furious—'is a face. One human face. One day I wiped it away,' he said, 'easy as you'd sponge a blackboard. He's never asked for it. But that doesn't mean I don't owe it. Like I owe Berenice. Owe you.'"

That was the first I knew that Vico was alive. And knowing he was alive, I also knew where he'd gone. He was with the Faceless Man. Lisa must have seen in my eyes more than I wanted to show.

"Farley," she said. "It wasn't you, then?"

I shook my head.

"But you know who he is, don't you? The Faceless Man?"

She was waiting for my answer.

"You do, don't you?" she whispered. "Who is he, Farley?"

I'd wanted my confession to put an end to lying, at least with her. The only way, with her looking directly into my eyes, that I could answer without lying was to tell her the truest thing I knew. I stepped closer, put my hands on her arms. What I wanted to say was that I loved her, that all I'd done was for her, that I'd been looking my whole life for her.

"Lisa," I said, "the moment I laid eyes on you, I felt I'd met you in a dream."

If I hadn't been touching her, she might have been able to disguise it, but with both hands on her I felt a jolt like an electric shock. Then she had wrenched away, had backed a couple steps toward the sliding door to the sundeck that overlooked the path down to the beach.

"What is it?" I said. "What's the matter?"

I took a step toward her, but the way she gasped made me stop. It wasn't fear. No matter what I'd done, she couldn't be afraid of me.

"On the phone that night," she said, and it was hard not moving closer, because I could barely hear. "Just before the line went dead," she was murmuring. "Those were the last words he ever said to me. And I said, 'You saw me in a *dream*? Is it a dream you married? Who do you think I *am*?' There was a thunderclap. When I could hear again, the line was dead."

I told her I hadn't meant to mock. I told her I must have picked up Vico's words from the papers, the report of her testimony.

"No, Farley," she said. "I never told Hoensinger about that."

She opened the sliding door and walked out onto the sundeck. She stood in the far corner where a triangle of early sunlight slashed across the wall. I followed her. As far as the door.

"I called you," I said. "Remember? Right after the cops let you go."

"I never told you either."

Now I was frightened.

"He was never even here that night, was he?" she said. "It was you, doing your Vico impersonation, just like you had Arnold Katchemire do in your letter." Then all her bewilderment and bitterness and rage at everything she'd been through since that day in Saratoga when Vico lifted her salt tear to his tongue took shape around a single question, the last she would ever ask me: "Who do *you* think I am, Farley?"

4. Script Trouble

NEVER, I SWEAR, till the moment she said it, did I recall that Spyhawk in his sly-drunk way had thought it might be clever to fake the voice of Vico to his wife. Slick guy, Spyhawk. Full of tricks.

We stared at each other, both I think surprised by what she'd said. I was afraid for her, pressed against the rail. A cry, a sudden reach, might pitch her backward. Our speechless stare extended.

Why had she chosen that night to tell me things I'd pried and peered for weeks to glimpse? Did she finally believe Vico was dead and the secrets of her marriage no longer binding? Or did she use her secrets as a lure to coax out secrets of mine?

Or—just now—this thought occurs to me: Nobody knew we had come to the beach house together. We were alone, far beyond earshot of her nearest neighbor, and I had been speaking to her with what a fruity prosecuting attorney might interpret as disturbing intensity. Could she have told me Vico's secrets out of sheer terror, afraid that if I let my own mask slip too far, I would feel I had to make my secret safe?

But if she suspected, she never would have let me know when I blundered. Unless she was more simple than I thought. Or crafty enough to believe she could convince me she—understood. Forgave.

Oh, Lisa, you are pure enigma. Whether that wide blue stare of yours was full of terror or guile, love or contempt, I shall never never never know. Never. Never.

I can't even say, though I would if I were more ignorant of the twists my Spyhawk took with those he loved, that I would never have harmed you.

I had to tell her something. I told her not to be afraid. Everything, I said, can be explained. It was a joke. A slap to open his eyes. But after what he did—ripping her gown, punching

Bolger—I knew I'd gone too far. That evening, I said, I drank and worried. I went home and worried some more, drank more, finally drove out to the beach house to tell him everything. He didn't answer my knock, but a light burned from the hallway. I thought he was asleep and I was drunk enough and thought what I'd come for was important enough to wake him. I tried the door. Once inside, I heard water running upstairs. He must be showering, I thought, that's why he doesn't hear me. That and the rain, the thunder. I hollered up the stairs that I was here. No answer. I thought he was angry. Stood at the foot of the stairs yelling. Drunk talk—joking, goading, pleading. No answer. It wasn't like him to sulk. It scared me. I went upstairs. I froze at the bathroom door. The tub was still filling, but there on the floor was the blood-soaked towel, right where she would later step on it, and bloodspots in the sink, and a big pie-wedge piece of glass from that Chaney photo that used to be in the study. I read the room like a camera setup, knew as if I'd been there that he'd tried to die Beth's way, but without her hate for me to see it to the end. I tried to recall whether some drunken night I'd told him how she'd died, given him this scene, too, so he could mock me with it. Then it hit me—Vico could never die this way, bleeding into a tub. He would know it, too—know it was wrong, like a scene that wasn't working. He wouldn't be Vico if he settled for a tubful of water when down the path he had a whole ocean in the biggest storm of the decade. I knew where I'd find him. Down on the beach, romantic as hell with the hair plastered wet on his brow, waiting for just the right breaker to throw himself against, and looking for it too damn hard to be serious. The blood he'd drawn in the bathroom would have scared him sober. He would walk on the beach awhile, setting up the shot, getting the right angle on the stretch of sand where he would imagine Lisa finding the body. Then he would climb the hill and find me in the study, and I'd say, "Helluva night for a swim, ain't it?" and we'd talk.

"You have to believe me, Lisa," I said. "I was worried, even scared. But I never believed he'd do it. I knew he'd be back, and I knew if I went down to the beach after him while he was still working it off, he'd hate me. You know how he is when you try talking to him while his mind is on a problem. That's all I thought it was—just another scene that wouldn't play right. If I charged down there to the rescue, it would shame him. He'd never forgive me."

Telling her that much had been the easy part. While I did it, I'd been thinking ahead.

Then the phone rang, I told her. All I could think when I heard her voice, I said, was that I couldn't alarm her. I babbled anything, all that stuff about sunbursts and Gila monsters was scooped off the top of my head. I was drunk and wanted her to think Vico was too drunk to talk so I could get off the phone and go find him. I was going to put him to bed and then call her back to tell her he was okay.

And when I couldn't find him, I told her, I got panicky. Went home to think.

As I talked I'd been edging along the porch rail, closer to her. At everything I said she nodded, nodding and blinking, and a dimple on her chin came and went like the shadow of a bank swallow on the smooth water far below us. When I got close to her, she put the hand that had been on the rail on my arm, and kept nodding, her eyes skating all over my face and back to my eyes and I never looked away, because I could tell what she was seeing was me—not Uncle Farley, but the person Spyhawk and I together had become.

That's what made me finally say the last thing I'd come that night to tell her. That night on the phone, I said. That business about her in my dreams. She nodded. It was Vico's voice, I said. But that was me talking. She nodded. Ever since I was a kid, I said. Sometimes I'd see her in my grade school, standing at the end of a hall, standing alone in a shaft of sunlight. Wait for me, I'd say, only by the time I got to where she'd been, I'd hear footsteps going upstairs. And when I'd got to the next floor, there would be another hall, and her at the end of it. Later, after Beth died, sometimes I'd be trying to find an inlet for *The Merry Widower* and see her waving from a cliff and by the time I'd docked and scrambled up, the cliff was the empty school. And always when I woke up, I would try to keep her face sharp in my mind and it would do a slow dissolve until I would forget what she looked like till the next time I dreamed her.

"Until I saw you," I said. "I recognized you."

Lisa was silent. How long did it go on, her silence? Was it really just long enough for her to press the back of her wrist against her forehead, then lower it and look at me again? It was long enough for me to know that I'd done what I came for. Like Vico in the ritual scene at the heart of each picture, I'd torn away the mask.

I watched it so many times, Vico. I should have known that the unmasking, the final seduction, was for you a moment of ultimate jeopardy. If it worked, the rest of the picture fell into place around it. But if the unmasking, the confession, failed to seduce, it left you naked.

Lisa's silence went on, each second not twenty-four frames long, but fifty, a hundred, and while I watched the hand she had pressed against her brow pass slow as the earth's shadow crossing the face of the moon, I had time to imagine in intricate detail Vico preparing some new version of the ritual, with Lisa his sole audience, the ritual complicated by a strange game or test or discipline that forbade him to make love to her, but still required her absolute acceptance of whatever horror he might reveal. And as Lisa's head was rolling back, her hair floating on a leisurely underwater current, I had time to see that in each picture Vico would have to repeat the confession, the seduction, because no matter how well it succeeds, nothing that follows after he tears away the mask—*nothing* can approach the intensity of the moment he spends waiting for her response.

I saw, as if I were far from the earth observing the crawl of armies and generations across its surface, that love stories end at the altar because marriage is the long decline, with security the bribe, with someone to warm the sheets the bribe, a splendid arrangement for stockbrokers, but for Vico—Vico the actor—I saw that what the actor in him wanted was not security, not even love. What he wanted was intensity. That, I saw, was what he was trying to get back with Lisa when he left his note on her pillow. And while I watched her lips parting, the tip of her tongue drifting across her upper lip, I saw now for certain that it wasn't contempt he'd felt—it was knowing there'd been a moment when he risked everything, stripped himself bare under her eyes, and wanting to get it back, get back the moment just before she spoke. And there—while her eyes were still lowered, as they were beginning to rise, rising, meeting mine—I realized *that* was the connection—that intensity. It was a drug, and Vico and I were both hooked. It was the giddy *moment* that I tried to freeze on film, the moment he could get only by circling back in each picture to the same scene—his twisted striptease of the soul.

I kissed her. She was heavy in my arms, said I'd better go, she needed sleep.

That's when I knew my confession had changed nothing. There was still a wall, like a wall of glass, between me and the one I wanted, so that I could never touch, never really touch. Only look.

Me too, I said. Sleep. Only I didn't close my eyes till a long time later, that afternoon high in the mountains in a shady spot alongside the road where I parked the car for a couple hours and stretched out along the front seat, because I'd been blurring and seeing double and was afraid I'd drive straight off a cliff into a cloud. I didn't dream my Lisa dream. I dreamed that deer bursting out of the woods and bounding off over the hill, the most graceful shot I ever put on film, only instead of tracking it with a movie camera, I had the stock of a hunting rifle to my cheek and my eye squinting down a good scope sight. I woke with my right arm hanging off the seat of the car, my fingers curled around the barrel of the gun I'd dreamed. I'd thought I could strip away a lifetime of lies in one night. But Spyhawk wasn't so easy to kill. If only one of us could survive, he thought, let it be him. I'd bought the rifle that morning after I left Lisa and laid it on the floorboards under the passenger seat along with a bag of ham-and-cheese sandwiches and a half-dozen oranges and a thermos of coffee and some pint bottles of whiskey.

I ate sandwiches and drank some coffee and drove again, and it wasn't till I was over the hump and winding down the mountain, the glinting ocean far behind and nothing ahead but the shimmer of the desert floor and the distant purple wall of mountains where I would find Singleton and Vico, that I realized Lisa must have known that if she had arrived at the beach house an hour after I said I'd left, she couldn't have walked into a cloud of steam in Vico's bathroom.

CHAPTER XXII

1. The Valley of the Shadow

FOR THE FINAL scene of his last film Vico would return to that shot of wood grain on the study desk where he drafted his scripts. We'll double-expose it, Farley, he would tell me, blend wood grain and wind patterns. Then we slow-dissolve the wood grain, let them see the desk was always only a disguise, and what's left, what's underneath the wood, is that stretch of sand dunes that spills out of Emigrant Wash. Just like that, he would pretend to discard his last disguise. As if the core of the mystery I'd tried seven years to trap on film could dissolve as easily as the flesh on Don Juan's cheeks. I've worked it out, he'd say. We can land a plane right behind the Stovepipe Wells Hotel. Think of it, Farley. A ten-mile aerial track up the salt flats where von Stroheim finished *Greed.* We shoot a prairie hawk winding up the valley, then we put your lens inside its eye. We soar and dip, mile after mile, we keep the landscape pouring off the bottom of the frame, till the audience is parched for the sight of something alive, anything: a prairie dog, a sidewinder rippling down a dune, a face—a human face. And then he would lean toward me, shoot me that up-from-under sly-lizard look, and say, Here's the best part, Farley: Once we make them want a face, what do we give them instead? *Think,* Farley. Remember Gibson Gowland out on that desert clubbing Jean Hersholt to death with the pistol butt? Hersholt's body goes limp, Gowland gets to his feet. And Hersholt's arm rises after him, even the ghost won't let go. Hersholt has handcuffed them wrist to wrist. Gowland stands there—long shot—looking around him. Off in the shimmery distance: mountains. The mountains he has to cross to get water. Between him and them: not a tree, not a shrub—only a dead burro, an empty canteen. So what we give them, Farley, what we circle in on, is the bones—first the burro, the saddlebags sunk through its ribs, gold pieces spilled in the sand, crusted with salt. Then Hersholt and Gowland. We shoot straight down on them, still wristbone to wristbone, then pan up the bone arms for a tight shot of the skulls, staring eye sockets, burned hollow by the sun.

Sometimes he would do that—take an idea out beyond what was possible just to make sure his big-star publicity hadn't got to me, impressed me so much I was scared to haul him down. He needn't have worried. And he would always leave me to work out the connections for myself, to trace the handcuffs back to the "Strangler's Hands?" slug and figure out that he knew all along it should have been my wrist locked to his, the two of us getting out of the police car in the newsreels, climbing the station-house steps through the press of the crowd.

2. Shooting Script

AS SOON AS Lisa mentioned the Faceless Man's letter, I knew I'd find Vico in Death Valley. I didn't even need the sand that spilled from the envelope. I'd always, in a way, known Vico was alive, and where. Known it the way I knew things that Spyhawk stashed like a pack rat in that part of my brain he kept sealed off from me. Why should I complain? Everybody needs a private place. Spyhawk more than others. He had a lot to hide. I knew about the letter, because the night of Vico's disappearance, when Spyhawk came to the beach house, to kill him or beg his forgiveness, he found it on the study desk along with another—Vico's goodbye to his wife. The two sheets—with Vico's goodbye on top—had their upper corners slid beneath that photo of Vico and Chaney linking arms with a wooden dummy. Spyhawk had them in his hand when he answered the phone and heard Lisa's voice.

He'd been there more than an hour already, wandering Vico's empty rooms, rooting through his dresser drawers, reading his old diaries, letters from Berenice—and something else, too, a real find for Vico's biographer. A slender, rubber-band-wrapped packet of letters he found at the bottom of a shoebox full of colored rocks and a split milkweed pod. They were from a woman he never mentioned to me, who told him in December of 1926, in a hand slanting in precise copybook parallels, that the lace mantilla he had stuffed in his pocket that night on the Cape had belonged to her grandmother and he was welcome to keep it because it could never now mean to her what it had, but she wished never to see his face again. How many times this past decade, I wondered, had she turned away from a movie marquee or a page in a newspaper?

While he read Vico's mail, Spyhawk had been playing dress-up, too, just like when he would pose in front of the mirror with his old man's trousers rolled to the knee, his head capped to the eyebrows in a mothball-smelling fedora. In a bedroom closet he'd recognized the khaki uniform Vico wore in *City of Sapphires,* and tried on the jacket. By that time of night and that stage of his drunk, it was the most natural thing in the world for Spyhawk to answer Lisa's voice with his Vico voice, and because he didn't know how Vico would deal with some of her more intimate questions, he used Vico's own words as a script. The letter explained that he wanted the desert to burn him away, burn him down, burn him to a core he could control. Lisa said, Eric, I think we should be apart awhile longer, maybe for good. And she heard Vico's voice say, A Gila monster will lock its jaws on your arm and not let go till sunset, even if you beat it to death. And when she said, I'm thinking about divorce, Spyhawk read her a line about the summer heat, how all day the sun could murder you, burst your brain like a grape, but at night there were stars you'd never seen. And when she wept and said, Don't you care at all? he told her in the next month he could catch the desert spring, the flowers spreading petals in the sun. But I've got to hurry, he said. Can't let too much time lapse. They bloom a few weeks and they're gone.

After that conversation had been edited by the staticky phone line and a few thunderclaps and Lisa's memory, and found its way from Lieutenant Hoensinger's notebook to his official, filed-in-triplicate report, and from there to the pages of the *Tablet,* it was a fine verbal version of the Kuleshov experiment. Truth is whatever explains what you see. The only problem with that is you never see more than about ten frames a second, and everybody knows it takes twenty-four to get a passable imitation of life.

Spyhawk played Vico better than Vico on the final take of the best scene he ever shot. For love scenes Vico had a voice with a yearning, almost mourning throb, a voice that wanted something so deep in a woman she didn't know it was there till he'd told her. That was the voice Spyhawk used when he said he'd met her in a dream. It was the voice he counted on to bring her out in the storm to the beach house.

I've spent a long time piecing together what happened next. Once he hung up the phone, Spyhawk ripped the cord out of the wall. When she comes, he thought, I don't want any interruptions. He hung Vico's uniform jacket back in his closet and put the Faceless Man's letter and Vico's goodbye to Lisa in the pocket of his suit coat. Lisa's hour-long drive to the beach house would give Spyhawk some time to fill. He stared for a while at the Chaney-Vico photo, then smashed the glass frame on a corner of the desk. He took Vico's fountain pen and gave the face a new disguise—the Groucho mustache and glasses. By now, still floating but feeling a few feeble tugs of sobriety, the idea of Lisa's finding him in the beach house worried him more than it pleased him. He poured another drink and felt worse. He had a couple more while he thought about what he'd say to her. Maybe he fell asleep. He woke sometime after one o'clock and decided she wasn't coming. Then he saw what he'd done to Vico's favorite snapshot. He ripped it into little pieces and cried awhile. After that he thought he would go for a swim in the ocean. He took off his shoes and socks and left them neatly by the back door, and walked out to the path. Once he felt the rain and the suck of the mud on the path, he came back inside. His wet clothes made him chilly. He went to the bathroom with a jagged piece of glass from the photo frame. He turned on the tub water hot as he could stand it. The clothes he stripped off were a disguise he would never need again. The bathroom filled with steam. Behind the foggy mirror glass something fleshy moved. He rubbed a knothole-size space in the mirror and peeked inside. An eye caught him peeking. The eye looked raw, peeled. It made him think of a photo he'd seen of a body on an autopsy table, the skin cut like a full sack and pinned back to the table, parts of the body where the sun ought never to shine exposed. Lust and hate crawled in the eye like maggots. Watching the eye, he touched the jagged glass to his left wrist. Maybe he thought it would be fun having Lisa find Farley bled to death in the bath. Maybe by that time he'd forgotten about Lisa, he was calling her Beth and telling the eye in the mirror he'd show her what she'd put him through. He made a cut. A little cut. Not enough blood to drain a rat. But it scared him partly sober. He wrapped a hand towel around his wrist and held it there while he searched the medicine chest for gauze and adhesive tape, then he wrapped the cut with that.

He felt his heart beating and was dizzy. He got in the bathtub and lay down eardrum-deep, resting his bandaged wrist on the rim. After a while, he thought, he might rip off the bandage and let his wrist bleed into the water. He turned off the roaring taps and lay gazing along his body. With his ears underwater he listened to whalebelly gurgles and cracks and wondered what they might be saying. At opposite walls of the tub his knees broke water, leaning away from each other. A dreamy shift to a long lens made them twin rock crags, the last high ground in the flood. A great shot: the water rising, people clawing a hold on the cliffs. It was a scene he'd shot before. When he was five, his mother gave him a book of illustrated Bible stories that she'd used in a high school religion class. The best picture, the one he'd lived in for hours at a time, showed a flooded town, heavy lines of rain slanting down the sky, streaming off the tile roofs, and people in the rain, some thrashing in the water, some struggling onto the roofs, looking down at the rising water with white-eyed snarls. On a rock cliff more people hung on to bushes and boulders that would soon be swept away. Far in the distance Noah's ark rocked snug in the storm. For weeks in the bath he would watch the water tighten its ring around his belly, close over it while drowning sinners struggled toward the distant peaks of his knees. As the rain poured on, he lowered his knees in the water till the last one drowned. One day he decided that lowering his knees to drown them didn't give it the right look. He had to keep his knees still and make the water *rise,* as it did in the real flood. It was one of those details that had to be right, and later when Vico would go for another take in a scene anybody else would have called a print, he knew why. He turned on the tap and stuffed a washcloth into the holes of the overflow drain. The water covered his knees and drowned the last sinner and when his mother came in and saw the water spilling over the tub rim, she yanked the washcloth out of the drain and yanked him out of the water. Now, in Vico's bathtub, no mother to stop him, he stuffed the overflow drain, poking in the washcloth with his toe. In a dreamy trance, with a gurgle in the eaves like the drowning rain in the *Bible,* he turned on the hot water, lay back in the tub with a sigh. The water rose, drowning all the sinners, till only the cherry tip of his cock kept its head up, and then the lapping water made it stretch its neck. No mother now to lift him out of the flood, he was thinking, when he remembered Lisa was on the way.

At the same moment he heard a car door slam. He burst from the bath, scooped his clothes and shoes off the floor, and dashed naked down the hall to a spare bedroom. In it a stairway led to the attic. Tiptoe sprint up the attic steps. At the top step he stopped, his teeth clacking, afraid to step on the creaky attic boards. The attic ran the length of the house, with a window at each end and two gable windows making nooks in each slope of the roof.

Up here, with only the roof between him and the storm, the rain beats louder. The long bare room is alive with trickles and sucks. He listens for movement below. No sound but the rain. If she's there, he thinks, the puddles in the hall will lead her straight to him. Let her at least, he prays, find me dressed. He pulls on his wet clothes. Still no sound below. Maybe there was no car, maybe it was only a shutter slamming in the wind. He is about to go back downstairs when headlights sweep the front windows, the shadows of the rafters stretch and shrink. He sprints to the window. Lisa's car is climbing the hill. She'll see my car, he thinks, then remembers: Turning into Vico's private road, he had cut his car lights, nosed slowly up in the dark, and turned off into his usual place under the pines, so he could approach unannounced.

Standing at the attic window he sees lightning in quick diminishing pulses toss up the silhouette of a palm tree, and he prays, Oh God, don't let her find me. He stifles a sneeze, then another. He hears her below him, moving from room to room, turning on lights, calling Vico's name. He hears her call the name softly as she climbs the stairs to the second floor, then hears her calling it outside the bathroom door, and hears the louder gushing of the tap as the door opens. Thinking of the shot Farley could get of her walking into the steamy room, the steam closing around her silhouette, he hears her soft yelp as her foot comes down on the blood-soaked towel. Then her footsteps chatter down the steps, her breath a single keening cry, jarred like a hiccup as her weight hits each step. He hears her jiggle the cradle of the dead phone, hears her whimper as she realizes she is cut off, alone. When he hears the screen door that opens onto the back driveway crack against the doorframe, he crosses the attic to a back window and looks down on her car, the headlights she left on while she was inside dim through the rain, the sound of the starter faint. The starter sounds like someone trying to retch, feeble, fainter each time. Then she leaves the car, running through puddles, not back to the house but down the drive. Crossing back to the front window, he watches for her to appear, and when she does, lit by the lights from the living-room windows that slash out over the lawn, freezing raindrops in slanting lines, she is still running, stumbling along the gravel road in high heels, those open-toed pumps, but before she gets beyond the light's farthest spill she has slowed to a fast walk. In the dark, he thinks, in the dark and the rain, and frightened, she will pass the pine trees and not see my car. Without a car she will be a long time finding a house to phone the police. A few minutes later, hunched low over the wheel, whipping around a highway curve, he spots her trying to flag him down, and turns his headlamp beam up bright to blind her as he sails past.

All the way back to town the retinal ghost of her face hovered above the slick, pocked, hubcap-deep streets.

At first, soaked from his dash to the car, he felt a prickly chill and thought that's why his teeth were chattering. Then all the steamy heat of the bathtub seemed to rise and press against his skin, and his teeth still chattered. As he coasted into his apartment garage, the roof of his mouth had a familiar sour ache. He started up the inside steps from the garage, sneezing. By the time he reached the lobby to collect his mail, he'd given his body back to me.

3. Invitation to a Coward

EARLY NEXT MORNING I woke up choking. My pneumonia was drowning me. Coming back from the bathroom I saw the rain on my windowpane. It made the street below undulate the way we showed it in *City of Sapphires*, when Count Boris sits at the café window filling the ashtray and peering out at the wet desolate street, slowly coming to hear the mockery that had been in Isulte's laugh as she urged him to go on ahead and she would cross the frontier on the midnight train. Then I sank into sleep again, wondering why sleeping in the rain didn't cool me off, why in the middle of a storm that was filling my lungs with water, my body was still parched. I slept and stoked my fever all through the first radio reports and the first editions of the papers telling about the washed-out bridges and drowned people and Vico's disappearance, and I never saw till later that photo of Lisa in Hoensinger's office, sitting in the same chair where I'd once sat, a wing of her raincoat collar raked along her cheek, her eyes gone blank from the glare of flashbulbs and headlights, and the tilt of that cup in her right hand bringing the coffee so close to the rim you knew exactly how slight a jolt it would take to spill her into hysteria. I slept on, dreaming my dream of Bolger telling me I would have to wade into the ocean to get a shot of a man-of-war, until the phone rang and Simmons announced that Vico's house was full of blood and Lieutenant Hoensinger was wondering why I hadn't reported for work. As soon as I hung up to get ready for Hoensinger's visit I knew it would be a question of hiding clues, because the last thing I clearly recalled before Spyhawk took charge was sitting in a bar some time after my shouting match with Bolger, rotating a glass on the table top as if it were the combination of a safe, and deciding as I spun the glass left, right, left again, and the tumblers fell into place and the chamber of my true desire sprang open, that the way to be free of Vico was to kill him.

About what really had happened I knew nothing. I knew that what was a wish to Farley could be an act to Spyhawk, and that Spyhawk had been prowling. I knew that I had less than half an hour before Hoensinger rang my bell. I raked my eyes over the spilled glasses and strewn clothes Spyhawk had left in my room. I noticed the bloody bandage on my wrist. I thought how to hide it. Only one way: be in bed when Hoensinger comes, keep the arm under the covers. Tuck your hairy ears under Grandma's night cap and try not to show your fangs. I remember that as I gathered my damp clothes and dumped them on the closet floor, I felt a stiff crinkle in the pocket of my suit coat and thought it was probably a wad of bills. During the quick search Hoensinger gave my apartment while I drifted off into delirium, all that kept him from proving that I'd been in Vico's house the night before, reading Vico's letter to Lisa over the phone, was the drunken vomit on my suit coat. What else would have made Hoensinger pass up the chance to search the pocket? After he'd gone and I was packing, knowing by the time he returned I would have to be far away, I was running water from the bathroom faucet over the jacket when I felt again the papery crinkle in the pocket and pulled out the papers I'd found on Vico's desk.

Phrases from Vico's letter sounded like things I thought I'd dreamed of telling her. Things about Gila monsters, murderous heat, the desert sun bursting your skull like a grape. Singleton's letter to Vico talked about some of the same things, but in his invitation I could almost hear the familiar, taunting drawl Singleton always used when he was telling Vico how he intended to drop from a treetop into the lap of an awning, then grab the awning's iron frame and kick himself through the window. Singleton always spoke to Vico with the faint sneer of a professional explaining his tricks to an outsider. Vico pretended not to notice, but he grilled Singleton all the more, made him review his timing to the second. At first I used to wonder whether he was worried about Singleton's safety or just making sure that if he got hurt somebody would be able to tell his replacement how to do the job. Then I decided that the elaborate grilling was Vico's way of reminding Singleton that he depended on Vico's approval. Finally I noticed that while Vico was listening to Singleton, his head was constantly nodding, his eyes full of sick dread. For all his daring as an artist, I decided, he was a physical coward. Sometimes with the help of his compulsion to do everything from choosing camera angles to designing costumes, he would make himself do a mildly dangerous stunt. Other times he would squirm with shame and let Singleton take a risk he had refused, and cover it with that elaborate calm grilling, proving to Singleton that the stunt was just one more aspect of the production that he wanted to get on film exactly as he saw it in his artist's eye. Singleton had developed a thousand subtle ways of saying, "Shit, boss, it's so easy you could do it yourself, wanna try?" It was that tone I recognized, a tone so familiar I didn't even need to glance at the signature to know who was writing, saying he was making a trip to the city soon to sell a piece of property he'd got tired of paying taxes on and Vico was welcome, if he was really fed up as he claimed he was, to hitch a ride back with him to the valley and learn how to live with nobody watching.

The road along the mountain had a logic like water or a snake, and as it meandered toward the desert floor I wondered what it was in Vico that had made him an easy sucker for the old taunt and mock of Singleton's letter. And then, with the road looping me out for a glimpse of the white-gold glare below, it hit me: cowardice. His trembly, chicken-heart cowardice. I remembered the day the gas tank exploded, the grim set of Vico's mouth as he plotted the exact landmarks of his sprint across the gravel fan to the airplane, his breathy voice as he asked Thorny to show what he could do with the machine gun, and the spasm that jerked Thorny's arm when the gun stuttered, the way it tossed up splashes of sand and how the silence after it stopped had sizzled and tasted of gunpowder in the back of my throat. And then I knew that Vico's twisting his ankle during the rehearsal had been no accident. For Vico an explosion ripping away his face would have been a perfect fate, an aesthetic climax. But he'd seen it coming, heard a whisper, a dry hiss of sand in a desert breeze, and drawn back. He'd sent Singleton in his place.

When the crew dragged Singleton away from the burning plane, his hands were pressed over his face as if they were holding it together, and I took a quick glimpse of Vico the instant before he overcame his own horror and moved in to help. His hands were up, frozen an inch from his own face. He was the actor, trying out the gesture, remembering how it would feel.

I never saw Singleton after they took off the bandages, but hearing he was back in the desert hadn't surprised me. One night a couple days before the accident he'd come into the dining room at the Stovepipe Wells Hotel, where the crew was staying during the shooting, all excited about gold and silver. We'd been doing only close work that day, and since he had the time off, he'd done some exploring. He'd found his way through the Panamints to a ghost town called Ballarat, where he spent the day talking to an old prospector who prowled the hills with a pick and a string of burros.

In the months after the accident, months that dissolved during the next year into casting calls and costume fittings for *The Mask of Don Juan,* we got at intervals of days or weeks, mostly from Vico who kept in touch, news of Singleton, mostly a series of operations. Snipping away the dead time lying in hospital beds while the tightening scar tissue itched under the cocoon of bandages, you could splice together the story. A montage of ether masks descending on Singelton's face, each with five fingertips peeking around the rim, and then the eyes of his surgeons, framed between skullcap and facemask, dissolving from confident to doubtful to grim as Singleton's voice counting backward from one hundred stretched to a slow-motion baritone and faded to black.

The first week we were shooting *The Mask of Don Juan,* Vico came on the set one morning while I was checking setups and lighting for the day's shots and said Singleton had gone under the knife for the last time. "You don't mean he's dead," I said. After a pause Vico said, "No. He's just not letting the doctors play mud pie in his face anymore." And Vico's gaze drifted off so that if you didn't know him better you'd think he was staring straight into a sun arc, and he said, "He's back in Death Valley. Got some idea he knows where to find the Gunsight Lode." I was standing thirty feet up on a ladder. I slotted a gel in the liko I was setting and said, "We ought to load up a camera and follow him. Sounds like a good plot for a movie." It was a tossaway line, something I said while I waited to see what Vico was feeling, and I ought to have known it would have occurred to him, too, and the difference between us was that I tossed it away and he hoarded everything till he could use it.

The Gunsight Lode had been a legend since a party of Forty-niners got lost on its way to the gold fields and wandered for weeks, winding up one canyon after another, and when the survivors had scrambled up a high ridge of the Panamints and one looked back at the blinding white salt bowl and kicked a rock down the slope and said, "So long, Death Valley," the name stuck like a cactus needle. It wasn't till they'd got to Los Angeles and had a bath and spent some days drinking long drinks from glasses they could always refill, that one of them took a shiny rock he'd carried out of the valley to a blacksmith and said, "Can you make me a gunsight out of this?" And the blacksmith said, "You sure you don't want to take it over to the assay office first? It looks like you got a vein of pure silver running through there." And even that wasn't enough to warn him, shush him, because he blurted out to the blacksmith that by damn, he'd picked that rock off a whole mountain full of the same, and by the time he got together a string of burros and supplies, there were already two other parties waiting at the edge of town to track him back to the valley. He never found the silver mountain, but men who believed it was there could eat sand and granite and drink from sinkholes that would poison a horse, and they'd been disappearing into the Panamints ever since. Singleton was only the most recent in a long line of believers, people who get a little crazy when the Santa Ana blows through a gap in the mountains. They feel that dry heat full of Mojave grit and think they hear a voice in the wind that calls their name.

"He says he knows where to find it, Farley," Vico said, and I can see him now, standing with his hand on one of the iron staples that were used to chain the asylum inmates to the wall, looking straight up at me. "Remember that day we were shooting on the salt flats, and he wandered over to Ballarat? It wasn't just talking to prospectors that had him so excited that night he got back. He never told us. While he was out roaming, he came over a canyon ridge and got struck blind. With him standing just where he was and the sun at just that angle behind him, the whole vein glittered, he said, just like sunlight on water. He said he thought it was a waterfall, water pouring down a gash in the mountain. And when he'd closed his eyes a minute till he could see again, and walked sideways so the shine glanced away a bit, he saw it was a vein of silver, so wide you couldn't hide it under a barn roof. Just like the old Forty-niner stories. 'You got your pile of silver up on that silver screen, Vico,' he told me. 'I'm gonna get mine, too. Right out of the ground. Want to bet which vein gets played out first?'"

And I freeze on the ladder, Vico's eyes staring me dumb, daring me to say the Gunsight Lode is only an excuse, that you wouldn't find raw silver shiny as a table knife, and the real reason Singleton went back to Death Valley is that it's a place where he can walk all day with only pack rats and sidewinders to stare at his ruined face.

CHAPTER XXIII

1. First Person Singular

SOMEWHERE IN THE mountains cupping Death Valley, Singleton had scratched himself a burrow out of the sun's eye, a place where he could hide. Wherever he was, Vico—with his own monstrous face—hid there, too. The road down the inland slopes of the San Gabriels unraveled, dropping me toward the flat Mojave floor.

I drove out into the desert. I read the horizon with a nervous eye, as if I were scouting location shots and not finding them. All I saw was a scorched landscape—a stubble of mesquite; cactus plants that guarded their lives with thorns; and then, the first sign of spring: a stand of Joshua trees waving white pompoms at the ends of their arms. The Joshua tree was named for the Old Testament Joshua who stopped the sun in the sky by holding his arms up to God. My true ancestor, I thought. I do the same thing with a click of the shutter and don't even need to pray.

I drove along the main street of Mojave in mid-afternoon. Diner, gas station, feed store, bar and hardware, a few houses with paint flaking like dead skin from a sunburn. And a grocery. I stopped there for more supplies, a frying pan and a pot, a fork and spoon, a pocket knife with a can opener, and food and water for a week. People behind the plate-glass windows of the diner and the feed store didn't seem to be interrupting any other work to watch me pass. A wind streaming out of the mountains blew grit against my cheek. I closed the driver's-side window until the cab of my old Packard grew stale as a coffin. Ahead to my left a man-size clump of tumbleweed flung itself at my hood, scraping for a hold, then—as my foot hit the brake—the left front wheel yanked it out of sight, snarling and scratching, caught in the fender. My heart was pounding as if what I dragged were a live thing clawing to be let inside, and when it fell away and I saw it shrink in my rear-view window, crushed and skidding in the breeze, I stepped on the gas and sped away.

As I drive, I'm thinking: Time the blink of an eye. A quarter of a second? Call it that. Six frames. How far—in a quarter-second—can a '32 Packard travel on smooth blacktop? How far can it go—dart along, toward a vanishing point in the Panamint foothills? One of those word problems at the end of the chapter. And how far in the still, thin air of a Death Valley spring can a fresh-oiled deer rifle toss a bullet? An eyeblink, a moment of darkness—and you blink awake to find that all your years behind a viewfinder were good practice for this long patient stare down a telescope sight mounted over a rifle barrel. It's simple, as any final thing is. No need to worry about adjusting lamps, balancing tones, erasing shadows under the nose. Enough light to see by is all you need. A balanced composition? Again—simple. All that gives the space inside that circle meaning is the place where the crosshairs meet—over the heart; between the eyes. Not much difference, really, between a viewfinder and a gunsight. Both are simple tools for people who want to stop time. Emile Vico, 1899-1938. Cut it and print.

Only this time, I'm thinking, it won't be Vico who chooses the ending. The script is mine. I choose the angle. I call for a take, anytime I want. And this time, the final cut is mine. There's no Spyhawk with his scissors, snipping the best shots to the cutting-room floor. I'm wide awake, staring my eyes raw, because sometimes all he needs is a moment in the dark, the blink of an eye—and he takes over.

I'm wide awake so that after it's over I can say I was the one. I was the one, stretched along a granite ledge with the smooth stock of a rifle to his cheek. I was the one, sighting across a gravel fan to the dark mouth of the mine shaft. I was the one, waiting for Emile Vico's last entrance. I'm wide awake, so that later—after I walk across the canyon floor and nuzzle my toe under the shoulder to flip the body onto its back for a last close-up—I don't have to gag on the hypocritical stench of my own breath when I say: My God, what have I done.

2. Where Time Stopped

BEYOND MOJAVE, ROUTE 6 angled northeast, and I was pricked with the same excitement I had felt roaming the empty rooms of the beach house, ransacking drawers and scanning the documents of Vico's ancient betrayals for clues to what had made him who he became. This bleak country, too, would spell out pieces of the puzzle, if only I could learn to see what his eyes had seen. I looked out over the mudbed of a dry lake. If the storm in which he had disappeared had hit the desert, too, he might have seen real water there, and flowers in bloom. Now, six weeks later, all that was left for me was a mirage, a quicksilver shimmer. To my left the mountains made a silent leap like when I switch to a long lens, that brought the horizon near and high, blocking the sky. What was here, I wondered, that could feed his eye—and the next second I rounded a curve and spotted a trail into the mountain. I braked and turned up it, my breath coming quicker, trusting a memory elusive as a smell to tell me why. Just when I was looking for a wide place in the trail to turn back, the spike-tip pines dropped away and the chaparral and creosote bushes thinned to a bald hillside. Somebody had put up a sign: "ROARING RIDGE PETRIFIED FOREST, admission fifty cents, children free." Four years earlier Vico had lurched me up this same road, scouting locations for *Mark of Cain.* We had paid fifty cents and spent an hour wandering among the trunks of a forest centuries dead. They lay in sections like broken icicles, all their living sap and pulp hardened to agate and jasper and onyx—preserved like an image on film. "More beautiful dead than alive," I say, and Vico turns to me, shading his eyes with his hand. "In a different way, maybe," he says.

I stopped the car for a minute to let the engine cool. The ticket taker lost his greeting smile when he saw I wasn't going to buy my way onto the hill. A false scent, I told myself. I knew he wasn't here, yet I found it hard to leave. Here in the forest where not even death made things decay, it seemed needless to worry over lost time. I was tired, my long night with Lisa catching up to me. Languidly tired, with all the time in the world. I knew I would find him, and when I did, it would be just as it had been when I spotted the trail up here to this rock hill: a sudden recognition, my heart knocking like an alarm clock, and me doing what came next without a thought.

I drove on, remembering that the rough trail eventually drops back toward the road. A couple miles farther on I passed through a canyon where a string of dugouts hung in the wall, some fitted with doors and windows stripped from abandoned houses. I remember Vico slowing the car. He sticks his head out the window. "They're like cliff swallows," he says. "What makes them live like that? Does each one think he's going to be the one to strike it rich?" "You better put on a hat," I tell him. "You'll get sunstroke."

A prospector winding along a path with a burro stopped when I stopped the car and hollered: "Hey, you seen any strangers up there?" He gaped at me without speaking. "Somebody new," I said. "Just in the last six weeks. Big forehead. Full lips. Eyes—" He flicked a switch at his burro, moving on into the mountains. "Eyes a little bulgy," I hollered. "You seen him? Hey! You take a goddam vow of silence or something?" He rounded a fold of the path. I was left with a tumble of my own echoes.

I rejoined the road and shifted into second up the grade into Randsburg and stopped for coffee at a diner with a red Coke sign blazing on the wall beside the door. At a corner table a leather-skinned man with watery blue eyes lowered his voice and continued a conversation with another man in a low buzz. The waitress who served my coffee wore an apron streaked with hamburger blood. Now and then some urgency roiled out of the buzz at the corner table and I caught the words: "...it's the *lode,* I tell you, the *real* lode...just get me a *stake,* that's *all I ask*...out there, waitin'..." The words all circled back on one another, like a fly on the counter that kept returning to the same sticky paste of cherry-pie juice, and the buzz of the voices in the dry heat blended with the buzzing fly and I felt as if I were overhearing sins in a confessional box.

I curved down the mountain and bumped across the railroad track and drove uphill again and then down and crossed the tracks again near the jigsaw-cracked mud of another dry lake. Then I threaded a pass between two mountains and came out heading straight across a valley toward the Panamints, where the empty town of Ballarat got its last hour of sun.

"Where was that again?" somebody had said, and Singleton joined his lips in a delicate line—his lips in repose so like Vico's I sometimes found myself staring at them, the same pouty ripeness, the same fleshy beak. And the crowd around the table in the bar of the Stovepipe Wells Hotel, where the crew is drinking away the day's thirst, pauses to watch him say: "Ba." And then, "La," like a voice teacher demonstrating articulation, and then, with a ripping sound, "Rrrat!"

"Ballarat," he says, telling us all how he spent his day off wandering through the hills in a flatbed truck, until he came to a ghost town called Ballarat, where he met an old Indian prospector.

And he tells us what the Indian told him about a desert mirage called the Lost Gunsight Lode. He doesn't tell us he's seen it.

That's how I knew I'd find Singleton's trail in Ballarat.

3. The Western Street Set

AHEAD, STILL A WAY out from town, there was an abandoned shack—a couple boards nailed over the window. I swung in alongside it, putting the shack between the car and eyes from the town. If Vico was near—and my neckhairs tingled as if I'd caught his scent on a breeze—I wanted him in my sights before he knew me. I walked back to the road and was starting toward town when I saw mountains and desert through the shack's front door. The side wall where my car was parked and the charred boards of the front wall were the only ones standing. What was left of the other walls had been drifted over. Here and there they broke the sand like fractured bones. A blackened brass bedstead had been dragged a little way, then abandoned. I squatted behind it a minute to line up a shot of the town through its bars. An arty shot, the kind Vico would have gone for up till he made *Mark of Cain,* but not since. The bars kept nothing in or out. There was no movement in the town.

I went back to my car and reached under the seat for a flat pint bottle of whiskey, still in its brown bag. I slid it into my hip pocket. Trinkets for the natives. Then I walked down the road. The sun dropping at my back laid my shadow out long ahead and made the empty sky blue. Then in what seemed like a dozen steps a shadow flooded the valley and the mountains beyond the town went purple-gray. They loomed above the squat, weathered buildings ahead like a tidal wave stopped by the click of a shutter.

I passed tin cans and a bucket with a rusted-out bottom, then a broken pick handle, a couple stove-in barrels. Then I noticed broken whiskey bottles, the glass purpled by the sun, more and more of them, cluttered thicker the nearer I got, till they made a mosaic pavement that took me into town.

The wood shacks and adobe huts didn't worry much about facing onto the street or crowding in close. The biggest of them was a long wooden building with a plank sign over the door that read: "Chris Wicht's Saloon." Between "Wicht's" and "Saloon" someone had slashed a caret and printed above it in a wobbly primer hand the word "FORMER." Except for a couple huts that still had a tin roof, the adobe walls were bare to the sky. Wind had rounded off the edges of the walls. The wood shacks kept sharper edges. Some were tar-papered and thc tar paper peeled like blistered skin. One still had a stovepipe. Another had its front door and window boarded shut, but the side and back walls had been crowbarred away to kindle fires.

When I saw that I knew why the street seemed familiar. It was a movie set, a western street facade, all front walls for the camera to glide over, but nobody moving behind the windows, nobody making breakfast or playing the radio, and if you stepped behind the facade, nothing but bare beams propping them up.

Behind me a board ticked in the still air, and there, leaning in the doorway of a shack where a minute ago there had been nobody, was an Indian. He wore a black vest and a brown fedora with a pinprick hole in the vee of the crown. He stared at me as if he'd been looking a long time.

4. Shoshone Bob

HE HAD DECIDED I would be the first to speak. I walked over and put one foot on the shack's porch step. He didn't move his head, not even to keep me in focus. If his eyes moved, I couldn't tell. They were squeezed between folds of flesh so thick no whites showed. Everywhere but his high, smooth mahogany cheeks was covered with ancient wrinkles. On the end of his chin a few gray hairs were twisted to a point.

I said, "Howdy." Then I stiffened. My foot on his step seemed like a dare. The other foot stayed in the street. Against his own thigh the Indian held a revolver. It wasn't pointing at me, just hung in his hand as if it had been there when he heard somebody in the street and walked over to the door to find out who. But I had the idea that it could be brought up very fast.

I took my foot slowly off the step and held my hands away from my sides to show they were empty.

"I didn't know anybody still lived here," I said. "I'm looking for a guy, maybe you know him."

The gun barrel didn't seem to have moved, only the hand. Now the gun was being held, gripped. The forefinger against the trigger.

"He's a guy with a scarred-up face," I said quickly. "An old friend of mine. Came up here a while ago, looking for gold. No, silver. I guess it was silver." I tried to laugh.

The palm gripping the gun relaxed a little.

"Faceless man, you mean?"

For a second I wasn't sure he had spoken. His lips and jaw had stayed rigid. I had an eerie feeling that his use of Lisa's private name for Singleton was no coincidence. He had read my thoughts.

"Faceless?" I said. "Yeah, that's what I hear. Myself, I haven't seen him since the bandages came off."

I had tried to remember what Singleton's face looked like before the accident, but in my mind it was smooth as an egg.

"Can you tell me where to find him?" I said.

The Indian's gun hand came up. He did a jerky imitation of a Tom Mix twirl and sank the revolver up to the handle into the side pocket of his bib overalls.

"Whatcha gimme if I do?" he said, and his rigid face split in a three-tooth smile.

He invited me inside and offered me a cup of cool tea, brewed before sunup in a huge crock and taken hot till about nine in the morning, he told me, then allowed to cool, and drunk through the day.

"Sometimes after sundown," he said, "I put in a little whiskey."

I grinned and slid my pint bottle out of my hip pocket and planted it on the table. It was one of those dreams where complications disappear and whatever you need, you find in your hand. The Indian grinned back at me. I lifted the bottle out of its bag and broke the seal, then passed it. The Indian added a skimpy dollop, like a dose of medicine, to both our cups.

"Call me Shoshone Bob," he said. "Everybody does—but I ain't no Indian. Lived with 'em a while, but that don't mean I'm one of 'em."

"Sure," I said, and looked around, while Shoshone Bob went on talking. His shack was dark inside, the wood dirt-gray. He had one chair and a hogshead at a kitchen table, a mattress on the floor, and a steel-cornered trunk on its end against the wall. On it was spread a yellow doily and on that sat a scalloped wooden picture frame. The frame held a postcard-size daguerreotype of a man with hungover eyes and shoulder-length hair that curled up at the ends like a waxed mustache.

I looked back at the Indian when he stopped talking. It wasn't a smile, but on one side his lips were twisted up into his cheek. He slid his eyes sideways to the portrait, not to see it but to show me he knew I'd been taking it in.

"Years ago," he said, "I killed a man with a gunfighter pappy." He sipped his tea. "That's how come I pack a six-gun," he said, and sipped again. "Out of habit." He took small sips but lots of them, letting information leak out between sips. "That pappy swore to kill me."

He cocked his head at me and waited. I could see it would be a while before we would get around to Vico and Singleton. I wanted to ask where he'd got a picture of the man who'd sworn to kill him.

"I used to live on the coast," he said, his voice soft but tense, wanting to sound casual, but weighing each word as if he were making a case and didn't want any part of it lost. "Worked awhile around Santa Barbara. Monterey. Los Angeles." He sipped again, tilting the cup and his head. "That's where that pitcher got taken."

"That's *you* in the picture?"

Shoshone Bob looked surprised, then nodded.

I looked at the firm flesh and thick hair in the image. I thought how time had ruined them, rotted away the teeth, scored the flesh, sucked the eyes deep inside the skull as if they couldn't take the light anymore. Then I knew Shoshone Bob was lying to me. However time had handled the sleepy-mean face in the picture, it couldn't have pushed those flat Anglo-Saxon cheeks into the high spoon-bowl cheeks of an Indian.

"Sat for it," Shoshone Bob was saying, "so's I could give it away. Girl in a dance hall. Got back that night, she'd took up with some dude. We had some words. He pulled on me, so I killed him. Next thing I hear, his goddam pappy's coming to town. I didn't wait. Took the pitcher with me."

The lie rang true. Not his story, but somebody's.

The next cup of tea he poured had a bigger dollop of whiskey.

"You've been here a long time, then," I said.

"Nobody come out here that don't have to," he said. "White men, like us, call it Death Valley. That ain't its true name. Shoshone named it before the white man ever come here. True name is Tomesha."

"Tomesha?"

"Yeah. It means Ground Afire. Shouldn't call things by different names. God meant for it to have one name—Tomesha."

His gaze had slipped away from my face, drawn back to an old argument with the face in the daguerreotype. He blinked, looked back at me and poured whiskey in my glass and then his, forgetting to add tea.

"The guy I'm looking for—" I said, but he was leaning toward me across the table.

"What you say to *this,*" he said. "Man out here—*years.* Lotta years. Lives with Shoshone woman." His forefinger thumped the table, making each point. "Not just squaw-screwing. I mean, *lives* with her. Far as Shoshones figure it, they're *married.* Now what you say about them kids?"

"What about them?"

"What *about* 'em? What *about* 'em?"

His hands were spread, gripping the table edges as if he were holding it down in an earthquake. He filled the room with a sour fierce smell.

"Them kids bastards?" he said. "Or *not*?"

His eyes, deep in the shadows of his skull, had already made up their mind.

"Course not," I said softly. But Shoshone Bob wasn't listening. He stood up and shuffled over to the trunk. He leaned on it with both hands, looking at the picture, staring hard, keeping the room from swaying, keeping the picture from drifting into space, the face from turning away.

"That pappy, he wants to kill me bad," he said. "Better luck out here. See him comin' anyhow, huh?" He spoke between long pauses, like an interpreter waiting for someone else to finish talking. He seemed to have forgotten he'd told me the man in the picture was himself. Fifty years ago, I thought, the face might have been a good likeness of the man Shoshone Bob was hiding from. Or waiting for. "He be back someday," Shoshone Bob was saying. "I scoot up one of these draws. Pack a carbine. What good's his quick draw then, huh? Goddam quick-draw six-gun. I kill him fifty yards away. I kill him." It seemed like an idea he'd been over before, but kept forgetting.

He lurched back to the table and stood across from me.

"That's why you after that faceless man, ain't it?" he whispered. "He's yer pappy. Run out on you, huh?"

"No," I said, and felt my skin prickle.

He sat down stiffly, nodding, suspicions confirmed.

"Maybe I got it wrong," Shoshone Bob said, but not as if he believed it. He peered across the table, calculating. The glint in the deep sockets narrowed, refining the one truth he knew. "No good," he said. "Even you find him, it's no good. Once he gets it in his head yer just a bastard..." His head shook in resigned sympathy. "Cheer up," he said grimly, and poured me a big slug of whiskey.

I had to break through the tight circle of his logic.

"He's not my father," I told him. "He's my brother. Our mother's dying. She wants to see him before she dies."

"Mine, too," he said.

"What?"

"Know just what you mean. She'd go up the mountains. Drag me up there with her. Sit all day looking out to the coast. He played poker, you know. Santa Barbara. Monterey. Taught me to shuffle a deck. Then took it off with him, so's I never got no practice. She sent me off to find him. Find where they shuffle cards, she told me. He'll be there." He took a long gulp of whiskey. "What I never tole her," he said. His lips trembled. "What I never tole her is—I never woulda knew his face. Nights I'd close my eyes and try to see it. But all I'd get in my head is that damn pitcher." He nodded at the picture on the trunk. "No good, see? It weren't nothin' like him at all. I looked six months afore I give up. I mighta passed him a dozen times on the street. Didn't matter a goddam, though. Time I got back, she was gone. Just like yours."

"Like mine?"

"Your mammy," he said, his voice husky. "Rest her soul. I'm a Christian, y'know. Just like you."

I took a long breath.

"The Faceless Man," I said. "I've got to find him. Where is he?"

Shoshone Bob gulped and rubbed the back of a thumb in one of his eyes.

"Sure," he said. "Last month he was in Skidoo, way north. Then I heard he's moved on. Up Surprise Canyon, somewheres around Panamint City. Workin' one of them played-out shafts. Still there, 'less they moved again."

"They?"

"Had a partner with him."

"How do I get there?" I said, and he told me.

I got up to leave.

"Guess you can always try," he said. "Ever play cards? Maybe yer card-lucky. Like some."

I was out the door, reeling a bit under the desert stars, when I heard him calling.

"You come back here," he cried.

I went back to the door.

"You listen to me," he cried, and there was a callow crack in his voice. "You jus' siddown a minute." But he wasn't looking at me. He was staring across the room at the hard young face in the daguerreotype. "Tell you what you are," he whispered. "Yer nothin' but a squaw-screwer."

I walked away, and far down the road to my car I could hear him calling, "You come in here, Pappy. You *listen* to me."

5. Snake Dreams

THAT NIGHT, SLEEPING in the backseat of my car, I dreamed of ways a rattlesnake could reach me. I dreamed a snake with unstoppable intelligence that would stand high in its coil and loop itself around the rear bumper and from there stretch itself onto a fender and mount the hump of the car trunk till it could peer in the back window at me sleeping. I heard its smooth sliding on the metal roof of the car and as it dropped its head from the roof down to the open window, I woke stiff and breathless, and studied the outline of the window till I was sure the head wasn't waiting for me to move so it could strike. Then I realized it could just as easily be at the window above my head and I cocked my head back slowly as I could bear, sweat running through my scalp hair, till I could be sure no shadow hovered above me. I sat up and cranked both windows closed and lay back down, but the air seemed close and heavy. I was afraid I might suffocate. It's only claustrophobia, I said, and tried to fight it. I couldn't hold out. I cranked the windows down half an inch, thinking a rattler couldn't get its head through the opening. I was still wheezing. I cranked down one window all the way, thinking I would only have one space to watch, and lay back, staring hard for any movement, until at last, fully awake and with the dream cleared out of my head,

I decided it was unlikely that a snake could actually climb the smooth surface of the car the way it did in the dream, and if one did get on my roof and tried to stick its head in the window, it would be in a bad position to strike and would probably fall off.

I cranked down all the windows again and lay back on the seat. As I was drifting off, I heard something out on the desert squeak and scuffle. It gave a big scream and then broke off, and when I slept the snake came back, too smart this time to try to make me believe it could climb the outside of the car, but exploring the bottom, the axles, the complicated underbelly, easily heisting itself into the motor, finding a hole along the steering-wheel shaft that it needed only to gnaw a bit larger in order to coil up the shaft into the cab, and this time I woke convinced it was on the front seat, ready to strike as soon as I raised my head to look.

By now the desert night had cooled. My shivering was only partly from the dream. It's sleeping all cramped up, I said to myself. It makes me dream. But I still had to poke a flashlight into all the corners and make sure the place where the steering wheel entered the cab hadn't been gnawed larger. Finally I slept again and woke once or twice more with a stiff back and dreams I couldn't remember, except that in one of them Shoshone Bob was trying to give me a daguerreotype of a Gila monster and I was afraid to take it into the car, because I'd heard that if you kill one, its mate will always come and lie beside the body.

At dawn I got out of the car and stretched. My dreams had left me hung over with dread. I walked around, willing my blood to move and flush the dread away. It was cool enough now and the long sunrise shadows lovely, but when I had wandered forty yards out from the car something too far away for me to make out moved—slithered—and I turned back quick. Snakes are sleeping this time of day, I said. But I watched each step and couldn't swallow down my loathing. At least I was awake.

I had to make my mind grip something solid. I broke a couple boards from the shack to make a fire. I wasn't hungry, but I boiled some of the water I'd got in Mojave for oatmeal and coffee. I thought hard about measuring the right amount of water for my oatmeal. I listened to the snap as my teeth broke the skin of an apple, felt the juice that squirted my jaws when I chewed. I drank my coffee, I cleaned up my dishes. I was still calm. I felt ready. I leaned over the hood of my car and studied the map of Death Valley, thinking how best to take Vico from behind.

The day before, I saw, I'd been a fool with a fool's luck, strolling right into Ballarat. I couldn't count on luck. I had to learn to stalk. I'd already decided that if I took the direct way, up Surprise Canyon, Vico and Singleton might spot the car ten miles off. But I could make a long loop south and cross the Panamints at Goler Wash. That would bring me out in the middle of Death Valley. I could drive straight up the salt pan and take my pick of the canyons that gouge the valley's eastern wall. He might be on the watch for somebody from the coast, but not coming out of the salt pan.

It made sense. When I'd left Bolger's party and started downhill in the dark, I had no idea how far I'd have to go. I still was going down. Even in spring the valley heat was no joke. I was headed for the lowest spot on the continent, a furnace, where a leaky radiator could kill me. But it made sense. It had a logic I couldn't shake, only follow down. I'd lived my life in a trance, watching shadows on the wall. To break out of it, I had to go where there were no shadows, only sun. Out there, two hundred and eighty feet below sea level, whatever I saw would be real, not some damn Vico trick. I'd let the desert be my teacher. I'd crack the nut of every natural fact to find the way I had to go. Then I could start to climb. When the road gave out, I'd climb on foot. Another five or so miles. Over mountain trails. Then I'd have Vico in my sights and break the trance for good.

I folded the map. I'd made up my mind. I was sick with dread, but no longer willing to live with the person I'd have to remain if I didn't go.

6. Brother Hawk

THE GOLER WASH turnoff was only about fifteen miles from Ballarat. Once the road began to climb, I felt the mountain flex itself against me. I shifted into second gear and snarled along, rounding the massive shoulders it turned to block me, slowing to thread a rockfall that had scattered stones to explode my tires, sensing an ambush and slowing even more just as the rock shrugged away to let the sun smash across my windshield. The first time that happened, I'd braked so hard the car stalled. I was sitting there, my eyes squeezed shut, watching the red pulse of my blood and the floating purple disks the sun had burned, thinking of popping flashbulbs in the precinct hall, when I felt a gentle movement. I jammed my foot on the brake just in time to keep the mountain from easing me backward over a thousand-foot drop.

At the crest of the pass the mountain gave me a glimpse of the valley floor, the white glare of the salt pan shimmering like the ghost of water.

Now I was very frightened, and things I passed had the sharp, precious outline of things I was leaving behind forever. The road dropped me into a shallow valley stubbled with shrubs and purple flowers. There was a rock, a particular rock, ribboned with tan and gray and yellow. I climbed the rim of the valley and dropped again, leaving it behind. I passed through a gully dotted with tents. Two men in shirtsleeves were hanging clothes on a line. I left them behind.

Then, as I bumped along, trying to swallow my fear, a bush seemed to explode, I saw a splash of wings lurch up, a quail, soaring now, finding its balance in the air, and just then a brown streak sliced its glide apart. The quail tumbled, bucking, squawking, borne down, down, out of sight behind the mesquite. Then it was lifted, splay-winged and limp, in the talons of a redtail hawk. The hawk flapped heavily, lazy as Babe Ruth rounding bases on an out-of-the-park homer, and I thought: Brother Hawk. That's how I'll take him—that quick—only he's got to have one second to know it's me. And I wasn't afraid anymore.

Then I went through a canyon where strips of white talc ribboned the brown walls and miners grubbing for the talc had hollowed the cliffs. I came out in a series of steep, short hills and long declines onto the vast flat plain of caked salt with its poison wells and bitter, borax-running river.

7. Ground Afire

IT'S ONE OF those fairy tales where your wish comes true as a curse. I'd wanted to aim a lens and stop time. And I've done it. Only what's there, printed behind my eyes, is not a woman's body but the plains of hell. Whenever I close my eyes, the desert—just as it was, and is, and will be—sifts into every pore.

Here on the valley floor, the mesquite grows sparse and dwarfed. Where the road passes through the salt-crusted mud, nothing grows at all. Nothing makes a shadow. An aerial shot would show a beetle, a glittering metal shell, crawling up the desolation of salt. I pass a couple tracks heading left into the mountains, worried that I might be missing the one I need to take. At the next turnoff I stop for another look at my map, sitting on the running board with the car door open. I shrink in a shallow pool of shadow leaning away from the sun. The heat dries my sweat and leaves salt itching in every pore and crack. When I'd told Shoshone Bob I didn't want to go up Surprise Canyon, he'd said, Why, and I told him the simple truth: Because I want to surprise him. He smiled his three-tooth smile as if he understood, but I don't trust his directions. I study the canyon roads for the place where I can make the deepest penetration before I have to abandon the car. A place marked "Starvation Canyon" seems the most direct route, with Panamint City just over the ridge, but the map shows no road. That leaves Johnson Canyon and Hanaupah Canyon. The road up Johnson seems closer, the elevation less than ten thousand feet, but Shoshone Bob had said, Take Hanaupah. I try to figure why. I'd have to drive the salt pan another dozen miles. It would take me steeper into the mountain, make me climb another thousand feet. I decide that's a dumb idea, but once I'm behind the wheel, I go for Hanaupah, Shoshone Bob's way. The time for questioning is past. Besides, I tell myself, it's what I want. When he sees me, he'll see me against the sky.

Driving again: On my right a thick clump of brush comes up fast. Rising out of it, a slender, wood-ribbed tower, a platform at the apex, and above it the still spokes of a fan. A splintery daisy waiting for a wind. The valley floor is where people leave things behind. I pass rusted wheel rims, strands of baling wire, a Model T fender, the ribs and skull of a mule. Then a pair of gray-bleached boards. They stand at the head of two mounds of earth circled by stones. Then the saltbed changes its complexion, sprouts jagged crags and fangs. I've missed the turnoff, driven into the place the map calls the Devil's Golf Course. I stop the car to judge how much room I've got for a turnaround. I step off the road, kick at one of the spiky salt crystals. It breaks off, brittle, with a crack like a burning pine branch. The crack rings away to the canyon walls. Suddenly, thinking how a rifle shot would gorge the air with echoes, I find myself shivering. I sit awhile on my car fender, weak and chilly. But it's not fear, I tell myself. I'm past fear. When I feel better, I maneuver the car around. The turnoff will be at Badwater. But when I come up on the poison lake I'm shivering again and have to stop for a few minutes. Then I drive again.

I find the turnoff and head for the mountains. Distance in the desert stretches as you go. Driving up the slope of a gravel fan, the mountains ahead seem nearby and low. From this distance the channels cut by cloudbursts are slender veins that branch and spread and disappear behind the nearer rises, and it's only when you've been driving a long time, and still longer, that you see where far ahead the veins must broaden into chasms, and you begin to pass boulders the size of houses that they've spilled onto the fan. Sometimes I have dreams of driving, never getting closer to the mountain where Vico is, and I get out of bed dry-mouthed and shaky and go to the bathroom for a drink of water, feeling relief, yes, but also an ache to get back on the road.

I come back to bed, and I'm driving again. At last my eyes drop in a momentary doze behind the wheel, and I blink awake to find myself in second gear again, crawling up the narrow winds. Halfway up the mountain the road gives out. After I switch off the engine I hear a busy crackle, like flames. Above the trail water trickles down the rocks. A sandy slope below swallows it, swallows all that comes. The trickle feeds a few fat willows, a few grapevines. From a nearby slope a mesquite had sent roots groping toward the spring. Before they got there the wind had exposed them. They had whitened and dried in the sun. The leaves were brittle and dead. I look up the steep trail, wondering what would have happened if I'd taken my chances driving up Surprise Canyon to Vico's doorstep. But Shoshone Bob had said, "That road gonna take you far as the spring. Then you find trails, Indian trails. They take you over the ridge. Take the one to the left, away from the high peak." When I asked him to show me the place on my map, he'd traced a square, ragged forefinger between Telescope Peak and Sentinel Peak.

I make a sandwich of the last of my ham and put oranges into a canvas pack along with my thermos, filled with water. I shoulder it and the rifle, and start up. By the time I've climbed for an hour, my calves are aching. The smooth blanket I saw from the playa prickles with cactus and thorny shrubs. Higher up, where nothing grows, black boulders sprout like eyeteeth rotting in their gums. I climb, talking as I climb, talking to Vico, talking to Lisa, talking to Beth. Talking, I come to a turn in the path, and there, waiting for me, is what was promised in my dreams. A diamondback rattler curled in the shade of a Joshua tree. I can see its neck in a menacing coat-hanger curl, the hovering poison-tipped wedge of the head. I hear the sizzle of its rattles. I raise my rifle. But the shot will echo through the canyon to Vico. I back slowly, then leave the path, scramble up on hands and knees. The gravel spills away beneath my weight. When I've circled back to the path, where burro hooves and Indian moccasins have trod the earth firm, I sit and catch my breath.

I calm myself. I open my pack for a drink. Standing, looking back, unable at this distance to spot the rattler, I hear a chink at my feet. My thermos is tipped on its side between my feet, glugging water into the sand. I grab it, but it slips through my fingers, hits a rock. I hear a muffled implosion of glass. It's okay, I tell myself. I right the thermos, then strain what water is left through my handkerchief, pouring it into the cup. I drink. I pitch the cup downhill, kick the thermos after it. It's okay, I've still got oranges in my pack. And by tonight I'll be drinking Vico's water.

I shoulder the pack, lighter now, and walk again. I carry my rifle by its stock. In the desert you leave behind whatever breaks, whatever will do you no good. Leave behind pity. Leave behind love. Let the sun clean the fat off the bones.

8. The Lure

IT WAS A couple hours after noon when I reached the crest, and a couple hours after that before I found myself stretched in the shady angle of a boulder halfway down a wide ravine. All around me other ravines slashed down from the rim. I was in a rock bowl high in the Panamints. There were flowers on the low slopes. Far below, Panamint City scattered its few deserted shacks. Through the telescope sight of my rifle I was watching a shadow in the facing wall of the ravine. It was a little below me, not much further away than I could throw a rock. A place where men with picks and dynamite had hacked the mouth of a cave and wedged it open with timbers. From the cave mouth a path fell down the rock-strewn slope, jumped a narrow cut, and came out on a more gentle slope that led up to a shack with a wire-rigged stovepipe.

When I got tired of watching the cave mouth, I would shift my focus to the shack, try to see if anything was moving behind the window. What I'd at first taken for the sleeve of a shirt had turned out to be a muslin curtain catching a faint breeze.

Coming over the ridge, I'd seen the shack right away, but it wasn't till I spotted the cave above it that I was certain enough to set up my ambush. Shoshone Bob had told me what to look for: an abandoned mine shaft in the hills above Panamint City. But it was more than that. There was something about the way the landscape led your eye—the shack, the path to the cave mouth, the cut of the mountains that ringed it all in, then the rooftops far below. It made the silence seem to be waiting, hinting at a secret meaning. It was the feeling I always got when Vico framed a scene.

But I couldn't be sure. Vico had done something I'd never imagined, had secrets I'd never guessed. After an hour I was worried. "One of them shacks up beyond Panamint City," Shoshone Bob had said. There were a hundred ravines and cuts and canyons; there might be a shack and an old mine shaft in any dozen of them. I had to be sure. I had to explore the shack.

It was risky. If one of them was in the shack, I'd tossed away my ambush. But I'd watched for an hour and there'd been no sound from the shack, no movement. They were both in the mine. If they came out while I was in the open, I was finished. But they wouldn't. They'd stay in the mine till sundown. I weighed all the chances. But I knew I'd have to do it. I'd always been a Thomas, needing to put my finger where the nails had gone. If I can see the bed where he sleeps, I thought. The dishes he eats from. Something there will tell me for sure. Maybe a picture of Lisa. Maybe the script for some new film. Some clue, I thought, and I can put it together with the silence in these hills, and it will tell me why he *chose* all this. I don't want just to kill him, I thought. It's never been only that. I want his secret.

I took the rifle and crawled on my belly along the ridge till I got beyond the sightlines of the shack window, then leaped and skidded on my heels downhill to the back wall.

9. Prowling

THIS TIME IT wasn't Spyhawk on the prowl. I don't have any trouble remembering. All I need to do is close my eyes to see what I did.

I'm leaning against the wall of the shack, panting, shallow as I can in case there's someone inside. Then I edge around the corner out of sight of the tunnel. There's the window with the muslin curtain, open but screened, a table just beneath it. I flatten my back to the wall. Only someone in a corner of the room could spy me. Through the muslin I make out a coffee mug, just the rim, and the corner of a page. I risk a closer look, more exposed. The hairs on my neck tingle: It's the same size paper as the sketchpads Vico uses to script a film. I show my face at the window, keeping the rifle out of sight. Shadows. Hard to make out through the screen if anyone's there. I glance around the next corner, up the path to the tunnel. Nobody in sight. I skim tiptoe along the wall to the door. At my touch the door moans, swings a foot or so inward. I hide the rifle along my right leg, try to compose the grin I always put on my face when I knocked on the beach house door. I step inside. Nobody there. With a glance uphill to the tunnel, I close the door. I cross to the window for another look at the tunnel mouth, a careful look. I take a deep breath, relax. I'm there, in the cool dark, alone again in one of Vico's burrows.

It's the feeling I used to get as a child in my parents' bedroom. Summer afternoons when I'd been put down for a nap, I would tiptoe in there while my mother downstairs was ironing or washing dishes. I would search their dresser for clues. In the bottom drawer I found my mother's high school yearbook, and turned past the page with her picture on it, and came back to it, puzzled, and sounded out the letters under the picture till I was saying, W-h-i-t-f-i-e-l-d, Whitfield, here's someone with Grandma Whitfield's name, and I worked the strange word "Gwendolyn" back to my father's voice on the phone saying, "Just a minute, I'll call Gwen," and then I knew the woman with the hair puffed out all around her head and the eyes that had never thought of me was my mother. The next drawer held her silk stockings and slips, that I would press to my face, breathing in along with her perfume a feeling that I was already old enough to wonder how I'd lost.

One of my father's drawers smelled of tobacco and had in it two things I waited all through my childhood to hear him mention. The first was a pistol with a cracked ivory grip. Even when I was in my teens I would sometimes go to my father's drawer and hold the pistol in my palm and pose with it in front of the mirror. I was certain that all my father's days with us were only a hiding from the ones who were after him, and any night a knock on the door might make him spring up the stairs to the drawer, climb from his bedroom window onto the back-porch roof, shooting, killing, dropping to the driveway and shooting his way to the garage, aiming the car through a storm of bullets out of our lives. This heavy, silent man. The next secret in the drawer was a pigskin tobacco pouch. In it he kept three stones, and not one—even when I was four—too large for me to close a fist around. At last I had fondled them so long I came to believe they were mine, and stole them, and waited for my father to accuse me of theft, and when a long time passed—months, it seems to me now, but it may have been only days—and he hadn't found me out, I convinced myself that whatever meaning the stones once had for my father they had lost. That bothered me—the idea that he could *change.* No longer care.

It came back to me, the feel of those afternoons in my parents' bedroom with leaf shadows nodding on the drawn shade, when I was alone in the beach house, and it came back again in the shack where Vico lived with Singleton. From four years old—from the time I first came awake in the world, it seems—I knew that it could only be in some place forbidden to me, where I was a trespasser, a thief, that I might find the clues that would tell me who I was.

At first, in Vico's shack, my head is throbbing, my breath still coming in gasps, but soon, as I look around the room, it calms me. Near the windowless back wall there's a small woodstove. Skillets and pans hang on the wall. There's a breakfast table with a coffeepot on it, and two cups. Dirty dishes soak in a pan on the counter. On the wall above it is a calendar with a picture of a busty girl. The old-fashioned swimsuit makes me look close at the date—August, 1921. The model, if there was one, if the artist didn't just invent her, is now seventeen years older, if she lives, that lewd wink just one more crease at the corner of her eye. But here in the shadowy room she is August of 1921 for as long as I care to look.

There are two narrow beds set in opposite corners. One is of two-by-fours aged to the same hue as the walls. At its foot is a duffel bag. The other is a folding cot. Underneath it is a brown leather suitcase. It might be the one Vico carried once on a trip to New York. Beside it is a straight-back chair with an oil lamp on it, and a book—Lawrence's *Seven Pillars of Wisdom.* I start reading at the bottom of a page where a sentence is underlined in pencil: "I had strung myself to learn all pain until I died, and no longer actor, but spectator, thought not to care how my body jerked and squealed." And I think, No longer actor? Not likely. Learning another role, I'd bet.

Under the window I'd looked through from outside, a table is drawn against the wall, just as Vico's desk in the beach house was. I sit at the table looking out, wondering why Vico would exchange that lovely shot of his leaf-fringed, winking blue ocean for this scalded rock. Far up the slope I see the place where I lay in ambush. I go on looking. In the gravel, strips of gray and tan emerge, then gold and crimson, shades I didn't see at first. A string of stumpy mesquite shows where underground water must be. Near a bare ridge where the rock rises through the gravel, the trail I came down winds up past the window's upper edge. Then I find my hand on Vico's sketchbook.

10. Learning to Stare

WHEN I OPEN it, I think at first I've made a mistake, it's not Vico's after all. I've been expecting the comic-strip layout he uses to plan a script. Instead a single design fills the page—an abstraction full of jagged angles. I skip to the next page, then turn back. It's not an abstraction, not quite. An inch down from the top edge a line crosses the page in a familiar rhythm. It's a horizon line—what I saw when I got to the shoulder of Telescope Peak and looked back over the salt pan: the far, haze-gray line of the Funeral Mountains, cut off by the nearer, sharper Black Mountain ridges that cup the salt pan's eastern rim. Below the mountains the perspective shifts. He seems to be belly-down on the bank of a lake watching great chunks of dirty spring ice drift off to the horizon. Again I'm about to turn the page, when I recognize on the surface of one of the ice blocks an echo of the line Lisa's hair makes lying along her cheek. Another block holds Bolger's toothy snarl. Then, starting from a pattern of sworls that might be a naked female breast, I trace across several converging surfaces a blurred arc that ends as a fist in Bolger's gut. And it all comes clear—not blocks of ice, but the shards of a great mirror smashed across the salt pan, printed with the last image they reflected.

The next page is an attempt to sketch Lisa, eyes closed in sleep, mouth slightly open, the upper lip stretched across a thin crescent of teeth. Hasty work, the lines nervous, unconnected. An X slashed through it. On the next three or four pages he's tried the same image, sometimes several faces on the same page, shooting from different angles—Lisa tossing in a restless nightmare. In the last of the series the eyelids are not just closed but clenched, the lips drawn tighter against the teeth, and the X that cancels it is heavy.

On the next page is a self-portrait, the angle like the shot they'd used in the lobby poster for *Cain*. It had started as a fine shadowy self-dissection. In the left eye each line rays inward toward an agony you can almost see reflected in the pupil. But that's the only eye visible. Once he'd finished, he slapped on the face a pair of bull's-eye spectacle frames, as if he'd read about how I defaced the snapshot on his desk. The glass in the other frame is starred like the shattered mirror on the first page. The ears are bloated black hoops, and he's pulled the nose, which he always disguised with makeup in a film, into a raisin-tipped Mickey Mouse snout. The next page has a single line, his own profile. He hasn't even bothered to X it out. The page after that is blank.

It's like watching a projector tear a film: First, when the sprocket fails to catch, the image blurs, then the frame empties to a still white rectangle. The blank page is a punctuation—the end of the Vico I've known and can understand.

What follow are the first of Vico's desert studies. It seems to have taken a while after he arrived for him to see where he was. Once he did, the desert poured in through his eyes. As I flip through the pages, I can follow his track, roaming from Telescope Peak to Bad Water and up the salt pan to the Devil's Golf Course—the same route I took. All the way he was sketching. At first his style shows the quick, impatient skim I knew from his camera setups, one subject crowding the next in a tumble of images, so that on the same page but not part of a unified composition, I see a prairie dog casting a shadow, the shaded strata of a cliff, a weed with lapping petals, sidewinder tracks laddering up a sand dune.

Gradually the line develops a steadiness I've seen before only in isolated moments—in the one good eye of the self-portrait he ruined, or that study of Lisa he did in the script of *Loves of a Spy*. Then I turn over a page, and hold my breath.

Vico had learned how to stare.

He was a Saul knocked off his horse, and the first thing he saw when he had eyes again was the fulfillment of a prophecy—maybe a promise—that he'd made in his farewell letter to Lisa, that I'd read her over the phone in Vico's voice. It was a Gila monster.

One reason I never took seriously Vico's yearning for the desert was that his fear of reptiles was even greater than my own. I'd made a joke of how an old prospector had saved me from squatting on a Gila monster, but that night when I told the crew about it, Vico's face went white. "God, Farley," he said, "in the desert you keep your eyes peeled *every minute*, or you die." We'd spent the next hour telling stories about snakes and scorpions and Gila monsters, and joked about how even if you chop one off at the neck you can't pry the jaws apart till sunset, and how impressive I would have looked setting up shots with a two-foot lizard hung to the seat of my pants. But Vico was silent, and drank more than usual.

So what strikes me right away, looking at Vico's sketch, is that it's not the kind of thing he could have done by looking from a distance, or from memory. The Gila monster is profiled against the sky. To get it like that, to get the pattern of beads under the jaw, the way the elbow of its foreleg tucks against its fat flank, he must have lain flat on his stomach less than two yards away.

At the bottom of the page are the book's first words. "Yesterday I was on my usual ledge. It won't let me get closer. I watched a mouse skitter past its nose. It dropped behind a rock *out of its sight.* Then zipped down a hole. The thing waddled after it. Never find it, I thought. It went right to the hole, scraped away gravel, made two sharp chomps—dinner. How? I pictured it: the waddle; the pause; the tongue flicking the rocks—what was it *doing*? A blind man with his cane! It had been *tasting* the trail. I thought about that: It's almost blind; if I can be on the ground an hour before sunset and *not move,* I'll be close enough to spit on its nose, and still just part of the landscape.

"It worked."

I flip through pages, my hand trembling. Now that I know

it's Vico's book, now that I've even seen his handwriting, I've got to get out of here, back up to my ambush. But I can't look away, can't stop turning pages. More studies of the Gila monster, maybe ten pages. Or is it the same one? That stops me. I go back to the first one, turn the pages slowly. I look close at the curl of the mouth, the bead patterns, I count the beads along the upper lip, and compare. It's true: not a *typical* Gila monster, not even a particular *one.* Four, at least, that can't be mistaken for each other. And I think—So what? Does he think he can see better than a camera? And then, looking hard at the pattern on a flank to make sure it's not like another, my eye seems to sink through the surface: I find myself studying the eggshell cracks in the skull of a mouse, then a profile of the Funeral Mountain range—drawn, I'd swear, from the very spot near Bennet's Well where I stopped that morning to look at my map.

All the drawings that follow, the ones I can recall, give me the same feeling—that the precisely rendered surface is a transparent skin covering a world of intricate harmonies. Vico seemed to have discovered that if he stared hard enough at anything—Gila monster, tumbleweed, salt crystal—he would see, first the atoms that composed it, their electrons whirling in their lawful patterns, then their secret twinship with the delicate gravitational poise of the solar system.

The notations he made, sometimes on the overleaf, sometimes on the same page as the drawing, usually begin as a rendering of things the drawing can't say: the Gila monster's hiss when it warns him off, the way colors on a mountainside shift as the sun crosses the sky. Mixed with these notes, growing out of them like green branches on a bush, are strange thoughts and speculations. Most of them I can't recall now, but one stands clear.

The sketch shows a sidewinder rattler, the eyes like a hypnotist's, drawing me in, but something wrong with the tongue. He's forgotten to make it forked. How odd, I think, that his eye should fail him. I wonder if he was afraid. But the notes explain it. He speaks of coming upon a long tail writhing in a crevice. He made himself come closer. He was close enough to count the rattles on the tail when the head jerked out, dragging the hind legs, rump, and tail of some desert rodent.

"It was practically at my feet," he says, "but I knew it couldn't go for me so long as its mouth was stuffed. At first the legs still twitched. The thought of something conscious, even dimly conscious, being sucked down that hole, nearly made me faint."

He describes the ripples squeezing along the snake's neck, forcing the rodent down, the look of patient ecstasy glazing the snake's eyes. Then, with only the tail still visible, lolling from the snake's mouth like a pink, pointed tongue with downy whiskers, the snake stopped swallowing, went stiff, alert. It lifted its head, still drooling the tip of the pink tail, and seemed to listen. "It knew I was there," he says, "knew someone was watching. Its eyes found me."

At that moment Vico felt hot piss in his trouser leg.

"It surprised me," he says. "It wasn't as if I'd *decided* to let go, or even realized I couldn't hold it. There was no struggle, no yielding. It flowed." And then, a strange question: "What has my body got to do with *me*?"

Somewhere up in the shack's rafters I seem to hear the question repeated, very faint, in Vico's whisper. I strain to hear it again. And slowly, slowly in the silence, I realize that what I'm listening for is not Vico's voice, but some sound, some chink or rustle of gravel on the path down from the mine. An instant later, I'm pressed against the wall beside the door, peering through a quarter-inch crack. I listen, hold my breath and listen. Nothing. I notice for the first time the other window, above Singleton's bed. It frames the upper path, that I can't see without opening the door. Nothing. I'm safe. It was only some kangaroo rat with bad dreams, maybe a lizard scraping itself a cooler piece of shade. Safe. Looking back from the window, I see my rifle propped against the desk where I'd been reading. So many paces away. I'd never have been ready.

I'm trembling. I can't be found here. But once my eyes drop again to Vico's sketchbook, I can't look away. I scan ahead to see how long the entry continues. Two pages on, in the last paragraph, I read this: "There's a pattern," he says, "and the pattern is in *it,* not in me. Where you find order, you've got to believe there is mind. Mind. That glaze in the rattler's eye—where have I seen it before? Why am I thinking of Pearl? Pearl as a baby, Pearl at Sharon's breast. That's it. The same glaze. A rattlesnake—and my sister's baby, nursing. The same glazed look. What mind could *imagine* that? Did it want me just to see the joke? And walk away? I want to *know.* I want not to piss my pants when one of God's creatures looks me in the eye."

Now it's rage that makes me tremble. I want to rip the page, spit on it. And I think: Know? You want to *know*? There's nothing to know but this: You've lost your nerve. Who needs your staring, you're no da Vinci. You're Vico—you stare *inside.* You find what we're afraid to look at *there,* and drag it into the light. For me to get a shot at. I try to calm myself: It's my fault. I'm the one who made you look so hard you had to look away. And I think: God's creatures! One of God's creatures? What a pious stink! Can't take it, can you? First time I've seen you blink, Vico. First time you've had to look away.

I rip the page from the notebook, stuff it in a pocket. I'll paint the snake on the stern of *The Merry Widower,* and re-christen it. *One of God's Creatures,* I'll call it. I'm on my feet, I'm at the door, it opens wide and whacks against the wall. Let him see me, it doesn't matter. At last—I can despise you. You're not worth killing.

Not having to kill him—I'd thought it would be a relief. But as soon as I said it I choked on a sob. What was I without him but an empty mirror? I went back to the desk, to the sketch-book, praying he'd give me a reason to kill him.

I skipped through the pages. Fewer drawings, more and more words. The book was becoming a diary. On the last page, dated the previous night, he talked about the tunnel.

Singleton had been working it all along, I gathered. Now and again Vico would forgo a day of roaming the hills to help him prop a beam, but for the most part they came together only at evening. What finally lured Vico underground was something I could understand a lot better than I could his fascination with the eating habits of rattlesnakes. The day before I arrived Singleton had discovered a pair of corpses.

That morning, instead of deepening the main artery of the tunnel, he had turned down a branch. He'd ignored it before, Vico wrote, taking it for a vein that had been worked dry. He spent the whole day clearing rubble from what looked like a cave-in, and finally, toward evening, squirmed his head and shoulders into a chamber. The smell was thick. He lifted his lantern to see how deep it went, and saw the corpses. That first look was a quick one. He came back with a report that he'd discovered two Indians, recently dead. That night after supper Vico went with him back to the chamber. They stayed only a few minutes, but long enough to decide the corpses were not after all recent. In the airless chamber the bodies had partly mummified. The flesh had shrunk away, leaving a papery, darkened skin over the bones. All so long ago what lingered of the smell was sweet enough to bear. Vico held the lamp high and they looked around. Neither corpse had been hurt by the cave-in, but a smashed lamp lay on the floor. There were two picks, one with the handle broken off short, the other buried under rock, only an inch of the handle showing. The two prospectors had probably groped for it in the dark.

Vico speaks of his revulsion at the thought of touching the corpses. Yet he says he will return the next day. He plans to go through their pockets to look for some clue to who they were. Then, he says, he will learn what he can by drawing them.

He imagines their slow suffocation, even connects the mine tunnel with the throat of the rattlesnake. He ends by saying the two bodies were lying each with its head cradled in the other's arm. "Not an embrace," he says. "Not the kind of nuzzling lovers do. But they'd been scraping in the dark for days. Their fingers bleeding, canteen empty. When the thin air finally wore them out and they lay down to die, there was some comfort in touching." Those were the last words. The book was filled up.

Just like always, you above it, finding the meaning, I thought. You think you're so far ahead I'll never catch up. But you're wrong. You're worth killing after all.

I left Vico's sketchbook on the table where I'd found it. All I came away with was what I'd been able to see. I climbed back up the mountain and lay with my rifle aimed at the cave.

11. Blurred Focus

I LAY THERE—patient as a lizard. I watched the sun hit the western rim of the bowl. I'd learned waiting years ago. If you wait long enough, you'll always get the shot you want. Finally in the shadow beneath the timbers at the mouth of the tunnel I saw a floating ruby glow. I made out a man in the shadows, smoking a cigarette as he looked down on the rooftops of Panamint City. He threw the butt into the sun and stepped after it out of the shade, and as he started down the trail to the shack below, I got my first look at what had happened to the Faceless Man's face.

I could tell it was Singleton. He still walked with a regal roll of the shoulders that he'd learned from Vico. But what should have been a face made me blink and look to see if a drop of my sweat had blurred the scope's eyepiece. Where there should have been an eye and a cheek, I saw a concave smear of flesh. There was one good eye, and I kept coming back to it, because when I tried to see what had happened to the other, my gaze would pull back the way you snatch your hand from a hot burner. I had to force myself; and then, it seemed, I had the eye of a hawk, seeing through the scope with a kind of detail I'd think was impossible if the images weren't fixed in my memory: The bone above Singleton's left eye had been crunched flat. There was no shelter for an eye, and no eye, only a sewn crease of flesh. The nose was gone, too, except for a stubby fang of bone above two almond-shaped holes. The left side of his face had no upper lip, just a crack-toothed snarl. But I could swear the corner of the good eye had shrewd squint-rays like the eye of the man I used to call Singleton, and it was a clear blue, full of his old cocky wit.

He ambled down the trail and entered the shack.

12. Vico's Instructions for the Final Shot

I WENT ON WAITING, puzzled and relieved. Puzzled, because I had expected they would come out of the tunnel together. Relieved, because I hadn't come to kill Singleton, and killing him just because he happened to be at Vico's elbow would have been—an excess. An offense to aesthetic economy. I had pictured Vico's scorn, thought of him tugging at the lobe of his upper lip—his hawkbeak lip that worked with his raptor eyes to make him a secret cousin to my Spyhawk. I thought how he would sigh, sliding the story board onto the desk, and say, "No, Farley, it won't work. We can come up with something better." And he grabs his sketchpad, blocks out frames for a new page, and as the frames fill with figures and shadows, all trapped in a web of converging perspective lines, he tells me the story, the new story, the version we'll shoot: "You're far away—stretched along that slab. You see us through the scope. You get a clear head and shoulders of us both, then slide Singleton out of the shot and pin the crosshairs right between my eyes. To Singleton, in reverse angle, you're just the top of a head. Keep your hat low and he can't even tell what color your hair is. With your eye behind that scope, your cheek against the stock, you might as well be wearing a mask. He'll never recognize you."

"But you will."

"Yes."

"How?"

In the still afternoon, while I lie baking on the rock, blinking away heat shimmers and mirages that keep forming in the gravel below the mouth of the tunnel, his voice reaches me in a sizzling whisper:

"Because I know you, Farley. I've always known you."

"So from my point of view the trick is simply to give you a split second to recognize me, to know what I'm going to do, but not time enough to tell Singleton who I am."

"You can do it, Farley."

"Maybe it will happen too quick, not give me a chance to—"

"You can run it in slow motion. Loop it back and run it again. Run it often as you like. All the rest of your life."

So as I lay there waiting, I realized that even if they had emerged side by side from the tunnel, I wouldn't have killed Singleton. There would have been a simple cut—from him, on his knees watching Vico's blood spill out of the hole between his eyes, to me, scrambling up the side of the ridge. I'd be in sight for a few seconds after I broke from cover, climbing, but I'd be a running man seen from behind, the size of a thumbnail. Before he could think to follow, I'd be well on my way over the mountain and back to my car.

But Singleton coming out before him was better than I'd hoped. It was my moment—mine and Vico's—and I didn't want anybody else watching. It would be Vico alone coming down the trail, glancing quickly up at the little chuckle I make to get his attention, and his eyes widen in that instant's recognition of all that will happen, all that I am, all that I was, as far back as the night I approached the restaurant table where he sat arguing with Berenice, and said, "Sure, I'll shoot your next picture. You need somebody with a lens that can peel away your layers."

He had smiled: "You talk like I'm some kind of onion."
I smiled too. We were friends.

13. Grade-A Prime

ALL DAY, IT SEEMED, shadows had slept inside the mountain, or crept along the faults and crannies. Half an hour after I saw Singleton the sun grazed the peaks on the valley's western rim, and a great shadow leaped out. It pounced on the distant rooftops of Panamint City, pounced on the shack on the slope below me. Now inch by inch it climbs toward where I lie and toward the mouth of Vico's cave. Above the shadow-blue the gravel has a sunset blush the color of molten iron beginning to cool. On the tongue of the cave where he will appear, light slices deeper, more narrowly every second.

I might have expected this. In every picture there was no shot you gave more time than the one that uncovered your new face. Open looking past his shoulder, Farley, so all they'll see is a rim of light on cheek and chin. Shoot him in shadow, Farley, up to the eyes in shadow, like a bandit's mask. Track in on the man with field glasses to his eyes. We'll get cannon smoke—not foggy, just puffs, torn to rags by the wind—and when he lowers the glasses we'll see through the smoke that he's been grinning at what he sees.

That last, of course, from *City of Sapphires,* was one of your early mirror tricks, wasn't it, Vico? Did you think I wouldn't recognize myself? Or were you counting on it, counting on me seeing *only* myself, so that you could keep in shadow that image of *you* that each new disguise exposed? I lay along a boulder, waiting as always for you to appear—to lower the glasses, step into the light, glance over your shoulder at my lens—and I thought: Whatever else about you will be strange, you haven't lost your touch for the fine tease. Yes, Vico, I could hardly wait. I squirmed inside my skin to see what the desert had done to your face.

I lay waiting, watching the cave. Some dead mesquite leaves

rattled. Up through Surprise Canyon there must have been a faint wind. Where I was I couldn't feel it. Only hear the dry rattle, as if the leaves were trembling, getting ready to come back to life. After a while I seemed to hear them whisper. I found myself whispering back. I heard myself saying: But it's a moral thing. I seemed to have waked up in the middle of a conversation. I wondered if my fever had come back. I never closed my eyes, I could have sworn. But I went on talking, telling Vico all the reasons why he had to die. And from time to time, like the refrain of an endless litany, I'd hear my voice, a whisper winding through the caverns of my ear, a voice-over in a dream montage, and it would be saying, It's a moral thing, a moral thing to do.

Berenice had been—so far as I cared—your own, to use as your genius required. Yes, your genius. That numbness in you to her pain, that power to stare with such a fierce concentration that you could block out whatever fell beyond the frame—it stamped your genius grade-A prime. Only genius could excuse it, so it had to be genius. I envied it.

When I noticed that each time you threw her image on the screen, the woman herself became more pale, chain-smoked and spilled her drinks with a laugh a little more thin, a little closer to hysteria—I only shrugged. It was only Berenice, and if she could take it, why should I worry. But it scared me when she died, when you—when *we* killed her. And the night you read me the shooting script for *Loves of a Spy,* I felt your fangs sink in me, and I thought, My God, I've taken her place. I didn't like how you'd guessed that I must have betrayed you to Hoensinger. It made me writhe with shame. But at the same time, seeing the first rushes, seeing what I did thrown across the screen—it wasn't small and sneaking anymore. You made even my cowardice grand. I was proud. I'm strong, I thought, stronger than Berenice, and I've got fangs of my own if he gets too rough. But it got worse. You shot scene after scene to shame me. And more than that: By a hundred decisions, from the day you cast her to the clothes you hung on her and the lines you gave her and the way you had me light a scene, you made it clear that going after me wouldn't be enough. You wanted another Berenice. You were after Lisa, too.

And Lisa—you didn't own. No matter what threat or charm you'd dangled to make her eyes go glassy, you didn't—couldn't own her. No dream I dreamed of woman was not her. Could I say, Here, take her—from this day I'm dreamless, I'll never close my eyes?

So I decided that—for your art: to keep it, if not you, from hypocrisy—it would do you good to see your own face, with all the makeup scrubbed away, as well as you'd seen mine. You were too good at nailing people in your art, too good at hiding yourself. Sure, you looked at places in yourself where other people didn't have the guts to look, you dragged out of yourself all sorts of nasty desires. But once they got on the screen, they were pumped up like a bullfrog's throat. You stabbed and strangled and set fires and kept women in cages, and the splendid way you suffered while you did it set a new fashion for heroes. With you on the screen, who would bother to notice that your victims suffered, too? Not you. Least of all you.

Don't you think I cringed each time someone brought in a paper with one of Monty Druhl's venom-dripping slurs, and you glanced from eye to eye around the set—but never to mine, never to the dark-scooped, hungdog-faithful eyes of Farley—and made some lip-curled comment for the benefit of the spy on the set? But it was a moral thing. Each note I passed to Druhl was a mirror for you. All you had to do was look. Let it shake you out of that sense that she was something you could own. I'd never have gone further, never have hit you with such an arclight *glare* of truth, if you'd only looked. Just long enough to say, loud enough for me to overhear: Yes, I'm a genius, but I don't own her. Yes, I'm a genius, but if it weren't for me, Berenice would still be alive. Yes, Farley betrayed me, but—

But you wouldn't look. I had to go further. It was a moral thing. Telling Bolger that Lisa was ripe for plucking—a moral thing. Writing the Kill-You-Annabelle Letters—my parable of you in your ruthless art. That, too—a moral thing. And when I saw that, despite all I could do, you'd sliced up Lisa's soul and fed it in bite-size chunks to your fucking genius, then I say it's a moral thing—most moral of all, to shoot the last frame of Emile Vico's last film with a bullet.

To split a hole for sunlight in the skull of genius.

The rifle's telescope sight is a tunnel and I stare down it. My eye is locked to a close-up of the tunnel mouth cut in the facing ridge. Locked in a seamless stare that joins tunnel to tunnel. Frames away the ravine between us, the shack on the lower slope, where Singleton—not part of my design—putters at cupboard and cookstove, making a supper you'll never eat.

I keep blinking away a dull whiteness that washes out the image in the scope. At first I think it might be a reflection bouncing off the outer lens. I shift my elbows and look again. I think it's gone, but catch myself blinking again. Did I somehow smudge the lens? I wipe it with my pocket handkerchief, nervous, thinking: If he comes now, I won't be ready. Something deep in the cave, maybe a belt buckle, throws out a glimmer. I quickly bring the scope to my eye. Deep in the cave, in a place the last of the sun can't reach, there's a darker shadow—and again, that dull white blur. A rectangle of white floating in the dark. It's the folded-back page of your sketchbook, the one that continues the book I saw in the shack.

The sun is almost gone, and I think: Take two steps down, Vico. Come into the light.

And he does.

14. In the Crosshairs

EACH YEAR WHEN I climbed the hill to the beach house for that first session outlining a new picture, it would be in the cicada-humming heat of August, and you with all the front windows closed and draped tight—not just because you worked in the study cooled by a breeze off the ocean, or because your mother had always said, Drawn drapes keep a room cool. But as if some part of the house you inhabited while the story shaped itself in your mind had to be sealed away from the sun. A place of damp and darkness where the images you quarried dripped like stalactites from the ceiling. And when you opened the door it was from that room—full of shadows and soft-focused edges that I only glimpsed, because you always threw an arm across my shoulder and steered me past the doorway—it was from that room the smell came. The earth smell that mixed with your sweat but was more than your sweat. The smell of the cave with the stone rolled back.

Oh, yes: every film a resurrection. You spent more time in that front room, the room where you never invited me, than you ever told. The night you disappeared Spyhawk prowled there, trying to find its secret. But it was just a room: an old stuffed sofa and chair, doilies to cover the faded nap; an upright piano with gouges and beer-glass circles on the top; mantel photos of what must have been your parents. Mother in ankle-length dress, seated, while your father stood at her side in his celluloid collar. Neither looked a bit like the bohemian circus performers of your studio biography. All I could guess was that the room, furnished in a style not yours, was a mausoleum of the people in the photo, full of inherited chairs and lamps you'd been too sentimental to sell or give away. The room held nothing. If it was the source of your art, you made your art from nothing. You were my true antithesis. My art the interpreter's art, the art of molding light around the shapes of someone else's dream.

He stands at the mouth of the tunnel, just where Singleton stood a while ago. It's not quite the same shot. When Singleton stood there, the shadow of the overhang clipped him at the knees. The only part of Vico in shadow now is his face. Of course. Still the artful tease.

Is there a breeze scudding across the valley? I could swear

I smell the old smell—sweat and earth. He stands another minute, then starts down the slope.

Again that preternatural clarity of sight locks into focus and what I see is etched in acid inside my eyelids. A floating circular frame cuts him off at the waist. The crosshairs of the scope flutter a bit, but keep lighting just above his eyes, like a fly that's found a spot of grease and won't be shooed away. The skin has gone a rich Indian brown. The creases alongside the mouth, that used to come only with pain—that shot in *Cain,* say, where the sting of the bullwhip makes him a killer—those creases are permanent now, deep-grooved, and his cheeks sucked tighter to the mouth, and I think: Only forty days, and he's got thin. And then—a clutch at my throat for all I'll never be able to ask him, the films we'll never make.

Only a second more, I think. Let him get down to that creosote bush. And watching his lazy, loose-shouldered jump from a two-foot ledge, his lips in a half-smile like nothing I've seen before, not in all my years behind the camera, I keep thinking. Why should I believe you? Haven't you spent a lifetime putting on masks and peeling them away? Why should I believe this one is more flesh than the rest?

I wanted to shoot him quick before he could change into something I wouldn't have the right to kill.

My cheek sweats against the stock. There's plenty of time. He hasn't seen me yet. I sight along the crosshairs, line them up on his brow, his lips, his heart. I think of Lisa, crossing herself with the back of her thumb. It's no good, Lisa. Prayer can't keep off stares. It can't stop bullets. I line up the crosshairs. Where shall I kill him? In his mind. On his lips. In his heart. My lens drifts up. From breast to brow. He's stopped walking, he's looking this way. Maybe the barrel glints in the sun. I see his eyes. Sunk deeper than I knew them. Familiar in a way I didn't expect: the sleek skull, bone hooding the eyelids; the down-drawn reptile curl of the lips; even the cock of his head, alert, ready to strike. And then I see what he's done:

The snake in his sketchbook is a self-portrait.

The snake eating the mouse. Vico at last seeing *himself,* catching in his own eyes the self-absorbed glaze of the predator. Artist, eater of souls. Berenice. Lisa. Myself. Vico, looking at last at the victim, too.

I'm low behind the rock. He can't see who it is. He's afraid. He's not acting. He's looking. I can't stand his looking. *Shoot,* I tell myself. And Spyhawk tells me: *Shoot.* In the tunnel of my lens all that separates us is the fine crosshair joined over his brow, his lips, his heart. My finger on the trigger tightens.

Just before I turned the camera over to my operator, the last thing I always did was to take a final look through the lens at Vico's face. I let the scope drift back up to my last close-up: he's looking back at me through the scope, already beyond his fear, that steady calm in his eyes that I always saw on the take we wound up printing.

I stand up. I shuck the cartridges out of the rifle. They bounce and clatter on the rock. I swing the rifle by the barrel and the third time I swing it down on the rock I hear the glass in the scope smash, and then the gun is sailing out butt over barrel and it lands bouncing on the trail far below him. He looks at me. I'm sobbing, gulping, naked Spyhawk at last, no lens between us, and I think he was reaching up his hand, but I couldn't look anymore. I turned away, stumbled toward the crest, and when I got to the first ledge, I did look back at him standing where I'd left him, because we'd be alone together only another minute and I wanted to tell him why, but I knew it would be a long time before I could see anything straight, so I hollered down, "I'll catch up later—when I can." By the time I reached the crest the sun was gone and as I picked my way down the canyon trail the quick dusk deepened till the salt pan was a faint silver pool where flickering shadows might take any shape at all.

15. Fade to Black

I'M ALONE ON *The Merry Widower,* rocking somewhere off Big Sur. I didn't paint out the name. I've got money enough in savings for another month or two before I have to go back to work. I don't know what work I'll do.

I turn off my desk lamp and lie on the bunk. Only darkness above me. I no longer miss my old room in the Silver Palms or the square of light from the Palace marquee that fell across my ceiling. I no longer miss the shadow of the blowing curtains that would twist and flutter there. I no longer imagine that the shapes I saw in that gray flame can tell me what I need to know. The only light I allow in my window at night is moonglow. It creeps across my floor where I can't see it from my bed. I prefer darkness at night, so that I can see stars, and I don't trace lines between them to make pictures of heroes in the sky. I'm content to know that they are distant fires, nothing I can touch or claim to understand.

That's not true. It's only how I wish I were. The truth is, I think of you constantly. Are you still in the desert? Still with Singleton? For a while I wondered why, if you wanted to disappear, you chose to go with him. Was it guilt—a way of forcing yourself, day after day, to look at his ruined face? That's part of it, I think. That, and a certain fascination. You can look at him, and see which way your Don Juan might have turned if he hadn't found himself a mask. But even before his accident something about Singleton fascinated you, frightened you. Some possibility in yourself that his presence made more real. The day after I saw you last, I stopped in Mojave for gas and a sandwich. When I reached into my hip pocket for my wallet, I pulled out the page I'd ripped from your sketchbook, the page with the rattlesnake. On the other side of the paper I found your ink sketch of Singleton. At first it seemed like an illustration for a medical text—you'd looked away from nothing. But the old Vico would have seen only the grotesque, only the suffering. You got something more. You found it looking back from Singleton's one good eye. What you found was that it wasn't to escape the stares that he'd gone to the desert, any more than he'd gone to find a silver mine. What you found was what you'd always craved in him—that anchorite serenity.

Once or twice a month I stop in a library to scan the papers for news of you. Last week I read that Lisa's gone back East. Some newshound caught up with her on the library steps at Columbia University. What's a pretty girl like you want with a college degree, he wanted to know. A way past you, she told him. The picture he got shows her in a brisk stride, a very determined lady with her blurred right hand rising to block the lens.

Surely by now you've told her you're alive. And she, it seems, is keeping your secret. Why? Did you talk through lawyers, or work something out together? Are the people you've become less strangers to each other than the ones you were, or more? There's been no word of a divorce. Not yet.

Sometimes I imagine you're only researching another role. Even if you think you've given it all up, think you'll stand out there in the gritty wind till it hones your flesh away to bone, you must know, in some cell of your brain, that when you come back, when you come out of the desert and down the mountain to the city, you'll come like Moses with the tablets. I think what it would be like, picking up the phone, hearing your voice: Farley, we've got a film to shoot. It's like nothing we've done before. How soon can you get to the beach house?

It would be like the first time. We'd be strangers, testing each other out, probing to see where bottom was, where we might exhaust each other or not be after the same thing. Maybe it could never be. Maybe some things you do to another person you can't go on after. It's just that I'm itching to work again. I can't go back to the old work, figuring ways to light the old feelings. The old reasons for it don't make sense.

When I think of the new hollows in your cheeks, the sharper cut of your jaw, when I think of your eyes, the way the new lines at the corners lead us inside, spin us down, down to the blue fire with the hot black coals at the center—I know how it will be. The air around you will crackle with flashbulbs. You'll make every front page in the country. You must know it, too. Your timing was always perfect. It's been almost a year now. I'm waiting.

Vico—oh Vico. I'm hungry for where you'll take me next.